THE EVENING REDNESS

THE
EVENING REDNESS

THE BLUE TRAIN
·
THE RIVER BETWEEN
·
EL MORRO
·
PORTRAIT
OF MY FATHER

The Collected Four Novels of
LAWRENCE CLARK POWELL
with Notes on his Writing – 1930-50

CAPRA PRESS
SANTA BARBARA
1991

Cover design and typography by Ward Ritchie.
Type set in Palatino by Stanton Publication Services, Minneapolis.
Printed and bound by McNaughton & Gunn.

Library of Congress Cataloging-in-Publication Data
Powell, Lawrence Clark, 1906–
    The evening redness / by Lawrence Clark Powell.
        p. cm.   `
    Contents: Introduction—The Blue Train—The river between—
El Morro—Portrait of my father.
    ISBN 0-88496-335-7 : $ 22.95
    I. Title.
PS3531.0954A6   1991
813'.52—dc20   91-11401
                                                         CIP

CAPRA PRESS
POST OFFICE BOX 2068
SANTA BARBARA, CA 93120

CONTENTS

PREFACE

As a young librarian at UCLA my beat included the shipping room. A crate from a Dutch bookseller held the final volumes in the huge set of Stendhal's *Oeuvres Complètes* which had been in process of publication over the past twenty years.

Other jobs included completing the Library's holdings of 19th century French and German writers, and I had been reading critical works to help determine what should be added. One was a life of Marie-Henri Beyle whose pseudonym was Stendhal. Those final volumes of the Le Divan edition proved the winning ticket which Stendhal had played when he declared that a writer's work is a lottery, the drawing for which would not take place until one hundred years after his death. The year was 1942 when I unpacked that crate. *Stendhal died in 1842.*

What vanity to link my name with that of the great novelist! Such is, alas, a trait which looks to preoccupation with my own work— yet it is also what drives me to write and to seek approval.

Several earlier novels—practice work—will probably never be published. Not until I followed the practice of Willa Cather in her best work did I jettison needless verbiage, did as she did and threw the furniture out the window, leaving a bare stage.

Three of these works collected here were written during my seventies when the Evening Redness lit the sky. With social dues finally paid, I could now work at my own pace and with my own choice of subjects and form. From 71 to 80 proved the most fruitful years. By then I had gained an audience for my books on reading and collecting and the literature of California and the wider Southwest. For those who wondered why I turned to fiction, here is my answer.

5

Emily Dickinson asked the first critic to whom she had sent her poetry, "Is it alive? Does it breathe?" If these words of mine should bring an affirmative answer to those queries, I will be content.

L.C.P.
Tucson
Bajada of the
Santa Catalinas

NOTES ON MY WRITING, 1930–1990

NOTES ON MY WRITING, 1930–1990

I

It was during that deceptive lull between wars, when its ominous nature was apparent to only a few, that I first saw Paris. The summer of 1930 was ending. In that halcyon time France was still insulated from the American crash of the preceding autumn. With the franc down to four cents, what little money I had went a long way.

After Fay and I had spent two weeks together in Paris, troubled by our uncertain future, she returned reluctantly to California for her third year of college. Yeats's words described us as we were then—"bodily decrepitude is wisdom, young we loved each other and were ignorant."

We parted at Gare St. Lazare from where she took the boat train to Cherbourg. Although more in love with her than ever, or had ever been with anyone, still I knew that I was not ready for marriage. Nor did I believe that at nineteen, she was mature enough for a life without material assets. I thought we should finish our education and then see if we still wanted to marry. Little did I foresee that three years were to pass before we met again, older, wiser, and poorer—yet also fated not to part again.

I was not left alone. Ward Ritchie and I were to share a room in the Hotel Crystal at 24 rue St. Benoit, a few doors off Boulevard St. Germain. He had already checked in. Over a bottle of vin mousseux he sought to console me. He was due to begin an apprenticeship with Francois-Louis Schmied, the great Art Deco printer, and I was headed for graduate studies in the University of Dijon, 200 miles southeast of Paris.

We were *not* expatriates of the so-called Lost Generation. Far from it. When with a Tauchnitz paperback of *The Sun Also Rises* in hand, I saw Hemingway at a nearby table in the Brasserie Lipp, I was too fearful to ask for his autograph.

I was coming up on my 24th birthday, Ritchie had passed his 25th in June. We had been friends since childhood in what proved a lasting union of opposites. I deferred to his seniority, then and now. We had a few weeks before settling in for what appeared to be an untroubled future. How were we to know what lay ahead when our leaders didn't?

Fresh from the heady teaching of professor MacIntyre, poet Jeffers, novelist D. H. Lawrence, and a year of sharing a studio at the Abbey San Encino in the Arroyo Seco, where Ritchie began to print and I to study pipe organ, we set out each morning with our own agenda, to meet for late lunch at Lipp's. There we relished Alsatian *choucroute garnie avec saucissons*, with sandwiches of ham or gruyere on long split rolls, all washed down by the dark Strasbourg Walsheim brew—Das Bier der Kenner.

What little money we had bought a lot. Our room cost only 50 francs a night. Meals were even cheaper. At the Restaurant des Beaux-Arts in the Rue Bonaparte, a steak with pommes frites and watercress cost only 6 francs. Once, when feeling flush, we ate two apiece.

I wasn't sure what my friend did on his mornings—probably made the rounds of bookstores, printing shops, libraries and museums, looking rather than buying, and interested primarily in typography. We depended on occasional remittances from home. Our mothers were widows, and we were the youngest of three sons, spoiled of course. Before leaving California I had sold my Chevy for $400, my sole capital.

I knew that Richman (which I have always called him) carried a notebook and I learned later that when he stopped at a cafe for a beer, he wrote the verses of what was later handprinted by him as *XV Poems for the Heath Broom*. What he meant was "Hearth" broom, however the line lacked space for the "r."

Where did I go and what did I do on those mornings? Although I barely knew my way around in the great city, I already felt at home.

I went straight to the nearby Luxembourg Gardens where Fay and I had lingered. There I began to write my first novel. I was more determined than Richman to be a writer, and still am. In that idyllic setting I made an uncertain start on what was intended to be a magnum opus. Wasn't the Great American Novel waiting there on the threshold? Why shouldn't I write it? Ah Youth! *La Belle Jeunesse!*

I had sat down on one of the iron chairs beside the round pond where children were already launching their toy sailboats and begun to write, when I felt a tap on my shoulder. It was a crone in black, with a leather pouch hung from the belt around her waist. She held up two fingers and grunted what seemed to be *deux francs.* So there was a charge for an official chair! I had everything to learn about French ways.

I paid and was given a torn off billet and a second grunt which I figured out was *merci m'sieu.* Such was my literary debut—at a low point of ridiculousness.

I had no idea of what I was going to write—no plot, no characters, no notes or outline, nothing. My student notebook was blank. In my subconscious was a setting for the novel, already magical in memory: the college campus where I spent six years off and on, and where two years before, I had first met Fay and left music for literature. Now seen as it were through the wrong end of the telescope. Southern California was an enchanted land. That was all I had to bring to my first novel. *Nostalgie du pays,* the French call it.

After living through the 1920s as a dance musician and bohemian student (to the extent that Los Angeles was Bohemia) I could have entered the 1930s as a performer. I was a natural entertainer.

After a trip around the world as a ship's musician, during what would have been my second college year, I developed more mature taste in music. Jazz had proved empty of form and feeling.

Traces of talent were in my writing for college periodicals and in letters about D. H. Lawrence in the *Saturday Review of Literature.* Discovery of Beethoven (and Fay) led me for the first and last time to write poetry. It proved only a way of discharging emotion.

In a college course in Harmony and Composition, I learned that I had no gift for either. The college gave no courses in writing. If I quit music, the only way to make a living was teaching literature.

A discovery of the poetry of Robinson Jeffers and the wild seacoast of his work, to which I was led by my classmates Ritchie and Gordon Newell, who had left college to be a sculptor and was living in Carmel, encouraged me to go on for graduate work and seek a doctorate on the poetry of Jeffers.

11

No American university would accept work for a degree on a living poet. I learned that it might be possible in France. Fay's former classmate, Mary Frances Kennedy, and her husband Alfred Young Fisher were students at the University of Dijon in Burgundy. A welcoming letter from MF said that my proposal would likely be accepted there in a new department of American studies, headed by Professor George Connes.

France had long favored Anglo American studies. Poe, Whitman and Melville were the first Americans to be studied at the Sorbonne where Jeffers now had a critic and translator in Professor Charles Cestre, head of American studies.

So there I was in Paris in the fall of 1930, a young romantic, footloose for a month, breathing the city's bittersweet air of coal smoke and Chanel, and beginning my first novel.

After several false starts, I conceived a plot with two characters: a young graduate student in music (guess who), and an older woman, a college teacher of music, determined to make a creative musician out of our young hero, despite his desire to forsake music for literature. The woman was modelled on the drama coach under whose stern direction I played in college productions, including "You and I" by Philip Barry. She was actually not musical. What she had was vitality and certainty, and an impersonal yet challenging femininity which I proposed to make serve my literary purpose.

And so I kept writing, making it up as I went along. It gave me a new sense of freedom as I kept unloading emotional baggage. For the first time I had two purposes, to earn a degree that would enable me to make a living, and to be a novelist.

Each night Richman and I made the rounds of cafes—the Deux Magots and the Flore were our favorites—to sit and sip a porto blanc and munch chestnuts from the crone on the corner, guarding her glowing brazier. It was not my first taste of sidewalk cafe life which was quickly so much of Paris's charm for us. On that earlier trip on shipboard, we had called at Marseilles, and the scene along the Cannebiere was what I remembered the most.

Toward midnight we returned to our room and read aloud our day's work. Mutual acceptance was all that mattered. A litre of the sparkling wine lasted until we grew sleepy and turned in.

Alas for high hopes, that novel became my albatross, yet I was ashamed to abandon it, even when unsure of where to go or of how to get there. After I resettled in Dijon, it took a poor third to my studies and the emotional life which began in the provincial city. Before Richman went home at the end of his Paris year, he came for occasional weekends in Dijon. Thence my only listeners were the Fishers. He was writing his dissertation on Shakespearean comedy.

I had unhappily begun a new draft of the novel, compelled to keep writing. Fisher suggested instead short stories of my shipboard experiences. "Take a smaller canvas," he advised, "and write only of precise events with specific details. You've been reading too much Lawrence and Conrad."

He was right. To my fondness for the Lawrentian novels, *The Rainbow* and *Sons and Lovers*, I had added *Lord Jim*, all of which Fisher judged badly written. I took his advice and wrote several episodes of my musical adventures and read them to the Fishers in their chambers on the top floor of our pension. While he puffed on his pipe and she knitted, I amused them with outlandish happenings. Years later those evenings were recalled by her in *The Gastronomical Me*.

Fisher helped me even more with the method and organization of my dissertation. His critical detachment was essential when my mind was overly affected by my emotions – a teacher both stern and kind. My thanks were two complete typings of his thesis – a bit more Shakespeare than I wanted.

When MF went home that summer of 1931 for a family visit, he and I were together every night, as Ritchie and I had been the year before. We argued about literature, especially the comparative merits of Jeffers and Eliot. Fisher urged me to translate passages from their poetry as the best way to discover what they really meant. His knowledge of literature was wider and deeper than mine.

We were not always serious. Dijon's classiest brothel was Madamed by the wife of a town councillor. Each Wednesday morning on the way to the clinic for their official health inspection, her girls passed by the cafe where Fisher and I took aperitif before lunch at the pension. In badinage we were invited to visit them during working hours. That appealed more to Fisher, a minister's son, than it did to me. To have to pay for it seemed an unnecessary expense.

We were welcomed by Madame herself with a tiny glass of port

13

in the old-fashioned parlor. Fisher made it clear that as he had once been a reporter on a New York newspaper, he came only to interview one of the girls about her work. When Madame returned from escorting him upstairs, she found me seated at the Pleyel, playing soft whorehouse jazz, what else? "I'll be down to get you in a taxi, honey, better be ready about half past eight." Soon the girls trickled downstairs, lured by the music, and upon Al's return, he was pressed into service as a dancing partner.

It was the first time I had played since leaving California. I could have continued all night, as I sometimes used to do. This was not what the house needed. Before long Madame sent the girls back upstairs. Whereupon she offered me a nightly job for dinner and perks. I begged off, although it was tempting.

A year later Madame made a fleeting appearance at the public defense of my thesis before a jury of savants, Professor Cestre having come from the Sorbonne to administer what could have been the coup de grace. When I saw her at the back of the hall, blowing me a discreet kiss, I took her for a talismanic presence—and such she proved.

I rarely touched a piano during those years abroad. The pension where we lived was at 14 Rue du Petit Potet, in the heart of the old town, in Gallic times a Roman fortified camp, a *castrum*, with its narrow curving streets and tall dwellings. An upright piano stood in the parlor, and sometimes I allowed myself the nostalgia of playing the music I knew by heart. Writing those jazz stories brought it all back to my hands. In moments of revery they fingered imaginary keyboards and woodwinds.

While Fisher's appreciation of music was intellectual—Bach was his god, as Beethoven was mine—Mary Frances's was more emotional. She would slip into the parlor when she heard me playing, and remain silently at the back where I heard her humming along on "Blue Skies," "Stormy Weather," and "Sophisticated Lady." If I urged her to sing, she vanished.

We never talked about my playing, nor about Fay of whom she was fond. To my insistence that I was not prepared for marriage to anyone, Al only smiled and said "Nous verrons." When his degree was awarded and the Fishers moved to Strasbourg for more study, I began in earnest to write my dissertation. I would never have made it without his guidance.

14

That was a dreamlike summer of 1932, awaiting my final oral examination, as I divided my time between bicycling and reading. In addition to defending my thesis on Robinson Jeffers, there were two subsidiary subjects upon which I was to be prepared to be examined. Both related to Jeffers' subjects and vision. The first was the use of incest in the poetry of Byron and Shelley. The second subject I chose was a comparison of Jeffers' and Whitman's vision of the Pacific coast.

In reading and boning up, again I took Fisher's advice and concentrated precisely on what the poets had written and not on commentaries of others. In addition to Jeffers' published work, my texts were the Oxford edition of Byron and Shelley and Whitman's *Leaves of Grass, Democratic Vistas* and *Specimen Days In America.*

I was also thinking ahead to what I would undertake after Jeffers. It would focus on D. H. Lawrence's works laid in France and Italy. He had been dead only two years. While writing the final draft of my thesis before it went to the printer (in the same Dijon shop where Joyce and Hemingway had been printed), I holed up for six weeks on the Riviera near Nice.

Only a few miles inland was the town of Vence where Lawrence had died and was buried. For relaxation from sweating out my thesis, I went to see Lawrence's grave in the little cemetery of Vence. His letters had just been published, and I steeped myself in them and in his many books.

At last my moment of truth came. With more than a bit of luck, I was awarded the degree and a writeup in the local paper. An unexpected legacy of $1500 from my maternal grandmother enabled me to stay on another year in Europe. Word from Richman of the deepening Depression held no hope of a teaching job if I returned home. Why did I think I could make it as a freelance writer? There was nothing to show that I could. I was still young and ignorant of my ignorance.

Almost mechanically I began still another draft of the novel while living on the Riviera near Nice, advanced it in Florence and Rome, and finished it the next summer in London on the eve of returning to California. I had no choice. Although living remained cheap in Europe, the legacy was nearly gone.

I had been away for nearly three years and was growing homesick. I heard that Fay had married an older man and was expecting a baby. How did I feel? Not good. Richman reported signs of a literary awakening in Los Angeles. He urged me to come back and take part in it. Jake Zeitlin wanted to publish my work on Jeffers.

A San Francisco bookseller had bought copies of my thesis and was selling them for $4.00. With forty dollars from him, I had a suit and overcoat tailored in Florence, my first new clothes since leaving home. The Italian lire was as low as the franc. If I had had any income, however small, I would have stayed on in Europe.

I had not been without encouragement to persist in writing. While I was living in the south of France, a Frenchwoman journalist perceived more in me than an academic or a literary imitator. She had been the mistress of Francois Mauriac. From her came a copy of his book of poems called *Orages*, with its epigraph "les derniers grondements d'une jeunesse qui s'eloigne." We translated that as "the last grumblings of a vanishing youth." She was ten years older than I and the first mature woman I had loved. It was a big step toward growing up.

Our parting was painful, bringing misery felt only once before at Gare St. Lazare. When *The Blue Train* appeared years later, and also in French, I hoped she would read it and learn of how I remembered her and what she had taught me. Alas, she had apparently been swallowed up in the fall of France.

After reaching London, two books chanced upon increased my homesickness for the Golden State. *Two Years Before the Mast* was the first. Dana's descriptions of the California coast recalled the shoreline on which I had grown up and sailed. In Mary Austin's *Lands of the Sun*, her closing pages sounded a call I dreamed of myself as the one to answer:

On lamenting the destruction of much of what she had once known, she concluded, "In two or three generations, when towns have taken on the tone of time, and the courageous wild has re-established itself in by-lanes and corners, a writer may be born, instinctively at one with his natural environment, and so able to give satisfying expression to that wholeness." Was I that writer?

On my last night in London, the latest draft of the novel finished that day, I lay awake until daybreak, planning to sell the book to the movies and play the hero at the piano. Sleep ended that fantasy.

I sailed in the R.M.S. *Majestic*, the former North German Lloyd *Bismarck*, Southampton-Cherbourg-New York. The great White

Star liner was nearly empty. I was the sole occupant of an eight-berth stateroom for which I paid $75, borrowed from a penurious aunt in London.

Dancing was at the stern where vibration from the quadruple screws rattled everything not fastened down. Fellow passengers included young academics returning from the summer in Europe, all as poor as I.

In addition to the wind and weather, the joy of that crossing was the band playing nightly in Third Class. The constant vibration made the couples appear to be dancing the Shimmy. The band was from Cornell, and I sat in with them, welcomed as relief pianist and also saxophonist. I hadn't lost either fingers or bite.

That was the last time I ever played for dancing. Now in old age the connections between brain and fingers are breaking, and a once large repertory of popular music of the Teens and Twenties is slipping away. Sometimes my fingers resume the old positions on keys and valves and play me to sleep.

II

Back in California life soon became real and earnest and also magical as I sought out the old landscapes and a few old girl friends, sadly changed, or was it I? Fisher had been right when he said "Nous verrons." Fay and I remet in October of 1933, and it was as though we had never parted.

We were married the following March. With her and her baby and then one of our own, plus another degree funded partly by a loan from an old high school friend and fellow entertainer, I settled down on February 1, 1938 to a beginning library job at UCLA. I stayed there for 28 years, although for only six years at the bottom!

"Jazz Band" went into deep freeze while for the next three years I wrote bibliographies, articles, reviews, all drawn from my reading and the work I was doing with books, libraries, and printing. Before going back to school in Berkeley for the MLS degree, I had apprenticed for two and a half years with Jake Zeitlin. He had indeed published my thesis, designed by Ward Ritchie and illustrated by Rockwell Kent.

When it was printed, my picture appeared in the *Los Angeles*

17

Times, alongside a flattering review by Paul Jordan-Smith. That brought a lecture to a women's club which earned fifteen dollars. Richman had been right when he urged me to come home and take part in all that was happening. What I was doing brought much joy and less money. Jake Zeitlin was to call it a "Small Renaissance, Southern California Style." Now fifty years later, Kevin Starr has written its history.

My world continued to widen and enrich as I found work and play to be the same. I was immersed in projects, none of which brought in any money. By 1938 the country was still depressed, yet rent and food were as low as wages and salaries. At UCLA I began at $1620 a year. In six years it rose to only $1980. Thanks to Fay's ability to manage our household and raise our sons, we made it.

Then one day she asked me what had become of the novel that was intended to make our fortune. She didn't see anything coming in for what I gave so much thought and time to. We had no savings. I had lost weight, she said, and had become more serious than she had ever known me to be. It was true. I had changed from the playboy she had first known, and yet so gradually that I didn't recognize what had happened.

Only I saw what lay ahead if I continued to work and have faith, even though the prospect was unclear. I knew that my destiny was to remain at UCLA. Thus I spurned offers from other libraries, some of which would have more than doubled my salary. The only answer I could make was a half joking, "I'm investing in a reputation."

Her reply was not in reproach when she said, "I'm sorry you've given up your creative writing." Yet no longer did I have any time for sustained thought and effort. Now I regretted those idle hours when on a cafe terrace I dreamed of the future. All I could manage were shorter things on the energy left after the day's work.

Only I knew that what I was doing was preparation for the time when I would manage that library. Such was my vision upon first entering its rotunda in April 1935. I began to keep a ten cent notebook, similar to the one in which I began the novel, writing down what I saw as needed to bring the library to the strength UCLA would require. If I were to undertake another work of fiction, it would have to be longer than a story and shorter than a novel. One look at the moribund manuscript convinced me that it was dead beyond revival.

Although I wanted to respond and make Fay proud of me, I was at a loss. Part of my mind was troubled during long days of typing, checking, filing, wrapping and unwrapping. On my own time I was dressing the library's public exhibits, as I had done the years before in the Los Angeles Public Library.

I kept remembering Europe with regret for what I had both known and missed. Was I far enough away to lend perspective for what I might write? Those vanishing places and people had now replaced the romantic college milieu of the novel.

On August 10, 1941, I wrote in my journal: "Increasingly troubled by the urge to write a European book. Everything must go into it in essence. It must be simple and unpretentious, straightforward and moving. Must not wait too long. These are my best years. Soon I'll be 35, the halfway point. Mustn't get to far from my youth before I try to recapture it."

What I began to write was triggered by a chamber music series at our alma mater. On several Sunday afternoons we drove to Eagle Rock, leaving our boys with my mother, to attend a Beethoven cycle by the Pro Arte quartet. While hearing the final work on the last Sunday—his Opus 135, in which Beethoven bade farewell to the string quartet, a terse work so different from the expansive quartets which preceded it—suddenly, *tout d'un coup*, came the form for what had been haunting me. It was a startling experience so suddenly did the vision appear.

Hardly before the music ended and on the drive home to Beverly Glen, my mind was at work. What I would write would be to the novel what the string quartet is to the symphony—a work for few voices and themes, free of virtuosity and rhetoric. It would boil down those European years, distilling the essences and also resolving dissonances and reconciling differences between men and women as they struggled to meet and then to part.

It came in an unbroken flow, even as I went about checking faculty orders, unpacking and entering shipments against invoices, one part of my mind dealt with author, title, publisher and cost, while the other planned what to write that night after supper, story hour and reading time, when the family was at last asleep. At work in the cathedral-like building, immured by books, I fancied myself

19

God's spy. I had tapped a new source of belief and energy in a time of sustained exaltation when I talked to no one of what I was doing, lest the current be broken.

Only a few times did I cheat the library by slipping into the stacks to consult town plans of Neuchâtel, Nice or Villefranche. None was needed for Dijon.

Not long ago Richman came upon a letter from me which said, "You once declared that never would I be able to write of my life in Europe until time brought retrospect. Since last autumn I have been working on a story of those years. Scholarly, bibliographical studies are not enough. I have juice that cannot be forced into utilitarian receptacles. The story I write now is an erotic one—restrained though, no naughty words. I hope to have it finished and typed this spring. A hundred pages or so. Don't talk of it." No longer did I need applause or critical listeners.

Unlike "Jazz Band," this shorter book was quickly written in several drafts over three months, at night and on weekends. Again I knew the exaltation felt in London upon completing that earlier manuscript, poor though it was.

It was the most sustained period I had ever known and proved harder to regain as my burdens grew heavier and I aged. Only after I had written the book did I realize that an unconscious morality underlay it: that the more demanded in love, the less is given, and that the deepest relationship can also be one without consummation. It was also a reader's lesson in taking hold and letting go, in which the *before* and the *after* are more meaningful than the *during*. Which is, in this present time of explicit sex in book and film, what makes my work so old-fashioned.

At last I proudly gave my first notebook draft to Fay, saying that I had done what she said I should do—not let my creative gift die. She read it, then protested that she didn't mean *that* and that I had idealized those women and everything else, including myself. "You know very well they weren't like that," she said, "and neither were you."

"*Now* they are," I replied defiantly, trying not to show my hurt. "Now they're what I've made them. Now they'll have life beyond life." I must have sounded unbearably pompous.

Yet I was convinced that this was indeed a function of the creative writer as alchemist, to harmonize and resolve the discordants and to transform the common into something precious.

Despite her initial rejection, Fay gave it a careful re-reading. What I mistakenly took as a complete rejection led me to seek approval elsewhere. That misunderstanding opened a gulf which was never completely bridged, for never again did I want to risk being hurt. Any fault lay with our being so different in our basic natures, she private, I public. We had yet to learn who the other really was.

Next a draft was read by William Everson, my new friend in the San Joaquin valley, for whose first book of poetry I had written a foreword and arranged for its printing by Ritchie. I was awakened one night by a phone call from where he lived on a vineyard farm near Fresno. He voiced such incoherent delight that all I could make out was his shouted "Man O man!" over and over. No matter. That was all I needed.

My next reader was our new neighbor in Beverly Glen, a writer met in passing, ten years earlier at Dijon. I had read his *Tropic of Cancer* with delight and admiration. Now Henry Miller had come west to make his fortune as a screen writer. He nearly starved to death. In addition to my bringing him library books, Fay invited him sometimes to lunch or dinner.

This evening he came returning the manuscript. He proceeded to get high on Escondido muscatel and Fay's casserole of ground beef heart at five cents a pound. He strode about the room, sounding my praises and chiding her for not recognizing what I had done. I couldn't shut him up, retreating instead to my study. That same night, back at his place down the Glen, he wrote me the ardent letter which waited thirty years before appearing as the published book's Afterword.

Miller brought me that letter the next night. I had been writing in my study, and about ten o'clock I put my work aside and resumed reading Elie Faure's *History of Art*, a work to which I had been led by Henry's praise.

I heard a tapping on the curtained window. It was Miller. While he browsed among my books, I read what he had written the night before. It left me speechless. With tears in my eyes I embraced him and he left. For the first time I sensed my worth as a writer. Since that night I have never doubted that it was within me to take place, albeit a small one, in the company of American writers.

In the resulting euphoria I sent the manuscript to Knopf, calling it "Quintet," with each episode bearing its own musical signature. It went under the pseudonym "Stephen Coast," for I knew that the book would not further my career as a librarian in the state's employ. Back it came with a kind letter from Knopf's editor, Emily Morrison, rejecting it not for what it was but for what it wasn't nor was intended to be—a story of character development and dramatic culminations. It was, she said, only a single story told five times over, during which the narrator shows no change or growth.

Precisely! What I had intended was variations on a theme—the way of a man with a maid, five of them in fact. A romantic unity was achieved by the coming and going of trains which brought and took away. It also said something about an easy taking hold and a harder letting go.

What had been perceived by Everson and Miller went unseen by Knopf's editor, who concluded by asking to see my next work. Although tempted I did not reply by quoting Remy de Gourmont, who declared that every original work of art creates its own aesthetic and must therefore be judged by what it is and not by what it is not.

Although steeped in Lawrence, Hemingway and Miller, I never imitated them. What I admired was their dedication to writing; in that they were my role models. As a reader I have sought writers with their own recognizable voices, never thought I had to learn what mine was and how to use it. That I proved a slow learner was because I had so much else to do, none of which was forced upon me. Though my burdens were heavy, I bore them lightly, nay joyfully.

Years later when in his old age, Alfred Knopf and I became friends, I recalled that rejection by his editor. He was mildly amused and informed me that she was the daughter of the famed historian, Samuel Eliot Morrison. I did not confess that I was *not* impressed. Knopf had long since won my admiration as our greatest publisher whose Borzoi imprint I had alas failed to win. Yet it proved in the end that I did not have to have it.

Fay now conceded that while it was easy for me to write of romantic happenings in a foreign land, she doubted that I could write of everyday life in the USA. I set about proving her wrong. This time I began another college novel with her in it, although I knew that she would resent this invasion of her privacy. So I kept mouth shut and Scripto busy.

Meanwhile the world changed. A global war was being fought, with the prospect of only losers. In spite of our children I was classified 1-A in the draft. Though by conscience I would not fight, I would do non-combatant service that might help end the senseless killing and destruction.

When I learned that Greyhound bus drivers were exempt, I applied for a job. I had driven since I was twelve—cars, trucks and tractors.

Those intensive years of research and publishing had brought me to the notice of the powers in the book world, notably William A. Jackson of Harvard, with whom Richman and I had grown up. Others were Randolph Adams of Michigan's Clements Library, Louis Wright of the Huntington Library and Henry R. Wagner, the legendary father of them all.

All were of the opinion that I was unappreciated and underpaid by UCLA. They were right. Yet in spite of this lack of recognition for what I did beyond my regular duties, I knew that my worm's eye view of the library would serve me well when my position was reversed. That proved to be not long in the future. I was right when I told Fay what I had been investing in. Dividends were now coming in.

Early in the summer of 1943 Northwestern University approached me (upon Jackson's suggestion) to be their head librarian. Upon Fay's urging I dropped my resignation into the mailbox at the Union Station and boarded the "Superchief" for Chicago, headed for interviews by the president and faculty committee on the campus in Evanston.

After two full days there on the northside lakefront, I returned confidently to Chicago's venerable Blackstone Hotel to await the next available berth on the westbound limited. With the prospect of a new life ahead, I celebrated by shopping for presents at Marshall Field's—a silver compact for Fay, handkerchiefs for my mother, and toys for the boys.

Back in California President Robert Gordon Sproul appointed me university librarian and director of the William Andrews Clark Memorial Library, as of January 1, 1944. He too was a gambler, in giving charge of an exploding library system to a man still in his thirties without any administrative experience. Of doubts I had none, sustained by that vision of 1935.

For the remainder of 1943, after withdrawing the Greyhound application—disappointedly, I should add—I obtained deferment as a laborer in a war plant which made Arctic sleeping bags for the Army and kapok life jackets for the Navy. It was the hardest work I had ever done, learning how to truck 300-pound bales of kapok from freight cars, then opening and feeding the long strips into a shredding and blowing machine. It was also hazardous, for shredded kapok is highly inflammable. The blowers who were filling the jackets worked in a netted enclosure through whose flimsy walls they could roll to safety when everything blew—which was a couple of times every few hours.

I left for work in the dark, six days a week, to labor from 7:00 to 3:30 at $1.00 an hour. The sprawling plant was in industrial Los Angeles, 22 miles from Beverly Glen. At the end of each work day after a shower and the last daylight hours with Fay and the boys, I went to my study and worked until late on the new novel, now called "First Symphony."

In three months, during which I helped make a hell of a lot of bags and jackets (and won a few bucks shooting craps on my lunch hour in an empty boxcar, money spent on rationed luxuries such as butter and olive oil), I wrote 300 pages, then revised and typed as many more. Still the book was only half done. My strength seemed limitless, although my doctor warned me that my lungs were getting congested from down dust and kapok fibers.

After returning to campus in my unlikely new role, I kept writing. So rich was the material and steady the flow that I had no choice but to make it a long novel, replete with characters and incidents. The setting had become secondary, so well had I purged it in "Jazz Band."

I intended proudly to show Fay the finished book. Yet as the war ended and my responsibilities increased, I ran out of gas. Although I tried to keep the manuscript alive, it withered and died. I had reached my limit, and private creativity yielded to public responsibility.

I buried the manuscript, belief in myself and my work lost, I feared forever. I was too busy to grieve. Faith in my gift returned only as I entered my sixties and left all that had bound me for so many years.

III

For twenty-two years, 1944 to mid-1966, I did other work, wrote other books and shorter things, mostly about books, reading and collecting and the obligation of librarians to be well read as well as useful. In addition to regular writing for *Westways*, I contributed to *Arizona Highways*, *New Mexico* magazine, and the *New York Times Book Review* for which I wrote lead articles and reviews.

I became known in the book world at home and abroad, going to Europe several times to acquire books for UCLA, once on a sabbatical, supported by a Guggenheim fellowship, during which we lived in Chelsea.

In 1960, after fourteen years of active belief in the need, I led in the founding of a UCLA graduate school for educating librarians. As dean I began a new career of teaching and educational administration, preaching what I had practiced. After six years I retired at age sixty.

In twenty-eight years at UCLA I had done all I was capable of doing. Needed now were new vision, new strength, new voices. I was still unrecognized for the writing I knew was in me and beginning to demand release.

William Targ, an editor at World Publishing Co., for whom I had written three books on reading and collecting, expressed interest in the manuscript of 1941, about which he had heard from Henry Miller. I took it out of storage and while teaching a final summer session course, I refined the work as belief came flooding back.

It was an exalted six weeks, doing what I loved most, teaching and writing. Mornings were for lecturing and advising, then after lunch at the Faculty Club, usually at table with either lawyers or doctors (the most literate of faculty colleagues), I holed up in the lounge and worked over the old manuscript. My joy was boundless.

Sometimes I talked with two unusual visiting professors who also took sanctuary in the lounge—Norbert Wiener, the psychologist from M.I.T., and Walter Starkie, the Irish folklorist and gypsy fiddler. We shared a single copy of the *Manchester Guardian*.

Fay and I planned to celebrate retirement by living out the year in England. As we left on a midnight flight to London, my briefcase held the newly typed manuscript, a copy of which had been sent to Targ in New York. It had taken a quarter century for the book to come this far. While the Pan Am 707 flew over the Arctic Circle route, I stayed awake, reading for typos. Fay slept beside me, more necessary than ever for whatever lay ahead.

Alas, Targ's rejection awaited me in London. Again the manuscript was faulted for lacking what it was not intended to have. I could only accept the verdict. If a reader did not respond to the book on first reading, nothing I could say would make any difference. Now it had to make its own way. I lay down on the couch in our Dolphin Square flat and heard a B.B.C. broadcast of the second Rasoumovsky quartet, its music best of all therapies.

Later I wrote to Henry Miller, now an old man living in Pacific Palisades, after the hippy invasion had driven him from Big Sur. Although without a publisher, I asked to include his 1943 letter as an Afterword. He responded with these restorative words:

"Pay no attention to negative criticism," he wrote, "even if from people you believe in. Just believe in yourself—completely. Avanti! Fuck the critics, editors and their ilk. I do remember the warm sensuous feel of your book. You'll never lose that. And of course you may use my original letter. And if I may say so, don't go for perfection. Turn out one after another—time is short. You have dozens in you. Bless you, my dear Larry."

Is there any wonder I loved that man to his death at eighty-nine? His monument at UCLA is the archive we created in homage to the most generous man I have ever known. Again he confirmed my belief, as the creative euphoria, long hidden even from myself, flooded back. Knowing that it was still there to be drawn on, was a new source of energy.

In a burst of writing during thirty days, I wrote an autobiography looking back from sixty. It was published two years later as *Fortune and Friendship*, the record of my professional career. In the twenty years since then, I have fulfilled Miller's prediction of the books left in me.

Still another ten years remained before the European book saw print. First I took it to a London publisher, one of several suggested by Miller. I left it at their chaotic office. No acknowledgement. On the day before leaving for Portugal, en route home for Christmas, I retrieved it, obviously unread.

Two years later in the spring of 1968, as a Fellow at Wesleyan University in Connecticut under Paul Horgan's wing, I asked him to read the manuscript. Although he too faulted it for being a repetitive story without character development—it never occurred to me that those critics might have been right—he suggested calling it "The Blue Train." Weren't trains the book's leitmotif?

A final obstacle remained. Upon my completing the Arizona volume in the Bicentennial series on the states, the publisher's editor asked to read the European manuscript, heard about from someone. His prompt rejection was that it was "rather quaint and dated, and yet there are things about it we like a good deal."

Thus was I told that romanticism is out and explicit sex in. He also said that it should have been published when it was written, thirty years ago. No! The book's fortune was that it wasn't, for it would then have sunk from sight in that time of war.

With that final rejection, I all but resigned myself to posthumous publication. Yet I still believed deep down that the book was destined to have readers in languages other than English. Small consolation came from Robinson Jeffers' advice to young writers that posthumous fame was the only kind worth having.

Then my belief was revived by a young woman's reading of the manuscript. If the book were important to me, she insisted, even though to no one else, I must keep trying to get it in print. I remembered a publisher in Santa Barbara who had sought a manuscript from me, preferably on a California theme. At least I was a sometime coastal resident now domiciled in the desert; and so with small hope I sent the manuscript to Noel Young of Capra Press.

To my astonishment he liked it, although he foresaw difficulties in marketing it, "Today when sex has little more significance than sneezing, your accounts of the female citadel won't have much credence. Henry's Afterword eloquently describes my feelings about the manuscript. Your work is clean and spare, and so evocative of a romantic era. I too lived in France and Spain for a year and know well what they are—the trains and l'amour."

His interest rose as our correspondence continued. "Times are

27

changing," he wrote, "there is a new hunger for romantic places and gentler sex." That these were the gist of Miller's letter made it appropriate as an Afterword. The clincher was that Young had become Miller's publisher in his old age.

Capra gave the book a handsome format, reproducing on the jacket Monet's smoky blue vision of Gare St. Lazare, painted in 1876. That the actual "Train Bleu" leaves Paris for the Riviera from Gare de Lyon would disturb only a French train dispatcher.

And so at last *The Blue Train* began its run on the main line. It was exactly a century since Monet created that oil of the soaring wrought iron Paris railway station, similar to the one in Dijon evoked in my book. My poor man's cathedral, I called it in those years as a young and unknown Dijonnais.

If a first novel by a writer, whose reputation has been gained from different sorts of writing, does not win approval from a critic with a following, its success is unlikely, especially if published by a small press on the west coast. That the author was a former librarian made its chances even unlikelier.

Habent sua fata libelli declared the Roman poet Terence, which is to say that even little books have their fates. Mine's was to be favorably reviewed by the two best critics in California, both familiar with my earlier work. Robert Kirsch of the *Los Angeles Times* and Kevin Starr of the *San Francisco Examiner* were those who built my bridges to readers.

It was not long before his early death from cancer that Kirsch saluted *The Blue Train*. "Some may find it surprising," he wrote, "that Powell should turn at an autumnal age to fiction. I think it a natural development, and one which was a blossoming of style and matter. The poignance and power, tenderness and excitement Powell was always quick to recognize in others came out of the material of his own experience. It is the work of a journeyman novelist and one of the best pieces of fiction I have read in a very long time. For those who want what novels once gave in life and enchantment, *The Blue Train* is just right."

From that one review came a decade of motion picture options taken successively by hopeful producers, the latest by Leonard Nimoy who hopes to direct the film in France. That the book is essentially French in feeling as well as setting, was recognized by its faithful translation into that language by Nicole Tisserand.

Kevin Starr's perception went even deeper. He heralded his review with a postcard: "Your book is soaked in life, alive with Mediterranean fullness of the senses and a back-feeling of Virgil's *sunt lacrymae rerum*—there are tears for our sorrows. Where was it all these years? Or did the knowledge that you had it secreted away provide you with a hidden source of strength, a feeling that is, that you were something other than what you appeared to be?"

"What a wonderful paradox!" his review in the *Examiner* began. "The library administrator contains within himself a dialectical opposite—a passionately sensuous literary artist, capable of capturing the incandescence of awakened flesh. The bookman, responsible for the growth of an institution, holds in delicate tension the free-and-easy bohemian, capable of throwing it all away for love or art."

That last sentence recalled an evening in the early 1950s spent with Henry and Eve Miller at their candle-lit eyrie in Big Sur, that dramatic coast where the great cliffs plunge into the sea, when it was Eve who urged me to chuck it all and return to a bohemian life in France, whereas it was Henry who urged me to stay the course at UCLA. "God knows we need librarians like you," he argued. He was right. I stayed.

The French translation also had a good review in *Le Point* by Francois Nourissier, who asked, *'Qui est cet écrivain inconnu? Quelle fraicheur, quelle delicatesse! Il faut lire ces cinq inoubliable portraits de femme."*

By now the evening redness lit the western sky. I had reached my seventies, thirty-six years since the book was first written. How strange it must have seemed in our youth-oriented culture! With my social dues nearly paid and still with ambition and energy, I went on to write three more short novels, published by Capra in 1979, 1984 and 1986. The last appeared on my 80th birthday. The sunset years in truth!

We had been living in Arizona since 1970. After leaving UCLA our life was enriched with travel and teaching from New to Old England. In 1971 I yielded to the persistent president of the University of Arizona and agreed to come to Tucson for one semester as a consultant on libraries and library education.

Although Fay was at first reluctant to leave Malibu for good, she came to recognize that we had put down roots in the arid earth of the *bajada*; and so we remained beyond that first semester, going back for summers on the shore, until in 1978 fire destroyed our Casa dos Vistas and everything in it not yet removed.

I gradually became a part of Arizona culture, writing and speaking statewide, continuing to meet my social obligations. As a writer I took a closer, deeper look at the Southwest, and many articles and books followed, including these novels.

I was sometimes mocked by machine-oriented colleagues for preaching a bookish gospel. My paternal grandmother, a zealous Quaker reformer (as had been her brother, a worker in the Underground Railroad) once said to me when she was not telling me to stop snapping my chewing gum, "Lawrence, thee must become a minister." Although she did not live to see it, I came to view my library work as a ministry. It was her legacy that gave me that extra year in Europe.

Sixty years have passed since that summer in the Luxembourg Gardens when I sat down on what proved to be a rental chair and began my first novel. Why had it taken so long to arrive at where I now am? It was hard for me to realize that I was an old man. And yet as my eighties waxed, my life force began to wane in a loss of recuperative power. I ate less and rested more. No longer true was what I once read lettered over the fireplace in Tor House: *Time and I against any two.* Now Time was leaving my side.

When in my twenties I first began to write, Aurora was the goddess of the dawn and the morning redness lit the eastern sky. Now in old age, Hesperus rules the west as sunset fires the heavens. My fate was a long wait for those who took my work for what it was and not for what they thought it should be. At first I was the only one who knew that I could write in no other way. In achieving the freedom of creative writing, I had to reimagine and reorder my life. To harmonize and reconcile discordants and disagreements was my intent. That fulfillment took the best of the life that remained to me.

IV

What was practiced in the first of these works gathered here, I continued to apply to the others. In them was realized the wish of

Willa Cather, expressed in her essay "The Novel Démeublé," that is *unfurnished*. "Wouldn't it be wonderful," she imagined, "if we could throw all the furniture out the window, all the unnecessary descriptions of nature and of the characters' emotions, and leave the stage as bare as in Greek tragedy or Elizabethan drama."

In "Jazz Band" I had overfurnished the house in a need to recapture beloved landscapes and emotions of unformed characters. Then I heeded the advice of Alfred Fisher and wrote of specific events and precise details.

There's little in these books of inner feelings, or of the character development expected by those early editors and critics. This new character who was and was not the writer, merely saw and then acted, which was to woo and win and then reconcile himself to loss. "All love is prelude to loss," Lawrence wrote. "Bodily decrepitude is wisdom," Yeats observed. Most of the people of *The Blue Train* are young, some wise, none decrepit.

I did not order the books' lengths, nor did I work from a strict outline. My words said what I had to say, following my instincts for form and time and memory of places. Capra published what I wrote after useful advice from Noel and Judy Young. I was also guided by a line from that visionary Fisher poem of our Dijon years: *Crack the rock if so you list, bring to light the amethyst*. This I tried four times to do.

I knew that I was out of sync with the publishing practice of our time to reward the blockbuster book and to persuade the buyer that he was getting his money's worth if only in weight. Reviewers bowed to the behemoths. Perhaps I was influenced by the shorter European novels of my years overseas—those of Schnitzler and Mann, for example, or Mauriac. As for Proust, Romains and their *romans fleuves, non merci*! Thus I was at odds with popular and critical taste as well as with publishing.

If I had needed to depend on income from fiction, we would have starved. The money earned from my other writing was not enough to support a family. Only university library work, free of academic jockeying, allowed me the liberty to be the writer I was compelled to be by my own nature, and in the bookish milieu in which I was at home.

By the time I entered my seventies, life lay behind me, a reservoir into which I had only to dip for material. Fay came to recognize my seriousness of purpose, and she was also aware of growing public responsiveness to my writing, however small. I came better to appreciate her kindness and compassion, to which I was at first blinded by my own compulsive egotism.

In the setting for *The River Between* I left Europe for the Southwest, and conceived an allegory of the struggle between California and Arizona for the water of the Colorado River, the life-giving boundary between the states. This was personified by the conflict between a man and a woman from opposite banks of the river. Despite their love, they were fatally sundered by the woman's primitive struggle between love for one man and loyalty to an ideal. It was intended also to account, however ambiguously, for my move from seacoast to desert and the unanticipated years of service at another university.

Although first broached in 1960, *The River Between* took seventeen years to complete. At least I had gained speed! As it took form I was given responsibility for the new school at UCLA, to which the book took second place. There were still dues to pay.

Again Paul Horgan, Noel Young, and the same believing young reader were necessary to its completion. In frustration over my warring needs I left home, hoping to escape the doubts and fears threatening to paralyze me. Those epigraphic words in each volume of the Everyman's Library—"I will go with thee by thy side, in thy most need be thy guide,"—I heard as my inner voice.

Respite was found in a remote community to the north. There I followed my instincts for content and form. Periods of writing were relieved by walks on the juniper slopes of Mingus Mountain and by swims in Oak Creek near its confluence with the Verde. Evenings were spent around the fire pit, burning trunks of mesquite and cedar shoved into the flames. As the last light went from the Rim and Mingus turned from blue to purple to black, on its side the lights of the old mining town glowed like a lit honeycomb. High above, the transcontinental jets flew over in a heavenly host, trailing vapor across the darkening sky.

By daytime my beacons were the Sacred Peaks beyond Flagstaff and the tip of Bill Williams Mountain, barely visible above the Rim. A hundred years earlier that solitary landmark had guided Martha Summerhayes, as she followed her lieutenant and his Army troopers on their march from Fort Mohave to Camp Apache.

I took a trip that summer with an architect who was building a solar house. Our destination was a quarry on the mesa north of Ashfork where a bed of Coconino sandstone rose to the surface. In the warm air the incense of pinon and juniper woodland was intense.

We saw the stone quarried in slabs, then trucked down to the Santa Fe railroad at Ashfork for cutting to order and shipping to distant parts. A Texas architect was there, dressed in white, supervising an order for a Dallas subdivision to be built of this stone. The colors he chose were subtle shades of red, beige and lavender.

By the end of the summer, when I thought my manuscript was finished, I was persuaded by Noel Young to add a story within the story—a gentler tale to soften the brutal one of the witch's daughter. Its ending was too horrible, even for today's bloodthirsty readers.

I had come at last to know who I was, after seeking definition in book after book. *"Qui est cet écrivain inconnu?"* my French critic had asked. I learned that a creative demon shared my body and had to be appeased and then exorcised. Writing was the way I discovered to do both.

That proved a productive summer. Not only did I advance the novel, a book of essays was gathered, my re-discovery of Van Dyke's *The Desert* led to its reissue by the Arizona Historical Society, and to Ansel Adams' book of Southwest photographs I contributed a lyrical essay on the land.

When two young geologists learned that I was writing a series for *Westways* on the rivers of Arizona, to result in a book, they came with a persuasive proposal. Both had skills in addition to geological science. Michael Collier was a photographer, Christopher Condit a pilot with his own Cessna 172. They had done aerial mapping for the U.S.G.S. Now they proposed to illustrate my book with aerial color photographs of the state's river system. It was irresistible.

We made our first flight from a field in the Verde Valley, more like a cow pasture than an airport. This was a new way of seeing the relationship of history and literature to geography. I had first read of its significance in an article by Bernard DeVoto, written after a flight with Army engineers the length of the Missouri River.

It was clear that man goes where water flows, and those words gave title to the book. Ours was a good tradeoff: for their knowledge of the earth's surface, I gave them a course in Arizona's history and literature as seen from above.

The book was published two years later by Northland Press, designed by Mark Sanders and with a foreword by Governor Bruce Babbitt. He had offered to take us up in his Queenaire if the Cessna couldn't fly high enough to get a picture of the double bend of the Gila. Chris made it to 12,000 feet and no oxygen! It was in December and I had never been as cold.

Meanwhile, I bought an International Scout and travelled the lengths of the rivers. Few writers on the Southwest had what I doubly gained during that gypsy year. I had nearly stripped away what had for so long kept so much locked up in me. Such was the imperative I was responding to. It was Kevin Starr who first perceived my paradoxical needs and demands, the one for freedom, the other for confinement which paradoxically also held freedom.

As that second summer waned, the time of choice came. The angel with upraised sword at my back would be put off no longer. Much of what I had lived and written had disregarded convention and the warnings of an aging body. There was time left only for a last trip through the landscapes whose beauties I had long extolled.

Back home in the autumn I knew that I must find a way to commemorate what proved to be the last summer. My body was also hurting. A hernia repair relieved pain felt all summer. Equipment which had served me for a lifetime was wearing out.

For the first time I admitted that I was old. Would I, as Yeats foretold, never again know the supreme experience possible only to the young? A rereading of Melville and Hawthorne heightened my foreboding. Was this the end of my creative life? In my confusion I did not know how to give form to what I was feeling.

With those uncertainties I went into university hospital early in December for a prostate operation. It was an unusual desert day in winter, dark, rainy and cold. The hospital was overflowing with patients, many obviously worse off than I. My room was long, narrow and two-bedded, opening on a light well. Day and night became one.

The bed nearest the door was occupied by a high school football player whose knee had been shattered. He was in agony. I had never heard anyone cry so piteously. We were separated by a hanging curtain, through which I urged him to be brave and also be quiet. He cried the louder. He was joined by his teammates who brought their own beer. He finally yelled for them to get the hell out. Bad theater!

In addition to toilet kit, I brought a bedside radio, a few books, and my pad and Scripto, unsure of the uses I might make of them. The books were the Portable Melville and Hawthorne. They too had come though deep depressions when they had feared their creative death.

My doctor was a reader, including my books. We talked more of writing than my health. After he continued on his rounds on the eve of the operation, I dozed off with Melville's review of Hawthorne's "Mosses from an Old Manse," and its peroration, "For genius, all over the world, stands hand in hand, and one shock of recognition runs the whole circle round."

I was wheeled down early in the morning to surgery to enter a holding pattern for patients. A spinal injection floated me free of worry, as at last I looked up at doctors, nurses, and students, while my doctor friend performed a prostoscopy with mirror and scalpel.

He came by on his rounds that evening to report that all had gone well, and that he wanted me to stay in hospital a couple more days. When I complained of my failure to find form for what was haunting me, he assured me there was plenty of blood flowing in my body. "There are two kinds of old," he said, "the old old and the young old, and you are the latter." He also warned me that after 75, aging accelerates. Before I could say that was the urgency I was feeling, he smiled and left.

My roommate had been rolled away for orthopedic surgery. Alone in the darkened room, I was monarch. The night brought evidence that all had not been lost to the scalpel. I woke at four and rang for nurse and coffee. Medication first, washed down by the first cup of brew. My mind began to race. Notes for what came to be *El Morro* came fast.

Throughout the day between visitors and calls, I mined the golden vein, fearful that it would not last nor come again with such clarity. Insulated from the outside world, not knowing whether it were night or day, with music of radio, rain on the window and wind in the light well, I felt confident come whatever.

Notes of plot, setting, and characters flowed with increasing clarity. As I felt what would prove my last book, I knew I must hurry before it vanished. At the back of my mind were those two great authors.

Fay brought a bowl of ripe persimmons which found place in the book. Everything was grist to the mill as back over the summer's journey my characters moved to their fulfillment—eastward to Montezuma Well, and from the South and North Rims to Shonto, Betatakin, Chelly, Chaco and Chama, on to Santa Fe and beyond to journey's end at El Morro.

Back in the Library, now nearly deserted in the holidays intersession, a first draft came in twelve days, making 254 pages for revising. Everything in the book had to be kept within the time frame of two weeks.

Only the setting was not imagined. The main and supporting personages—Stone and Arla, Hester Crane, Jennie La Porte, Maria MacPherson, and even the dog Sheltie—had prototypes, some more obvious than others. In the background was Willa Cather who admonished me to keep throwing out the furniture.

This I did to the degree that one reviewer faulted my laconic descriptions of landscapes. I had indeed stripped the pages to bare bones. Marrow bones! *El Morro* is the most deliberately written of all my books. The characters gain definition by what they say and do. Everything leads to their final destination. I believed that was my farewell as a writer to the Southwest.

I wrote with the certainty that life ends in death however eternal it seems along the way; and death at El Morro comes at the other moment of supreme ecstasy. Thus was acted out my own ritualistic end in an elegy for beloved places and people.

Three years passed before the book was done. At times it took an effort to sustain it. Was I not fulfilling my doctor's prediction that after age 75 . . . ? Publication came as I reached 78, in a bold design by Ward Ritchie.

Although *El Morro* celebrates death, its vitality won approval from Edward Abbey and Charles Bowden, reward enough. Still more precious was the response of Peggy Pond Church, the New Mexico writer and friend of thirty years. She had made a similar journey with her husband as he was unknowingly dying of a brain tumor. She was destined to die soon thereafter by her own hand, though not without a farewell to me: "If there is a life hereafter, let's do a bit of haunting—at El Morro."

V

It proved a delusion that *El Morro* was my last book, nor was it my death as a writer. I returned to a long deferred project I had been unable to complete in the forty years since its conception – a biography of my father. It was the hardest to write of all my books. Its origin followed the loss of my eldest brother, Clark, dead at 38 in South Africa. His ashes were scattered on a hill in a Transvaal game refuge where he had photographed the herds and their predators.

In the absence of a biography of my father and with urging by my mother, I set about writing the life of him who had died at 50 when I was only fifteen. Higher priorities forced me to leave it unfinished. Although my mother was disappointed, there was not enough material to make it an engaging book. His life appeared to be strictly public. Most of his contemporaries were dead. Now years later they were all gone. What records did exist lacked personal evidence.

Then upon my mother's death in 1957 I inherited startling new information about my father. Included were his only diary, of a few months in 1908, and a packet of ribbon-tied letters to my mother from him in Paris, written at the time of the diary. This material laid bare a love found and lost, a love denied by my mother who because of us boys and his career refused to divorce him. His hitherto unknown personal life was suddenly illuminated in his own passionate words.

I realized that my mother had waited until her death for me to tell the story of the unfilled life she had denied him – and to tell it in his own words in the letters he wrote to her. Was she also avoiding my judgement of her denial while she was still alive?

My task was how to merge the public and private lives. For twenty years after her death I sought form for the telling. Even when found, gaps could be filled only by imagination.

Fay and I were in England in the summer of 1976 on a visit to my niece Marcia, Clark's daughter, and her English husband Sir Guy Lawrence where they lived near Ascot. Their country home was next to Windsor Great Forest, with its many alluring footpaths. As once done in Burgundy, I brooded while cycling among the old trees, my mind seeking to organize the book about my father.

Then one summer morning, during a prolonged drought over

southern England, there in the burning heart of Berkshire, the answer came. In a shaded corner of the garden, under a great beech tree (Yeats's great-rooted blossomer!), I began what proved both fact and fiction.

Back to France in imagination I went for the setting. Was it not there that it had begun for him as it had for me? I recalled a narrator and a listener to hear my account of his life and love, as told in his own words to his wife. It was from Paris that my father wrote those burning letters which revealed the complex man the world never dreamed him to be. Had he too not walked with his love in the Luxembourg Gardens? Thus the lives of father and son were rejoined.

Another stream blocked the first flow. It was the demand of the unfinished *The River Between* which, according to Noel Young, needed a final revision. I needed someone to mull it over with. My family were not the ones, dear though they were.

I lay awake that night listening to a tiny radio under my pillow, broadcasting from Covent Garden the premiere of Hans Werner Henze's opera "We Come to the River," an anti-war work of violent music and exalted singing. I heard it as a summons to return alone to Arizona and finish the earlier book. Again I felt the pain of tearing apart.

My father's book would have to wait—for another ten years. Part of a not to be denied imperative were lines of Mauriac recalled in *The Blue Train*:

> Au jours ou la chaleur arretait toute vie
> Je cherchais votre coeur comme je cherchais l'ombre

With *The River Between* completed and published, I was free to return to my father's book. Yet it was not until nine years later that it came with a rush, even as *El Morro* had. Fay and I were in Santa Fe that summer. I was propped in bed early one morning at La Fonda when I began the first true draft.

So well was it focused in my subconscious that it came clearly and was quickly finished, with only carpenter work for which no listener was needed. Nor was there a need to return to Paris, Vézelay or Auxerre so vivid were their settings in memory, even to the French capital's bittersweet perfume which has never left me.

Portrait of My Father was published by Capra in Santa Barbara on my 80th birthday, its jacket bearing the portrait made by Edward

Weston not long before my father's death in 1922. Reviewers were puzzled by the book. Was it biography or novel? It could not be both. Who was this upstart writer who said that it could?

I had also confused readers by leaving the field of the Southwest in which I had made my first reputation and to which my non fiction and my second and third novels were linked. It was too much to expect readers to understand my return in old age to the land where I had begun as man and writer—and also to the man from whose loins I had sprung.

The *Portrait* did find a few receptive readers, including a writer whom I have never met. He wrote me, "What an enchanting heroine! She seems to me the most accomplished of your women characters, *Blue Train* and all, and not just because you've had more space to develop her in: she has a beautiful complexity, and it certainly comes through. By and large, too, you've been very skilful in handling historical facts that are hard to account for . . . "

VI

I can see now that this tetralogy is a single work, encompassing one writer's creative lifetime. Responses have been Yes or No, the No's from those who judged the novels for what they are not, expecting them to be more conventional and expansive in character portrayal. "Underpopulated" one reviewer called *The River Between*, a work in which only desert and river were important, the few people meaningful only as they drew strength from the austere environment. Such an ambiguous response was better than none.

These books are *sui generis*, the form of each determined by its mode and content. Each deserves to be read and judged as a work with its own shape and style. Even those who rejected them were compelled to read them through, even while the intellect protested. "I read it straight through immediately, marvelling as always at your gift of readability, the most indispensable of the writer's gifts, which you have in abundance." The words are Paul Horgan's.

In this gathering, readers are offered an opportunity of reading the linked achievement of one writer in reorganizing and bringing meaning to a lifetime's experience. They can also be seen as rebellions against their author's fate, which was ultimately to find freedom in the confines of a disciplined life. All are undertoned by deepening sadness.

Until they receive such reading, I'll have to content myself with Charles Bowden's response to *El Morro*: "At a time when most men have long since given up work for the golf course or rocking chair, Powell continues to wrestle with this slab of American earth that has dominated the life of his mind."

At first I did not understand the imperative to learn who I was and what I was meant to do with my gifts. To attain self-discipline took many years, so attractive were the ways of self-indulgence. So much time was wasted in those early years in France, seeking to complete that first seemingly endless novel. I remember the words in the newspaper the morning after my final examination: "A work about an artist, written by an artist." Although I didn't know it then, that proved a challenge to make it come true.

And now in "old" old age I am living out my final years under the beneficent dominion of Hesperus, lord of the Evening Redness. Once when feeling frustration as man and writer, I consoled myself with lines from the *Rubaiyat*: "Ah love, could you and I with Him conspire to grasp this sorry scheme of things entire, would not we shatter it to bits—and then remould it nearer to the heart's desire!"

Now at last those words seem unreal. I prefer instead those of Whitman, "Reconciliation, word over all, beautiful as the sky," Am I reconciled to waiting a century for posterity's verdict? Readers of a hundred years from now, if there are any, prithee be kind to this book.

THE BLUE TRAIN

THE BLUE TRAIN

This is a romance, intended to be to the novel what the string quartet is to the symphony—more compact, chromatic, evocative. It plays variations on a single theme. If it should be thought that actual persons were portrayed, even though it had been so meant there could be little resemblance. Time alters reality, filtering it through memory and imagination, so that what remains is the magic of being young in a foreign land, unburdened by the weight of living that comes later. If Life once sounded discordant, Art has here rendered it harmonious. What then was agitated is now serene. The dedication is to Henry Miller, old friend and encourager.

I
Nancy

On a Friday afternoon of a cloudy day in early November, the wind from the northeast, I stood on the station platform ten minutes before train time, waiting for the 13.36 *rapide* from Paris. I often came to the station late at night when my eyes grew tired from laboratory work, merely to witness the arrival and departure of the express trains that left the capital in the early evening. There was the Blue Train to the Riviera, the Rome, and the Simplon Orient bound for Italy, the Balkans, Athens and Istanbul. For the price of a 50-centime ticket I could gain entry to the platform and watch the trains make their brief stop for servicing.

This time was different. I was bound for Switzerland to what promised to be a romantic rendezvous. I was already excited as I walked up track from under the high ironwork shell that arched over the boarding area to where the freight yards widened out. They were congested and noisy with the crashing of shunted cars. Brakemen were gesticulating and shouting to drivers of the small engines.

The main line was clear, all lights green, the high rails gleaming as I watched for the *rapide* from Paris. Then I heard it approaching, heralded by a shriek of the engine's whistle; and there it was, bearing down with the overpowering majesty of the black and green, copper-banded P.L.M. locomotive, cleaving the confusion of lesser equipment with the authority of the crack flyer, two hundred miles out of Paris, scheduled to pause only long enough to take on coal, water, and passengers.

I stood back and let the long train pass and then halt with a sigh of relaxing air brakes, before I followed it back into the station. I found my car next to the rear *fourgon*, a black Swiss coach with red and white Maltese cross and placard on its side, reading "Paris-Berne via Dijon, Pontarlier, Neuchâtel."

I boarded the second-class end of the carriage and looked for a smoking compartment. All were full. Even the aisle was crowded. I found a jump seat in the vestibule next to the door window, and there I settled down for the journey to Switzerland. I could hear outside the seemingly disorganized uproar of a French train departure; and yet, precisely on time, the shouting ceased and the train rolled out of the station, gathering speed along the banks of the Burgundy Canal, through the stucco suburbs and past the signal tower where a division occurred, one line going down the valley of the Rhone to Lyon, Marseilles, and the Riviera, the other branching off to Switzerland and Italy.

We followed this latter and were soon in open country, running fast over the plain that stretched eastward to the foothills and mountains of the Jura. I did not relish the four-hour journey on the hard seat, and to distract myself, I unfolded and read for the nth time a letter—a letter from a girl I had never met, and curiosity about whom was leading me to Neuchâtel.

"Dear Jack," it read, "Your letter was wonderful. You must come. I need you. I haven't been able to find a place for you to stay. My French is hopeless and no one speaks my kind of German. Can't we leave your bag at the station and walk around till we find a room for you? It's not a huge town.

44

"I'm such a child it's ridiculous to react so vitally to unfavorable health and I think and hope I'm wrong that I have something simply awful the matter with me. What it can be to cause me to lie awake every night I really don't know. I hope you will.

"Please Jack, you will come, won't you? I can't abide one more weekend surrounded by chattering black uniformed French-Swiss jeunes filles. If you don't come soon I'll have to go home although I'm not expected until Christmas. The school doctor speaks and understands nothing but French and I with only English and German, really it's quite hopeless. Why did I ever come here? This is the most urgent plea of my life and funnily, it's not because you're my girl friend's boy friend's former roommate and someone from home I can talk to or a former med student who can possibly help me, but honestly because in a way it's you, the you of your letters. Am I hopelessly incoherent?

"I know you are terribly busy with your studies and all but it's awful to think there's a sane reason for your not coming. I wish you would let me wire you the money. I've never spent my allowance. I feel like a sick little cold little timorous yellow dog (did I hear you say bitch?). You will come Friday afternoon? I'll meet you at the *gare*. This is amusing, my crying out for help but so I am.

"Your needful, Nancy Clary."

I put the letter back in my pocket and mused over its contents, as the plain began to undulate into the first hills, and the bare trees be darkly interspersed with pines and firs. I would miss only the Friday laboratory. There was a *rapide* back on Sunday evening. I was curious about Nancy Clary, a student of the pipe organ, and said to be both beautiful and rich. And it was my first visit to Switzerland. It was called playing by ear. Would we make harmony or discord? I had no money to spare and would not take hers. It had been long since I had known an American girl. I was susceptible and yielded, and now the train was speeding toward a denouement. I dozed.

Pontarlier was the point of no return. From there most of the train went on to Geneva and through the Simplon Tunnel to Italy. My Swiss coach was coupled on to a waiting train drawn by an electric engine, and soon we were climbing through the last range of the Jura Mountains that separated France and Switzerland. Snow lay on the ground and clung to the branches of the firs. Crows flew up as the passing train disturbed them. Deep below in narrow pockets of the mountains were isolated villages, their houses plumed with chimney smoke. Here and there among the conifer forest, autumn-fired deciduous trees burned in shades of red and yellow. Then we crossed the frontier at Vallorbe, and soon were switchbacking down to the city on Lake Neuchâtel.

I saw her on the platform as the train came to a stop: windblown blonde hair, expectant face, thin, worried and frowning, wrapped in a gray tweed coat. I went to her as she came along the platform.

"Thank God, you've come!" she said, as we shook hands in continental fashion.

"Did you sleep better?"

"Not really. But I think it was excitement over your wire. Do you have more baggage?"

"Just this one. I'm not coming to stay. Let's find a place for me to sleep."

"I already did, just this morning. It's a *pension* room near here. I wish you would have let me pay for a hotel room."

"I can't afford to be in your power. A *pension* room is the limit of my budget."

"You'll let me take you to dinner."

"Where?"

"A perfect place on the lake front. I've already booked our table."

"Bart said you were bossy."

"He told me about you, too."

"I hope so."

"That you are a rebel."

"What else?"

"That you left a brilliant record at med school in San Francisco to bury yourself in a lab in the dreariest of provincial cities. Dijon must be frightfully ordinary."

"I suppose it would be for you. I am working and happy."

"Do you know any girls?"

"What kind of girls?"

"Girls you make love to."

"A different one each night."

"Bart said you were misanthropic."

"A love affair takes time. I've been busy."

"I warn you, I'm not going to have an affair with you."

46

"That's not why I came."

"Why then?"

"Because you asked me to."

"Do you always do what women ask you to?"

"When they are as blonde and beautiful as you are."

"Flattery will get you nowhere, Jack Burgoyne."

"I suppose it was really curiosity that brought me to Neuchâtel."

"I have never known how you came by your last name."

"My paternal grandfather was French, named Bourgogne. When he emigrated, he anglicized it. It means Burgundy."

"Is that why you chose Dijon?"

"Subconsciously, perhaps, but really for the endocrinology laboratory I'm working in. It has a wide reputation."

We chatted in pauses of climbing the steep street back of the station that led to the *pension*. At its door we turned and looked down on the terraced town, dropping to the lake. The sky was cloudy, the lake colorless, the Alps veiled.

"It's supposed to clear," she said, "and be milder. We're going on a picnic tomorrow."

"With the school?"

"Heavens, no! Just the two of us."

"Will I be safe?"

"Silly."

"Will you promise to stop frowning? You're getting a permanent wrinkle."

"It's worry. You must help me."

"I'm not a doctor."

"You'll let me tell you my symptoms?"

"For dessert."

"Don't tease me. I'm serious. I'll call for you at seven-thirty. You'll have time to change. I don't suppose you brought evening clothes."

"I don't have any."

"It *is* a chic restaurant."

"I have a dark suit on under my overcoat."

"I already tipped the headwaiter and told him we must have a quiet table where we can talk. May *I* dress?"

"In black."

"Bart said you were not to be trusted."

47

"A platonic affair will be a restful change."

"Don't count on anything more from me."

She went off down the steps and I settled in a large room with wash basin and wardrobe, and undressed for a nap. She posed a challenge. Was it really only for advice that she wanted me to come? The answer lay in pressing all the way. Except for the frown and a brusque way of speaking, she was a lovely girl, although the heavy coat had concealed her figure.

A few minutes before seven-thirty I stood in front of the *pension* and waited for her. The sky had cleared. The stars glittered. Leaves from the plane trees rattled along the cobbled street. The air was sweet with woodsmoke. Below and in both directions were the lights of Neuchâtel.

Then I heard a horse and carriage toiling up the street. It stopped and the driver swung down and opened the door for me. Nancy Clary was in the back seat. I got in and sat beside her. The driver wheeled, set his brake, and we went back down the hill, the horse's hooves ringing hesitantly on the cobbles, the brake shoes grinding on the iron-rimmed wheels.

"I have never ridden in a carriage," I said.

"I know you are going to help me. I just know you are."

She grasped my hand. I held hers. She withdrew it.

"I can't help it." I said. "You smell good. You and the woodsmoke."

"The townspeople lit fires in your honor. Do you like my perfume?"

"I thought it was you."

"Bart warned me."

"Can I help it if I'm responsive?"

"I've heard that before."

"So you know about men!"

"I'm no virgin, if that's what you are trying to find out."

"I wasn't, but I'm glad to know."

We reached the lake front and the horse began to trot along the avenue that followed the quay. We drew into a brilliantly lighted garden restaurant at the water's edge.

"Will you ask him to wait?" Nancy whispered to me.

"You mean through dinner?"

"Of course."

"I heard you were rich."

"I am—although the news from home is not good. Daddy says that the Depression is getting worse."

I did as she asked, and followed her into the restaurant. The headwaiter bowed and showed us to a corner table overlooking the lake; and as we gave up our coats and were seated, I saw Nancy's approving gaze.

"Did you expect me to be in corduroys?"

"Bart said you were unconventional."

"I wouldn't be here if I weren't."

"Thank you for dressing nicely. After all, we are a civilized people and should live that way."

"You talk like an old lady."

"I *am* twenty-five."

"And beautiful."

She was—in a low-cut, bare-armed, black evening gown, her hair done up and banded with a narrow black ribbon. Her eyes were blue, her lips a bit too thin.

"Do you like me?"

"If you'll stop frowning."

"But I'm worried."

"Stick out your tongue."

"I'm serious."

"I'm beginning to realize it. Can't we eat first? Pleasure before business. I'm starved."

"I'm sorry, Jack. I'll be patient."

"Be mine."

She wrinkled her nose at my pun.

Nancy had ordered the dinner, and it was a good one: filets of lake fish sautéed, with a local white wine, chilled and naturally sparkling, followed by *chateaubriand aux pommes frites* and watercress, and a bottle of Romanée.

"In your honor, Monsieur!" Nancy toasted, when the queen of the red Burgundies was served.

The food and drink made me expansive.

"Now, tell me your troubles, poor girl. Why can't Nancy sleep o'nights?"

"That's not it. That's not my real trouble, although I *might* just have a loathsome disease."

49

"You look disgustingly healthy, like a Swiss milkmaid."

"Horrible thought."

"Tell me."

"It's sex."

I laughed. *"That's* no trouble."

"Stop being so predatory."

"Men naturally are."

"Please listen to me." I went on eating and drinking while she talked. "I've known only two men. An English boy in Cheltenham and an Austrian man in Salzburg."

"As lovers?"

"Yes, but Jack," and she was almost in tears, "I never felt anything. Aren't I supposed to?"

"Normally."

"I've never—what do you call it what you have an orgasm?"

"Never come."

"I've tried so hard to. At first I blamed it on Roger, he was so young. Karl was a man though and very experienced."

She stopped, her eyes tearful.

"What happened?" I encouraged her.

"He cursed me. He said I was a blonde American bitch, as cold as the Arlberg Glacier."

I laughed.

"And you aren't?"

"It wasn't funny. I was never so humiliated. I loaned him money, too."

"And he never paid you back."

"How did you know?"

"I've read the classics."

"You keep making fun of me."

"After a meal like this? You're a marvelous cook."

"I hate to cook."

"Of course."

"What's wrong with me, Jack? Why can't I come? Don't all girls?"

"It's probably psychological."

"What do you mean?"

"You're too self-conscious."

"How do I go about forgetting myself?"

"It's late to start trying, if you haven't learned by now."

50

"Can you help me?"

"Do you want me to try?"

"No, if that's what you mean."

"You amuse me."

"I'm Irish, I warn you."

We listened to the string orchestra.

"Do you know what it is?" she asked.

"Yes."

"What?"

"Grieg's *Holberg Suite*."

"Bart never told me you were musical."

"I'm not. My mother was. She was a singer and a poet. I learned from her to love poetry and music. My father was a practical man."

"I came here for the course in pipe organ and found the Maître had gone on a tour. A young organist is in charge. I think he wants me to sleep with him."

"Well, why don't you?"

"I've suffered too much of a trauma."

"Didn't you ask me here to make love to you?"

"I did not."

"Why then?"

"For advice."

"You make it hard for me to help you. I might as well go back to Dijon."

"Not till Sunday, please."

"Will you stop frowning?"

"I'll try."

"You spoil your looks when you frown."

"Am I pretty?"

"Beautiful."

"Do I still smell sweet?"

"As all Burgundy."

"O Jack, I want so much to be normal."

"Let me hold your hand."

"Mother told me not to. She said the road to ruin began with holding hands."

"It's not a dirt road."

And so we held hands across the linen, and the meal ended har-

51

moniously. As she was due in at eleven, I suggested that the driver take her home first and then deliver me.

"Take this," she said, handing me a wad of francs. "Please pay for the meal and the carriage. Don't overtip, though; they don't expect it here in Neuchâtel."

It was no place to argue. I took the money, paid the check and left a generous tip.

The driver had blanketed his horse, and he was great-coated; their breaths made frost on the air. The night was even sweeter with woodsmoke; and in the carriage, as we rolled smoothly along the lake front, Nancy's fragrance went to my head.

"You may leave your arm around me," she conceded.

"And kiss you?"

"Just one."

I was astonished when her mouth opened to mine and she relaxed in my arms.

We were at her school too soon.

"I said just one," she warned, as I sought to kiss her again.

"Tomorrow?"

"I've planned an outdoor day."

"I'm a great outdoorsman!"

"Meet me in the market place at nine-thirty," she said. "The driver will tell you where it is."

The concièrge opened the great front door and she slipped in and was gone. I paid the driver there, after getting directions to the market place, and found my way back up hill to my *pension* through drifts of wind-blown leaves. The night was cold, and I walked fast for warmth.

I was early for the rendezvous in the morning and wandered about the stalls. The foodstuffs were displayed with Swiss care and elegance—game, poultry, fruits and vegetables, breads and cheeses and sausages. The scene was bustling yet orderly, unlike the disorder of a French provincial market. The forecast proved true: it was a clear day of mild sunshine. The Alps were almost unreal, silhouetted against the pale sky.

Nancy found me in the throng. Again we shook hands.

"I slept!" she said.

"I lay awake."

"Thinking of me?"

"Thinking of it."

"You are a lecherous man."

"And you are a beautiful woman."

"Do you like me in this?"

She was wearing a tan skirt, a green flannel shirt, her hair in a loose knot at the back of her neck, green wool socks and ankle-high boots.

"Who wouldn't?"

"When you wrote that you wanted to walk in the autumn woods, I went shopping."

"I like women in skirts. They're more vulnerable."

"It's chamois—and so am I! You'll never catch me."

We packed her haversack with gruyere, ham, rye bread, and grapes. I slung it over my shoulder, and we set out for the *funiculaire* which took off from the highest terrace. A short steep ride brought us to the mountain top, high above city and lake, the woods at our back. A dirt track led deep into the colored fire of oak, chestnut, and ash; the last leaves of the year drifted around us like butterflies.

"This is my first real walk," she said. "We must not go too far. I'm not terribly strong."

"Is this the road to ruin your mother warned you of?"

"You'd better forget last night."

"That meal?"

"You know what I mean."

"Haven't you forgotten how to forget yourself?"

"I did, didn't I! But we really can't, here in Neuchâtel. It's a very proper place."

"Aren't we beyond the city limits?"

"I'm not going to let you, so there."

"Well then, let's take it out in walking."

Toward noon we were passing a farmhouse, and I turned in and bought a litre wine-bottle of warm milk from a roomful of dung-booted peasants. They were gathered around a table in an open shed, husking a mountain of chestnuts.

We walked on out of sight, turned off the path, and while Nancy unpacked the food, I heaped up a drift of dry leaves. We devoured the nutty cheese, the smoky ham and coarse bread, all washed down with milk, then savored the sugary grapes for dessert. I lay

53

back on the leaves and looked up through bare boughs at the sky, while Nancy took a book from the haversack.

"Do you like German poetry?" she asked.

"Read me some and I'll decide."

"I bought this Insel Bücherei just for your coming. The poems are arranged by season."

"Is there a section called Indian Summer?"

"It is such a beautiful day."

"I didn't bring it with me. Dijon weather is horrible. It's fall in case you aren't sure."

"Of the leaves, not me."

"You can't seem to get your mind off it. You'll end up giving *me* ideas."

"As long as you don't want to do more than talk."

"But I do!"

"I'm afraid of getting pregnant."

"You can trust me."

"Maybe someday. Could you come to Salzburg?"

"Paris would be the limit of my budget."

"I don't like the French."

"But I am American."

"A persistent one, too."

"Would you like it better if I were a woman?"

"I've never tried it with one."

"You're obviously made for man's enjoyment."

"But not yours, Jack Burgoyne. Please get that through your head."

"Well," I said, resignedly, "If we can't do it, let's read about it."

"I told you these are nature poems."

"Isn't it natural?"

"You're hopeless."

"I trust the situation isn't."

"I'll read you *Oktoberlied*."

"It's November."

"Be quiet and listen."

She read beautifully. I stretched out in the crackling leaves, closed my eyes, and listened to her voice reading.

Der Nebel steigt, es fällt das Laub,

54

Schenk ein den Wein den holden;
Wir wollen uns den grauen Tag
Vergolden, ja vergolden.

"Translate, please."

"It means that in October there is rising mist and falling leaves and someone comes along and pours vintage wine, and the days are made golden; yes, golden."

"Yesterday was gray and windy and last night the world was all flying leaves. We drank wine and voilà; today is blue and gold." I caught her hand and sought to draw her down beside me. "O Nancy, your eyes are lake blue, sky blue, your hair is yellow gold, golden yellow."

She pulled loose. "Unhand me, varlet."

"Milk always makes me mellow."

She laughed. "You are an entertaining guest."

"Read me more, Miss Iceberg."

"Just don't call me a you know what."

"Don't be one and I won't."

She read Storm and Goethe, Rilke and Georg, and as I listened to her soft voice in the strange tongue, I heard only the music and not the meaning. I mused on what she would be like if she could forget herself. It did not seem hopeful. There was not time enough. And I was not patient.

I must have fallen asleep. When I opened my eyes, Nancy was asleep beside me, no trace of frown on her thin face, her breathing deep and regular. I leaned over her on my elbow. She opened her eyes and frowned. The spell was broken. I stood up.

"En route, mademoiselle," I said, helping her up.

We walked slowly back out of the woods and again looked down on the terraced town and lake and across to the Alps, rosy in the afternoon light. We saw a dirt road leading to terrace after terrace, and instead of taking the *funiculaire*, we decided to walk all the way down. We heard the sounds of children at play, of barking dogs, tramcars, and church bells striking the hour. Peasant women were gleaning in the vineyards. We leaned on a stone wall and rested, while a gleaner crept toward us along the row. When she reached the end at the wall, she straightened to turn and go back, saw us and croaked, "Bon soir, m'sieu, 'dame. Vous vous promenez? Qu'il fait beau aujourd'hui! Mais dépêchons-nous, il va pleuvoir." She waved toward the Alps and the gathering clouds, then resumed her gleaning.

"I'm so glad we came this way," Nancy said, squeezing my hand.

We kept descending toward the town. The air was perfumed with smoke from burning leaves, rising from many points in town. Nancy began to limp from a tight boot, and as we neared my *pension*, I suggested we stop there and rest. I expected her to say no. Instead she agreed. At an *épicerie* I bought a kilo of Algerian dates and a bottle of vin rosé.

"I shouldn't have come," she said, as I closed my room's door and locked it. "But I am so tired."

"Lie down, and let me take off your boots."

She was passive as I unlaced and removed them and then her heavy socks. Her legs were smooth and white. She wiggled her toes in relief. I wet a washcloth.

"That's heavenly" she murmured, as I bathed her feet.

"Your role's reversed, Mary Magdalen."

"I never walked so far in all my life."

"Drink this." I poured her a glass of wine, and I, too, drank a full glass. We ate dates. I sat on the edge of the bed. Her eyes were closed. I began to caress her forehead and to stroke her hair and neck. Her arms reached up and drew me down, and our mouths met again in a wet and winy kiss.

She finally broke away. I said nothing.

"My skirt will be ruined," she murmured, arching her back. "Be a good Jack."

I pulled it off and threw it on a chair.

"Hang it up, please," she whispered.

"To hell with it," I said, fearing to break the spell. I found her mouth again and she returned my kiss, even more passionately. My hand slid down to remove her panties and again she arched her back.

There came a stern rapping on the door.

"Who is it?" I called.

"The landlady. You have left mud on the hall rug. Kindly remove your soiled shoes hereafter when you enter."

"As you desire, Madame, I shall not give offense another time."

I had gotten up to go to the door, and now turned back to the bed, groaning, "Ah God, the tidy Swiss!" Nancy was sitting up.

"Give me my skirt. I've changed my mind."

I pushed her down. "Change it back."

"I won't."

"I'm going to make love to you, if it's the last thing I do."

"It will be the last thing if you do. Let me up."

I held her down. She struggled silently. I pinned her against the wall.

"Come on, Jack," she said, matter of fact, "you can't make me."

"You've heard of rape."

"What pleasure would that give you?"

"Lots."

"You're an egotistical bastard, Jack Burgoyne, and I hate you. I'll *never* let you now. Please give me my skirt."

I threw it high on the wardrobe.

"Don't do that! It's an expensive skirt. You'll ruin it."

"I'll ruin you."

"You've ruined it all, just as I was giving in."

"Give in again."

"Jack, listen to me, I must get back and change, and there's the concert at 8:30. I bought box seats for us."

"We'll make our own music."

"You tried to get me drunk and you almost did." She turned face down, sobbing.

Time passed. I sat on the edge of the bed and would not let her up in spite of her alternate pleading and scolding. I drank the rest of the wine. I was a little drunk, and disgusted by the way things had miscarried.

At last I relented. I stood on a chair and threw her the chamois skirt. She slipped into it, unlocked the door and was gone. I looked at my watch. It was ten o'clock. I went to the window and threw it open. The street and walks were glistening. The wind had risen and rain was blowing.

I started to undress, and then I relented, hurried into my clothes, took my overcoat, and went out. She was sheltering under a nearby fir tree. I threw my coat around her and we hurried silently back to her school. I was cold sober, ashamed of having overplayed my hand. While waiting for the concièrge to open, she removed my coat and I put it on over my wet clothes.

"Thank you at last for being a gentleman," she said, coldly.

"At your service, Miss Blondebitch." I bowed and walked away, as the door closed. I trudged back to my room through the empty streets. The leaves underfoot were sodden.

I was awakened in the morning by a soft knocking on the door.

"Who is there?" I called, expecting the landlady to answer.

"It's me, Nancy. Let me in."

I got up and unlocked the door. She pushed by me.

"How did you sleep, Mr. Caveman?"

I did not answer, and began to wash my face and comb my hair.

"I slept," she offered.

"I didn't expect to see you again."

"I came for my haversack."

"It's there in the corner."

"Don't be cross with me, Jack. Kiss me good morning. Or do you insist on shaving first?"

"I'm taking the noon train."

"It's an *express* and it stops everywhere. Please take the 20:30 *rapide*."

"What would I do with myself until then?"

"Be with me."

"What do you mean?"

"What I say."

"We behaved badly."

"I'll take the blame, if you'll stay. Please stay. I need you. I've felt so well since you came." She took my hand. "I lost my head when she knocked. Forgive me." She embraced me. I breathed her freshness of hair and skin and soap. "We can go back to our bed of leaves."

"It rained."

"We can stay here."

"What if she knocked again?"

"Keep our heads under the covers."

"This is a new Nancy."

"Don't be cross with me. Nancy loves Jack. Nancy will offer proof of her love if Jack wishes."

"Carnal?"

"Utterly."

"Nancy Clary in the role of Delilah. Instead of cutting my hair, will you shave me?"

"Put on the lather."

We laughed. "Wait for me out front," I said "I'll shave and dress and be right down."

"Will we come back here?"

"All I can think of now is my stomach. We'll take care of the other organs later."

"I have never known anyone as outspoken as you."

"I can't help it."

"I'm accustomed to more genteel persons, but I'm beginning to like you, Jack Burgoyne."

"I'm willing to start over. Are you going to wait outside for me?"

"No, I want to watch you shave."

"Where will we eat?"

"I know a nice place on the lake front where we can have petit déjeuner."

"I want breakfast, lunch, and dinner. Dates is all I've had since yesterday noon."

"Poor man, Nancy will feed you."

I felt my interest rising as she showed this contrite side of her nature. The day was fair after rain, and it was an attractive outdoor restaurant on the quay, under pollarded plane trees, the water of the lake all but lapping our table as we ordered a mushroom omelette and ham, bread and sweet butter and jam, with café au lait. Under the morning sun the lake was dancing with whitecaps. Fresh snow had whitened the Alps. The promenade was peopled with the Neuchâtelois in their Sunday best. They were a staid folk all dressed in black.

While I ate hungrily Nancy nibbled at her plate; and she, too, was silent until finally she looked at her wrist watch and said,

"You've missed the noon train. I was afraid you might change your mind. Now you're mine until tonight."

"Possessive, aren't you? I must say, though, I like the new Nancy."

"You've done it. I hate myself for panicking. I knew it would have happened."

"What would have?"

"Do I have to say it?"

"Yes."

"I felt myself having an . . . I felt myself . . . coming."

"What was it like?"

"Fire under the ice. I felt myself beginning to melt and flow."

"There's hope for you. You haven't frowned once this morning."

"You don't hate me?"

"You're too selfish."

"So are you. You came just to have a good time at my expense."

"To have a good time together. That way we cancel each other's selfishness."

"I ruined it."

"You'll do it again if you keep talking about it."

"I want more than anything to be normal—and not pregnant."

"No danger with your Uncle John."

"Do you know why I am not frowning? Because I know that something nice is going to happen to me."

"You *can* be sweet, Nancy Clary."

"And we will turn the gloomy days to golden days, yes, golden."

"Did you bring the little book?"

"Only my fair young body and my long golden hair."

It went the way she wanted and that I had hoped, the day before, it would go. We returned to my room, undressed, and lay on the bed. She was beautiful and good to love, with no trouble between us and no knock on the door. Somewhere in the *pension* a violinist was practicing Bach sonatas; and as we lay quietly afterward, Nancy hummed along with him. Sunday in Neuchâtel was dead quiet. No noise rose from the street. We slept and then made love again.

When it grew dark, we dressed; I packed my bag, and we walked to the station for supper in the buffet.

"I'm starved again," I confessed.

"The stomach is terribly important in your scheme of things."

"I have a rapid rate of metabolism."

"I'm so glad I'm normal. It was so good. For the first time in my life. But I wonder?" She clung to my arm, and I saw that she was frowning.

"Now what's the matter?"

"Jack, are you sure I'm all right?"

"You mean pregnant?"

"Silly! I mean *not* pregnant."

"Of course you won't be. Didn't I explain to you?"

"I know, but what if there was a leak?"

"Should I have blown them up?"

"Don't be sarcastic."

"Then don't worry."

"Women are born to worry."

"Give me one that doesn't and I'll make her my goddess."

"You're not the one who will swell up and be horrid looking."

We had reached the station, taken a table in the buffet, and ordered dinner of roast lamb and white beans and a chicory salad. Nancy would not eat. Her hair began to come down and she went to the rest room to pin it up. When she returned, she was frowning.

"I know you think I'm impossible," she said, "but I really think I'd better go home and take a douche."

"Eat something first. See me off, then take a carriage. You'll be all right. Let me pour you some wine."

"I know you think I'm always spoiling it for you."

"You are."

"And I'm frowning horribly."

"You're not pretty anymore."

"I don't care. I just can't eat." She smiled wanly. "I think I have evening sickness. Please get me a carriage."

"Do you mean it?"

"Please, I must go."

I followed her outside to the carriage rank.

"Get in with me, Jack, and sit a minute. Kiss me good-by."

"You have a genius for ruining things."

"Wasn't it worth it?"

"A thousand times no," I said cruelly.

"Won't you kiss me good-bye?"

"No."

"Will you take this money?"

"No."

61

"You are heartless."

"Only when you make me so."

"Please, Jack." She began to cry.

I turned away and went toward the buffet door. I heard the carriage door close, the wheels grinding on the cobbles as it turned, and the horse's hooves beginning the deliberate klop, klop, as it drove away.

Though full of self-disgust, I ate both portions of the lamb and beans and salad and was on the platform as the *rapide* from Berne came in, silently drawn by an electric engine. This time I found an empty compartment in the through car to Dijon and Paris, stretched out on the wide seat with my overcoat for a blanket, and soon fell asleep to the clicking of wheels over the rail points.

II
Erda

What draws a man to a woman—that draws one man to one woman when they are only two among thousands? In the beginning it was probably because she went bareheaded even in the coldest weather. Her hair was the color of ripening cornsilk. It hung to her shoulders in rippling waves and gleamed in the winter sunlight. She was short and solidly built, with a strong stride. Each noonday when she passed the café window as I was taking an apéritif, I watched her come up the Rue Chabot-Charny, probably from the Faculty of Letters, cross the Place du Théâtre to the sidewalk outside the window where I sat, then on past the Church of St. Michel and out of sight.

She was obviously not French. High cheekbones and aquiline nose indicated what race? Slav? Magyar? Finn? I came to await her daily passage, a kind of princess among the provincial throng that streamed by each day on the way home to lunch; and though I stared at her coming, her passing profile, and her going, never did she notice me.

After she had gone, I mused over my vin blanc-cassis. Should I follow her and learn where she lived? Or block her way and introduce myself? I did neither. I was wary of all blondes after Neu-

62

châtel; and yet, though I was occupied in laboratory work, with little free time, I wanted the company of a woman. No Dijonnaise drew me. The sweetness I had tasted with Nancy, although it had turned bitter, was like honey at the back of my tongue.

Then one afternoon, because I was interested in the Symbolists, I went to a five o'clock lecture, given by the Dean at the Faculty of Letters, on Rimbaud, the wonder boy of French poetry. She was there. I saw her a few rows below me in the petit-amphithéâtre. Throughout the Dean's crisp, logical, and elegant *explication*, I stared down at her, seated to one side so that I could watch her face partly in profile, strong yet not masculine, wide, generous mouth, large forehead. She seemed spellbound, never turning her gaze from the short, dark, fox-like speaker. The hour went by. My mind was divided, following the Dean's lecture and at the same time dreaming of her who fascinated me, wondering how to draw her to me as I was drawn to her.

"Lucid, yet mystical," the Dean concluded, "as in these lines, saying all, meaning what? Take them with you, listeners, as a talisman in memory." He lowered his voice, and read:

J'ai fait la magique étude
Du bonheur, que nul n'élude.
O vive lui, chaque fois
Que chante le coq gaulois.

The applause was loud and long. The Dean acknowledged it with a sardonic smile. The students waited for him to leave the platform, then they crowded into the aisles. I stood at the back, watching her come up the steps; and then as she approached, drawing on her gloves, I took a deep breath, stepped in her way, and heard myself say,

"Je demande pardon, mademoiselle, mais puis-je vous accompagner chez vous?"

Her blue eyes stared into mine, and for a second I feared defeat. Then she smiled and said in English,

"If you like."

"But . . . but . . . " I stammered, "you are not English."

"I prefer it to French."

"You speak it beautifully."

"How nice of you to say that."

63

"English English, not American English."

"Will you teach me American English?"

"How did you know I am American?"

"I am a wise woman."

"What are you?"

"Do you wish to see my papers?"

"Forgive my curiosity."

"Guess."

"Finnish? Esthonian?"

"You speak like a world traveller."

"Hungarian? Russian?"

She shook her head.

"I give up. I only know that you are the most beautiful woman in Dijon."

She laughed delightedly. "I'm an ordinary Swede from Stockholm."

"I am an extraordinary American."

She laughed. "From San Diego."

"How did you know?"

"The nephew of the lady who keeps the *pension* is a colleague of yours at the Faculty."

"Who?"

"Raoul Dupont. He has told me of you, the lone American, the recluse, the woman hater, so regular in his habits, so intelligent and brilliant—a genius *enfin*."

"I thought the Swedes were serious, but you are a tease. What is your name?"

"Erda."

"Erda what?"

"Erda Lindström."

"Erda means earth. What does Lindström mean?"

"It means linden stream."

"I'm John Burgoyne."

"May I call you Johnny?"

Throughout the conversation we were partly blocking the aisle, oblivious of the push and jostle of the students; and it was she who finally took my arm and steered us out onto the street.

It was dark, the street thick with bicyclists, furiously ringing their bells as they rode home from work, candled lanterns swinging from their handlebars. We walked along the sidewalk toward the Place du Théâtre, and when it narrowed, I dropped off into the cobbled gutter. As we crossed the Place and approached the café, she squeezed my arm and said, "That's where you sit at noon."

"You've seen me?"

"Like a fish in an aquarium."

"And I thought I was studying you."

"Don't you know how perceptive women are?"

"Sometimes I forget. An apéritif now?"

"I am not supposed to, unchaperoned. Yet I will with you."

We entered the warm, smoky café and sat side by side on the leather *banc* against the wall, under an ornate gilt-framed mirror, with another across from us in which we could see ourselves. The room was rumbling with Burgundian French, over which her English accent sounded exquisite.

"You like poetry," I said.

"Not particularly."

"Why were you there?"

"Madame Décat says that the Dean speaks the purest French in Dijon. He bored me, so logical, like a scientist dissecting a butterfly."

"He looks like a fox that's raided the hencoop."

"She says he has a very bad character."

"Did you see me?"

"I felt you."

"You knew I was there?"

"Why didn't you come sit with me? I thought Americans were friendly."

"My grandfather was French."

"The French aren't shy."

"I'm not very typical anything, I guess. Are you enrolled in Letters?"

"I go for the learning, not for a diploma."

"What are you doing in Dijon?"

"It's called *absorbing culture*. I was in Germany, Italy, England."

"Where next?"

"Home."

"When?"

"In three more weeks."

"May I see you again?"

"Madame Décat has not encouraged me to have rendezvous."

"She's not running a convent, is she?"

"Madame is strict. Raoul will vouch for you though. In fact, he already has."

"You know more about me than I do about you."

"It is a woman's way."

"How old are you?"

"Guess."

"Twenty-four."

"I am only eighteen."

"You are so womanly."

"We women of the north mature early."

"I have been led to believe that Swedes are a somber people."

"Laplanders and Norwegians, perhaps; Swedes and Danes— *toujours gai!*"

"You have had men friends here?"

"The Dijonnais do not interest me."

"What do you like to do?"

"Ski. The Côte-d'Or is no place for skiing."

"Do you like to walk?"

"Very much. I am strong."

"Music?"

"Oh, yes!"

"Would Madame allow you to go to the opera with me a week from Saturday?"

"Come home with me and ask her."

"And for a walk this Sunday?"

"I'll say yes to all that you ask of me."

Such was our beginning. Erda was extroverted, unsentimental, vigorous, and healthy. We shook hands in meeting and parting, and her grip was as strong as mine. In the beginning we were like brother and sister. She resembled an American college girl in her forthright manner, but with flashes of an exotic foreign cast of mind. I called her my blonde Viking. She did not show any romantic interest in me or in anything.

Our night at the opera changed that. It was a one-night stand by a company from Paris. Dijon's shabby municipal theater across from the café was packed with the town's élite. Erda was beautiful in a sea-green gown which revealed her strong white arms, shoulders, and neck. Her hair was done up in a severe coiffure. She was eye-catching amidst the overdressed, heavily perfumed throng, and I saw several of my professors stare at her, then wink knowingly at me. I was enormously pleased with myself.

The opera was Moussorgsky's *Boris*, its music passionate enough to overcome such handicaps as rickety scenery, dusty stage, ragged orchestra, an off-key soprano and a restless audience used to Puccini and Massenet. The bass who sang Boris, however, was superb, and the bells of the Kremlin, rung off-stage, were deafening. At the climax of Boris's death, I saw tears on Erda's cheek. Her hand reached mine and squeezed it hard.

As we walked home from the theater, she clung to my arm and was quieter than I had ever known her. It was a clear night, the stars like bright powder, and our breaths made frost on the air.

"You were moved by it," I said.

"Oh Johnny, I never knew music could be like that."

"Hearing it together does it."

"With you, Johnny, with you."

She was transformed from the tomboy I had known before. All my senses were heightened by the knowledge. As we neared the Rue de Metz, our heels ringing on the cobbles, we saw a glow ahead and hurried toward it. A building was on fire. The occupants had fled to the street in night clothes and coats. A crowd stood transfixed, their faces raised like flowers to the fiery spectacle. Firemen were coupling hoses and raising ladders and commanding the people to stand back. No one moved. Blue flames spurted from the metal gutters. Window glass cracked and crashed. The roof suddenly burned through and a fountain of sparks played into the windless sky. The crowd gasped.

We shoved into the thick of it, Erda clinging to my side and there we stood pressed together, surrounded by people oblivious of each other. Erda began to tremble.

"Cold?" I whispered, drawing her closer.

She did not answer.

I felt my way beneath her fur coat. Her body was hot. She pressed even closer and whispered in my ear,

"I hope they never get it out."

My own excitement mounted as I realized that the fire had

aroused her. I moved so that I stood in back of her and let my hands, still beneath her coat, begin to caress her breasts and belly. No one paid the least attention to us, their faces ruddy in the glow. My lips found her warm neck. My hands grew more ardent. Her breath quickened and suddenly her body went rigid. My arms tightened around her until she slowly relaxed and would have slumped to the ground had I not held her fast.

"We must go," she whispered finally. "I promised Madame I would come home after the opera."

We forced our way out of the crowd and hurried the rest of the way to her *pension*. As she searched in her bag for the door key, I sought to kiss her. To my astonishment she broke free, slapped me hard, and cried, "Let me go." She opened the door and it slammed in my face.

I stood for a moment, then walked home through the empty streets. The wind had risen and window shutters were banging in the still of the night.

A week passed. My puzzlement changed to anger at the way she had reacted. I moved across the Place to the Café de la Comédie for my noontime drink and did not see her pass. Then on the following Saturday morning Raoul Dupont brought a note from Erda, asking me to have Sunday lunch at her *pension* and go for a walk afterward. I told him to tell her yes. I wanted badly to see her again.

Madame Décat was well known in Dijon for her culture. Before she had been widowed by the war, her home was a salon. Now it was an exclusive *pension* for foreign girls. She was petite with gray hair and pale blue eyes and a lovely sad face. Luncheon was formal. Erda and I were elaborately polite to one another. I had no eyes for the other girls, but directed my attention to the hostess. Raoul was in Paris, and except for the butler I was the only man present. Madame Décat led the talk through topics as varied as the comparative sweetness of Spanish and Californian oranges, the preparation of Burgundian snails for cooking, the amount of honey in the best Dijon gingerbread, the limestone formations of the Côte-d'Or, the music of Rameau and the sermons of Bossuet, two of Dijon's most glorious native sons. The talk was lively. She knew something about everything. The food was elegant, and in my honor she opened a vintage bottle of Clos Vougeot, a heady red Burgundy.

After lunch, and the girls had dispersed and Erda was changing into walking clothes, I found myself alone in the parlor with Madame Décat.

"Let me get to the point," she said softly. "You are aware, I am sure, Monsieur Burgoyne, that Mademoiselle Lindström's parents have charged me with responsibility for their daughter while she is under my roof."

"I assumed she must have parents," I countered, "although she has never referred to them."

"Although she obviously possesses some of the attributes of a woman, she is still a girl, and of fluctuating emotions. Since you escorted her to the opera, she has been in a rather high state of nerves."

"Music affects some in this way."

She smiled faintly, then said, "As a student of human nature, as well as of the more exact sciences, you are familiar with the psychology of infatuation."

"I assure you, Madame, of the honor of my intentions. Erda will testify to the platonic nature of our relationship. To speak the truth, I have not seen her since that evening."

"Just so. I know something of your lineage, Monsieur Burgoyne, or you would not be my guest today. But I must inform you, inasmuch as she tells me that she has not done so, that Mademoiselle Lindström is affianced."

"To whom?"

"To one of Stockholm's most substantial financiers. A banker, to be precise, and a widower of an age, it is true, considerably more advanced than hers. A most distinguished individual, I am told, and of great means. She is spending these months abroad at his instance, chaperoned, to be sure, in order that she may prepare herself to be the lady of his house."

"We do not favor such marriages in our land."

"Customs vary, as we observed in our conversation at the luncheon table. One learns tolerance."

"I am not planning an elopement," I protested.

Madame Décat arched her thin brows and shrugged her shoulders. "I am convinced of the truth of all you say. But here is the point my dear young man, here is the point I have taken far too long to arrive at—and I beg of you to forgive my prolixity—I should not care to see your relationship with her transformed into something more ardent. Mademoiselle is young, I repeat, and though fully developed as a woman in body—indeed most seductively so, I am fully prepared to admit—and accomplished beyond the average in such diverse interests as sports and languages, the creature is still essentially a naïve."

"This is indeed part of her charm."

Madame Décat again ventured a small sad smile. "Raoul was right. You are truly not a crude foreigner; so unlike the Americans we are accustomed to, thick tongued and heavy handed. Your perceptions and reactions are altogether Gallic."

"My grandfather was French," I reminded her. "From Auxerre."

"The purest of Burgundian. And you, my esteemed friend, are a very likeable young man."

"Thank you, Madame. What is your price for this fine compliment?"

She chuckled. "Raoul did not sufficiently emphasize your roguishness." Her face hardened. "I will tell you. It imperative that Mademoiselle Lindström leave Dijon in the same state in which she arrived in my care."

"And that is precisely what?"

"A virgin, my dear son, a virgin."

"But my dear Madame, we have been as brother and sister. We have never exchanged—I hesitate to say enjoyed—a single kiss."

Again she gave me a tired, wise, and compassionate smile, then flared her eyes and said, "This is her last week in Dijon;" and added with icy precision, "I am counting on your honor as an erstwhile neophyte of Hippocrates to see that she leaves Dijon—and may I borrow a phrase from your discipline—that she leaves Dijon *virga intacta*."

Erda entered the parlor at that moment, and I made no reply. I thanked my hostess for a delicious lunch, bowed and kissed her hand, and Erda and I took our leave.

As we walked through the curving narrow streets and reached the apse of Notre Dame, Erda halted and drew off her glove.

"You must also remove yours," she said, and when I had done so, she took my hand and placed it on a little owl carved in relief on the stone of the church.

"What is it?" I asked.

"The wishing owl. See how smooth it is worn?" She put her hand over mine. "Now wish together." And after a pause, "Have you wished?"

"Yes. Shall I tell you what?"

"Then it wouldn't come true."

"Tell me yours."

"Guess."

"The same as mine?"

"Yes."

The afternoon was bitter cold, and we walked fast to keep warm, stride for stride, her arm in mine, neither speaking, until we reached the park on the edge of town. It was about a mile square and had been created in the seventeenth century by Le Notre, the great landscape architect. The incidental details of his original design had long since vanished, and there remained only the basic geometrical pattern of unpaved walks and intermediate groves of ancient trees, now stripped bare to a company of skeletons. The park's southern limit was the little Ouche River, and there on a stone bench at its edge we rested. Although barely four o'clock, the sun was low in the sky and there was no warmth from its rays. We gathered leaves and twigs and lit a fire, took off our gloves and warmed our hands. Crows rose from the stubble field across the semifrozen river and cawed their heavy way toward the low sun. The time was winter and everything was numbed and slow. The sweet smoke from the fire rose without wavering.

"Why have you avoided me?" she finally broke the silence. "Was it because I slapped you?"

"Partly."

"Is there someone else?"

"No."

"I was frightened by my feelings. I have always been sure of myself."

"You were so responsive."

"It was the music and the fire—and your hands and lips."

"I didn't want to let you go."

"All week I have longed for you."

"We are together now."

"Madame Décat would surely reprove me for my boldness, but I must say it. Do you want to hear it?"

"Tell me."

71

"I love you."

We stood up, and I took her in my arms and sought to kiss her.

"No," she said. "You must tell me first what you and she were talking about."

"More about snails and oranges."

"Liar. I saw her face."

"She told me what is going to happen when you go home."

"Oh, I hate her for that! Johnny, I swear I don't love him."

"But you are going to marry him."

"Yes, I am."

"You foreigners have quaint ways."

"Don't be sarcastic. I am going away in another week. Have you thought of me at all?"

"Every night."

"Oh Johnny, kiss me now."

Our first kiss was long and deep and tender, while her gloved hands stroked my face. She was radiant as my hands found her again under her coat.

"I am so happy," she said. "Can we walk again before I leave?"

"Lab keeps me until five every day and by then it is pitch dark. Can you come at noon?"

"Madame made me promise not to, even with you."

"Evening?"

"I am all but locked in my room."

"She is a veritable watchdog. A pity she has forgotten her youth."

"She has never forgiven life for having left her a widow."

I looked at my watch. "If we hurry, we can hear a concert from Paris."

"What do you mean?"

"Sundays before you came, I always went to a friend's house for the five o'clock radio-diffused concert from the Conservatoire. It won't be like the other night, but I think you'd enjoy it."

My friend was an old French *confiseur* from the Vosges who had retired to a family property in Dijon, a great eighteenth century *hotel* in the Rue Berbisey, where he spent hours huddled over the loudspeaker, tuning in music from all over Europe. He lived alone and welcomed my weekly visit while we sat silently in the formal parlor, listening to the broadcast and nibbling a plate of his sweets, with a liqueur.

We found Monsieur Bonespoir fighting static, as he struggled to bring in the Paris broadcast.

"You honor me to return," he greeted us, "and to bring with you such a charming creature. I must apologize for the cold. I suggest you leave on your coats."

The pink-eyed, walrus-mustached, portly old candymaker had on his coat, hat, muffler, and gloves, while he muttered and twirled the dials and cursed the crackling interference. Then all of a sudden Radio Paris came in bell-clear and the concert commenced with the *Roman Carnival* overture.

"Enfin!" he beamed and brought out a plate of cookies and gingerbread and poured us tiny glasses of kümmel, where Erda and I sat at a great square table, covered with green baize and over which hung a beaded chandelier with one bulb of low wattage.

The Berlioz was followed by a song-cycle for soprano and orchestra, a *première audition of Les Heures du Foyer*, a suite of lullabies sung by an expectant mother, seated at the fireside, to her unborn child. It was followed by the *Daphnis and Chloe* music, an orgy of sound that made Erda's eyes shine and her hand reach for mine.

Old Bonespoir joined us at the table during the entr'acte.

"You also like music?" he asked her.

"Oh yes!"

"You must come again with Monsieur Jean."

"Alas, I leave in another week."

"Where do you go?"

"My home is in Stockholm."

"Tiens," he exclaimed, "the other side of the moon."

"You have travelled?"

"Once to Grasse, for a particular perfumed condiment."

The final music was the César Franck symphony. We were carried away on the flood of sonority, holding hands, staring at one another across the table in the dim light.

The concert ended and the old man saw us to the door.

"Did I ever tell you?" he asked me, "that Sophie and Mirabeau occupied these chambers on their elopement from Paris? Your coming here, so close do you seem one to the other, reminded me of those passionate ones." He shook our hands and murmured, "Ah, *la belle jeunesse!*"

The door closed. We crossed the flagstone courtyard in the biting air and the great wooden street door slammed on our backs like doom. We hurried through the narrow streets that formed the mazy heart of the old town, for it was after seven and she was late. We stood a moment at the door of her *pension,* but when I sought again to reach beneath her coat, she pushed me away.

"I dare not. We must say farewell. Adieu, my love." She kissed my cheek and was gone. I walked away down the curving street, my desire not cooled by the snow that had begun to drift down in the dark.

The days passed. I kept vigil at the café. In vain. Perhaps she had left before the appointed time. Then I learned from Raoul that Erda was still in Dijon and was leaving on Friday. On Thursday all of the faculties of the university were closed, along with other state institutions, because of the funeral in Paris of a war hero. The day was cold and rainy, and I remained in my room. As the bell clock on the municipal library tolled three, there was a knock on my door.

"Come in," I called, seated at my work table, my back to the door, believing it to be the chambermaid with clean towels.

The door opened and a moment later from in back of my chair cold soap-sweet hands closed over my eyes.

"Guess who!"

"Erda!"

I stood up and took her in my arms. Her cheeks were cold, her lips warm.

"I have longed to see you," I said.

"You sent no word."

"I waited each noon."

"I took another route, pausing each day at the wishing owl."

"I went there one day and wished. And now do we not have our wish?"

"I was afraid. I have promised Madame Décat that it would be our last rendezvous. I hoped that somehow you would find me and then I would not break my promise."

"I despaired, particularly when you parted so casually."

"Oh Johnny, you must not say that! I am not casual. I am a frightened girl. I have never known these feelings."

"I thought you northern women matured early."

"I was teasing you. I will not tease you any longer. When Raoul reported the faculty closed today, I had an overpowering desire to be with you. Promise or no, I came."

"In the wind and the rain. Take off your coat and let me hang it to dry."

"I brought you a present for your little phonograph." She took a parcel from the bed. I opened it and found a recording of Franck's *Variations Symphoniques*. I put it on. Erda looked around my room at books and pictures. She found a bottle of Sandeman's ruby port and poured us each a glass.

"Skaal!" she toasted, and sat cross-legged on the floor beside my chair.

I removed her wet beret and her hair fell loosely to her shoulders, silky and fragrant. I whispered in her ear, "Look up. Let me see your face. You are thinner. There are circles under your eyes."

"I have thought of you in the sleepless night. Yesterday while shopping with Madame, I heard this record and I returned today and bought it for you. I wanted us to hear it together."

"My darling."

"I brought you something else."

"What?"

"You might not want it now. How can I say it?"

"Whisper in my ear."

I slipped to the floor beside her and for a moment we were joined in a kiss. Then she freed herself and said,

"It is myself that I bring you." And then, even softer and in French, "*Parce que je vous aime. Je vous . . . je t'aime, tu sais.*"

Again we kissed, but I could not forget our predicament. It was a student *pension*. There were no locks on the doors. People came and went in great informality. The nosy chambermaid was everywhere at all hours.

I lifted Erda up and we went to the window. I opened it and we looked down on the rainy street and across to the wine merchant's courtyard where workmen were rolling barrels across the cobbles to the cellar chute. The lamplighter was making his rounds in the darkening afternoon and stopped beneath us to raise his long, lighted taper and thrust it up into the bracketed lamp which in a moment began to glow with golden light.

"Do that to me," she said, seeking my lips, "Oh Johnny, do that to me."

"We must cool off," I said. "There is no privacy, and besides, we deserve at least a night, not an hour."

"But how? The Décat has become so vigilant. I leave tomorrow. She knows that I love you. I told her so. I want to tell everyone. I wanted to call down to the lamplighter."

The rain blew in on us as we stood together and kissed.

There came a knock on the door and even before I could call "Entrez!" the chambermaid burst in with the towels.

"Pardon," she said, "I was unaware that Monsieur had company." She gave me a knowing look, arranged the towels with elaborate care, and finally went out.

"See what I mean?"

"Play the record again. Music fertilizes my brain."

We stood at the window in a close embrace all through the *Variations*, and then she spoke.

"Would you love me in Paris?"

"What are you saying?"

"Could you join me there?"

"But how? You are going home to be married."

"To a man I love not. That old Croesus shall not have me first."

"But how?"

"I am not supposed to tarry in Paris, of course. Madame is putting me on the train tomorrow and I am to taxi from Gare de Lyon to Gare du Nord and take the Nord Express to Hamburg where my fiancé's agent is to meet me."

"You are booked through to Stockholm?"

"Stopovers are permitted."

"With whom?"

"I have excellent friends there whom my family would trust to chaperone me. A young Swedish married couple studying at the Beaux-Arts."

"Would they delegate the chaperonage to me?"

"I stopped over with them on my way here in October and they were sympathetic to my plight. They would gladly aid me in a deception of Old Moneybags. They would join me in a telegram to my parents, and then you and I could be together for a few days, even for a week, if you did not tire of me."

"A week of nights."

"As you desire. Can you leave your work?"

"I can make it up."

"I have enough money left for us both."

"I have some," I lied, knowing that I would have to borrow. "When does your train leave?"

"The two-thirty *rapide* from Lyon."

"What class?"

"First. You must board without her seeing you. She's hardly worried now though. She believes her little lecture cooled you off. I, too, feared that it had."

"Raoul won't give us away?"

"Tell him you've been called to Switzerland again."

"Of course. On banking business."

"Oh Johnny, I want you to have me first!"

"And I want you. Wait and see."

We pledged the rendezvous with a kiss and she left. I leaned out the window and saw her wave as she hurried up the Rue de Petit-Potet.

I went early to the station the next day, taking a back way along the canal path, carrying a suitcase and wearing my overcoat, for the cold had settled down for the winter and the sun was seen no more. I checked my bag to Paris, then gained the platform and walked along in the direction of Lyon out into the freight yards, and there I waited for the *rapide* to arrive, certain that I was out of sight even if Madame Décat should accompany Erda to the platform.

Once again I was going to a romantic rendezvous, but this time in place of the curiosity that was a main part of my motivation in meeting Nancy in Switzerland, I felt mounting desire to be with Erda in Paris and to satisfy the passion I knew she was capable of. Compounding the intensity of my feeling was the excitement of eluding Madame Décat's vigilance and of cheating the old Swedish banker of his interest due.

I heard the *rapide's* shriek as it entered the yards and then saw the huge engine bearing down on me and the long train roll past and come to a stop a few cars up track from where I stood. I boarded the carriage in front of the *fourgon* and remained in the rear vestibule until the train began to move and gather speed. I waited until it had cleared the station and the yards and was running fast along a ledge

at the bottom of the limestone walls of the Ouche, before I began
to make my way forward from car to car, seeking Erda.

Had she boarded? What if she had changed her mind and taken
an earlier train? Or if Madame Décat had decided to accompany her
to Paris? It was too late for me to don a disguise. My uncertainty increased, and the sweat began to trickle down my body under my
clothes, as car after car did not hold her. Passengers looked at me
suspiciously as I peered into each successive compartment. The
train was running at full speed now, swaying on the curves as the
line climbed the low hills separating the watersheds of the Yonne
and the Seine. The wintry landscape was a blur through the steamy
window. Erda, Erda, darling, darling, I kept muttering, hoping to
evoke her. Although I had lost count of the cars, I knew that I was
near the front of the train, for I began to hear the locomotive's exhaust, powerful and regular, overtoned by the cry of the whistle as
we approached a level crossing or flew through a village. The *rapide*
was due to stop only once, at Laroche-Migennes for engine water.

And then, when I had nearly given up hope of finding her, I
heard my name called.

"Johnny!"

I turned. It was Erda, standing in the corridor of the first-class
coach, with an older Frenchman. I had passed by the couple, not
recognizing her in a black tocque, veil, tailored dark suit, a fur coat
on her arm.

Relief turned to jealousy. How could she be so casual? We chatted a moment. The man regarded me as an interloper, evidently believing he had made a pickup, I grew angry. I saw his face stiffen.
Erda intervened. She took my arm and said to the man. "You must
say good-bye now. I am to have tea with my fiancé."

He and I bowed stiffly and I began to relax as she and I made our
way back along the train.

"There *is* a restaurant car, isn't there?" she asked.

"It is in the middle of the one hundred cars that constitute this
train. I had despaired of finding you and then to encounter you in
the company of that *cochon!*"

"I feared you were going to strike him. I, too, had despaired of
your being on the train, when you were so long in finding me. And
so I let that stupid shoe salesman engage me in conversation."

78

"I thought I would never reach the front of the train, and then I passed right by you without knowing it."

"Do you like me in this?"

"Lift your veil and I will tell you."

We were at table in the restaurant car. I ordered English tea, toast, and port.

"She suspected nothing," Erda exulted.

"I'll not relax until we have left the Gare de Lyon. She might have telegraphed someone to meet you and escort you to the Gare du Nord."

"It is unlikely. We will telephone my friends from the station and obtain their permission to telegraph my family in their name. They'll think it a charming deception."

I watched her remove her gloves. "Need help?"

"Later."

"You'll want me to?"

"You'll despise my woolen underwear."

"I, too, wear it in winter."

We laughed in relief and anticipation.

It was dark when we left Laroche-Migennes. The lights of villages and farms flashed by. We reached the Gare de Lyon at seven o'clock. It was swarming with passengers, brilliant with lights, noisy, confused. Would there be someone looking for her? I began to sweat again. I waited outside the P.T.T. office while she telephoned and sent the telegram to Stockholm. The Blue Train was beginning to board passengers for eight o'clock departure to the Riviera. The Simplon Orient and the Rome expresses also stood waiting.

When at last we gained a taxi and the porter stowed the bags at our feet and beside the driver and the door slammed and the car entered the traffic flow in the rainy street, I collapsed with relief. Only for a moment. I roused myself and took her in my arms and my hands went beneath her coat.

"We made it," I breathed in her ear. "Now they'll never find us."

"Oh Johnny," she murmured, turning her body to mine.

She lifted her veil. We kissed. Our mouths remained fused all the way to the hotel. My hands roamed over her body.

It was a small hotel near the Place St. Germain-des-Près. Our large, high-ceilinged room was papered with enormous birds of

79

paradise in red and blue. The first thing Erda did was to open one of her suitcases, dig to the bottom, extract a garment and hold it high.

"I bought it for our honeymoon," she exulted. It was a sheer black silk nightie. I took her in my arms.

"Now?"

"Isn't Johnny going to feed his girl?"

"Do you want to go out?"

"I'm hungry, and besides I want to see the boulevard at night."

And so we walked to the Place and after dining at the Restaurant des Saints-Pères, we moved across to the Café de Flore and sat on the *terrasse* next to a glowing charcoal brazier. I had never known Erda so gay and talkative. Finally she sensed my impatience.

"You want to go to bed, don't you?"

"With you. Tonight."

"Soon."

"Now."

"Isn't it nice to know we can?"

"Then let's!"

A crone hobbled up with a basket of hot chestnuts in cornucopias, freshly filled from her roaster at the corner.

"Buy me some to eat in bed," Erda teased.

Another peddler had stopped, sensing a sale, and I took a bunch of violets from his basket and pinned them on her suit lapel.

"You eat the violets," I said, "and I'll eat the chestnuts. Aren't you getting cold?"

"Poor Californian! At home this would be a mild evening."

"Shall we go now?"

"Will it be like at the fire?"

"Hotter."

"Then I'm ready."

Erda proved a vigorous lover. Her body was strong from sports and it took all my strength to lead in her clumsy ardor. When she finally fell asleep on the torn-up bed, I opened the window and looked out. Daylight had come. Snow was falling between the high buildings that lined the narrow street. The room smelled of her and me and us and violets. I lay down beside her, pulled the sheet over us, and fell asleep.

Paris in the winter, the coldest winter in years, the city shrouded in a blue-gray veil. The damp air smelled of coal smoke and Chanel. It was perfect weather only for lovers. Erda lived in delight with everything, especially the great department stores where she went shopping every afternoon. I accompanied her the first time, and then we had our first quarrel, when I said that I preferred the museums and galleries. Neither of us would yield and for the rest of the week we spent our afternoons apart, I going to the Louvre, the Luxemborg, Orangerie, Cluny, Rodin, and others I had read of and never seen. I would return to our room late afternoon with a pocketful of postcards, and soon after, Erda would burst in, laden with parcels, throw them on the floor and herself in my arms.

Then we would race to see who could be naked first, flinging our clothes around the room and falling together on the bed. Afterward I would doze and when I opened my eyes, Erda would be sitting naked on the floor, tearing open parcels and exclaiming over each thing she had bought—gifts for half of Stockholm, I teased. She always brought a gift for me—a tie or handkerchief or pen and pencil set, saving my package till the last. She was irresistible.

One day a small trunk was delivered into which she began to stow her purchases. She was like a child at Christmas, gay, responsive, and also willful and spoiled. No quarrel ever lasted for long. She would end by pulling me onto her with Viking passion. Her strength was nearly equal to mine.

Evening found us in harmony, for each night we heard music together, feasting on riches of symphonies, chamber music, recitals, always half a dozen events to choose from.

The unbroken cold brought misery to many. Along the lower quays men and women huddled around bonfires, grotesquely wrapped in rags and newspapers against the cold. The Métro platforms were peopled with the homeless. In the Rue de Rivoli I saw a coal-wagon horse fall and snap a foreleg with a sound like a pistol shot.

We were young and in love, bearing Blake's "lineaments of gratified desire," and the suffering of others did not touch us deeply. We saw it and did not like it, but were not moved thereby; if anything, it increased our own self-absorption.

Then one morning, while we were sitting up naked in bed with café-au-lait, croissants, and confiture, Erda announced that her money was gone.

81

"You should have told me," I scolded her. "I have only enough to pay for our room. The rest I spent on our meals."

"Don't be cross with me, Johnny."

"But you will need money for the station and meals on the train and you're not leaving till Saturday. We must eat and we planned on chamber music tomorrow night, our last night."

She laughed. "Oh, Johnny, you are so serious. Don't worry. I'll go see Sven and Gertha tonight. They'll give me money. I must go alone though."

"Why must you?"

"I just must, that's all."

"Was Sven your lover?"

"Of course not. You're the only one."

"Perhaps."

She burst into tears for the first time. "You're hateful and jealous. Why must you be?"

I embraced her. We didn't get up until noon. She had her way though. I spent a lonely evening while she went by taxi to her friends in Montparnasse. Hours passed and she did not return. I went time after time to the window, pulled the flowered drapes and looked down. Snow was falling. Taxis passed; none stopped. She did not come. I grew worried. I tried to phone. No one answered. I began to read a Tauchnitz edition of *Lord Jim*. No use. I stared at the flamboyant wallpaper and counted the birds. The bell in the tower of St. Germain struck the hours, hour after hour, and still she did not come.

It was three in the morning when she finally burst in, laden with parcels, as fresh as ever, excited and laughing.

"Don't scold me," she cried. "I have lovely presents, all for you."

"Beware of Swedes bearing gifts," I growled, half angry, half relieved.

"And money," she cried, opening her bag and flinging a handful of paper francs on the bed. "We're rich again."

"Did you sleep with Sven?"

"Johnny, you mustn't talk that way. You know I'm your girl."

"Why were you so long?"

"He insisted we go dancing, and as I'd had a thousand francs from him, I couldn't refuse."

"Why didn't you come and get me?"

She hesitated. "Well, there was another Swede there — a boy I grew up with in the Ostermalmsgatan — and Sven thought it better not to let him know I've been with you all week."

"And so the four of you went dancing."

"Don't be jealous, Johnny, please don't be."

I was not to be appeased, and for the first time we fell asleep back to back.

The morning brought another day. We awoke and turned to one another again and lay abed until early afternoon.

That last afternoon, reduced to just enough money to get her home, Erda let me lead. I took her to some of my favorite places. In the Luxembourg Museum the virility of Bourdelle's bronze Herakles Archer made her eyes shine. We walked through the bare gardens and on to St. Clothilde where César Franck had been organist, and back along the Boulevard St. Germain to the Faculty of Medicine, where I showed her the museum of monstrosities in jars of alcohol. She shuddered and clung to my arm.

We dined our last night at the Voltaire, opposite the Odéon, on trout from the Auvergne and a bottle of flowery Chablis whose bouquet brought pleasure to diners at the next table.

"I like you better poor," I toasted her. "I've had you all to myself since you came home last night."

"This morning."

"And tonight."

"Our last night."

"Don't be sad. Be glad I'm marrying a banker."

"Selling yourself."

"I gave myself to you."

"Only for a week."

"You're so serious. I thought Americans were frivolous and gay."

"Is that why you wanted to meet me?"

"Please don't be stupid."

"I want to hurt you."

"You will if you don't stop."

In spite of the food and wine, I was glum, and she gave up trying to amuse me. We took our seats in the Salle Pleyel and waited for the music to begin. We did not speak and did not hold hands. It was an all-César Franck concert, his string quartet and piano quintet. The richness of the strings brought me to life. My hand found hers.

"Oh Johnny," she whispered, leaning toward me, "isn't it beautiful?"

We were reconciled by the music to our differences and our parting. When it was over, we walked back to the hotel, seeing the great department store façades illuminated with animated toy displays for the Christmas season.

"Even if I had any money," she said, "I couldn't spend it. They're all closed."

"Do you want to stop at the Flore for a last drink?"

"Yes, and I have a confession to make."

"You mean you are?"

"I won't know that till after Christmas. Do you want me to be?"

"Would it bring you back?"

"Johnny, listen to me. I've lost my passport."

"What?"

"I must have left it in one of the shops when they asked to see my papers. I can't get through Belgium and Germany without it. What shall I do?"

It was not until we were seated at the café, with little glasses of Remi Martin, that I had an idea.

"Go to your consulate in the morning and ask for a transit passport to Sweden. They have a record of your being in France and will surely issue you one."

"They ought to, but will they?"

"Show me the man who could say no to you."

"You don't know the Swedish functionary. He's as cold as a frozen herring."

"Wear what you did coming up on the train."

"I'll try."

"Maybe he'll refuse and then you won't be able to leave."

"Be honest, Johnny. You'd grow tired of me. Or angry. You're grown up. I'm still a girl. I don't really want to settle down."

"What will *he* say about that?"

"I'll wear him out and inherit his money. Then I'll come to you."

"Mad girl!"

"You don't know how impoverished my family is. They have been living on borrowed money until my marriage is consummated. I'll wait a week, then give him a bag of bills to pay."

"Mercenary Swede. It's a horrible system."

"I don't know any other. You know now, don't you, that it's you I love."

"Are you ready for bed?"

"I'll really show you that I love you."

She did indeed. It was the best night of all. We were utterly compatible. In the fire of her surrender my destructive emotions were burned away. Delight remained in purest essence. And sleep, the deep sleep of complete fulfillment.

We rose at nine after breakfast in bed, and somehow managed to pack her things, loaded all into a cab, and drove to the Swedish consulate. I waited while she went in. I lay back in the cab, beyond feeling, and waited. The lapel of my overcoat was sweet from where her head had rested. She returned, waving a paper in her gloved hand.

"I did exactly what you said. Never lifted my veil. Removed one glove and touched his hand, oh so timidly. He issued me a transit visa—and asked me for coffee. I said no thank you, my grandfather is waiting for me." She kissed me. "Wasn't I polite?"

I leaned over the driver. He was reading *L'Ami du Peuple*. I tapped his arm.

"Alors, m'sieur 'dame?"

"Gare du Nord."

We arrived half an hour before the Hamburg *rapide* was due to depart, and after checking Erda's baggage, we entered the station buffet.

"There are shadows under your eyes," I said, "as there were that day when you came to my room."

"And for the same reason. Lack of sleep."

"I slept."

"I watched you."

"You were so good last night."

"Have I learned the American way?"

"All ways."

"Oh Johnny, you've spoiled me. You'll forget our quarrels, won't you? They were all my fault."

"Darling."

"Can you make up your work? Will Raoul aid you?"

"I'll work terribly hard to keep from thinking."

"You won't forget me?"

"Never."

85

"Now may I have a kümmel?"

"That's all I have left. The price of one kümmel."

"Take these francs."

"You'll need them."

"Will you go right back?"

"I hope I can make the eleven-thirty *rapide*."

"Tell the old gentleman I loved his cookies. You'll go tomorrow?"

"Every Sunday."

"I'll be listening." She raised her glass. "Skaal, Johnny."

She sipped and handed me the glass.

"Skaal, Erda."

We were in the stream just above the falls.

Then we found her car, a first-class black and red Deutsches Reichsbahn carriage, with placard reading "Paris-Hamburg." Steam was billowing from between the cars. We walked forward just as the engine eased into the coupling with a soft clash of steel.

"You did that to me, Johnny," she murmured. "You did that to me."

We looked up at the gloved driver. He looked down at Erda. She blew him a kiss. "Drive carefully," she said. He looked at his watch. The air was bittersweet with the ancient smell of Paris.

Five minutes.

We walked back to her car and mounted to the vestibule. I found her beneath the fur and for the last time I ran my hands over her body. Our eyes sought the lasting image each of the other.

Two minutes.

"En voiture!" the conductor called.

Erda grimaced and wiped a tear from each eye with her gloved hand. I kissed her with all my might, until I tasted her blood in my mouth.

"Adieu," she whispered. "Good-bye, Johnny."

I kissed her again, as though I could arrest the train by the force of my desire.

Useless. The train began to move. She broke away and pushed me toward the open door. I jumped off and nearly fell. She leaned out and waved. I waved back.

The train gathered speed with incredible swiftness, and in a moment the *fourgon* glided by, faster, faster; and through a smother of steam I saw its two ruby lights, like the eyes of a beast.

III
Joyce

I spent the Christmas holidays in the laboratory, making up the lost week; and to repay the money I had borrowed, I gave English conversation lessons to French students. The cold weather endured. Streets and walks were icy and treacherous. Erda wrote twice, and sent me a copy of *Gösta Berling* in English; and though I answered and wrote again, I heard from her no more.

I was effortlessly chaste. Nothing diverted me from study. I slept late, went to the café for apértif and lunch, was in lecture or laboratory from two until seven, dined at the *pension*, sometimes went to the movies, then returned to my room and studied and read to music, or joined in a bull session in another student's room, until going to bed long after midnight. I lived on stored-up heat from Erda. She had irradiated me for the winter.

Old Bonespoir had returned to his natal village in the Vosges and there were no more Sundays in the Rue Berbisey. I acquired my own radio receiver, and it brought in the musical riches of Europe from London to Warsaw. At my work table, which was covered with sailcloth and lighted by a lamp with an orange-colored shade. I heard music through earphones, while I labored on a translation into English of an endocrinology text by one of my research professors. Pinned on the wall above my table was a print Erda had given me, of Bourdelle's glowering bronze of Beethoven, its inscription reading, *"Moi je suis Bacchus qui pressure pour les hommes le nectar délicieux."*

After midnight as the stations began to go off the air, the house grew still and no sounds came from the street; then was heard only the striking of the hours on the town's many bell clocks. For the first time in my life I had broken the sensual barrier and attained a serenity in which my mind was free to flower.

And then one day in early spring when I had finished lunch and was about to leave for the Faculty, a British couple named Penfield entered the café. They were students of landscape design, living in Dijon while writing a thesis on ancient Burgundian parks. I had met them one weekend at Vézelay where we had gone to see the Basilique de la Madeleine. Burton Penfield was tall, thin, and bespectacled, his wife Mildred a plump Irish woman with rose-petal skin and honey-colored hair.

A woman was with them I had never seen before. The café was crowded, and mine was the only table with empty seats.

"May we?" Penfield asked.

"Please do. I'll be leaving."

"Stay," Mildred Penfield said, "and meet my friend Mrs. Davies."

The woman's eyes met mine, and I was the first to look away. Hers were green eyes in a blank white face.

"We've been trying to persuade Joyce to see Vézelay now that she's this close," Mrs. Penfield said, "but she insists on going through."

"To?" I asked, to be polite.

"Cannes." Mrs. Penfield replied. "Have you been to Vézelay again?"

"I've been too busy."

"What occupies Mr. Burgoyne so urgently?" Mrs. Davies asked.

"Jack is a science student at the medical faculty," Penfield said. "A slave to his studies, especially since he was in Paris last winter."

"I do not care for doctors," the woman said.

"Jack would never actually cut into you," Penfield explained. "He's more apt to dissect you philosophically."

"Jolly brilliant, these Americans," Mrs. Penfield said.

"I would not have taken Mr. Burgoyne for an American," Mrs. Davies said.

"Would you like to see my passport?" I asked.

"The Americans I have known have all been rotters."

"One finds what one seeks," I said.

Our eyes met again, and this time hers dropped. She lit a cigarette and blew the smoke in my face.

"Thanks," I said. "I happen to like the *Gauloise bleu*."

The Penfields were embarrassed. I rose.

"Back to the formaldehyde vat," I said, "Where life is less hazardous."

Mrs. Davies smiled faintly. I shook hands with all three and left.

All afternoon in the laboratory her perfume lingered on my hand, an exotic smell soap and water did not remove. I recalled her chic clothes, her long legs crossed high up, her thin face with wide mouth, and above all, her green eyes. I had not seen her hair, for she was wearing a tightly wound dark green silk turban.

I went to the movies that night to see Charlie Chaplin in *Les Lumières de la Ville*. It was the third time I had seen it, enthralled by the master pantomimist and the musical score he had composed for the picture; and I walked up the aisle afterward, humming the little flower girl's song.

Then in the crowded foyer I found myself pressed against — Joyce Davies. She was with the Penfields. When she turned to see who was crowding her, our faces nearly touched. Hers cut like a knife. Only for a moment; then her eyes widened in recognition and I saw that their green was amber-flecked.

"Monsieur le docteur," she murmured, with the faintest of smiles.

"We're going to the Miroir for coffee," Penfield said. "Will you join us?"

"Please excuse me," I said. "I have work to do."

"It would give me pleasure if you would come," Mrs. Davies said in French.

"I thought you didn't like Americans?" I countered, also in French.

"Are there not exceptions to all rules?"

"I assure you of my profoundest gratitude."

"Do come," she said in English, "I'll behave."

A whiff of her perfume decided it. I went with them up the Rue de la Liberté to the Brasserie du Miroir. A string orchestra was playing the ballet music from *Le Cid*. The Penfields and I got into a discussion of Cluny in southern Burgundy and the merits of Viollet-le-Duc's work, while Joyce Davies listened, watching the face of each speaker, her own veiled in smoke from the strong cigarettes she favored.

"Are you always this silent?" I challenged her, in a lull of our talk.

"Afraid of angering you again."

"Joyce is still fatigued from her journey," Mrs. Penfield explained. "She came across on the Trans-Siberian."

"All the way across?" I asked. "What kind of equipment do they have?"

"Horrible. And the food was even worse. It took two weeks."

"And she wants to leave tomorrow," Mrs. Penfield said. "We are frightfully annoyed with her."

"Go on talking architecture," she said. "It's so reassuring."

She intrigued me. Who was she? Not French, although she spoke it fluently, I kept trying to place the perfume. Was it Chinese? I did not leave early as I had intended to do. It was Monday night and the Miroir and the town's other cafés all closed at eleven.

"Just as I'm waking up," Mrs. Davies protested. "Is there nowhere open that I may stand a round of Pernod?"

"The *buffet de la gare*," I said, "is open all night."

"Shall we go there?" she asked.

"We'd better not," Penfield said. "Jack, you go with Joyce. A bit of night life will do you good."

I did not protest. And so we separated, the Penfields going off to their apartment and Mrs. Davies and I retracing the Rue de la Liberté to the Place Darcy and on to the railway station. We walked silently under an arch of plane trees in new leaf.

In the smoky buffet she removed her coat for the first time and I saw that she was a mature woman, full-breasted, round-armed, thin only in face and shapely legs.

"I see that you approve of me," she said. "I suppose you'll be wanting to sleep with me before the night is over."

I stood up in anger.

"Sorry," she said, taking my hand. "I seem to be fated to annoy you."

"You are accustomed to men finding you irresistible."

"You speak the truth."

"Have you tried not wearing that perfume?"

"I do not wear perfume."

"What is it then?"

"It is on my clothes. Our closets were made of sandalwood."

"In China?"

"Indochina."

"So that is an Oriental mask you wear."

"For protection."

"Take it off."

"Why should I?"

"Where are you staying? I'd better take you to your hotel. We don't seem to be getting along."

90

Her face softened. She took a long swallow of the milky Pernod. "Please don't." She lit a Gauloise. "I'm beginning to relax."

"Why so tense?"

"The long journey, I suppose. Men on the train annoyed me. There was no privacy."

"I want nothing from you."

"I'm beginning to see that you don't."

"Who are you?"

"You know my name."

"Let's not spar."

"Do you want me to take my hair down?"

"It might help."

She began to unwind the turban.

"I wrapped it too tight. It's giving me a headache."

Her hair came down in a flood, thick and curly and copper red, clear to her shoulders.

I reached out and touched it. "Will it burn me?"

She laughed. "It's all my own. Nor do I tint it."

"Why do you hide such beautiful hair?"

"I attract enough attention without this bonfire."

"It is indeed an incendiary red. Now tell me who you are."

"Please don't be an aggressive American, just as I am beginning to like you."

"Do you dislike all men at first?"

"Mostly."

"I don't suppose I'm any different from the rest. I am just a man."

"That is obvious."

"Why don't we be simple with each other? Dijon is a poor place for melodrama."

"Don't you find it dull here?"

"I do not seek excitement."

"Why are you here?"

"To work. Why are you?"

"Passing through. And to see Mildred. Do you sometimes go to Paris?"

"Not since December. The severe cold burned me."

"Your paradox fails to hide the presence of a woman."

"You are perceptive."

"Tell me about her."

91

"She returned to the Arctic Circle."

"*Tiens*, an Eskimo. How exotic!"

We laughed.

"What do you do to amuse yourself?" she asked.

"We were at the movie, remember?"

"Was that tonight?"

"Last night. We met yesterday noon."

"Do you have a girl here?"

"No."

"Lucky you. Was the one in Paris good?"

"She was really Swedish, not Eskimo."

"Where is she now?"

"She went home to Stockholm to be married."

"Lucky you."

The train caller entered the buffet and poured out a torrent of words.

"I thought I knew French," she laughed.

"He's calling the Blue Train. It's due to make a ten-minute stop. Want to go see?"

"Whither thou goest . . . "

I put fifty-centime pieces in the vending machine for billets de quai and we gained the platform and waited beside the main line until the de luxe sleeping-car train from Calais and Paris came in precisely at midnight. Blinds were pulled on the windows of the blue and gold *wagons-lit*. A mechanic hurried along with a flashlight, crouching to check the journal boxes with a rap of his hammer. A few people boarded. No one got off. The Blue Train carried only through passengers for Marseilles and beyond.

We walked back along the train, drawn by a lighted, unshaded window. There we gazed up. Four red-faced Englishmen in shirt sleeves were sitting, rigidly erect, playing cards. We were so close that I could read the label on their bottle of Johnny Walker. One man looked down and saw us. His lips moved soundlessly. The other three turned and looked. Their faces were expressionless. We stared up at them. They turned back to their cards. The train began to move and gather speed. As the *fourgon* passed us, we saw the baggage-master standing in the open side door, his ill-fitting, red-corded, black uniform open at the throat, in the act of tilting a wine bottle to his lips.

"*Santé!*" I called, as the car glided past.

His Adam's apple twitched. He removed the bottle from his mouth. "*À la vôtre, m'sieu'dame*," he said.

Joyce squeezed my arm and laughed.

We walked the length of the platform after the departing train, until finally its rear lights disappeared around a curve. We walked out from under the shell and saw the yard signals turn red. The air was damp and smelled of coal smoke and hot oily machinery. I told her of the last times I was there and of Nancy and Erda and what I had learned from them.

Joyce clung to my arm as we walked in slow strides together and I spoke of my successes and failures. I touched her hair. It was beaded with moisture. The bitter smell of coal smoke blended with her sandalwood. We drifted back under the arch of the station.

"I call it my cathedral," I said. "Shall we eat something?"

"As you like. I seem to be yours without your asking for me."

"You've grown wonderfully gentle."

We entered the buffet and ordered ham and gruyère sandwiches, coffee and brandy.

"In a few more minutes," I said, "the Simplon-Orient is due. And then the Rome. And at 2:38 there's the Bordeaux-Strasbourg *rapide*, the only fast train in all of France that does not originate in Paris."

"I am coming to the conclusion that you like trains."

"I often come here at night to see them pass. If I do not visit the buffet, it costs only fifty centimes."

"I thought I never wanted to see a train again."

"Now tell me — are you an international spy?"

"Heavens no! The Russians took me for a whore. I might look like one, and I'm no virgin, but I've never taken money. Isn't that the definition of a whore? I would if I had to; but then I've never lacked money, so I shouldn't boast of my virtue."

"You have known many men."

"Too many."

"Is there a Mr. Davies?"

"That is my maiden name."

"You were married?"

"To a Frenchman."

"You will understand my natural curiosity about your antecedents."

"That is much nicer than 'Who are you?' "

"Our manners improve with practice."

She laughed. "My father was a Welch adventurer, my mother an English noblewoman. He earned his living by cards and when he was blinded in an accident, he killed my mother and committed suicide. I was sent to a convent in Rouen."

"I once thought of studying there."

"It is much like Dijon though busier because of the river commerce. They are all alike, however, these provincial holes. Well, at fifteen I was seduced by a high ecclesiastic and became his mistress, until he died of apoplexy from overeating. Then I married a wealthy importer and we moved to Indochina. Ten years in Saigon and then alcohol did for him, as it will do for me, I fear. I turned down an even dozen proposals, more or less legitimate, took my maiden name, and here I am in the *buffet de la gare de Dijon*."

"Where do the Penfields come in?"

"Mildred was in the convent. We've kept in touch. I was curious to see if she could still excite me the way she did when we were girls."

"Does she?"

She smiled. "You didn't give me time to find out!"

"Do I excite you?"

She finished her brandy, then said, "Yes, you do."

"Are you in a hurry?"

"No. I like talking with you. There's no hurry."

"What takes you to Cannes?"

"My husband left me a villa at Antibes. I want to see whether to keep it or sell it."

"Then you are not a spy."

"You are sweet, Jack Burgoyne. Have you forgiven me?"

"For what?"

"The rude things I said."

"That was yesterday."

"Is today tomorrow?"

"It grows late. Are you tired?"

"I am not sure. Perhaps in a state of ecstatic fatigue."

"We need fresh air. Which is your hotel?"

"La Bourgogne."

"It belongs to me. I own the entire duchy of Burgundy. It was my grand-patrimony."

"May I be your first duchess?"

"Joyce the Red, all hail!"

She laughed. "I don't know which has gone most to my head — you, the brandy or the trains, but I have never been so happy. Do you learn this art at school?"

"It is the Burgundian bedside manner."

"It's your not wanting anything from me."

"Don't I?"

"Do you?"

"Your hair."

"It's not removable."

"I want to bury my face in it."

"Did you say we needed fresh air?"

"You don't want to see the other trains?"

"Not tonight." She smiled, then said, "I was wrong. I *am* in a hurry."

We went out into the damp air and walked arm in arm up the street. A group of soldiers came toward us, walking in the middle of the street, clinging together and singing drunkenly. We stopped and watched them reel past. They paid no attention to us.

"You haven't told me," she said, "that I smoke and drink too much."

"Do you?"

"Yes."

"Then that's settled."

We reached her hotel on the Place Darcy. The lobby was deserted, the room clerk snoring. We leaned against the wall at the elevator.

"Journey's end," she said, and drew my face to her hair.

We stood for a long moment. Then she opened the elevator door and held it for me.

"Will you?" she asked.

"Willingly," I replied.

We mounted to her room on the fifth and top floor. She undressed swiftly and lay on the bed and waited for me to join her.

It was nearly noon when I awoke. Joyce was still asleep, her hair like fire on the pillow. We had enjoyed long, deliberate and deeply satisfying intercourse, and I felt refreshed. I dressed quietly, and as I was about to leave without waking her, I saw her eyes open. I sat on the edge of the bed. She reached up her arms. I held her and kissed her. She laughed and fell back. On her milk white skin, her body hair was all the redder.

"I had forgotten," she said, "how good it can be."

"You'd think we'd done it for years."

"I wanted you the moment I saw you."

"You nearly drove me away."

"Horrible thought."

"I'm late. Will you be here after lab?"

"I was going to take the seven-thirty *rapide*."

"Don't."

"You want me to stay?"

"Yes."

"What will we do?"

"What we did."

"You want more?"

"Yes."

"So do I. Is there a quiet café where I can sit and have a drink until you come?"

"The Concorde, directly across the Place."

"It will take me until then to get the tangles out of my hair."

"Don't bother. I'll only put them back in."

When I returned at six, I found Joyce seated on the leather *banc* at the Concorde, a Pernod in front of her, a cigarette in her hand. Before she saw me, her face was expressionless as it was when we first met; and then as I approached, her eyes widened, her face relaxed, the lines disappeared and she smiled. We shook hands and I sat beside her and ordered a *demi* of Vézelise, the blonde Pilsner-type beer featured at the Concorde.

"*À toi.*" She lifted her glass and drank it half down, then lit her cigarette and we were enveloped in a cloud of the acrid smoke.

"How is it," I asked, "that you smoke the workers' cigarette?"

"Did we not labor? The truth is, I like everything strong. You!"

"You are a strange one."

"Do you like me?"

"I haven't had time to think about it."

"Did it go well for you? Not too tired?"

96

"Recharged."

"I too."

"You are not leaving."

"You want me to stay?"

"You are good medicine."

Time passed as we drifted along in quiet talk, she on Pernod, I on beer, there in the peacefulness of the Café de la Concorde, its panelled, gilt-mirrored walls reflecting the older Dijonnais who frequented it as a club. Merchants and professional men and matrons, too, came for apéritifs and tea, chess, the newspapers, and talk. The waiters were old professionals, deliberate, impersonal and skilled. When ours brought more drinks, Joyce's face would resume her habitual green-eyed mask; then when he had left, she turned to me and smiled, her eyes widened and were again amber-flecked.

Toward eight she paid for the accumulation of saucers and we strolled up the Rue de la Liberté to the Place d'Armes and there at a table behind a hedge of potted privet on the *terrasse* of the Restaurant du Pré aux Clercs, we dined on steak, potatoes, salad, and Beaujolais en carafe. It was beginning to grow dark and the pigeons were settling to roost on the ledges of the Hotel de Ville, the great structure of honey-colored limestone which stood where the Dukes of Burgundy had once built their palace. The vanished rulers were symbolized by stone helmets which rose from the cornices in silhouette against the eggshell sky. A trolley car rocked crazily across the Place and disappeared down the main street with a squeal of flanged wheels.

Our waiter lit the candles on our table, and as we emptied the second carafe, Joyce took my hand across the cloth.

"Moeurs de province," she said. "Bearable only when one knows they are not permanent, that one can escape them."

"But not tonight."

"Not tonight."

I held her knee between my knees; our hands too were joined.

"When?" I asked.

"Let us live each day."

"And night."

"Again so soon?"

"It was long ago."

"We met only yesterday."

"A century ago."

"You are unusually romantic for one studying the sciences."

"You have heard of Arthur Schnitzler? Of Somerset Maugham? Of James Joyce?"

"I have small culture and large appetite."

"I will teach you."

"You have."

We strolled back up the street to her hotel. It was now dark and the bright shop windows offered beautiful displays of mustard jars, gingerbread, and confections, Dijon's specialties on view for the passerby. A soft spring rain was falling as we turned in and again mounted to her room. There we opened the tall windows that looked across a courtyard with elms and chestnuts in leaf to the cathedral of St. Bénigne. The air smelled strong of wet earth, sandalwood and tobacco. Our lips tasted of wine as we stood at the open window in a searching kiss, hearing the sound of rain on the leaves.

And thus a week went by, each day and night the same for us. We met at the Concorde, dined at the Pré aux Clercs, walked up the street to her hotel, stood at the open window and kissed, undressed and made love. Each morning I went away refreshed to the day's work at the Faculty. There were no variations in the slow and muted music that we made. I was not in love as I had known it before, nor even infatuated. When we met in the afternoon, it was as friends, and it was not until we had finished dinner and were holding hands across the table, our knees gripped together, relaxed, assured; and I saw her peaceful smiling face, that I began to feel desire again.

"Shall we go now?"

"It's lovely not being in a hurry."

"I am now."

"So am I. Go and I will follow."

The Penfields called us a stuffy old married couple. Our sole concession to sociability was to go with them one evening to the movie—René Clair's *Sous les Toits de Paris*.

"Those train whistles," Joyce said, as we talked after love. "They'll haunt me forever."

"He used them as a leitmotif."

"They'll be ours. That first night at the station! Those Englishmen! I've never known enchantment like this."

"Listen, you can hear the yard engines."

98

"And the rain on the leaves. Oh Jack, it's too good to last."

I kissed her words away.

Sunday afternoon we walked to the park on the only fine day since she had come. It was the first time I had been there since the winter walk with Erda. Now the trees made a green sky overhead. Thrushes sang. A cuckoo called. Children rolled hoops down the smooth walks. We reached the riverbank and sat on the stone bench. Across the stream the grassy field was the nesting place of larks and they rose up singing.

"I was reading Henry James's *Little Tour in France*," I said, "and it's here on this very bench that he brings it to a close. He did not like Dijon."

"He was probably alone. I'd go mad if I were here alone. I'll remember it because of you."

"You sound sad."

"Nostalgic, I guess, remembering Sunday afternoon walks along the river in Rouen. Now I'll add Dijon to memory."

"What are you telling me?"

"That I'll be leaving."

"No."

"You didn't think I'd stay forever."

"But it's only been a week."

"I intended to stay only a day."

"We could pool our money and share an apartment."

"Money's not the problem."

"What is?"

"You. You are losing weight. You can't go on with such a regime. What you have been lavishing on me belongs to your work."

"I have enough for both. I have never felt better."

"Nothing in excess, my husband used to say when I began on the second bottle of Pernod."

"I've never known one like you. You do not keep me aroused."

"I take that as a compliment."

"Stay. We'll find an apartment tomorrow."

"Now you're being that aggressive American. Don't forget, I've loved you because you weren't one."

"Be reasonable."

"I am. Oh Jack, you've been the first who's not sought to reform me. I truly have bad habits and a worse character."

"We have had other things to do."

"Lovely things, and all lovely things do pass. You're poet enough to know that."

"I refuse to be categorized."

She stood up.

"Let's walk. Talking is not good for this afternoon."

She had her way. We wandered back through the park, then returned to town along the riverbank and the canal path, past the hospital and the Faculty and the workers' quarter in the Rue Monge and the statue of Bossuet preaching, a fat pigeon on his head. I showed her a secret garden behind the stone wall of a deserted hotel. There against the side of the building was a well-shrine, with a stone cupid and the inscription. *"Tout par amor, 1539."* Lilacs had grown wild, the bushes were covered with purple blossoms, the air sweet with their fragrance.

"I could have loved you well," she said. "Why was it not you who came over the convent wall?"

We reached the Place Émile Zola as the fanfare of the P.L.M. began its Sunday afternoon concert—a dozen middle-aged railway workers in sloppy blue and red uniforms, blowing blasts of strident music. We found a table on the *terrasse* of the tiny Café du Midi. The leafy square was thronged with promenading Dijonnais. Children had scrambled atop the iron *pissoir* and were gaping over the crowd at the sweating musicians. We drank warm beer from green bottles. It was a spectacle Breughel would have relished. The music and shouting, barking dogs and roaring motorcycles made conversation impossible.

When it grew dark we walked on to the Pré aux Clercs for dinner. The Place d'Armes was also peopled with promenaders, the quieter bourgeoisie, and behind the hedge we were able to talk again.

"It's a poem by Rimbaud," I said. "Listen!"

> *Les tilleuls sentent bon dans les bons soirs de juin.*
> *L'air est parfois si doux qu'on ferme la paupiére.*

"Where was he when he wrote that?"

"Charleville."

"The dreary north. What escapists you poets are! If I shut my eyes, I'm back in Rouen. Oh Jack, why did it have to be the way it was?"

"Stay and we'll make it over."

"An old drunkard like me? Besides, you're my last man. I intend to live with women after this. Anyway, I'll be dead of lung cancer before I'm forty. Look at my fingers. You'd think I was Chinese. What could I give you? A child? No. The good father took care of that. He told me it was an appendectomy when he destroyed my ability to bear a child. My best gift to you would be my body in alcohol."

"Don't talk like that. You never have before."

"You're hearing the true me. I've hidden her for a week, thanks to you. Now you must face her, you fool."

"Please be reasonable."

"A lovely week for me. I've gained the weight you've lost. The lines are gone from my face. My hair is glossy again."

"Green eyes turned amber."

"You haven't asked anything of me. For God's sake, don't start now."

"Only that you stay for a while."

"You are a damn fool, John Burgoyne."

She began to laugh hysterically and I realized that for the first time she was drunk. I went across the square to the carriage stand, came back for her and we drove to the hotel. There she was quiet, and when we were in bed, she was violent in love, and then lay exhausted. It was nearing eleven when she pushed me gently out of bed.

"Go," she said. "Let us both get a good sleep."

She watched me dress, and then when I was putting on my shoes, she knelt naked and tied the laces. I buried my face in her hair, as she hugged my knees. Sandalwood, tobacco, wine, and woman were blended in one strong perfume. I drew her up and held her against me.

"You will stay?"

"Yes, but go now. I'm so tired."

"Tomorrow?"

"*Oui, à demain. Va t'en, mon amour. Laisse-moi dormir.*"

She pushed me into the hall and I heard the door lock.

All the next day I was impatient to see her. It was the first time I had not been able to concentrate on my work. On my way to the

Concorde I bought a nosegay of lilies of the valley—porte bonheur—the first time I had taken her flowers.

She was not in the café. I crossed the Place to the hotel. The room clerk stared when I asked him to ring Madame Davies.

"She has left."

"What?"

"She is no longer here."

"Do you mean that she has checked out?"

"That is the fact."

"Since when?"

"She left last night, soon after you did."

"Where has she gone?"

"She said that she was taking the *de luxe* at midnight."

"The Blue Train?"

"That's the one. For the Côte d'Azur. Some people have all the luck. They say it is fine weather down there."

"Doubtless. But did not Madame leave a message for me?"

"She left nothing at all, save the scent of a strange perfume."

"She was alone?"

"But certainly."

I thrust the lilies into my pocket and left the hotel. It had begun to rain. I crossed the square to the Concorde and sat down on the *banc*. The old flat-footed garçon came for my order.

"Monsieur desires?"

"The usual."

"Shall I bring Madame's?"

"She will not be here."

The waiter peered at me, then elaborately wiped off the marble-topped table with his towel.

"Then you are alone," he concluded.

"That, alas, is the exact truth. She took the Blue Train last night."

"I am truly sorry to hear that. You made a brave couple."

"That's life, my friend."

"True. One learns from experience that it is not all roses."

IV
Madeleine

The rainy spring merged into a rainy summer. The vintage failed. A cold wind blew from the east. The natives groaned.

I never heard from Joyce. The Penfields reported that she had sold the villa in Antibes and gone they knew not where.

I finished my studies and received my degree in early autumn. As my two-year fellowship had ended, I prepared to return to the United States and seek a laboratory appointment in or near San Francisco. Then one afternoon I received a letter from a legal firm in San Diego, transmitting a draft for $2,000, drawn on the Dijon branch of the Société Générale. It was the residue of my mother's estate, the very last of her gifts to me; and it decided me to stay on in Europe until it was gone. From all accounts, prospects of employment even for trained scientists were bleak. The Depression was becoming worldwide.

I hoped to write a book for which I had long been reading and making notes, a book on tuberculosis and art, studied in the works of Keats, Stevenson, Katherine Mansfield, and D. H. Lawrence. The latter two had died in France, and the first step would be to go to the south of France where Lawrence had lived his last days and to Italy where he had written *Lady Chatterley's Lover*. There I planned to interview doctors who had treated him and to soak up local color.

I was starved for sun. The golden limestone of the ducal city had lost its glow and gone gray. Dijon had become a morgue of grim weather. And so I closed my small affairs, said my good-byes, and on my last afternoon I called a taxi, stowed my bags therein, and drove to the bank on the Place du Théâtre. There I cashed the draft and took the fifty crisp new thousand-franc notes, folded and buttoned them down in an inner pocket of my coat. They gave me a feeling of great wealth.

Next, I directed the driver to the station, where I checked my baggage through to Nice on the seven-thirty *rapide*. Then I walked back the length of the main street to the Café de Paris, where I had first seen Erda pass and had met Joyce, said good-bye to the frog-faced proprietor and the waiters, and had a *porto sec* on the house. Then I paid homage to the bronze statue of Jean-Philippe Rameau, and in the courtyard of the Hotel de Ville to that of Claus Slüter, the Flemish sculptor, *imagier aux ducs*, standing aproned in the rain, his mallet and chisel upraised. I thought of them as friends.

Finally I climbed the circular staircase of the stone tower to the lookout platform for a last view over the town. In vain. Rain mist hid all but the nearest buildings, their multicolored tile roofs shining wet, their myriad chimney pots asmoke. Almost directly below was the Place d'Armes and the Pré aux Clercs where Joyce and I had dined every night for a week, its *terrasse* deserted, tables and chairs taken in for the winter.

Back on the main street I retraced my steps to the Place Darcy and entered the Concorde for a last *demi* of Vézelise. The old garçon approached, towel on arm.

"Monsieur desires?"

"The same." And when he returned with deliberate tread, carefully wiped the foaming glass and set it on the cardboard coaster, I declared, "You have worked here a long time."

"It will soon be thirty-seven years."

"I leave now. This is my last drink with you."

"I read in the *Progrès* that you completed your studies with honor."

"I have been fortunate here. It was a milieu that suited my temperament."

"It astonishes me that you endured our weather."

"It does not improve."

"It has become absolutely vicious. No spring, no summer, no vintage, and now the Gastronomic Fair is threatened. Soon we shall be entering the Ark."

"They say one enjoys fair weather on the Côte d'Azur. I leave for Nice on the seven-thirty."

"If this proves to be true, I beg of you to dispatch us some of their weather." He drew closer and lowered his voice, employing the subjunctive. "If it should not be indiscreet of me to ask, would you be rendezvousing with Madame?"

"You remember her?"

A slow smile spread over his moon face. "But certainly! She did not walk as an ordinary woman walks, but rather with a serpentine motion."

"That is well put, my friend. She was unusually supple."

104

He looked thoughtful. "You were fortunate in her company."

"I do not forget her, although let me say in all frankness, hers is not a troubling memory."

"It is curious, but I could never identify the perfume she wore."

"It was sandalwood. Her garments were permeated with it from having been hung in closets made of that wood."

"That is extraordinary. Certainly not here in France."

"In Indochina. In Saigon, to be exact."

"What you tell me is truly exotic. Does one enjoy such encounters in your country?"

"Hardly."

"I sometimes fancy that her fragrance lingers here where she sat with you so often."

"You are truly a man of sensitive perceptions."

"It is my *métier*. One learns from observing people."

I paid. We shook hands.

I went on to the station and dined in the buffet on steak, potatoes, salad, and a *demi-carafe* of Beaujolais. My sense of well-being was boundless.

The *rapide* was on time, its carriages shining from the rain, the couplings billowing steam. I boarded and found an unoccupied first-class compartment. Rain was falling as we left the shelter of the station, and I saw only a blur of lights through the streaming window. I pulled the shade, switched on the blue light, removed my shoes and coat and stretched out on the long seat with my overcoat for blanket. Soon I heard the wheels going over the switch-points at the Swiss junction and I knew we were on the main line south, via the Rhone Valley and Lyon, to the Côte d'Azur.

It was a smooth ride and I slept through the night. When I awoke we were somewhere east of Marseilles, running fast through low hills forested with pine and oak and a heather-like scrub, yielding to terraced olive orchards. The day was clear, and I knew the weather was warm by sight of the peasants in the fields, stripped to the waist. From Cannes to Nice the train followed the shore. I saw white sails on the water and the colored stucco villas. It was the Blue Coast at last.

My destination was the fishing village of Cros de Cagnes, eight miles west of Nice, where the *pension* called Le Soleil had been recommended by my professor of endocrinology as an unfashionable place of simple comfort and good food. The proprietor, Monsieur Torquet, met me at Nice with an old Citroën carryall. We loaded my bags, he picked up foodstuffs at the wholesale market, and we headed for home.

"As one of our dear friend's students," the proprietor said, "I shall ask you to look at my mother. A sad case, just home from hospital in Nice with what is declared to be a terminal case of cancer."

"I am not a medical doctor."

"Nevertheless, I should value your opinion as to the probability of her surviving through the year."

"I am at your service."

The Soleil stood on the beach, a few hundred yards west of the post office, café, general store, and huddle of fishermen's houses that constituted the village. It was a three-story faded yellow stucco building with a pink tile roof. I was given a front room on the top floor, overlooking the pebbled beach and the sea and along the coast in each direction. The few guests were French. The English tended to resort in Cannes or Nice; the Americans preferred old Cagnes on the hill in back of the beach.

The Torquet family of several generations staffed the *pension*, and I was asked by the proprietor to look at the old grandmother even before I had unpacked my bags. The entire family gathered around while I stood by her bed. She was stupified with morphine. Her heart was strong, her handclasp powerful. She would probably live thus until the malignant growth on the neck closed her windpipe.

"There is no hope at all, they told us at the hospital," the son whispered.

I nodded in agreement.

"Her room has a view of the maritime Alps," he said. "Mama enjoyed it more than that of the sea. Now she is indifferent, but we leave her here. I must apologize for the smell. Bandaging the dying flesh seems to do no good."

"It is only natural," I said, "when one approaches the end from such a malignancy. Keep her free of pain. That is all that remains. Is that not the main line of the P.L.M.?"

"You came along it this morning. There are good walks beyond it, if you care for such."

"I have a hunger for earth under my feet. They have become calloused from the cobbled streets of Dijon."

They gave me a small study in a summer house in the *pension's* garden; and there I spread out books and notes and spent my mornings in bliss. Before lunch I walked along the beach road to the café, and at an outdoor table under a trellised grapevine, I took an apéritif of the local white wine, mild and slightly sour, and nibbled on the plate of olives that was always served. On the beach across the road, the fishermen's women sat mending nets. The sun was warm, the sea blue and without surf or tide. The flora recalled California: bougainvillea and oleander, the trees of orange and lemon, olive, eucalyptus and pepper, mimosa and persimmon.

I led an idyllic life, at peace in body and mind. Evenings were spent in the *pension* parlor, gossiping with family and guests, listening to the radio, or reading *L'Eclaireur de Nice et du Sud-Est*. Several Frenchwomen came and went. They might have been my sisters for all the effect they had on my senses.

The autumn became winter, as at home, without any perceptible change of weather. The *pension* was absurdly cheap. I foresaw no change until early summer when I planned to move on to Florence.

Then one windy afternoon of early spring I was on the beach in front of the *pension*, practicing a boyhood sport recalled since coming to the Cros. The strand was composed of egg-size, varicolored igneous pebbles brought down from the Alps by the River Var which emptied into the Mediterranean a few miles east of the village. From two strings of rawhide and a leather pocket obtained from the village shoemaker, I fashioned a sling; and standing on the shore I hurled pebbles at targets along the verge or floating in the water. It was an old sport from which I derived pleasure.

On this particular afternoon when I was pegging away at a partly submerged crate, I felt eyes on me. I turned. A woman was watching me, seated out of the wind with her back against a blue dory. I had not seen her when I came out. She was not one of the *pensioners*. She wore a heavy coat and a red scarf around her black hair. She looked more Italian than French. I finally looked away and turned to walk farther on.

"Don't stop," she called, "I beg of you. You throw beautifully, like a young David."

I walked away without answering, resentful at having my sport

107

interrupted. I was wearing old clothes, and from her allusion, I believed she had taken me for a shepherd from the hills. I walked westward along the beach to a grove of umbrella pines called La Pinède which sheltered another *pension*; and there, beyond her sight, I resumed my slinging.

When I came down for dinner that evening, she was there, seated alone at a corner table, eating with a book in one hand. I felt my face turn red. She did not look up, nor did she gaze my way during the meal. After my embarrassment had passed, I observed her closely. She was beautiful, with creamy skin, black hair braided around her head, a long Greek nose, high forehead, full mouth with curving red lips, long lobed ears set with tiny red drops. An actress, I surmised, come for a secluded rest. I remembered her voice, free of the coarse accent which characterizes the speech of the south-eastern French. For the first time since Joyce had gone, I felt a quickening of emotion. Or was it merely remembrance of my rudeness on the beach?

She finished eating before I did, and gathering a shawl around her shoulders, she walked to the front door and left without looking my way. She moved with ease and grace, a small woman with slim legs and little feet, a mature woman of poise and elegance.

Instead of reading the *Éclaireur* and conversing, I walked to the café and enjoyed a cognac. I returned in an hour, hoping that I might find the newcomer with the family and be introduced. She was not there, nor did she return. I kept from asking about her, and finally gave up and went to my room.

I did not see her in the morning or at lunch. Perhaps she had come and gone. I could have asked. I did not. The current that bore me was languid.

I went for a walk after lunch, striking back across the railroad and the highway into the hills, bushed with wild lavender in flower. I broke off a bunch and tied it to my belt like an enormous sachet. Then I worked my way up and back to the low summit of the first range and there I rested, seeing below me the white-walled farmhouses, red-roofed and blue-shuttered, surrounded by vineyards and olive orchards. Brimming cisterns gleamed amid clumps of dark pines. I could hear the chop-chop of hoes, the sounds of children at play and barking dogs, and a man's high voice singing a folk song. Down below from where I had come, the blue sea was molded like a mirror to the shore. In the west I could see the Esterel range beyond Cannes. I stretched out and dozed.

The sun was nearly set when I started home. I passed terraced fields of night-blooming jasmine where peasant women were watering the plants. They would return before sunrise and harvest the flowers for the perfume factories at Grasse.

It was twilight when I reached the railroad back of the village. The northbound Blue Train was due to pass through at five forty-five. I was used to hearing it each evening as I washed up for dinner, flying by with a shriek of its whistle.

Now I leaned on the lowered crossing-gate and waited. In the half-light the tiny station was almost hidden by an enormous purple bougainvillea. Then the rails began to hum. The train was coming. I felt my skin prickle with gooseflesh. The whistle sounded, and suddenly there it was, drawn by the great black engine with copper-banded boiler gleaming in the fading light. Like a mad angel the train swept by, the blue and yellow *wagons-lit* with lighted windows and blurred faces. The red lights of the *fourgon* glared back, then vanished around the curve of track. I heard the whistle, wailing for the next village, and the diminishing sound of rolling wheels on iron rails. There remained a light pall and smell of coal smoke. And silence. My heart was pounding.

The old crossing guard hobbled out to raise the barrier. He saw me still leaning on it, and muttered a *bon soir*.

"It really rolls," I said, with a gesture down track.

"I should think so," he croaked. "It's making eighty when it passes here. They say it makes a hundred before it reaches Cannes." He tugged on the wheel and the barrier slowly rose. "They eat well, I'm told, and they sleep together. What follies those passengers enjoy!" He rubbed his hands together, chuckled, and crept back in to his meal.

It was that evening after dinner that I met her. Her name was Mademoiselle Montrechet. We remained in the family group at first, and then as they settled into their routines of cards and sewing, she and I withdrew to a wicker settee in a corner of the parlor.

"You are not still annoyed with me?" she asked.

"Was I ever?"

"Yesterday when I drove the young David from his favorite place."

"I believed you took me for a yokel. I regret the rudeness I displayed."

"It was I who was forward."

"Did you know I was a *pensioner*?"

"Of course. The little hunchback slavey pointed you out to me before I went to the shore."

"Emma is a beastly gossip. I have had to forbid her to interrupt my work."

"I would not have taken you for an American."

"They say my French blood shows."

"Only an American, however, would think of making sport with a sling. It impressed me as infinitely droll."

"I am not used to performing for an audience." I paused. "Nor such a beautiful one."

"Are all Americans such flatterers?"

"I do not see people in nationalistic terms. I see them first as human beings. I see you first as a woman. But I confess, I do not know your nationality, and I am curious."

"Let me test your cleverness."

"Are you Italian?"

"It is true that I am often taken for such because of my features and complexion. Actually, I am French. My mother is of Pau in the Basses-Pyrenées, my father Parisian, a professor of history. I was born in Paris, but I often go to Pau and its environs."

"Then you must have Basque blood or Spanish."

"I myself have never been beyond the borders of France."

"Do you know Burgundy?"

"Only the Morvan. My father directed researches there in pre-Roman Gaul. I used to go with him when I was little. There are many Celtic traditions to be found there, as well as menhirs and dolmens."

"And Vézelay?"

"Very well. A most beautiful sanctuary."

"If I may ask without being indiscreet, are you an actress?"

"Heavens no! Why would you think that?"

"Because of your beauty and your way of carrying yourself. Do not think me forward if I say that I felt an urge last evening to rise and follow you out."

110

She laughed. "Do you flatter all women this way? I must consult Emma."

"I have been a recluse for months. Tell me though, are you not connected with the arts?"

"Are all Americans as curious as you, or is it something you learned in your studies?"

"My interest *is* in research."

"And you regard me as raw material!"

"Don't say that. But you are a wonderful specimen."

"I assure you of the regularity of my natural functions."

"I have already taken your pulse."

"Without holding my wrist?"

"From the artery that throbs in your neck."

"Is it poetry that you write in the summerhouse?"

"No, but I am a devoté of the Symbolists. Myself, I am writing another kind of work."

"Do you ever read it aloud? My English needs practice."

"I might be persuaded." I paused. "You are the first woman I have talked with in a long time."

"I am honored."

"I do not mean it that way."

"What do you mean?"

"I feel drawn to you by instinct. Do not misunderstand me. I have no carnal motive.

She laughed. "You are a man. All men are carnal. Therefore . . ."

"Do not tease me."

"I do not tease you, my friend, but you say and do things that afford me vast amusement."

"Have you been here before?"

"Each year on holiday."

"You work then."

"Yes, I work."

"May I ask at what?"

"You are also a persistent man. I will tell you. I am a journalist. I am on the staff of *L'OEuvre*."

"I used to read it occasionally, but not since I have been here. *L'Éclaireur* is the local bible."

"I read no papers when I am on holiday."

111

"You live in Paris."

"Do you like my city?"

"Not in December. I am a southerner. I will visit you in Pau. I have never seen your Southwest."

"Why did you come to France?"

"Primarily to engage in endocrinological research. I had a fellowship."

"Then you are a doctor of medicine?"

"Of science. I was a medical student at home but gave it up to come to France."

"Why did you discontinue that line of study?"

"It was my father's wish that I follow him as an M.D. He died when I was in my teens. I sought to carry out his wish, and until my mother died two years ago, I did so, successfully—and unhappily. Her death left me free, and also with a small income. I determined to study pure science in the land of my ancestors."

"They say physicians are badly needed in your country."

"I am lacking in social conscience."

"You are an individual. That is what brought you home to France."

"I had tired of the group life we led as students. Here in France one is left alone."

"That is indeed our character."

"I thrived in Dijon, but once my degree was granted and I received a small inheritance, I came to this milder climate."

"Jean de Bourgogne is now Jean de la Côte d'Azur. Do you practice any of the arts?"

"I paint."

"Here?"

"Once in the refectory at the Faculty."

"An odd place for such."

"We painted the goddess of love under diagnosis by the class. All of us were involved in a kind of Burgundian Rembrandt."

"What was your part in it?"

"I painted a wart on her rump."

She laughed. "How very droll you are!" She looked at her wrist watch. "It grows late. I must go. We have talked at such length!"

"I ended up talking instead of asking."

"I must say good-night to my sister."

112

"Is she here with you?"

"She is with friends at La Pinède."

"May I accompany you?"

"Please, no."

She left again by the front door.

Although I saw her after dinner on succeeding nights, she was reserved. Had I been too bold? Had my eyes showed the hunger she stimulated in me? Though I was attracted by her, I also sensed that she did not welcome ardent attention. Each evening after we had talked awhile, she excused herself to say good-night to her sister. I managed to restrain my curiosity and cool my ardor.

Then one evening she went to her room after dinner and returned with a book. It was *Lady Chatterley's Lover*, in English.

"I bought it in Nice today," she said. "My friends in Paris have been talking about it. Will you help me over some of the difficult parts? My English is so slight."

"Do you know how naughty it is?" I teased.

"How so? The subject is love, is it not? Is that regarded as naughty in your country?"

"That depends on who does the loving."

"Just so."

She read aloud where we sat in the corner, haltingly with a thick accent, I helping her to pronounce and to translate. The parlor thinned out until at last we were alone. It was the first night she had not gone to La Pinède. At ten-fifteen we put down the book and heard the B.B.C. news from London.

"This Mellors," she said when the broadcast was over, "he is not like any Frenchman I have known. Do you as an American understand his psychology?"

"I don't know what you mean 'as an American.' As a man, yes, I do. His wanting to remain aloof. I have felt that way. I do feel that way. Or do I?" My eyes sought hers. She turned her face. Then she spoke again.

"A strange thing, this love out-of-doors. Lawrence seemed to have a passion for it."

"We love nature more than you do. I wish you would come with me for a walk in the hills. They are so beautiful now with the lavender in bloom. I am going again to Vence where Lawrence is buried to visit the sanitarium where he died. I need to copy his chart to use in my book. Go with me, I beg of you."

"I must be with my sister."

"Is she ill?"

"I can only say that she needs me."

She rose. I saw that she was troubled. She said good-night and went to her room.

I was puzzled. My life was so well ordered that I was reluctant to become involved, and apparently she felt the same. And yet we were mutually attracted.

I made the pilgrimage to Vence, found Lawrence's grave, and met the physician who had attended him in his last illness. He allowed me to copy the chart. There had not been an autopsy.

Back on the beach at day's end, triumphant at the success of my quest, I broke a spray of bloom from the mimosa tree in front of the *pension*. The pollen-heavy fragrance excited me. I wanted her to smell it. She was at table when I came in. My heart pounded. I gave her the little branch. She smelled it then looked at me curiously.

"From his grave?"

"From the tree of life. It is for you. Breathe its fragrance. Drink one of the golden balls in your wine. You will live forever."

"What makes you so fantastic this evening?" Her eyes widened.

"You do." Her eyes dropped. "May we talk later?" I dreaded her reply. She looked up.

"Yes," she said. "I'd like that."

Our eyes held for a long moment. Then I went to wash up. I stared in the mirror. The current had quickened.

We sat later on the settee while the parlor hummed around us. I was tongue-tied for the first time, afraid to speak lest I reveal my desire. Again she read from *Lady Chatterley* and we talked about Lawrence and my day.

Then the B.B.C. came on. "This is London," the distant voice spoke. We were alone. The others had retired, not caring for news in English.

Then for the first time I felt the heat of her leg next to mine. She must have sensed my awareness, for her body suddenly changed. What circuit had been joined? Had the mimosa proved a love charm? Or could it be Lawrence's ghost, drawn by her voice? Whatever it was, I knew that we had come together after touch and go;

114

and in that moment of revelation, I sought to control my trembling body, while the calm voice recounted the world's woe. My hand sought hers and closed over it. Now it was she who trembled. The news ended. The Mayfair Hotel dance band came on, playing "Penthouse Serenade."

I stood and held out my hand. She rose and I took her in my arms, and we moved slowly over the blue and white linoleum floor among the empty tables and chairs. I held my body away from hers. Only my hand, resting lightly on the small of her back, felt the warmth of her flesh, and my cheek next to her hair knew its softness. I breathed her fragrance, a perfume faint and delicate. The music quickened into "Sailing on the Robert E. Lee," and round and round we moved in tempo.

When it ended, she disengaged herself and went out the front door. Was she bound for La Pinède? I waited a moment, then followed. She was leaning against the trunk of the mimosa tree, the tree of life. The charm, the charm! A full moon cast a glittering track over the water. Her body was arched against the tree, her face uplifted to the moon like a priestess. The air was redolent with mingled scent of mimosa, eucalyptus, rose-geranium, and sea wrack. The only sound was of the little waves of the tideless sea, breaking softly on the shingle. The night was enchanted. I stood close, so that our knees touched.

"Aren't we getting behind in our reading?" she asked, matter of fact.

The spell was broken. She had run outdoors to break it. I leaned away.

"We are like Paolo and Francesca," I said. "Dante tells how they were reading together in the garden, and when they came to a certain passage, they turned and kissed and read no more that day."

"How persuasive you Americans are!"

"I am only a man."

"How persuasive you men are! But my arms are cold. I go in."

I followed. She was not in the parlor. I went upstairs. Her room was also on the top floor at the back of the *pension*, overlooking the mountains. A light shone from under her door. I knocked. She opened it.

"Madeleine," I pleaded. It was the first time I had used her name. "Madeleine, dear one, don't run away. Come to my room. There is

115

a marvelous passage in Lawrence I want to read to you. Not in *Lady Chatterley*. It is in another of his books, one that I bought in Nice. Come and hear."

She allowed me to lead her by the hand, and we tiptoed down the dark hall. We heard footsteps below, and then a door shut softly. We stood listening. In a moment the stink of death drifted up to us. The son had given his mother her eleven o'clock injection. Madeleine shuddered and clung to me. I led her into my room and locked the door.

She stood by the lukewarm radiator. All I could offer in the way of refreshment was an apple. She bit into it, then handed it to me to bite. In a moment I read from *Apocalypse*:

> What man most passionately wants is his living wholeness and living unison, not his own isolate salvation of his 'soul.' Man wants his physical fulfilment first and foremost, since now, once and once only, he is in the flesh and potent. For man, the vast marvel is to be alive. Whatever the unborn and the dead may know, they cannot know the beauty, the marvel of being alive in the flesh. We ought to dance with rapture that we should be alive in the flesh, and part of the living incarnate cosmos.

"That is beautiful the way you read it," she said, when I put the book down. "I am not sure I understand it all, but I won't ask you now to make a translation."

"You see it was not a deception. I *did* want to read to you."

I took the apple core from her and put it on the table. Then I stood facing her. She looked at me quizzically, as if to ask, how came we here? She was so beautiful that I could not keep from reaching out my hand and caressing her bare arm. Her eyes spoke to me. My arm went around her waist. I found her eager to be kissed.

We leaned against the radiator in the first long embrace. But when I grew bold, she gently freed herself, unlocked the door and slipped away. I followed and tried her door. It was locked.

I went back to my room, my body alert and glowing. I undressed and stood naked on the balcony. From beyond the village came the coughing roar of an African lion. A little ambulatory circus had arrived that day and pitched its caravan on the shore. I gradually cooled off, then chilled, and went to bed. Sleep came quickly.

I did not see her all the next day. She did not come down for

116

lunch. I knocked on her door afterward. No answer. I tried the knob. Locked. I walked along the beach past La Pinède, as far as the willow-grown mouth of the Cagnes. I did not see her. Had she left? I feared to ask. My mind kept turning over each detail of the night before. What had I done to drive her away? All I could think of was Madeleine Montrechet.

After returning from the walk I sat blankly over my notes in the sunroom. The door opened. It was Emma, the slavey.

"I thought perhaps your basket needed emptying."

"It is as empty as I."

The little hunchback sidled closer. "What troubles you, Monsieur Jean?

"Have you seen Mademoiselle?"

Her beaked face opened in a gold-toothed grin. "You're love-sick," she cackled.

"Answer me."

"Not since breakfast."

She fingered the edge of the table with a claw hand, then looked up, half sly, half wistful.

"Do you think she is beautiful?" she asked.

"Very."

"And desirable?"

"Utterly."

"And I? I am ugly. Is it not so?"

"Everyone loves you, little witch that you are."

"But no one wants to sleep with me. Only those stinking fishermen, so drunk they don't know who I am."

I laid my hand on her lank black hair, but she broke away, sobbing, and scuttled out the door.

I walked to the café later and drank a *chopine* of white wine that raised my spirits. When she did not appear for dinner, I despaired again. At eight o'clock there was a broadcast from Prague of the *Bartered Bride*. I pulled my chair close to the loud-speaker and sought solace in Smetana's joyous music.

During the first entr'acte, as I sat with my face bent over in my hands, I heard the front door open. I peered through the bars of my fingers. It was Madeleine, hair wind-blown, cheeks flushed, eyes sparkling. I rose eagerly. She greeted me impersonally and took a hand of cards from one of the family.

Her face told me nothing. She laughed and was gay. I closed my eyes and returned to the music.

Ten o'clock came and still she played cards. Finally she rose and came over to the radio. I stood up.

"*Bonne nuit,*" she said, holding out her hand.

I took it. A note transferred to mine. After she had left the room, I sat down with my back to the parlor, unfolded the note and read it.

"Come to my room, if it pleases you."

I could hardly sit through the London news. At ten-thirty I went to my room, took a sponge-off, donned robe and slippers, and stepped out on my balcony. Again the glitter lay on the water. The fishing fleet was scattered darkly over the bay. I breathed a prayer to Diana and went to Madeleine's room.

She answered my knock in a soft voice. I entered. She sat at the dresser with her back to me, brushing her long hair. Our eyes met in the mirror. Her face was grave. I went to the back of her low bench and stood. Her fragrance dizzied me. I laid my hands on her shoulders. She wore a thin blue silk kimono which did not insulate the heat of her body. She continued to brush her crackling hair.

"You wanted to come?" she asked.

I buried my face in her hair. She laid down the brush.

"Did you look for me today?"

"I thought you had gone.

"I had to go to Nice. I longed for you, my love, dear Jean." It was the first time she had called me that. "I feared you would be angry at my running away last night, like a foolish girl. I had to. I was not well."

She rose, still facing the mirror. "Tonight I am well."

Her kimono opened and and she let it slide to the floor. I saw her body in the glass, the rosy-nippled breasts, the love hair a dense black against the ivory of her skin.

I let my robe fall to the floor, turned her gently to face me, took her in my arms and carried her to the bed.

When finally we lay side by side, she said, "I have never loved an American before. Am I as good as the women of your country?"

"You have had my virginity."

She laughed. "Do you like me?"

"Do you seek another proof?"

"In a moment, but first, let me hear you say it."

118

"From the very first sight, sitting there out of the wind, black hair, red scarf, blue boat."

"You wondered?"

"No. I was mainly angry with you. But I did that night, when I watched you walk, not even glancing at me. I did not dream, however, that it would be thus."

"Nor did I."

"Are you ready now for the second proof?"

"Oh, but I am! Will you teach me the American ways?"

She turned on her side and drew me to her.

Day was breaking when I went to my room.

I slept until noon. On my way down to lunch I knocked at her door. No answer. It was locked. She was not in the dining room. I worked in the sunroom without the torment of the day before.

At four o'clock I heard the latch click as someone entered the garden gate. I knew that it was Madeleine. The door opened and there she stood, breathing hard, her face troubled. I moved to embrace her but she held me off.

"Oh my dear," she said, "a terrible thing has happened. My sister's friend committed suicide this morning. I can tell you no more now. I must return immediately."

My heart stopped. "To Paris?"

"To La Pinède, where my sister is. I ran all the way only to tell you where I am and that I cannot see you tonight."

"Can I be of help?"

"Friends have come from Nice. I must return now. *Au revoir.*" She kissed me and left.

I read the story of the tragedy that evening in the *Éclaireur*. It was an affair of Lesbianism. The sister's "friend" was an "amie." Madeleine had come from Paris in an effort to dissuade her younger sister from further relations with an older Frenchwoman, a dilettante who had seduced the girl and brought her to the Riviera. Madeleine had apparently succeeded in persuading her sister to break away and accompany her back to Paris. Whereupon the chagrined Lesbian superficially wounded the girl, then shot herself successively through both heart and temple, a feat which the newspaper termed, *"tout à fait miraculeux."*

Madeleine did not return to Le Soleil that night nor for breakfast the next morning. As I was walking to the café toward noon, a

119

Renault sedan overtook me. A handkerchief fluttered at the window. It was Madeleine, and a young woman and two men I had never seen before. I feared that she had had to leave without our meeting again. I worked all afternoon in blind concentration.

I went to my room after dinner and read in the only souvenir I had of her—a volume of François Mauriac's poems called *Orages* which she had loaned me. They were bittersweet poems of love won and love lost and of the burden carried by a sensual man. They spoke to me with a voice I had never heard in poetry. I read them now with new intensity and deeper meaning.

At last I turned out the lamp and went on my balcony. There was diminished light from the gibbous moon. No boats were on the water. The lighthouses of Ferrat and Antibes wheeled and stabbed. I ached for Madeleine. Had I lost her?

I lay down on my bed and must have dozed.

I was roused sometime later by a soft knocking on the door.

"Who is it?"

"*C'est moi, Madeleine.*"

It was she, in coat, hat, and veil, beautiful and melting. I held her close and she put her cheek against mine.

"I need you, my love, Oh how I need you!" she murmured.

"You have me."

"I feared you would not be here. Your window was dark and there was no light under your door."

"I thought it was good-bye you waved this noon."

"So much has happened. You read in the paper, yes? You know then. It is ended. I put her on the Blue Train before they could detain her for an inquest, then I came to you as soon as I was able, my American lover."

"Who were those men in the car?"

"Only my cousins from Nice. You were jealous?"

"I have had gloomy thoughts. Now you have turned them golden."

"Don't put on the light. I must look like a witch. Let me go and bathe. Will you come then? The night is yours."

It was a beautiful night. Madeleine had seen the body of the dead Lesbian—the first corpse she had ever viewed—and in response to her sister's wish had helped wash and dress it for burial. The effect had been to turn her back toward life, so that I found her needful

120

of my living body, her desire heightened to an almost unbearable ecstasy. We strove with all our might to perpetuate the life in us.

I awoke at daybreak and again slipped away to my own bed.

She rested in her room for the next twenty-four hours, then on the morning of the second day we went on an outing. I had read in the *Éclaireur* that the Italian liner "Rex," Genoa for New York, was due to call at Villefranche for passengers. We planned to be there when she put into the bay. They packed a lunch for us, and we set out by autobus to Nice, where we transferred to the Mentone bus.

Villefranche clings to the ankle of the Grande Corniche, a few miles east of Nice, its tall stucco houses forming a pastel conglomeration against the gray cliffs, two shades of green being supplied by terraced stands of olive and pine. The long finger of bay points seaward, bounded on each side by a narrow wooded cape.

We left the bus where the highway crosses the neck of the western cape, then followed a dirt road through pines on the crest until we had nearly reached the end of the cape. There we turned off and found a vantage point on the steep eastern slope. The blue bay was below us, its water unruffled under a windless sky. We were in a clearing among the pines, the ground carpeted with dead needles, the air fragrant with resin. I twitched a branch and a shower of pollen sifted down like yellow dust.

Madeleine lay on her back on the bed of needles. She wore a slack suit of fine-ribbed green corduroy, espadrilles on her bare feet. It was the first time I had seen her in casual clothes. I leaned on my elbow and watched the small boats coming in and out of the narrow bay.

"I brought your book," I said, reaching in my shirt and removing the volume. "Do you know Mauriac? I mean, know him personally?"

"I do. He is a man of great feeling and kindness. He has been very good to me with the tenderness that comes to a few older men who have lived deeply sensual lives."

"His poetry expresses much suffering."

"It is from the struggle between soul and senses. It is obvious that he is an ardent Catholic. I trust you did not overlook the book's motto: *les derniers grondements d'une jeunesse que s'éloigne.* How does one say that in English?"

121

"One doesn't, at least not literally. I believe I know what it means."

"So do I! Oh Jean, my friend, it is more and more meaningful as my own youth recedes."

"Dare I ask your age, O ageless one?"

She laughed. "You express yourself so nicely. I really believe you should remain in France and enrich our culture."

"You tease me."

"Indeed I do not I am a serious woman."

"Of what age?"

"You have been persistent almost from the first when, you will recall, you rejected my overture. But why do you need to ask my age, you who can take a woman's pulse without even touching her?"

"Thirty?"

"Oh thank you, you are truly a friend, but alas, you must add six."

"Such antiquity! All of eight years my senior. Soon we'll *both* be in our thirties."

"You will age well. You have learned good things."

"The most from you, my Madeleine."

At eleven o'clock, precisely on schedule, the bow of the "Rex" appeared from behind the eastern cape. She entered the bay and dropped anchor abreast of us, her twin black funnels banded with Italian colors, a red and white house flag flying from her afterpeak. Steam rose from the fore-funnel, followed by a deep blast that was hurled back by the cliff.

We sat with drawn-up knees and watched a lighter with passengers and baggage approach and disgorge into the ship. Then she backed out of the bay and disappeared behind the western cape.

"Do you wish you were on board?" she asked.

"If you were with me."

"Are you never homesick?"

"Only lovesick."

I kissed her, but after a brief surrender, she freed herself.

"No you don't, Mr. Mellors. Morning in the open air is not a proper place."

"We could go beneath the pines where no eye would see us."

"The needles would hurt my flesh, and besides my ensemble is not fashioned for such an act."

"I am nevertheless very happy."

"You have been in love before."

"Never like this. You are a kind of incarnation of all the women I have ever known."

"You are an incorrigible flatterer. Are you not hungry? I die of hunger, being unaccustomed to such a vigorous life."

We lunched on bread and cheese and meat, and there was a wicker-covered bottle of chianti. The wine made us glow and she let me love her a little and gently, but mostly she wanted to talk.

"Ah, but you're a city girl," I said, bending over her, "The wonder is you are so healthy with no outdoor life at all. Everything about you is perfection: skin, hair, teeth."

"I have never been made love to so clinically. I like it. Tell me though, how long before I fade?"

"Never, if you follow my prescription of the other night. One golden bloom in wine taken with the evening meal. It would be best if I could prepare it for you."

"But you will be returning to your country."

"Not until summer. Come with me to Italy, to the villa near Florence where Lawrence wrote the book. Let us honeymoon there."

"Do not torment me, I beg of you. It is a miracle that I am here now."

"Where should you be?"

"In Paris, of course. Imagine how difficult it was to send my sister back alone. Our cousins were angry with me. I can tell you now. 'For that beachcomber?' they asked, when I pointed you out as we drove by. I was furious that they saw only the worn clothes and not you. It was then that I decided to stay."

"Did you see more than old clothes that first afternoon?"

"I saw your thin face, your wiry frame, your brown hands, and, oh, the way you selected the small stones and most delicately rubbed them clean before putting them in the sling. The grace of your movements. It was a marine tableau, a poem of utmost charm. I was drawn to you in spite of my wish to remain aloof, and that is why I spoke to you. Only to be ignored. Ah God, I blushed and would not raise my eyes to you that night."

"Why did you wish to remain aloof?"

"I wanted only to free my sister. I did not want a love affair. I am not a green girl, you know, in search of experience."

"Are you married?"

"Do not catechize me."

"Why did you let me love you?"

"I could not help it. I sought to remain impersonal, but in vain. You provoked in me exquisite feelings that I thought myself no longer capable of; and when I perceived that you are an artist, as well as a scientist, and that you know something of the way women are and would not be foolish or clumsy, then I gave myself to you with all my heart."

"But you won't out of doors."

"It would not be successful here."

"You French are more cold-blooded than we are."

"And wiser. You have lived among my people and our blood is in you so that you are not alien to me. You and your ways are a seductive blend of the familiar and the strange. How could I resist you?"

"You will come with me?"

"You must not ask that. It is not fair, for I cannot. I must return to Paris."

"When?"

"Tomorrow."

"Tomorrow?"

"I had not meant to tell you until tonight when you were leaving me. I must take the Blue Train."

"Then this is the last time."

"We have all day, all night."

I lay face down on the prickly needles and sought to hold back tears of chagrin. I felt unable to match her resignation.

"I did not want to love you either," I said finally. "For long I did not touch a woman, even a handclasp, but gave myself utterly to my work. The Cros was like Eden, without Eve."

"It was unnatural for you to remain chaste so long."

"You are so utterly French."

"What else, my love, what else would you have me?"

"I will always be hungry for you. Can we be together in Paris? I shall be there en route from Italy to England."

"When lovers part they can never come together again the same two persons. Time alters them. Time and distance. Who knows what they will do to us? There will be war again. There is always the fear of the Germans, the modern barbarians. The paper I work for is international in outlook and policy, but in my heart I do not believe. I fear."

"You are too fatalistic."

"Life has taught me to be."

"I have yet to learn."

"You must learn to take all when the time is ripe, as ours was. You must never forget the nature of idylls. They bud, they bloom, they fade."

"You leave even before ours is through blooming."

"That is our fate. I would have you think of this enchanted coast and those who have loved here before us. Phoenicians, Greeks and Romans, the barbarians, Italians, French. And now we two, Jean and Madeleine. Think of us, my love, as two of the brightest links in the long chain."

We dozed, side by side on the pine needles under the blue sky and golden showers of pollen.

Twilight found us back in Nice at the Café Monod on the Place Masséna, where English tea and Sandeman's port engendered more talk.

"There is no point in a man enjoying women," she said, "if he does not learn to apply to the next all that he has learned from the ones before. You did not come to me a gauche shepherd. You brought things learned from those you have told me of, all of them, even Nancy. And do you know the greatest thing a man or a woman can learn?"

"Tell me."

"That it is more satisfying to give pleasure than to receive it. But you do know this. We both do. That is why we are so good together."

"But after tonight you will stop giving."

"Then it is your turn, to give me the freedom to go. What if I had gone day before yesterday, as every reasonable impulse told me to do?"

"I shall never forget your coming to my darkened room."

"It was a supreme moment for me as well."

"Tell me how it is that you are beautiful and not vain or selfish?"

"I was once both."

"What can I hope for in a woman after you?"

125

"Your new wisdom and strength will attract good women. Like unto like. You must marry and father children."

"You have borne children?"

"Yes."

"That is why you are tender with me."

"*Oui, mon enfant.*"

"One more?"

"Perhaps. It would be truly a love-child."

We walked across the Place to the Cagnes autobus stand, seeing the electric signs on the buildings—Aux Galeries Lafayette de Paris; L'Eté à Aix-les-Bains; Hotel Ruhl et des Anglais; Nestlé, Trésor des Mamans; Ostende, Belgique, Reine des Plages; Voyages en Italie—all the glittering signs, casting their light down on us.

We ate dinner at her table, and in honor of her departure, Monsieur Torquet opened an old bottle of St. Emilion. She was gay and adorable, and I loved her joyfully, hopelessly.

We went at once to her room after we had eaten, and undressed; and not wanting to make love in the dark, we dimmed the lamp with her red scarf. I remember that sometime toward morning she leaned over me and stroked my closed eyelids and whispered, "When you see me no longer, remember how I caressed your face." She lay back down and said, even softer, "Soon I will be old. And you as well, my love. How beautiful life is, how sad!"

I slept again until noon. She left a farewell note under my door. "I shall look for you when the Blue Train passes." There was also a sprig of lavender from a bouquet I had brought her.

Toward evening I leaned once again on the barrier and waited for the Blue Train to pass. It came with a shriek and a rush; and it went, leaving the dying sound of its wheels and the acrid smell of coal smoke. Was it she I saw at the window, waving? I could not be sure, so swift was the passage of the train.

The old man crept out to raise the barrier. This time I did not linger to talk with him.

V
Martha

My life at Le Soleil ended with the departure of Madeleine. I bought an excursion ticket to Italy that allowed stopovers in any city. Florence was the only one where I stayed a while, and there it was to visit the Villa Mirenda at Scandicci in the nearby countryside, where I sought vestiges of Lawrence's residence. From Rome I went to Naples and there obtained passage on a Dutch freighter to Rotterdam. A slow voyage with calls at Marseilles, Barcelona, and Casablanca saw my book finished, and I arrived midsummer in London with free time and a little money left.

I bought a Royal Mail freighter passage to California via Panama Canal three weeks hence, then settled into a Bloomsbury boardinghouse and passed the days in galleries, museums, libraries, and parks, and in the reading room of the Royal College of Physicians, examining the earliest editions of Vesalius and Paré, rare books that were never made available by French libraries to mere students.

The time was early summer, the weather fair, tourists few. The Depression cut deeply into foreign travel. London was sedate after Paris and Rome. It was my first visit to the British capital and I liked it more than I thought I would, responding to the sober English character, the friendliness of the people in the streets, and their sense of self-reliance and certainty.

I sought to understand what Madeleine had given me. I felt mature at last and ready for whatever life held for me. As for loving another woman, I could not conceive of one to match the gifts of the Frenchwoman I had known so briefly and yet with such powerful effect. Besides, the English women were unalluring.

Then one morning at the American Express I found a letter from my cousin Robert, the son of my mother's sister, a coffee and tea importer in San Francisco, which read in part:

> "Dear Jack, Mother gave me your travel letter saying you will be in London for a few weeks, and I hasten to ask you to be nice to my fiancée Martha Cameron. She'll be there about the same time as you with her mother on her way back from Munich. I wanted her to get married a year ago, but she insisted on going, and now she's due back and we'll get married

in Piedmont. I hope you'll be back for it. Business is very good for us in spite of the Depression—you know how people like their morning drink—and if you wanted to go into business I sure could make you a lot of money in this operation. Enclosed is a twenty for you and her to take in a show or two, and if there's any left over, bring me a Dunhill pipe, the kind with a short straight stem and a medium bowl. Be good to Martha but not too good.

Yours, Bob."

His letter was followed a day later by a note from Martha Cameron, giving her London hotel address. It was another few days before I overcame inertia and wrote, suggesting a rendezvous at the American Express office in the Haymarket; and it was there in the lobby that we met in mutual appraisal.

"So you are Bob's cousin Jack!"

"At your service, Miss Cameron."

"Out of a sense of duty."

"And curiosity."

"How do I look?"

"Cool."

"Do you really like it? I got it in Prague."

She was wearing a coarse linen skirt and a white blouse embroidered with red and blue flowers, and sandals on her bare feet.

"They say it's going to be another hot day. You are sensible to dress this way."

"Where are we going?"

"Lyon's Corner House. Do you mind eating there?"

We walked to the top of the Haymarket to the restaurant around the corner, and there we were seated at a marble-topped table in a quiet corner.

She was not pretty. Her eyes were small and close set, but a clear blue. Her nose was too large for her freckled face, her hair sand color. Her mouth was her best feature, wide and generous, the lower lip full, almost bee-stung. Her hands, as they played nervously with the silver before we were served chilled salads, toast and tea, were long fingered and blue veined. Her bare arms were white and also freckled. She was as tall as I, with shapely legs and feet. Her breasts swelled the flowered blouse.

"Well," she said. "Do you like what you see?"

"I can't decide whether you're a farm or a chorus girl."

She laughed. "I *was* born in the country, but on a vineyard, not a farm."

"Where did you meet Bob?"

"At Cal."

"I suppose you have been studying German business methods."

"Heavens no."

"What then?"

"Art."

"Art?"

"Why do you look astonished?"

"I can't imagine Bob . . . "

"I know. You think he's a Philistine. He is."

"Why are you marrying him?"

"Aren't you being rather personal, Dr. Burgoyne?"

"How would you like me to be?"

"Yourself."

"All right then, why are you marrying him?"

"He loves me."

"And you don't love him?"

"I didn't say I didn't."

"He and I are not alike."

"What are you like?"

"I like painting. Do you paint?"

"I try."

"Have you been to the Tate?"

"I haven't been anywhere in London. Mother is a hypochondriac. I've been devoting myself to her."

"When is the marriage?"

"This fall. Will you come?"

"If I get an appointment in the Bay region."

"Bob says you're a brain."

"I also have an organ called the heart."

"Tell me about its beat."

"Regular."

"I expected to find you terribly intellectual. You're really quite . . . "

"Ordinary."

"Entertaining is what I was going to say."

"I said I was at your service."

"It's a relief to be with an American man."

"Are Germans on the make?"

"They think art students are to bed down."

"Well?"

"I'm really a Puritan."

"All but your mouth."

"What do you mean?"

"It was made for kissing."

"I promised Bob I'd wait till we were married."

"Haven't you ever?"

"With him, naturally, but not with anyone else."

She put down her fork and took a swallow of tea and leaned forward on her elbows. "The marble feels cool, doesn't it. You're not an M.D., I know, but you have studied and know a lot."

"And lived a bit."

"I need to talk to someone."

"I'm here. What about?"

"Bob."

"Yes?"

"He can never make love to me without drinking a lot first."

"It sounds like he is the Puritan. There are many fetishes some find necessary before they can have intercourse."

"I'd like to think I'm fetish enough."

"I'd say you are."

She laughed. "I confess to loving it, fetish and all."

"The year must have been a long one to go without."

"Long in every way. I've had time to think."

"About marrying Bob?"

"About everything. I'm glad you'll let me unburden."

"Bob's a money-maker. And you'll never be out of tea and coffee."

She laughed again. "I've grown up with money. Dad owns the Beau Soleil winery and lots of other things. This year I've learned other values."

"My grandfather owned a vineyard. I went to see it in Auxerre. It's still there."

"Was he rich?"

130

"He had just enough vines to make his own wine. They say he regretted emigrating, but he made money in a San Diego real estate boom, and my father became a doctor, and here I am."

"I'm uncertain."

"Then why do it?"

"It's gone so far. The families have it all settled, especially what *they're* going to wear. Besides, I don't want to hurt Bob."

"Why not stay away another year? He'll wait, won't he?"

"I haven't any talent."

"We all have uncertainties."

"Is studying all you've done?"

"The first year. Since then I have had some interruptions."

"Interesting ones?"

"Educational ones. I'm not the same as when I first arrived in Europe."

"Women?"

"Women."

"I can listen."

"Let's walk. It would be too long a story."

I went with her along Piccadilly as far as Fortnum and Mason's where she was to meet her mother. I believed that this would be our only meeting; and then, as we were saying good-bye, something made me ask, almost against my will,

"Would you like to see the Tate?"

"With you?"

"Who else?"

"I thought maybe you were arranging a tour for lonely women."

"Meet me at Amexco again tomorrow at eleven."

"It sounds lovely."

That evening I dithered. I did not want an affair involving my cousin. I went so far as to draft a telegram saying I had been called away. It sounded flimsy. I tore it up. I went to sleep dreaming of Martha's lower lip.

We met on another hot morning, and Martha was again dressed in cool linen with bare legs and sandaled feet, like a flower amidst the wilted tourist throng, her homely face lit and friendly, as we came together in the crowded lobby. My inertia vanished as I realized that I, too, was lonely for someone from home.

We walked to the bottom of the Haymarket and boarded a Num-

131

ber 32 bus, climbed to the top and sat behind the windscreen as the red monster rolled through Trafalgar Square, down Whitehall, past Westminster Abbey, and along Millbank to the riverside Tate Gallery, its Portland stone a dirty gray from London's grime.

The interior was cool and colorful. We wandered through rooms of Turners, the pre-Raphaelites, and contemporary British painters, pausing before Stanley Spencer's fantastic "Resurrection," coming at last to the rooms of the French Impressionists. There Martha's grip on my arm tightened and I felt her response as we walked past the glowing walls of Renoir nudes, Gauguin's tawny Tahitians, the golden checkerboards and blue mountains of Cezanne's Provençal landscapes, Vincent's grain fields and wind-blown cypresses and little yellow chair, the ballet girls and beer drinkers of Dégas, and last of all, a Monet painting of blue poplars against white clouds.

Now Martha was pressed against me, her body like a harp under the touches of form and color. Thus had Erda responded to music. I knew that we were moving toward denouement. We did not speak. Painting was our tongue.

We stopped on the way out to look at the sculpture in the foyer — a stone woman with crushed lips and breasts by Gaudier-Brjeska called "Chanteuse Triste;" a crucifixion and an Eve by Eric Gill, demonstrating his twin loves for the religious and the erotic; Rodin's "Fallen Caryatid" and his head of Balzac.

When I saw that she liked these last pieces, I suggested that we go next to the Victoria and Albert Museum and see the collection of sculptures given by Rodin during the World War.

"We haven't eaten," I reminded her.

"You have fed me."

And so we walked hand in hand along the Embankment in the shade of the plane trees, seeing the Thames with its traffic of tugs and barges.

I asked directions of a bobby at the Albert Bridge, and then we boarded the bus that took us via the Marble Arch and Kensington to the Victoria and Albert. There we spent an hour in the cool dark rooms of the Museum where sunlight never reached, looking at the Rodins and the replicas of Florentine bronzes by Donatello and Giambologna. Martha paused in front of Rodin's "Fallen Angel," a bronze of two women in an intertwined position, their mouths joined, one woman on back, bent like a bow.

"I am not sure that I like it," she said.

I ran my hands over the cold metal. "He was a bull of a man. I can see him tearing the two apart and making love to them separately."

"It's a wonder the English would allow it."

"The title puts them off. They think it's something from Milton." She laughed.

We left the museum and crossed to Hyde Park and lay on the grass in the shade of great poplars. People drifted around us, dogs played, and in the distance the buses honked like geese.

"My feet are hot," Martha said.

"Let me unbuckle your sandals."

I held her bare foot in my hands and massaged it gently, then the other. She lay back and closed her eyes.

"It's lovely," she murmured.

"The feet are generally neglected. Men think hands are the only things worth holding."

"I never knew I could feel close to someone so quickly."

"Art does it."

"I'm glad you're not on the make."

"I thought maybe I was."

"Well, not obviously."

"There are other ways to make love than pushing a woman down on her back."

"How did you know the way to a woman's heart is through her feet?"

"A footnote in Gray's *Anatomy*."

She laughed. "Bob would think we're crazy."

"Art intoxicates."

"Art and Jack. I hate not being a good painter."

"Being a good woman comes first."

"What is good?"

"Said jesting Cameron and would not stay for an answer."

"I like you."

"And I you."

"I'm leaving tomorrow night."

"A good thing, too."

"Don't you want me to stay?"

"What would we do?"

"Man leads, woman follows."

"Your hands remind me of Rossetti's *Silent Noon*. 'Your hands lie open in the long fresh grass, the finger points shine through like rosy blooms.' "

"Why didn't you find me in Munich?"

"*Je ne sprache pas Deutsch.*"

"It was a wasted year."

"You'd better marry Bob soon, if you're going to."

"Mother wonders why I toss and turn at night. I can't talk to her, she's such a prude. She told me once her husband had never seen her naked. I hate what she did to him. He was once a virile man, I know. Now he's her eunuch. She said she wouldn't sleep in the same room with me if I didn't wear a nightgown."

"You sleep naked?"

"Don't you?"

"In weather like this."

"Bob's a prude, too."

"I don't know him at all. I already know you much better."

"We met only yesterday. It didn't take long, did it?"

"I know that the relationship between a man and a woman, the physical act, can be the most beautiful thing on earth. Not automatically and not always. Rarely, I guess. But then it can be so intense and creative as to make all the forms of art which flow from it mere echoes and reflections."

"You speak with conviction."

"Being in Europe has taught me everything."

"Tell me some you've learned."

"I can't tell it. I can only be it."

"I think I know what you mean."

The hot afternoon passed and we had neither lunch nor tea. We lay on the grass and talked and were silent, talked more and then dozed, in "a close-companioned inarticulate hour, when twofold silence was the song of love."

"Can we have supper together?" I asked, as we finally rose to leave.

"Mother has theater tickets. Dine with us at the hotel. Mother would like to meet you."

"Would I like mother?"

"No." She took my hand. "But you like me; you said you did."

134

"I do. You lead now and I'll follow."

We walked through Kensington Gardens, past the duck pond, the statue of Peter Pan and the sunken garden, to her hotel.

Mrs. Cameron was a reserved woman. I could strike no sparks from her, and we were able to converse at all only when I steered the talk to the subject of her own health.

Then we were saying good-bye in the lobby and again Martha's widened eyes spoke to me, and I heard myself asking her to dine with me the following evening.

"I'm sorry," Mrs. Cameron replied, "tomorrow is our last day. We are going to Hampton Court and won't be back until late. Our boat train leaves at one a.m. Something about the *Mauretania* sailing with the tide. Martha couldn't possibly see you again, Dr. Burgoyne."

She held out her hand. I ignored it and looked at Martha. She had blanched so that the freckles were jumping off her face. She looked at her mother, then at me. The denouement still lay ahead. I would not be denied.

"What time will you be back?" I asked Martha.

"By six."

"Meet me in front of Selfridge's at seven-thirty, I know a French restaurant you'll love. And there's Duke Ellington at the Palladium. I'll get you to the boat train on time. Your mother can take the bags in a cab. After all, Bob asked *me* to look after you in London."

Mrs. Cameron was speechless.

"I'm going to do it, mother. I'm not going to sit around this hotel until midnight."

Mrs. Cameron turned her back and went to the lift, Martha seized my hand. Her eyes were enormous.

"Thank God! I would have backed down."

"*Pour Robert et pour la patrie.* Do you want to see me a last time?"

She squeezed my hand. "Guess."

The next day seemed endless. I tried to bury the thought of Martha, the coolness of her garb, her fair freckled skin, widened eyes and bee-stung lip and the feel of her naked feet in my hand, but her image burned in me like a live coal.

Yet I made no plans. How could I? I had little money and less time. I sought to pass the day by walking, clear to St. Paul's, and there with a guide up onto the catwalk around the base of the dome from where we could see for miles around.

I returned to my lodging for tea and cucumber sandwiches, shaved again, took a bath and donned fresh clothes, and was waiting in front of Selfridge's in Oxford Street when Martha stepped off the bus. She was wearing a gray woolen skirt and a short-sleeved purple cashmere pullover, sandals on her bare feet. Her expectant face was lovely to see.

"Not too tired?" I asked.

"Oh Jack, why did you wait until the very last minute to ask me? Didn't you know I was praying all through dinner for you to ask me out my last night in London?"

"Is your mother still angry?"

"I shouldn't tell you this, but coming back on the boat, do you know what she said? She said she would be happier if I were marrying someone more mature than Bob. Someone like Dr. Burgoyne."

"You made that up."

"You buffaloed her."

"What did you say?"

"I said I didn't know anyone like Dr. Burgoyne."

"You'll be happy with Bob once you're married."

"He cabled that he's meeting the boat in New York."

"Don't give up your painting."

"When do you leave?"

"Next Thursday on the *Loch Clair*. It takes a whole month to San Pedro."

"I wish, I wish . . . "

"Dreamer."

We walked through Oxford Circus and on to Bloomsbury and the French restaurant in Charlotte Street called "Chez Antoine." There we sat at one of four candle-lit tables on the privet-hedged *terrasse*, and after plates of leek and potato soup, we ate cold roast beef, sliced cucumbers and tomatoes and French bread, and drank a bottle of chilled vin rosé. The garçon was pleased by the relish with which we dispatched the food.

"You're a healthy one," I observed, as we finished with coffee and cognac.

"Witty, not pretty."

"More beautiful each time."

136

"It's you."

"It was a long day."

"You wanted me to come."

"I wanted nothing else."

"You seem so serene about everything."

"I wasn't today. I could hardly wait for you to come down river. Now the time will pass too fast. What shall we do?"

"What *can* we do?"

"The Duke's at the Palladium. Want to go?"

"Do you?"

"I want what you want."

"Then can't we just talk? Maybe walk somewhere?"

"How did you know that's what I really want to do?"

"You make me feel that we're doing what I want to do, and yet I know that it's you who's leading. You know what a woman wants."

"What does a woman want?"

"Strength that's gentle."

"I didn't always know it."

"Live and learn."

"Live and love."

"I'm afraid it's too late."

It was nearly ten o'clock by the time we had finished the coffee and a second cognac. It was still twilight. The moon had risen from behind the row of high dwellings across the narrow street. Antoine came out for a breath of air. When he greeted us in French, I replied in his tongue.

"I thought you were French," he said, "but I cannot determine your region."

"California."

"But that is in America."

"I am American, but my paternal grandfather was French. He lived in Auxerre and made his own wine. Mademoiselle's father lives in California and makes his own wine. She and I drink the wine that others make."

"You have both the form and the spirit of a Frenchman. You are also an artist."

"I am a scientist. Mademoiselle is the artist. She is a painter."

137

"Many painters live in Charlotte Street. Your Whistler had his studio across from us. What does Mademoiselle paint?"

"He wants to know what you paint." I said to her in English.

"I am old-fashioned enough," she replied, "to believe that the human body is the best subject."

"But of course," Antoine agreed, "providing it is unclothed."

"We need your counsel, patron," I said. "Mademoiselle's boat train departs at one a.m., alas, and before then she wishes to take a walk. For exercise, that is, having eaten this enormous meal. And, I hasten to add, I intend to accompany her, although I ate much more abstemiously."

"Great liar," she said, ruffling my hair.

"She is far too precious and tender a creature," I continued, "to be turned loose in London on a night like this. Can you, will you, patron, in fact, you must recommend a likely promenade."

"No sidewalks or pavements," Martha said. "Remember, I'm a country girl from Calistoga."

"It is true, patron," I said. "This delicate slip of a thing was actually born and raised in a vineyard. For all I know, she was conceived in one."

"How charming," Antoine exclaimed, in English. "How utterly charming. Let me offer a liqueur in the nymph's honor."

"More cognac," Martha growled.

"Three for the road," Antoine roared.

We toasted exuberantly and then Antoine said, "I know the perfect promenade for you two nature-lovers. You are probably aware that London's parks close at nightfall—all but one. Do you know where Primrose Hill is? The other side of Regents Park, not far from the Zoo."

"I love monkeys," Martha said.

"Be serious," Antoine chided, "and hear me out. The Hill is London's only unfenced park. One can walk there all the night long."

"But we haven't all night," I said.

"How far is it?" Martha asked.

"Go to Russell Square and take a 169. It will set you down at the foot of the hill. In this prolonged drought, which I just heard on the news is due momentarily to break; in this dry weather the grass will be likewise."

"I beg your pardon, patron," I said, "It should be emphasized that we are friends, not lovers."

Antoine peered at us, then smiled. "It is better to be friends first and lovers afterward, than the other way around."

"You are a philosopher," Martha said.

"I am a Frenchman," Antoine replied, "which is the same thing."

I paid the bill and we set out for Russell Square. The bus came soon and in another twenty minutes we were at the foot of Primrose Hill. We walked arm in arm up the path to the top of the low hill, turned, and saw London far and wide beneath us. The sounds of traffic were muted. The moon was orange colored through the warm air.

"What time is it?" Martha asked.

"Eleven-fifteen."

"Can you keep track? I can't."

"Trust me to."

"I do, oh I do."

"This is our last time."

"I know."

"I'll surely see you again, but it won't be the same, with you Bob's wife."

"I know everything tonight. Remy Martin makes me clairvoyant."

"I'm a wee bit drunk," I confessed.

We walked on over the crest and off the path onto the grass. I reached down and felt it.

"Antoine was right. It's as dry as my mouth."

I took her arm and pulled her gently.

"Sit down here. It won't stain your skirt."

"What's a mere skirt on a night like this?"

She stretched out on her back, arms at her side, and stared at me. I sat down beside her. A faint breeze rustled the may trees. Crickets sang and we heard the sounds of switch engines. shunted cars, and an occasional whistle from a nearby railway yard. The dry grass filled the air with sweetness. I looked down at Martha. She smiled up at me. I lay down beside her. There were no words.

My hand was paralyzed. Only by enormous effort did I force it to find her bare arms with my fingertips.

"How cool your skin is!"

139

"Is it as cool as that marble you touched?"

"No, there's fire beneath the skin."

For answer her hand found mine and our fingers joined and began to woo "with the hot blood's blindfold art." I slid my hand beneath her sweater. Her breasts were bare. She began to tremble.

"No," she whispered, rolling free. "It's all or none."

I got up and walked behind a may tree and made water.

When I returned, she had turned on her belly. Again I sat beside her, and now I began to caress the length of her curved body, then gently turned her over and found her lips with mine. Ours was a deep, searching kiss.

She finally broke away. "If you do," she said, "I'll never leave you."

"Good," I said. "I'll never let you go."

I drew her roughly to me and again we kissed with hungry relief. We had gone over the falls. I had no power to stop, no thought of anything but the gift of her body, now open, arched and ready, the flesh on fire, burning, burning.

Then I heard a cough nearby. I started up. There at a respectful distance stood two helmeted bobbies. I waited, thinking they would move along. They did not. I helped Martha to her feet and we adjusted our clothes. The bobbies saluted and went on and took position at a respectful distance.

We walked back down the hill. In the arc light at the foot I dared look at my watch. Twelve-fifteen. We ran along Park Row until we reached the cab rank. A single vehicle was there. I spoke to the venerable driver.

"Waterloo Station. A one o'clock boat train. Can you make it?"

"With minutes to spare, sir," was the confident reply, and away we chugged through the quiet streets.

Martha lay in my arms and we kissed. Her face was wet with tears.

"Because I'm happy," she said when I sought to comfort her. "It was decided for us."

"There was no virtue in me," I said.

"I was yours, all yours."

"You've kept your promise to Bob."

"Hold me, darling, all the way. You don't feel cheated?"

"A thousand times no. It was more wonderful than any loving I've ever known."

"Remember, when you see us go down the aisle."

"Darling, darling my beautiful darling!"

We reached Waterloo Station at quarter to one. I tipped the driver half a crown and we rushed through the swarming station to the boat-train gate. There Mrs. Cameron fell on us with a cry of relief.

"I told you I would," I said. "Here's your darling daughter and all in one piece."

"God knows what you two have been up to," she said. "Martha's hair is a fright. And is that grass on her skirt?"

"Dry grass," Martha laughed, as we ran along the platform to Mrs. Cameron's compartment.

We boarded with minutes to spare, then Martha walked back to the vestibule with me and we kissed good-bye with hunger and tenderness in our touch.

Back on the platform I stood beneath their compartment. Martha put down the window and reached her hand to me. Her face was transfigured. Her lips kept soundlessly saying my name. The train began to move. I walked along still holding her hand, until we were pulled apart.

I watched the Southampton Express go by, its cream and red cars bearing the Cunard arms on their sides. Swift and swifter and then gone and the coal smoke drifting back. For the first time I felt cold sober.

I walked across Waterloo Bridge to Piccadilly and the all-night Lyons Corner House, and here I took the same table where we had lunched so long ago, only two days ago. I laid my hands palm down on the cold marble, and when the waitress came for my order, I said, "All I want, please, is a bowl of bread and milk."

"I say, that's sensible. You'll sleep well, sir. I always take one at the end of my day."

"It was beginning to rain as I came in."

"Pshaw, we planned a Sunday picnic. Now the grass will be wet."

"You should have gone tonight. The grass was dry."

She looked closely at me. "Are you from the country, sir?"

"Yes I am. From Primrose Hill."

She laughed and went for my order.

141

AFTERWORD

in a letter to the author from
HENRY MILLER

May 29, 1943
The Glen

Dear Larry,

I'm glad I had the chance to reread your book: it seems even better to me on second reading. For me it is the only book by an American which deals with *les amourettes*; it is also the first book by an American which gives to these little, passing loves the proper frame, the proper fragrance. It occupies a realm which is quite blank in our literature; it has a pagan, sophisticated quality which removes it from the sentimental or the immoral. It is thoroughly amoral—and aesthetic; its contour is spherical, finite and melodious. Each episode carries its own carnal glow; in each there is a blossoming, a ripening and a death. It is on the level of nature throughout, and it is this which gives one such a good feeling on putting the book down. It is true also that it is permeated with that melancholy which inspired the phrase—*la chair est triste*.

There are so many things about your book I like and admire that I scarcely know where to begin. Perhaps it has a special charm for me because of its European setting. Everything you refer to in your excursions and explorations, all your little observations, your discoveries and delights, I share intimately. In reading you I relive my own life abroad. With this difference—that I like your life better. I like what I must curiously call the "chaste" aspect. Behind the ardent lover there is always the serious student, and behind him the strange American that all of us are. For we are a strange species when set down in a foreign land. We are so awkward, so stupidly earnest, so childishly hungry, so inept, so inflexible. And yet we are loved, whenever we give the foreigner a chance to know us, to see into our hearts. And we are loved, and eventually respected, precisely for that quality which your Jack Burgoyne is always revealing—*tenderness*. That is the one thing we have to offer to the

European woman. And it is something for which she seems to be perpetually craving.

In the episode which concerns Madeleine Montrechet, for me the peak of the book, I was shocked at first, and then suddenly thrilled, to find your hero reading to her from *Lady Chatterley's Lover*. It was *her* book, I know, and perhaps that is why I read with such expectancy. What a strange figure this Mellors must have seemed to her! But what Mellors had was tenderness—and humor. No one has emphasized that enough, in studying this curious book of Lawrence's. It was the death-blow to the sickly English sentimentality which pervades their romances. And it is a humor unthinkable to a Mediterranean people, where carnal love is concerned. But, once again, I must compliment you on a little observation—which Madeleine makes when you take her to Villefranche to see the *Rex* lying at anchor in the bay. No love-making outdoors! It's unnatural! How French, that! And how right—for them. In the Lawrence book it was almost necessitous—to take Lady Chatterley outdoors and tumble her over. It was necessary to bring the pale, sickly English body out into the sunshine, to expose it to the light, to weld it to the sun-beaten earth which it had forgotten.

And while on this subject of Lawrence, how grateful I am to you for including the passage from "Apocalypse." How many times I have read that particular passage. Each phrase is burned into my memory. Nowhere in Lawrence is there anything to compare with this for truth and poignancy. It is as though he added something to the Bible, a coda concerning the flesh which had been overlooked by those who thought only of man's soul. "Man wants his physical fulfillment first and foremost, since now, once and once only, he is in the flesh and potent." What Lawrence forgot, in speaking of man's not wanting his own isolate salvation of his soul, is that in other times, other religions—I am thinking of India particularly— man did find salvation, fulfillment and God through love. The Hindus had their Bhakti Yoga as well as all the other forms of yoga. In Hindu lore the great love unions ended in bliss, in a sort of deification of flesh and spirit. In the West the great love sagas end in agony and death. But that, it seems to me, was always the fault of the man. He could not carry the woman through to the heavenly gates; he foundered in the sexual embrace.

But to return to specific delights . . . . This peculiar charm of

the American abroad, which so many writers have treated of —
Henry James at one pole and Mark Twain at the other — what a pleasure you give us in observing *l'education sentimentale* of Jack Burgoyne! Very wise of you to round it off with a quintet. Just as in the
musical form, there is in these five episodes a true progression.
There is a beginning which is harsh and strident and an end which
is utterly harmonious in its unresolved fulfillment. The whole development reveals precisely what a book of this sort should
reveal — mastery. Mastery in the art of love, I mean. It was absolutely fitting that the penultimate episode should revolve around
the very womanly figure of Madeleine Montrechet. It was like an
enriching and deepening of the second movement, with Erda. Two
earth feelings — one of the cold North, one of the warm Mediterranean. Erda gives the body, but the soul is not yet awake. Madeleine
warms the body with spirit. But with Madeleine, as one so often dis-
covers in this region, there is always the thought of "decay," of the
fading of powers and the loss of beauty. There is a scepticism born
of the sun's fierce heat, a false knowledge of death, I might say.
How accurate was your intuition in making those two references to
death in this episode. Particularly the latter one, when she comes
to you after washing the corpse!

But the greatest delight which the book brings is the atmosphere
that permeates it. A gentle, soothing atmosphere, even though it be
the bleak winter of Dijon or the mean, rainy season of Paris. An atmosphere in which food and wines play an important role. Your
cafés are especially redolent. Even the station buffets. And how
wonderful it is to go with you to the station and watch the express
or the "rapide" shoot by! In every chapter there are trains, it seems:
always "le voyage," always "le depart." These night trains come
and go, flash like meteors across the sky. Thank you for making the
trains come alive! Beautiful objects they are; each time we take one
they carry with them some precious part of us.

Yes, there are two atmospheres always — the one through which
the story is moving and the other which accompanies it like a re-
frain, the one evoked by longing and desire, or by pain and remembrance. "The Morvan country lay to the west . . . ." You have no
idea how enchanting it is to come upon such an observation. A few
lines and we are webbed in Celtic magic and imagery. Or take your
frequent little references to the names of those who once lived

144

here—of Rameau making his music in Dijon, of Henry James penning the last lines of his book on a certain bench, of the two famous lovers who spent a night in an old house. Or the "flowery Chablis" which made the nostrils of the other diners expand with pleasure. Or the reference to Vézelay and her Romanesque basilica. Or the blonde Vézelise beer of Dijon. Or you go into the hills near Grasse and you remember to gather a large sachet of wild lavender which is then in bloom. Or you stand on the beach near Cagnes and sling pebbles. Or you return and find her standing against the mimosa, her face uplifted to the moon. And you say—"The still air was heavy with the mingled scent of mimosa, eucalyptus, rose-geranium and sea wrack." Sea wrack! How lucky to recall that! How disturbing and just! Or to think to remind us of "the limestone walls of the Ouche." Everything brings us back to the senses and to their importance not only in art but love. So that when we come to the Rodin figure it is indispensable that you caress it with your hands, as later you will caress the flanks of the one you are making love to. Always a "making love"—a making love "to" and "with." Is it not one of the first things we Americans learn on reaching France—the meaning of *faire l'amour*? A making and a doing—something plastically creative—not just a state of being, however intoxicating. How grateful we were to discover that every French lover is if not an artisan an artist, or vice versa. It is as though we discovered that in love we had existed without arms or legs, that in conversation we had never enjoyed the experience of using the hands, the fingers, to say nothing of the face muscles.

Yes, food and wine, excursions to *la campagne*—and books and music. In every situation there is an ambiance in which the total being participates. It is this perpetual ambiance—like a perpetual temperature—which makes these episodes anything but obscene in character. All of them pivot on sex, true. In all of them it is the taking of the citadel which is paramount, yet how unimportant that becomes if we but glance from the bed and take register of the opaque atmosphere in which all is swimming. How beautiful those little moments by the big window—all Dijon outside, a museum of statues and light, a city groaning with fine wines and with memories of a splendid past. You stand by the window inhaling the fragrance of the street and it is so infinitely more than anything the girl can ever possibly give, though she gave her soul. And how marvelous a mood you evoke when you say of one of your characters—the dipsomaniac—"Each night we did exactly the same things. Beer and talk at the Concorde, steak and red burgundy at the Pré-aux-Clercs, a bottle of mousseux in her room, love-making and sleep." Exactly the regimen for that sort of affair. It will go on and on; it will make no sense to others. And then one day it comes to an abrupt stop. The very repetitiousness is what is exciting. It is like striking the same chord again and again—and then presto! the mood is gone, there is an end—but the memory is hammered in, and when the memory of it returns it is the blood that beats, the blood that remembers.

Perhaps the clue to the beauty of this little book lies in your own words to Martha: "I do know that the physical relationship between a man and a woman can be the most beautiful thing on earth. Simple and beautiful—sometimes. Not every time—just some times." To understand it fully we turn in our minds to some anterior epoch, to one of those periods when the adoration of woman, flowering from the myth of the Virgin, was coupled with a marriage between the male and female minds. There was a period, we like to think, when Love was enthroned. A period when marriages were consummated first in Paradise, soul meeting soul, and then again the flesh. But the road to the fleshly union lay through the mind. A mind trying earnestly to recapture the flavor of the past. You express it quite beautifully yourself. "Perhaps we are like Paolo and Francesca. Dante tells how they were reading together in the garden one day, and when they came to a certain passage they turned and kissed. Then they laid aside the book and read no more that day." A little *aperçu* such as this speaks volumes. It is as if now, in our own time, walled up in some ugly prison, we catch through the bars of our oubliette a fleeting glimpse of love enacted with passion and faith and intelligence. Then love was a global trine and the consummation was complete in every realm—or failed utterly, so that even the earth was mired. A man or a woman's portrait was made against a magical landscape; the human being was an integral part of the landscape.

Well, Larry, I suppose I could go on indefinitely. Enough, however, to show you how much I appreciate what you have attempted. It is the sort of book I should like to present to those about to venture into the realm of love. A little handbook, a manual of love, to replace the ancient Kama Sutra which was meant to be instructive and not pornographic.

Henry

THE RIVER BETWEEN

THE RIVER BETWEEN

This is a work of the imagination, a novel, not meant to be read as either history or biography.

They first met one morning in the library when, as they were working at opposite sides of a low shelf of reference books, each looked up at the same time. When he responded to her smile, she said, "Professor Graham, I'm Claudia Carter. You won't remember me, but I audited your final lectures."

"I do remember you," Carl Graham answered. "You always had a book open."

"But I was listening," she protested.

"What were you reading?"

"I was making my way through the collected Henry James." She hesitated. "I've been on the verge of asking if I could do a tape interview of you."

"You flatter me."

"It's for my M.A. thesis. I most recently taped your colleagues Professors Bryan and Wheaton, and now I want to interview you, if you're willing."

"What department are you in?"

"Communications. I hope to graduate in December."

"I've never known what Communications is," Graham said.

"I'm not sure myself. I needed the M.A. as fast as possible and it seemed the best way."

"Why me?" Graham asked.

"Because of your unusual career. And because your books spoke to my condition."

"Is thee a Friend?"

"As much as I'm anything. I know you are one."

"What do you want to learn that isn't in my work?"

"Whatever you'd be willing to add."

"What have you read of mine?"

"Everything in the Library. I have my own paperbacks of *Rivers in the Sand* and *Three at the River Crossing*."

"I don't know that an interview would be worth your while. Besides I'll be working on a book all summer. I plan to be on campus only once a week."

"I know it's an imposition," Claudia said, then added, "I'm sorry you retired. I'd hoped to audit you this fall."

"I could have gone on longer, but my time has grown precious. I need it all for myself." Graham paused. "I must seem old to you."

"Not really," she replied. "To an oldest child everyone seemed young, even my parents."

"Who else do you plan to interview?"

"No one. I left you to the last because I wasn't sure what field to put you in—history or geography."

"I was never sure myself."

"The university was wise to leave you free."

Graham was silent, then said, "I think I've said all I want to say, especially in those last lectures. Wasn't that enough?"

"My instinct tells me there's more."

He smiled. "I'm not sure I want to let you turn your instinct loose on me."

"I'll submit an outline of what I'd like to cover," she persisted.

"You mean it will take more than one session?"

"You *have* had a long career."

"What do you plan to do with the interviews—with the ones you've done?"

"I hope they could be made into a book on ways of researching in the Southwest. What I do is type transcripts and then submit them to the interviewees for editing."

"What if my answers should prove negative?"

"Then it just wouldn't be a good interview." Claudia hesitated. "Will you give me an appointment? I'd bring my outline, I must tell you though, whatever your answer is, that your books have helped me through a dull curriculum."

150

"Communications! I never could get a satisfactory definition when it came to the faculty for approval."

"I can come whenever's convenient for you."

Graham turned, then said over his shoulder, "I'll be on campus next Saturday morning."

"Tell me when and where."

"On the steps of the museum at 7:30. I like to beat the heat."

Claudia Carter came to campus early on Saturday and waited on a bench in the olive grove near the museum. In summer those hours were the best time of the day on the Sonoran Desert. Classes began at seven and were over at noon.

As she waited for Carl Graham, Claudia was both confident and apprehensive. From his books she felt closer to him than she ever had to a writer, and yet she had read enough to know that books were often masks that writers wore. Reading Graham's had made her curious about the whole man she sensed him to be. During his lectures she had glimpses. In his old age he had grown wary. And yet if that chance meeting in the library had not occurred, she might never have approached him.

At precisely seven-thirty she saw Graham approaching. She knew his walk, the way he would enter the lecture hall, take off and on his glasses, look around and then either proceed to lecture or read from one of the books that bulged his briefcase—a description of grama grass, or Lumholtz on the Pinacates, Sykes on the Colorado bore, or even passages from Harvey Fergusson or Frank Waters to illustrate how erotic understatement was more exciting than explicit description. She never knew what to expect, so unusual and wide was his reading.

As Graham neared she rose to meet him.

"Been here long?" he asked.

"I'm an early riser," Claudia said. "I left my children at my parents'."

"Children?"

"Two small ones."

"All I know about you is that you sat in the back by yourself."

"I know more about you—that is, everything you want the world to know."

"I've talked to my colleagues you recorded."

"What did they say?"

"That you are a very persistent person—and also a very nice one."

"Thank you, sir."

"And a very direct young woman."

"Am I too blunt?"

"You don't seem to have the usual young person's uncertainties. I believe you call them hangups."

"I'm not *that* young."

"How old are you?"

"Just half your age."

"You seem very sure of yourself."

"I'm not *that* sure. I don't want to presume, but do you live near campus? The directory gives only your box number at university station."

"I live up on Mt. Garcés."

"I should have known! Your first book was on Father Garcés."

"Most of the years since I came to the University I lived at the Sonora Inn. I had a cottage there, and a cabin on the mountain for summers. When I retired I moved up there for good."

"It's a long drive."

"An hour in good weather. I'll get a four-wheel drive next winter."

"Don't you feel isolated?"

"No. My mind has always needed solitude. I never had enough in these years at the University. Now the prospect of retirement makes me feel rich indeed."

"May I ask what you are writing?"

"What might be my last book."

"I'll try not to be *too* curious, and yet interviewing *is* the art of asking questions." Claudia smiled and added, "And of answering them. I'm glad there'll be another book."

"I've had other things that seemed more urgent." Graham rose. "These steps aren't the most comfortable place. How about a cup of coffee in the Union?"

As they crossed the Mall, Claudia paused at the bench where she had been sitting under one of the olive trees. Hidden in the branches a pair of Inca doves was cooing a monotonous antiphonal.

"That was the first sound to greet me when I came out here," she said. "I used to lie in the sun and let the doves soothe me."

152

"Why did you decide to record my colleagues and me? Why not some in your own field?"

"Although I was an English major, I was always interested in the natural sciences. I had a summer field course in geology in Norway and one in archaeology in the Dordogne. Then when I was faced with making a living, I had to acquire professional competence that would lead quickly to economic security. I already had graduate credits toward the M.A. in Communications."

"Whatever that is!"

"One of my brothers went to the River School—I hope to have a job teaching there next spring—and he showed me Montezuma Castle and Tuzigoot and then the digs at Betatakin, Keet Seel, and Chaco Canyon. That led me to your colleagues in archaeology and anthropology and now to you in historical geography—or is it geographical history?"

"Where were you an undergraduate?"

"Carleton. I had good teachers there—all but the one I married. He flunked the course!"

They found a corner table in the Union and Claudia went down the line for their coffee.

"You can drink it hotter than I can," she observed.

"Heat never bothers me. Look where I was born!"

"*Who's Who* says Laguna Dam, California. Was that a misprint for Laguna Beach?"

"I was actually born at Laguna Dam on the Colorado. It's across the river from Yuma and is one of the hottest places this side of Hell!"

"Wasn't that a strange place to be born?"

"My father, Samuel C. Graham, was a principal engineer on Laguna Dam—the first dam on the river and the first great project of the Reclamation Act of 1902. I was born on the day the dam was dedicated—April 23, 1909. There was a grand celebration—barbecue, flags, band, speeches. My mother had planned to have me in a Phoenix hospital, but she didn't want to miss the dedication. Well, she waited too long and I was born there on a blanket under a cottonwood, with a Mexican midwife and my father in attendance. They gave me a 21-gun salute!"

"No wonder your work has been so identified with the Colorado River."

153

Claudia went for more coffee and then Graham asked, "What's it like to be your age? I can hardly remember being thirty-five."

"It was the year you became chairman of the History Department at State."

"You *have* done your homework."

"I know most of the *whats*. It's the *whys* that puzzle me."

"And I'm supposed to solve the riddle for you? Did my colleagues give you their missing pieces?"

Claudia smiled. "There was no mystery about them."

"I don't believe that I've led a mysterious life," Graham said. "True, it's not gone in a straight line, and sometimes I've wondered which I am—historian or geographer. You're old enough to know that life is complex and motives are always mixed. What's your first question?"

Claudia laughed. "I should have brought the recorder. I wasn't sure that you'd say yes. Well then, why did you become chairman at State?"

"Because the dean asked me to."

"Then briefly an executive dean. Why was that?"

"Because the chancellor asked me to."

"Why did you suddenly leave State to work for the governor of Arizona?"

"Because he asked me to. You see how willing I am?"

Claudia laughed. "Why did you stay less than a year in Phoenix?"

"I'd done what he wanted—organized his historical office records and prepared a guide to them."

"Then you went to North Africa for two years. Algeria, Tunisia, Libya, Egypt, the Sudan—and wrote that beautiful book on the Nile and the Colorado—terse, rich, poetic. How do you account for that?"

"I'd reached a higher level than I had in *Three at the River Crossing* and the two before it."

"What had working as an archivist to do with it?"

"Let's say that it helped."

"It was the first book of yours that I read. I was taking graduate work at Yale then, my marriage breaking up, and it was a life saver." She paused and then said, "You were born a Roman Catholic. Why did you leave that faith?"

154

"When suddenly naked," Graham replied, "I found that I didn't need as many clothes as before."

"Students say you are a recluse."

"That's how I've gotten as much done as I have."

"What do you want to do now?"

"Reduce it all to essence."

"Your North African book did that."

"Because I was exalted when I wrote it — I was free. Then I let myself be tied again. Now retirement has freed me."

"These have been productive years here at the university even though you haven't written any more books."

"Other things seemed more important — teaching, directing theses, editing. When I say I was tied here, I should add that I've had great freedom within those bonds. I suppose it was my conscience — social, or religious, or whatever — that led me to lose myself in work for others — for students, for education. The years have passed, and now I want what's left to be for myself."

"I'll have to ask some of these questions again."

"Then I'll give you better answers. Is the interviewee allowed any questions?"

"Only if they are relevant! What's it like living on a mountain? What do you do other than write?"

"Saw and split firewood. Walk. Read. Meditate. Sleep."

"Are you ever lonely?"

"I'm pretty self sufficient."

"Do you regard yourself as selfish?"

"Self-centered. What writer isn't? Yes, I've known love — different kinds at different times of my life. Will you expect me to talk about my private life?"

"Only if you're moved to. I'll want you to set the limits. You *will* let me interview you?"

"When do we begin?"

"How about next Saturday?"

"Shall we use my study in the Library — Room 310."

"I trust it has an electrical outlet." Claudia opened her shoulder bag and handed Graham a paper. "I made these notes of the ground I'd like to cover."

"You *are* organized!"

"Superficially. Inside I'm a mess."

155

"I must warn you, cleaning up that inner mess never ends."

She watched him make his way among the tables, then she stayed for another cup of coffee. Had she been wise to be that frank? Her instinct told her that he needed to unburden. Her judgment told her to be cautious. He was indeed wary.

As he came to his next meeting with Claudia Carter, Graham felt ready for her questioning. He liked her directness, free of flirtatiousness. Her familiarity with his work flattered him. He also liked her strong handshake, the easy stride of her walk, her shoulder-length sandy hair, blue eyes and sturdy body, her bare feet in sandals, the absence of makeup, and her obvious good health.

She was waiting for him on the steps of the library. "What should I call you? Professor Graham? Doctor Graham? Or what?"

"My colleagues call me C. G."

"That would be presumptuous."

"May I call you Claudia? It's a lovely name."

"The girls at school called me Dia. I prefer my whole name. My brothers called me Bill."

"Were you a tomboy?"

"I had to show them I was as good or better than they were."

"Were you?"

"Until they outgrew me."

"How many are there?"

"Four at the last count."

"What does your father do?"

"Retired army. Still given to issuing commands. A gentle mother, strong though. I was always responsible and obedient to his commands, until I married."

"Were you an army brat? Dragged around the world and all?"

"As a child I was. Then when he commanded West Point, we settled down in the Hudson River Valley. We had Quaker neighbors. I used to go to meeting."

"Let me carry your recorder," he said when the doors opened at nine.

"If you'll let me take your briefcase. They must weigh about the same!"

"You seemed to be always carrying your weight in books. What were you reading beside Henry James?"

"Jane Austen. Or the Brontes. Or Balzac. I like prolific authors."

156

When they reached his study, she looked around the bare room and said, "You *are* a Quaker!"

"The backs of books are decoration enough."

"You must have more than this at home."

"These are odds and ends."

He watched Claudia unpack the recorder, then plug it in and thread the tape. "Did you look at my outline?" she asked.

"I did. The answers are all in my books. I tell you again, I'm a writer."

"She smiled. "That's why we're here."

"I know the kind of book I want to write now. I'm not sure that I can. I may have waited too long."

"You always seemed confident."

"Writing has to come from a deep source. That's why my earlier books have lived. What I had then I lost. I have been afraid to dive down after it."

"I've sensed this, that you were poised on the edge."

"You seem older than you are."

"And you seem younger."

"Do you have any occult power? Extrasensory perception or such?"

"Not really, I took Dr. Baylor's course in Folklore. She talked about witchcraft and divination."

"I've never cared for witches."

"Let me test this and we'll start."

"The machine makes me nervous."

"Dr. Graham nervous?"

"Is the damn thing turned on?"

"It will be."

"Your object is to get me off guard and draw me out."

"Precisely."

"I know what your first question will be."

"What?"

"Dr. Graham, tell me what kind of shaving lotion you use?"

"Be serious. I'm about ready."

Claudia pushed the button and the reels began to spin.

"Dr. Graham," she began. "Would you regard yourself as a simple or a complex person?"

"Let's say that I'm a simple man at the end of a complex career."

"Has there been a single all-important force or influence in your life?"

"You might say it has been a genetic one. The fusion of my father and mother made me what I am. He was strong and he gave me his strength. She was gentle, a dreamer, even a visionary. I don't believe she ever wanted to be a Catholic. He converted her. It took me half a lifetime to find a simpler faith."

"How did you manage to do that?"

"Simply by living—embracing life—buying life on credit when I was younger, and then paying off the debt by what I've done these past years."

"That's not a riddle, but I must think about it."

"Life gave me the gift I cherish."

"What gift do you mean?"

"The gift to be simple, the gift to be free."

"The gift to come down where we ought to be," Claudia echoed the old Shaker hymn. "Do you go to meeting?"

"It became too strident."

"I'd like to go again."

"This can be a meeting if we wish it to be. Now where are we?"

"Exploring the field."

"I like your dress," Graham said. "If I may change the subject."

"I made it. I make the children's clothes too. We also haunt thrift shops. I like old worn things."

"That must be what led you to me. I think you've missed your field."

"What do you mean?"

"You should be in psychology."

"I've always been my own best counsellor."

"Do you have problems?"

"Attempting too much on too little—too little time, money and brains. I was always over-motivated. I was determined to be the greatest wife and mother of all time, and I was pretty good at both."

"Then what happened?"

"He didn't want to be the greatest husband and father."

"You are divorced?"

"And blessed with two sweet kids."

"How did we get off track?"

"We're just warming up. You spoke of the genetic conditioning

158

from your parents. What would you say was the strongest environmental influence?"

"The river, of course. The Colorado."

"You mean from your having been born there? Did you grow up in Yuma?"

"No. My father died soon after I was born. We had moved to Phoenix. He was about to join the engineering force on the Roosevelt Dam. Then he died suddenly of a heart attack brought on, they said, by the heat and overwork at Laguna. He had always been in good health. My mother never wanted to talk about it, nor about their life at Laguna. She died when I was taking my doctorate at Berkeley—under Bolton in history and Sauer in historical geography. I was an only child. I used to go back to the river to hunt and fish, I always felt at home there. I still do. I even love the heat when it hits one twenty."

"Was this why your dissertation was on Garcés?"

"My dissertation was actually a leftover from Bolton's work on Anza. He would toss out bits to the seminar, hoping one of us would go for them. He had not followed all of Garcés' trails in the San Joaquin, and so I did. It was natural for me to go back to the missionaries' presence at the Yuma crossing. I was a Catholic then and their martyrdom seemed very real to me."

"Your next book was on reclamation. What led to that?"

"It was based on my father's material. You will recall it was dedicated to his memory. Like him I was an outdoors man. That's why I'm at home on Mt. Garcés. I couldn't have survived without fieldwork. Bolton also was a strong influence on me. Boots not bedroom slippers were his favorite footgear. He was a human bulldozer, pushing it all, including us students, ahead of him."

"Would you say that he replaced your father?"

"They certainly had a lot in common."

"What is your judgment now of your first two books?"

"Not very high. The Garcés was an academic exercise, although there *is* something more in it. The reclamation book was, as I said, an act of filial piety based on primary sources. It led to my early professorship at State."

"Then came *Three at the River Crossing* in which you wrote of Anza the soldier, Garcés the priest, and Palma the Indian chief. It's hard to classify. What did you intend it to be? Biography, history,

159

geography, anthropology, ecology, religion, philosophy—or what?"

"Now you're acting like a librarian—their insistence on classifying every book! I didn't intend it to be other than what it was."

"MacLeish says 'A poem should not mean but be.' How do you account for the break between it and your earlier books?"

"It reflected what I was becoming. I experienced a lot of growth at that time, and was increasingly interested in the natural elements of history."

"What caused you to break free and become more original?"

"Different things. *Three at the River Crossing* perplexed the critics as well as the librarians. It contended for the Pulitzer, I was told. They didn't know what category to judge it in."

"I can understand their dilemma. Unlike your first two books, it had no footnotes. Was that your idea?"

"Partly mine, partly a friend's. I wanted it to be read, not merely referred to."

"Did its publication have something to do with your leaving State?"

Graham paused. "Yes, it did. I wrote it on a sabbatical. Then I was made a dean and soon realized that I couldn't be both an administrator and the kind of writer I was becoming and that I would have to choose. And so I did."

"Was it a hard choice?"

"It would have been if it hadn't been made for me."

"By what?"

"What shall I call it? By destiny? By my own character? Character *is* Destiny, Goethe said."

"That's when you left State and went to Phoenix as an historical archivest. Would you call that a creative choice?"

"On the surface, no. But it was one that led to a more creative life—that led ultimately to here."

"It appears that you gave up a rising career for what seems a lesser position. Were you politically motivated?"

Graham laughed. "I find it hard to analyze that period. I will say that Governor John Clayton was a very important man in my life. Along with my father and Bolton, he was the most important."

"Why did he ask you to do this work?"

"He'd read a chapter from my reclamation book in progress. It

160

was essential for him as governor of Arizona to be informed about water. We met at a conference in Yuma. He respected my knowledge. We also liked each other."

"I know what it means to be drawn by a book," Claudia said. "If your move from California to Arizona was abrupt, how do you explain that even more drastic one to North Africa? I don't know what to make of that book on the two rivers—the poetic intensity of it. Will you account for it?"

Graham got up and walked to the window, then turned and asked, "Must I?"

"No," Claudia said softly. "Not unless you are moved to."

"The trouble is you are a good interviewer. I *am* moved to answer your questions."

"I told you it takes two to make a good interview. It requires a kind of rapport, of getting the flow between question and answer."

"Has it been that way with the others?"

"Not really. There is so much defensiveness in people. I know I'd be defensive if you questioned me."

"We all are if we've lived deeply. It's the machine that inhibits me."

"Do you want to take a break?" Claudia asked. "Or call it a day?"

"I'm sorry if I seem balky. My life and work were tangled back there. I don't know if they can be separated. I certainly don't want to try in any formal way."

Claudia pushed the button and the reels stopped spinning. "Now," she said, "I'm the only one who'll hear."

"So now you've got me where you want me!"

"You make me out a scheming female," Claudia protested. "I'm not one, really I'm not. It's the book that interests me. I sense that something unusual went into it. I only wanted to thank you for writing it. Perhaps the why and how of it can *only* be sensed. Perhaps I'm just too young."

"I'll tell you what went into it," Graham said. "It was my heart's blood. I wrote it from an exalted state of being I've never known since and certainly never will again. Some things happen only once. That's my problem now in this new book, of trying to reach a height I once attained. It can't be done simply by an act of will. Writing that book was an act of penance and also celebration, an act of death and

161

resurrection." He paused. "Turn it back on. You've got a project to complete."

"What you say is not final. You'll have the last word on the transcription."

"Push the damn button!" As the reels began to spin again, Graham resumed speaking. "My wife divorced me when I left State and moved to Phoenix. I had to go. Just went and never returned. Of course it was hard leaving her and our boys, but I'd never really been a good husband or father. I was too ambitious, too driven; I worked day and night. I often went back to the river alone. We had married when I was at Berkeley. I loved her. She took good care of me and our boys. I owed a great deal to her. Yet my desires were too strong. The tides of life in me were too high. I was like my father, my mother told me. I needed more, as he did, and yet I also needed a wife's love and care." He paused. "How shall I put it? Just say that my world blew up, and when it came down, I was single, a Quaker, an Arizonan, the governor's archivist. I had long been interested in comparing the two rivers the Nile and the Colorado; and then by chance I read a book on Tunisia called *Fountains in the Sand* and another one called *Les Nourritures Terrestres*, also about North Africa. I was somehow moved by them, called by them. When I finished my work at the capitol, the divorce settlement gave me what was left after nearly everything went to her. I took it and went to Algiers, Tunis, Tripoli, Alexandria, Cairo, Khartoum. It was an incredible two years. I found myself purged and clean and free. Reborn. My mind was crystal clear. My research on the Colorado had all been done. What I needed was in my notes or my head. Even before I had begun the fieldwork on the Nile, the book's form came to me in a kind of clairvoyant state."

"Were you taking drugs?"

"Not even alcohol. It was a state I had first approached in *Three at the River Crossing*. After leaving Algiers and Tunis, I worked my way east along the coast and camped with some French archaeologists at Leptis Magnae, the great Roman ruins near Tripoli. I was at home in Egypt, initially because I had contacts from my graduate years at Berkeley. There was always a contingent of Egyptian students there in agriculture and hydrology. I came to know them through the work I had already begun on my father's papers. Upon their return to Egypt they had risen to high government posts in agriculture and river control, and they made my work possible, gave me carte blanche. I also met a man who was writing on the Blue and the White Niles. I went on field trips with him to the head-waters."

"How did you keep your book from becoming a hydrological treatise?" Claudia asked.

"By listening to my inner voice. I used to write in my favorite café in Cairo. It was on the riverbank not far from Shepheards Hotel. The cafés there are very French. Really clubs, with newspapers, magazines, stationery, and the like. I loved the strong Egyptian coffee. I smoked then, Greek cigarettes – Nestor Gianaclis – light and fragrant Macedonian tobaccos."

"Were you also in Alexandria? Did you meet Lawrence Durrell?"

"No, but I did meet some of his Egyptian friends."

"Do you know the poetry of Cavafy? He was an Alexandrian who wrote in Greek."

"I only knew of him. His was a homosexual world I was never drawn to. They were already talking of the high dam at Assuan. I drew parallels between the dams on the two rivers. Our Great Dam on the Colorado was under construction. All of this gave me a sense of being bi-national. I could have stayed on and made a career at the University of Cairo. I gave occasional lectures on American subjects. It was amusing to see them reported in Arabic."

"Did you learn Arabic?" Claudia asked.

"French was my limit. It and English took me everywhere. I suppose you can say that those two river books were a gift to me from life."

"They were also a gift *from* you to life, to readers. You make me seem monstrous questioning you when you've been so forthcoming, and yet I feel that you are still posing riddles for me."

"I've told you more than I intended. Let's say I gambled and won. The book was a Literary Guild choice. It made money. It has been in print all these years."

"It was the dedication that first caught my eye. I was browsing in the Yale Co-op and came on it. 'To the river gods and the goddess.' "

Graham smiled. "Who else?"

Claudia pushed the button. "That's all for today."

"I'm just warming up!" Graham protested.

"I have a genius for stopping."

"Is it too early for lunch? I get up so early I'm hungry by mid-morning. Are you hungry?"

"I'll have a sandwich and coffee, thanks."

"It's early. The Union will be quiet."

Claudia and Graham carried their trays to a corner of the room.

"How did your marriage end?" Graham asked gently, when they had finished and were having coffee.

"The way yours did. He left."

"Was he unhappy?"

"Just lazy. After graduating I taught science and English literature and composition in a private school in Connecticut—and for a meager salary—while he quit teaching at Wesleyan to stay home and be a writer."

"Was he one?"

"I'm afraid not."

"Do you want to marry again?"

"I need companionship. He and I shared a lot, reading aloud and talking. We were friends. He gradually left it all to me. I *am* responsible, yet there *are* things a man should do. Now it's hard on the children. They need a father."

"Do you have any prospects?"

Claudia smiled sadly. "The wrong kind. May I ask, why haven't you married again?"

"I came back from North Africa a different person. It was as though I had entered an order, taken vows."

"Not silence!"

"Most of that deeply sensual part of me that irradiated my life and work left me, had been given away. If I were to have it again, it would have to be given back to me. It never was. No one had it to give. I knew that marriage without that wholeness in me would have failed, as it once did. I found other uses for what there was of me, which if it weren't the whole, was still a lot; and that has been my life here. Now I'm afraid it's too late. I say again, I must seem old to you?"

"And I must seem young to you."

Graham took out a pencil and figured on a paper napkin, then handed it to her.

164

Claudia puzzled a moment, then smiled. "Our median age! That's nice. Didn't you miss your children?"

"Only at first. I wasn't intended, at least then, to be a good husband or father."

"I'd die without mine."

"You're a woman, a mother."

"I'd like to be a wife again."

"It's good to talk."

"What I am is an old shoe and an easy chair. Aren't you lucky!?"

When they met again on the following Saturday, Claudia was carrying a large roll of paper. "Do you mind going away for a few minutes?" she asked, "so I can surprise you."

"I'll take these books to the Loan Desk and be right back."

When Graham returned he saw that she had covered the study wall at one end with a colored map of the state. "The room was a bit too Quakerish," she said. "It needed color."

"I like it."

"It's the new geologic map of Arizona. It makes the room glow."

Graham watched her unpack and plug in the recorder. "You're a take-charge girl. What are you going to ask me today?"

"I'd like to go back to Berkeley and Bolton. Not today though. Did you know Frederick Webb Hodge?"

"Up to his death at 92. I hope I can be as sharp as he was."

"I'd say you have a good chance, especially if you'll answer my questions with the truth and nothing but! Dr. Graham, I'd like to know what brought you to this university. Why didn't you go back to California, not necessarily to State? To Berkeley or Stanford—or to UCLA? It was rising then. Why here?"

"Because of Governor Clayton. I told you how important he was in my life."

"What did he have to do with the University?"

"He was a regent *ex officio*. As president of the board, he dominated it during the several terms that he served."

"Wasn't he a politician?"

"He was also an intellectual. I don't mean in the academic sense. He had only a bachelor's degree, but he kept growing. He was devoted to the university and to the whole state. He was a key

165

figure in the Great Dam affair. Helped push it through against the environmentalists."

"Was that right?"

"It was real. Jack Clayton was a third generation Arizonan. His people owned nearly everything south of the Gila, and he ended up with interests all over the state. Land, cattle, copper, cotton— you name it. He inherited much and added more. He also married the daughter of another wealthy old territorial family. When he'd had enough of making money, he went into politics. He knew his state and its people. He was smart enough to use the university for its brain power. If he was ruthless, he was also generous. He did things in a big way."

"Like bringing Carl Graham!"

"I told you he found my reclamation work of interest, and then when I was on his staff we became friends. I admired him, although I didn't always agree with his stands on water and power and told him so. We corresponded when I was in North Africa. He'd been dubious about my going, but when I sent him a copy of the manuscript of the rivers book, he responded in a characteristic way—he cabled me a ticket from Cairo to Paris and back. He was attending a conference there on hydroelectric generating. We were together all of his free time. My French was useful to him. It was good for us both. I told him of my dream of an academic appointment with no administrative responsibility, and one east of the Colorado."

Graham paused. "So what did he do? He created this chair that I've occupied. He and his wife endowed it and I was given life tenure. He had vision—plus the power and wealth to realize it."

"Were there political strings attached?" Claudia asked.

"None."

"I know that you published in several fields, but there were no more books like those two."

"I told you I was never moved again to that depth—or that height."

"Now what? You said you have hopes for the new book. Do you want to go that high again?"

"I may have given too much to others and not enough to myself. What *have* I done in these years on campus? Founded the quarterly review of geo-historical studies. Published many papers and

166

reviews. I've lost count of doctorates I've sponsored. My contacts in North Africa brought many students here to study."

"Will you go back?"

"I doubt it. This could be my last book. Again I have a kind of model. Perhaps we can talk about it before we're through."

"What would you have done if you had not known the governor?"

"Stayed abroad, perhaps, and held a post in North Africa or France."

"I'd like to go back to the Colorado River—to your use of your father's material in the reclamation book. Wasn't that the turning point in your career?"

"If for no other reason than it brought me to the governor's attention. It also told me about my father's ways of working. I wish I had begun it earlier. Much that I would have liked to know died with my mother."

"What did you do with his papers?"

"I still have them."

"What will become of yours?"

"Many I've already placed in the archives here. Everything goes there eventually. I'll put restrictions on the more personal material."

"Your biography will be written."

"I suppose so."

"Whoever does it should have full access to your papers."

"Is that what you are up to?"

"Heavens no!"

"Do you write well?"

"Not as well as I should, but better than I did."

"I should be interviewing you. You give good answers."

"I'm afraid the final transcript will be more of a dialogue than I intended," Claudia concluded.

And so the autumn passed.

Early in December, Claudia reported that she was ready to begin transcribing the tapes.

"Have I given you the answers you wanted?" he asked.

"You've given me some by *not* giving them."

"Is that one of your riddles?"

167

"You haven't let me into one of your rooms."

"Don't we all keep one locked? Don't you?"

"A closet perhaps."

"How large do you think mine is? Are you cross with me?"

"I gave up trying to get in."

"I heard you knock."

"I have only instinct to tell me what you haven't told me."

"What is that?"

"The explosive that blew up your world."

"I suspect you do know."

Claudia smiled, and said, "I'll bring some transcript next time if I may—at least as much as I can get done in the week. Things are closing in on me now as the semester ends."

"I'll miss our Saturdays."

They met briefly at the end of the week. "The children are in the car," Claudia said. "My parents are away."

"Would you like to take a ride with me tomorrow?" he asked. "Up the Santa Cruz and over to the valley where it rises. I need to look at the lay of that land again."

"I'd love to go. I'll have the kids though."

"Bring them."

"Do you mean it? They'd love it. I never have time to take them out of town. I was going to work more on the transcript."

"It will do you good not to."

When Graham called for Claudia the next morning she was wearing fitted black pants, a wine-red blouse and a gypsy scarf holding her hair back.

"Those don't look like old clothes to me," he remarked.

"Junior League thrift shop!"

Graham liked her children. They sat in the back seat and played games of their own devising. He and Claudia were quiet as they drove up river toward Mexico. Winter was late. The cottonwoods still showed color. The pecan groves were bare. There was a far view of the ranges from the Santa Ritas to the Baboquívaris.

"This is the quietest I've known you," Graham said as they neared the border and followed the river into the mountains.

"It's pure bliss that I feel."

"Because the interviewing is over?"

"I mean this." She gestured toward the trees in golden leaf and the blue slopes beyond.

"It's partly why I live on the mountain."

"I've seen you change this fall. The lines in your face aren't as deep. Those in mine are, alas."

"I like your face," Graham said.

"I've become reconciled to it. My husband used to say—though lovingly—I was homely as a mud fence."

"An old adobe!"

"Fall is my best time. Today I feel like a golden girl."

"Are your children always this good?"

"No," Claudia laughed. "But they're never really bad."

"You treat them as equals."

"I could do better, but I'm always on the run. Nothing really gets done. Where are we now?"

"We're crossing the Patagonias to the grassland where the river rises."

"Is there a special reason you came today?"

"The inner voice."

"Saying what?"

"Follow the river. Your book is there."

"You've never said what it is."

"That's because I've always been reluctant to talk about my work in progress. The thread is so easily broken. This is probably my last chance to approach those early books. I'm beginning to feel that I might."

"Why not? You're older, richer, wiser."

"Keep telling me!"

"It has been wrong to keep those riches to yourself. I'm not the only reader who wants more."

"I met E. M. Forster in Alexandria. I asked him if he was going to do for Egypt what he did for India—why he had gone so long without publishing another novel."

"What did he say?"

"He only smiled. Later I sent him *Rivers in the Sand*. He wrote me a beautiful letter about it."

"I'd like to read it."

"There were others who wrote."

"Why have you waited so long?"

169

"I've done other things. Perhaps too I've been waiting for belief like yours. If you should have access to my papers after my death, you'd find some answers there."

"But I'd be an old lady!"

Graham laughed. "What I'm doing now is seeing the land through the eyes of its discoverers—the first white men, that is. Coronado, Oñate, Kino, Garcés, Pattie, Kearny, Cooke, Browne, Martha Summerhayes. Imagining the way the land looked to them before we began to despoil it. My old theme, the influence of geography on history. It will be highly imaginative because those early ones left sparse records, laconic and impersonal. The later ones left more. I told you I have a kind of model, a commentary on the narrative of Cabeza de Vaca. Do you know who he was?"

"I've read Bishop's *Odyssey*."

"Have you read Long's *Interlinear*? No? That's the model I spoke of. It's an illumination of the Spaniard's laconic narrative—of what he *didn't* say in his report to the king of Spain. I've owned a copy all these years. A friend once had Long sign it for me. He lived in Santa Fe. I'm trying to get inside the others the way he did into Vaca. It will be a summing up, a simplification, and it will certainly puzzle my colleagues. They'll say I've gone balmy."

"Why should you do what others expect you to do? Haven't you done that long enough?"

"Too long. This will be my Indian Summer book—a celebration, a lament, and a thanksgiving."

"It should be a wonderful book."

"I've been working on it all fall since our interview began. It has come partly from the tension they created in me, of at once holding back and letting go. You see, I've both wanted and not wanted to open that last door."

"Ah me," Claudia sighed, "and now it's too late. Now I'll never know."

They had reached the summit of the Patagonias and parked at an overlook. Claudia gasped.

"Do you like it?" Graham asked. "It's why I asked you today. I wanted you to see it. I've never shared it with anyone."

Below them lay the San Rafael Valley hemmed by the mountains of Mexico in the south and the Huachucas against the eastern sky. In the north the Canelo Hills held the grassland against the encroaching city. The winter rains had not yet fallen, and the valley floor was still golden. Yellowing cottonwoods marked the wandering course of the Santa Cruz from where it rose in the cinnamon-colored hills and crossed the valley toward the border.

"Is it your Shangri-la?" Claudia asked.

"I'd like to think it was Kino's too."

"Did he build a mission down there?"

"Until a hundred years ago that land belonged only to the Apaches."

"Now who owns it?"

"A couple of big spreads. Grazing and erosion have been controlled. I think it's the most beautiful valley in the world. Where shall we picnic?"

"Can we go down by the river?"

"All you see is ours—for the day. Seeing it takes me back to another view down on a young river's valley."

"You sound pensive."

"You choose nice words. There are *cienegas* where we might see a blue heron or a banded kingfisher."

On the valley floor they found an open space in a grove of oaks. There Graham spread a blanket and Claudia unpacked the picnic basket. The children took their sandwiches and lemonade to the stream and began building a dam.

"Big family scene," Claudia remarked as she and Graham devoured their lunch.

"He was a fool to leave sandwiches like these!"

"Was I one to divorce him?"

"I would say he had his priorities confused."

"Did your wife like picnics?"

"I didn't have time for them. I was too driven. We had good things together. What we didn't have are things there are no names for."

"Did you find them elsewhere?"

"Found them, lost them. May I change the subject? Have you heard from the River School?"

"I'm hired if I get the M.A. at the winter commencement. And I shall. The kids will stay and finish school. They can live with my parents during the spring semester. I'll move first of February."

"Will you spend Christmas with your parents?"

171

"They are going to England. My brother Tom is at Oxford."

"Then you and the children will be together."

"They are going to their father. I had them last Christmas."

"Do you have other plans?"

"I haven't had time to think about it."

Graham paused, then asked, "Will you let me cook Christmas dinner for you?"

"Goodness! Isn't that a pretty big order? You mean take me out somewhere?"

"I mean *chez moi*. Have you been up the mountain?"

"Up and back a few times our first summer."

"Would you like to see where I live?"

"If you'll let me fix dinner."

"All right. I'll put the turkey in the oven. You can do the rest."

"It sounds nice."

When they returned to the city toward evening, the Catalinas were golden in the last light. In parting Claudia said, "Thanks for the glorious day. The kids and I needed it."

"How am I as a grandfather?"

"The best! I'll be gone next week. My San Diego brother is here. He's taking us to the Grand Canyon and then to make arrangements at the school. I'll have the transcripts with me."

"When do the children go to their father?"

"The day before Christmas. I'd like to go to Christmas Eve midnight mass at the mission." She hesitated. "Would it be too bold if I asked you to go with me?"

"No bolder than when you asked to interview me."

She laughed. "Would you like to? It will not be very Quakerish."

"I know Father Terence. He's a good historian. Sometimes we have a glass of wine together. I've never been to mass though."

"We could have late dinner and then go. They say the church is packed by eleven. Will you be my guest?"

"When shall I call for you?"

"Is seven all right? The children leave that morning. I'll be working all day on the transcript."

That evening after the children were in bed, Claudia took down her Yeats and let the poetry and letters of his old age compose her mind. She and Graham were still respectfully aware of each other, still in a mentor-learner relationship; and yet a new element was there, the recognition of a need to continue meeting. The picnic was evidence of this, and now their Christmas plans that had come about almost without planning, as though they were acting from a script. At such times Claudia turned to the poets. Wordsworth and Yeats were her favorites.

On Christmas Eve Graham called for Claudia at seven. "You're dressed up," he said as she met him at the door, wearing a tartan suit in dark green and black wool.

"Dressed warmly. it's supposed to freeze tonight."

"There's a weather front due this weekend. That is a lovely—is it a suit or what?"

"A what! I had it made in Edinburgh. We spent our first summer in Britain after we were married. He was supposed to be doing research in the British Museum. Instead he spent his time looking at French engravings. He had good taste in the obscene. He was a lot of fun. Now I depend on the kids for laughs."

"Did you get them off to New York?"

"Their father phoned that they had arrived."

"I'll try to amuse you, at least up until the mass."

"You're looking handsome, Professor Graham."

"Thank you, Mrs. Carter. It's the first suit I've worn since commencement. It's also one I had made—by my custom tailor in a back street of Nogales! Where shall we eat?"

"Somewhere nice, we're so presentable."

"Such as?"

"The Sonora Inn?"

Graham smiled, "I stopped there and reserved a table for seven-thirty."

Claudia laughed and gripped his hand. "I need some looking after. I get tired of being the whole show."

"Did you have a good week? Get a lot done? Find a place to live?"

"The answer is yes to all three questions. My parents invited me to go to Oxford with them. They were a bit put out when I said I had other plans."

"Did you tell them about your project? About—us?"

"I told them that you are our new grandfather. Daddy's jealous."

"Shouldn't you have gone?"

"I needed to assert my independence."

"Would he approve of me as your escort tonight?"

"Positively not! You are too successful, too distinguished, too old."

"Am I older than he is?"

"Older by five and younger by fifty."

As they parked at the Inn, Graham breathed deeply. "They burn only mesquite."

"I love it," Claudia said. "It smells like roasting coffee."

"I start my fire with pine or juniper, then mix mesquite with oak."

The maitre d' greeted Graham and led them to a corner table.

"I see they haven't forgotten you," Claudia remarked.

"I lived here a long time."

"They say it's dear."

"Not that bad. I leased my cottage by the year. I liked the serenity, the gardens, the quiet elegance, the maid service. Would you like a drink?"

"A marguerita, please. What are you going to have?"

"A sherry. Wine is all I drink."

"You are healthy."

"Probably weigh about what you do."

"Too much for me, not enough for you. I'm solid. I swam a lot as a girl."

"Where were you born?"

"St. Paul."

"Another river child."

"There'll be streams where I'm going—Oak Creek, the Verde. Have you had a good week?"

"Everything's gone well, including my book and my wood pile. My friend down on the San Pedro brought up a load of unsawed and unsplit mesquite. Feel my hands."

"I'm eager to see where you live."

"I'll come down for you in the morning."

"Let me save you the trip."

"You don't mind?"

"Heavens no! All you have to do is put the turkey in at ten. I marketed for the rest. You *do* have electricity?"

174

"I built near the radio and sheriff transmitters for the power line that was there."

Graham gazed at Claudia in the lamplight as she sipped her drink.

"What?"

"I've never seen you with makeup."

"Too much?"

"It's nice. What made him call you homely?"

"My face changes with my feelings. I wasn't too happy as a teenager and at college, I didn't pay any attention to my looks. I felt like Cinderella. My parents didn't help any. They never recognized me as a woman. They favored my brothers. They still do. No one ever said 'Dia, you're beautiful'."

"Is that what a woman wants to hear?"

"You know it is — most of all when she's freckled. I felt like dressing up tonight, including my face."

"It's why I wore a suit."

"Not for the mass?"

"For you, my dear Claudia."

"I thought it would end with the interviews."

"Do you ever see any of my colleagues? The ones you taped."

"Heavens no! They're all old men."

They laughed.

"I think of you as my grandson," Claudia teased.

When their prime rib was served with a bottle of Cabernet Sauvignon, Graham said, "I wish it were Tunisian red!"

"You've never gone back. Why not?"

"I'm an old stick-in-the-adobe. Things are stirring in me now though."

"You mean your book?"

"Things that give a book life."

"You are a very romantic scholar."

"I've kept it hidden. I grew self-protective. I can trust you. I've done a lot of talking this fall!"

"I did more than I should have."

"You said it takes two to make a good interview."

"Don't you miss people where you live now?"

"People tire me more than sawing and splitting wood. You must

175

find it hard to realize that everything diminishes. At your age I had no conception of growing old."

"When did you begin to recognize it in yourself?"

"Gradually. Now I suppose it is accentuated by your vitality, ambition, courage—by your handshake and your walk, as though you had been given the world and were on your way to claim it."

"The truth is I've never been so pushed as this semester. Some nights I've wanted to sleep in my clothes."

"But you didn't."

"I typed until half blind and then fell in bed at midnight."

"How long will the children be gone?"

"Until the day after New Year's."

"Are you finished?"

"All but the final tape. My course work's done. Busy work, most of it. Communications Arts is not one of the more demanding disciplines. It's nice here. Can't you hear my soul rejoicing?"

"That's what meat and wine do for the soul. We don't seem to have any communications gap."

"Old shoes are easy on the feet."

The night was cold, the moon past full as they left the city and drove along the far side of the river to the mission church on the reservation. They saw it in the distance, the whitewashed towers gleaming in the moonlight.

"San Xavier del Bac!" Graham said softly. "Paloma blanca."

"I'm glad you wanted to come. I thought perhaps . . . "

"You mean my having left the faith? I never looked back. I told you Father Terence is my friend. He liked my Yuma book."

Even though an hour before midnight, the church was already full, candle-lit, warm, and smoky. Graham and Claudia made their way down the aisle, looking for empty seats. They found places on a bench in the transept.

"We seem to be the only Anglos," Claudia whispered. "I'm glad I brought this black rebozo. I don't feel quite as blonde."

"They know me, many of them. I've spent a lot of time on the reservation. That's the tribal chairman there in front. It's as much social as religious for them. The older ones still have their own faith."

"It's a beautiful meeting house."

176

"Too ornate. I recall how George Fox saw the church as not the physical structure, but rather the living souls who meet there."

As the hour neared midnight, the church grew silent. The dark faces shone in the candlelight. The choir began to sing, its thin voices off key. An old Papago couple shuffled down the aisle, looking for seats. Claudia rose and beckoned to them. Graham also stood. The old ones, their wrinkled faces impassive, took their seats. Graham and Claudia stood against the painted wall of the transept, next to the crèche—a Papago ramada of boughs and thatch, with a tiny hammock in the middle.

The church was now jammed with celebrants. The air was stifling with incense and body heat. As the bell tolled midnight, Father Terence in white robe, purple vest, and lace surplice appeared with his red-robed, dark-skinned acolytes; and with smoking censer he led his little group to the crèche and placed the Infant Jesus in his hammock.

After conducting the mass in Latin, he turned and blessed the throng. Everyone rose and embraced his neighbor. Claudia took the hand of the Papago man on one side, then turned to Graham and they embraced.

They made their way back down the crowded aisle and out into the plaza.

"Smell the mesquite!" Graham said. "From their cooking fires. They'll go home and feast now."

"You didn't mind standing that long?"

"You were good to give your seat to the old ones."

"I was taught to rise for my elders. Wasn't that hammock dear!"

"I concede wisdom to the church in the way it recognizes its children. But the Latin mass is so inappropriate to these people. Father Kino would have celebrated it in Piman."

"Didn't I see Father Terence wink at you?"

"That's a tic!"

"Do you have to drive home?" Claudia asked. "Can't you stay in town?"

"I'm a homing pigeon. Will you sleep late?"

"I'll read myself to sleep. When shall I come?"

"Any time in the morning."

"You won't forget to put the turkey in?"

"Trust me."

They parted with a touch of cheeks.

Christmas Day was clear. Claudia allowed an hour and a half for the drive up Mt. Garcés, climbing in second gear and stopping at Windy Point for the far view over valley and city. Clouds were gathering in the southeast, heralding the weather front Graham had spoken of.

Freedom from children and studies allowed her to ponder the relationship with Carl Graham. She had none to compare it with. Although it had begun in mingled respect and curiosity and continued through a dozen sessions of asking and listening, of her probing and his backing away, she had come to be at ease with him. She thought at first that the relationship would end with the interviews and her imminent move north, and yet since the picnic and dinner and mass, and now this visit to his mountain home, she sensed there was more to come. Would he open that last door?

Although Graham had been impassive during the mass, she now remembered that as they stood against the stones of the transept his hand had found hers and held it firmly even while they made their way through the throng and into the night. Something had passed between them in that handclasp. It left her newly aware of his strength and of her own, and that together they were very strong. Now her face grew hot as she remembered.

These were new feelings, a new awareness of an older man. What was she responding to? Graham did not thrill her the way men of her own age sometimes did. Not often. Since the end of her marriage, her sensual needs had yielded to caring for her children and the pursuit of her degree. A brief affair with a fellow graduate student had left her unsatisfied.

Now as she approached their meeting, she imagined what he would be like as a lover. He seemed virile. What would it be like to give herself to a man older than her father, a man old enough to be the grandfather of her children?

Thus her mind wondered as she followed the narrow road that climbed from the life zones of saguaro, ocotillo and mesquite through oak and juniper to pine, spruce and fir.

When she reached the flat top of Mt. Garcés and looked for the turn-off to his cabin and then saw him waiting at the side of the road, her feelings coalesced in relief.

"Merry Christmas!" He came to her side of the car and took her hand.

178

"Hi! I made it."

"Did you get some sleep?"

"Enough. How about you?"

"Up at dawn. What a beautiful sweater!"

"It's my Joseph's coat. I made it of yarn ends."

"You'll need it. That front's moving in early. It could mean snow. I don't suppose you have chains."

"Are you kidding? This car barely has wheels."

"I'll get in with you. It's a quarter-mile to my place."

Claudia drove slowly over the rough road through a stand of ponderosa.

"You're a good driver," Graham observed.

"You have to be with this Chevy."

"Do you miss your children?"

"I've been too relaxed to know. Did you put the turkey in?"

"At ten."

The road ended in a clearing on the far side of which stood Graham's cabin.

"Did you build it?" Claudia asked.

"With the help of a Mexican contractor. I did the bookshelves."

They entered a big room walled with books and dominated by a great stone fireplace. A wide leather couch was ranged before the raised hearth. In the center of the room a long work-table was flanked by filing cabinets, easy chair and lamp. Navajo rugs covered the flagstone floor.

"Do you like it?" Graham asked.

"It's a great room."

A bedroom, bath, and kitchen completed the house.

Graham opened the far door and led Claudia out to a deck that ran the width of the cabin. She caught her breath. "You're on the edge of the world!"

"It's the very prow, the cutwater of the mountain. That's the San Pedro down there, and those are the Galiuros. When it's clear, you can see to the Grahams. They're a hundred miles."

"Your mountains!"

"There won't be many more clear days. They're going to build a smelter down there."

"I love the piney smell and the wind in the needles!"

179

"They roar when it storms. Are you warm? I keep the fire going day and night this time of year."

"I'll have a fireplace in my cottage at the school. I can have a dog too—an Airedale like the one I had as a child. You've kept it simple."

"All I need is time and grace for this last book."

"I'll get busy in the kitchen. We can't live on turkey. Show me where things are and I'll do the rest."

"I'll clear the table for us to eat on."

"I brought a couple bottles of Mountain Red. All you have to do is set the table."

By midafternoon Graham and Claudia sat down to roast turkey, sweet potatoes, green salad, pumpkin pie, and wine.

"You really are a take-charge girl," Graham said as they finished with coffee. "I like the way you eat."

"How do I eat?"

"The way I do! She used to nag me for eating fast."

"We should leave each other alone in those things that aren't important."

"Does the house seem bare and messy?" he asked. "Keeping house is new for me."

"Simplicity is better than tidiness."

"You're a pretty simple girl."

"I'd rather be simply pretty."

"Are you looking forward to the move?"

"Especially for the children. They'll have free tuition at the school. I'm tired of being broke. It's been hard to keep independent from my parents. They mean so well. But we haven't opened our presents. I have one for you."

"And I have one for you. Shall we open them out on the deck with our second cup?"

"It's a book!" Claudia exclaimed when they had moved outdoors. "Yeats! How nice."

"I found it in the campus bookstore. See, the photographs of the Irish countryside illustrate the poems. Have you been there?"

"London was the nearest. Have you?"

"I once went to see the burial mounds in County Antrim. I never knew about Yeats. I confess to having read in the Yeats when I got

180

home last night—I mean this morning—before I wrapped it. I hope you don't object to a used book!"

Graham felt her tissue-wrapped package. "The evidence points to a tie." He tore open the paper. "Did you knit it?"

"With these very hands! I like solid colors on a man."

"It matches the hair I once had. You like to knit."

"It's how I keep sane."

"What can't you do?"

"Stay married."

"You sound sad."

"It's the wine—and being up here. Take-charge girls sometimes need taking charge of."

"It seemed wrong for us to be alone at Christmas." Graham pointed to the southeast. "That front's ahead of schedule. I keep the university station on most of the time for the weather and music.

"Were you listening to that program on witchcraft along the Rio Grande?" Claudia asked. "I heard it on the car radio driving up."

"I told you I wasn't interested in witches."

"I wasn't either until I had an experience not long after I moved out here."

"What was it?"

"It was when I was trying to gain admission to graduate school. I'd been refused by the Registrar for what he ruled were irregularities in my credits. The department chairman said it was useless to appeal although he seemed to want me in the program." Claudia paused. "I was pretty close to despair—not like me at all. I drove home. The kids were at my folks. There was a car parked out front with a flat tire. A woman was trying to fix it and having no luck. As I drove up, I heard her swearing a blue streak. Sweating too. Her makeup was all over her face. I changed the tire for her."

Graham laughed. "Claudia takes charge!"

"I couldn't bear her frustration. Afterward I asked her in to wash up, then I made us a drink. She was a strange one. A gypsy, perhaps. Short and solid with an enormous bouffant hairdo and flamboyant makeup—slanted eyes, big red mouth, fingernails a deep purple. After she'd finished her drink and refused a second, she asked me, 'What's wrong? You're troubled.' All I said was that things were going from bad to worse. 'Do you believe in witches?' she asked. 'I don't know,' I said. 'I've never known one.' 'I'm a

181

witch," she said. 'A white witch. That's a good witch. Don't be afraid. I'll help you. Make three wishes.' She waited until I said I'd wished, and then she stood up and somehow—this is crazy, I know—she began to expand and grow larger. My mind suddenly felt empty and I was relaxed and free. She began to chant in a strange tongue. She raised her arms and made strange gestures. She wore silver bracelets and the room was full of their music. I was absolutely transfixed."

"Were you frightened?" Graham asked.

"Not at all. I felt wonderfully secure. I kept repeating my wishes. The first was to get into grad school. As she stopped chanting, she seemed to shrink to normal size. She went to the door. 'Don't worry,' she said, 'Doors will open for you and you will have a new life.' I saw her out to the car and watched her wave and drive off. Then as I went back in, the phone rang. It was the Registrar himself. He had talked by phone with Carleton. I was admitted to the graduate program. And from then on it went like silk."

"What about your other wishes?" Graham asked. "Did they also come true?"

"The second did—or at least it has so far. It was for the kids to be well and happy."

"And the third?"

Claudia smiled. "I'm still waiting."

"Give yourself time."

"You'll understand why I then took Dr. Baylor's course in Folklore. For my research paper I wrote on white witches and my own experience. Have you known anything similar?"

Graham was silent, then finally said, "Yes, I have. But she was a black witch. And it was long ago."

"Did you ever write about it?"

"Never."

When he did not offer more, Claudia asked, "How high are we here?"

"Nine thousand."

"The forecast said there would be snow to the four thousand foot level. Will it snow before I get home?"

"It depends on how fast it moves in."

"Do they keep the road open?" Claudia asked.

182

"Only for chains and four-wheel drives. I should have mine any day now."

"Hadn't I better get started? I don't like to drive though when I've had this much wine."

"Do you have something to do?" Graham hesitated. "Is someone expecting you?"

"No," Claudia said. "There's no one."

Graham pointed to the clouds now over the Galiuros. "The temperature is falling, the wind rising. Maybe you'd better stay here."

"Stay here?" Claudia echoed softly.

"I can make up a bed on the couch. It's quite comfortable."

"What would the neighbors say?" She laughed. "Besides I brought only what I have on."

"I have a notable collection of odd garments." Graham took her arm. "We'd better go in. I'll bring in more wood. There's an electric heater in the bathroom."

"I'll do the dishes."

"You'll stay?"

"Don't you have work to do?"

"Not if you do the dishes."

Graham went out to the woodpile before she could answer.

Claudia puzzled while cleaning up the kitchen. What would her staying mean? In the beginning the initiative had been all hers in seeking the interview and in pressing him, albeit gently, to say more than he was willing to. To admiration had been added curiosity. Since the picnic and the mass and now in his home, her feelings had somehow changed. She realized that he had taken the lead. Yet not aggressively nor ever flirtatiously. They had come to a point at which she was both hesitant and certain, and for the first time free of the fears that had troubled her since the failure of her marriage. She knew she could depend on him.

When she had finished the dishes, Claudia settled on the couch with the Yeats and a glass of wine. She could hear the sound of steel on steel. Darkness was falling when he came in with an armload of freshly split logs and stacked them on the hearth.

"Chores done," he said. "I'll share a glass with you."

"Is it snowing?"

"It will be soon if the wind keeps rising."

183

"How cold is it?"

"Nearly down to twenty. I've got a bottle of old port put away for the big snow. This might be it."

"Wine is good for the soul as well as for the stomach. I'm very mellow."

"I too. I don't suppose you brought the recorder."

"Should I have?"

"I never got around to telling you about my maternal grandmother."

"Was she the witch?"

"Some of this furniture was my grandmother's."

"I'm afraid I inhibited you."

"Are you comfortable? Why not take off those desert boots? Here let me help you. I'll lend you my second-best slippers."

"How would you like to interview me, Professor Graham?"

"Where's the Yeats? Let me read you one he wrote just for us. Listen: 'But I am old and you are young, and I speak a barbarous tongue'."

"You aren't and you don't, so there. Have you forgotten our median age?"

They laughed as Graham filled their glasses.

"I'm going to hate leaving my thirties," Claudia said, "even though they've been painful."

"Do you realize that your hair is demonstrating the alchemical process?"

"What do you mean?"

"Didn't you ever take Alchemy? What's sandy by daylight is turned golden by firelight."

"That's no barbarous tongue! May I tell you something? Your books are nice in the firelight."

"Smoke and ashes aren't good for them."

"I'd clean them but I'd get to reading."

"That's why I don't."

"I see a lot of things that need doing."

"You'll stay?"

"Should I?"

"I think it best that you do." He opened the door and called to her. "It's begun!"

Claudia stood beside him as they watched the falling snow. The wind had brought the pines to life. She finally spoke. "I'm glad you asked me to stay."

"There's no choice now," Graham said. "We've passed the point of no return. They won't plow the road till morning."

He closed the door and shut out the cold. Claudia brought in a fresh pot of coffee and they resumed their places on the couch by the fire.

"I wondered about that photograph in the bathroom," she said. "What dam is it? Not Laguna."

"That's Roosevelt on the Salt—the one my father would have worked on if he had lived."

"Did you take the picture?"

"A friend did. It was a wet year, both spillways were flowing. I have my father's college cane there in the corner. It's Scottish briar with his initial in silver."

"I can think of things I'd like to have asked you about him."

"Our interviews must have been frustrating for you," Graham mused.

"I sought more than you wanted to give."

"Besides the divorce, what caused you the most pain?" Graham asked.

"Just growing up."

"I see you surrounded by a magnetic field—an aura of health and vitality."

"That's what comes from your reading Yeats."

"From my reading Yeats and your being Claudia."

"I used to wait on my husband. I wanted my marriage to last forever. I was happy at first even though he never waited on me, never unlaced my boots."

Graham took her hand. "We both need spoiling."

"I don't need any more than you've given me."

"I liked our interviews."

"Will you visit me next year?"

"If you'll ask me."

"Must you have it in writing?"

"I don't have to have anything," he said.

Graham opened the door again. The blowing snow was heavier, the pines were now roaring. The sudden draft made the fireplace smoke, filling the room with bittersweetness. He shut the door and stood gazing into the fire. He felt at the very heart of his long life, both sure and unsure, certain and doubting, yet joyful and strong and ready.

Claudia settled again on the couch. "Now I know," she said.

"Know what?"

"What kind of shaving lotion you use."

Graham laughed. "Are you ready for that old bottle of port?"

"Any port in a storm!"

"You *are* a good girl!"

He uncorked the bottle and poured a dash of the amber wine into his glass. "It's good," he said, tasting it, then half-filled her glass.

Graham sat on the hearth facing her, with his back against the stone. She tossed him a pillow.

"Getting sleepy?" he asked.

"I'm a night owl."

"I was thinking while you were in the bathroom, do you still want the whys?" he asked softly.

"I think I do, and yet—I know we're on the edge of I don't know what—and I'm a bit scared."

"Don't be." Graham's voice was even softer. "Perhaps the time has come to open that last door. It might take long."

"We have all night," Claudia whispered. "All week."

"You can stay that long?"

"If you want me to."

Graham stood up. "It's my turn. Don't go away."

"I'll be here."

He rested his hand lightly on her hair, then went to the bathroom.

Now Claudia felt regret at not having brought the recorder, and yet she knew that it was her not having it that freed him.

Graham sat again on the pillow by the fire and began to speak almost to himself, so that Claudia had to strain to hear him.

"I found another poem in the Yeats—a few lines that seem to apply to all the talking I've done this fall. 'Speech after long silence,' it begins. Do you remember it?"

"Of course," Claudia said, and continued, " ' . . . it is right, all other lovers being estranged or dead.' I felt that you needed to speak to someone, that you needed speech after long silence."

186

"You were right. I still do." Graham was silent, then began again in the same soft voice.

"You asked if I had ever met a witch in the course of my research and I told you that I had, and that she was a black witch, not like your white witch." Graham hesitated. "I hardly know where to start." Claudia waited for him to resume. He went to the door and looked out. "We'd be snowed in forever if they didn't keep the road open." He refilled their glasses and began again to speak.

"It was when I was at State, finishing the reclamation book. I was invited to a conference in Yuma on cultural research in the Southwest. It was being held on the anniversary of the martyrdom of fathers Garcés and Barreneche. Because of my book on Garcés I was asked to speak on the opening morning. As a native son—a neighboring one at least—I had some ideas of how to commemorate Yuma's historical significance at the river crossing. A memorial fountain was one of them. It was a talk that almost wrote itself on the eve of the conference. In it I brought together the three protagonists—the soldier Anza, the priest Garcés, and the Indian Palma."

"That must have been the beginning of *Three At the River Crossing*," Claudia observed.

"I drove over on the day before the conference opened."

"Was your wife with you?"

"She had the boys to look after, and she wasn't that much interested. That I was busy interested her, but not what or why. Have you ever been in Yuma?"

"We flew over it once en route to San Diego," Claudia said. "The pilot announced that we were crossing the Colorado River at Yuma. I must say I wasn't impressed."

"It isn't impressive. The history doesn't show. The river used to be a giant in the spring when the snow melted on the Rockies. It would flood then, and later when the river fell, the Indians would hurriedly plant their crops in the silt. Squash and melons grew fast in the summer heat. When the dams ended those annual floods, they also ended the Yumans' agricultural existence."

"That's a main theme in *Rivers in the Sand*."

"As I neared the river that afternoon I came to the sand dunes— those great dunes thirty miles long by five miles wide. The Algo-

187

dones, they're called. In the light of the western sun they were golden, like a naked body on the desert. I decided to take the long way into Yuma, up the west bank toward the dams at Laguna and Imperial. When they built the latter in modern times, it made Laguna obsolete. I hadn't been back in several years."

"I suppose the psychologists would call it a return to the womb." Claudia remarked. "Is there anything there now where you were born?"

"Only the old dam," Graham said. "The diverted channel forms a pool below the dam; and when I stopped, there I saw some Mexican boys swimming and diving. They were naked. One of them, a handsome brown kid, stood on the bank, water dripping from him, and shouted up to me, Hey mister, you want to come down? No, thanks, I said. You want to meet my sister? She's naked too. No, thanks, I said. Hey mister, he shouted, you go to hell! And he dove back into the pool to the derisive shouts of his fellows. That excited me. It was so nakedly pagan, so different from the life I was leading. Can you understand?"

"I too would have been excited," Claudia murmured.

"I went on to Imperial," Graham continued, "and walked out on the new dam. The sun was going down and the mountains had turned purple. On the lake above the dam, coots were scattered like pepper. There was the rank smell of the vegetation—tules and arrow weed. The green water was sluicing into the desilting basins with a muffled roar. The spray felt cool on my face. The All American Canal takes off there for the Imperial Valley. I felt wonderfully well—the way I do now. Everything was rising in me, a sense of the beauty and power, yes, and the nobility of the world."

"Pure Wordsworth!" Claudia whispered.

"I thought of it as an epiphany. I was eager to give my talk. I knew that it would move people as it had moved me to write it. I also had the feeling that I was on the threshold of the certain unknown, the unknown certainty. It was a feeling I'd never had before nor since. My inner voice was loud and clear. Love this life, it said. Give thanks for it and praise it in your work. I know now that it was one of those supreme moments of prefiguration. I stood there in the gathering dark, the bats beginning to fly, and when it grew chilly, I crossed on the dam and drove down the Arizona side into Yuma. The motel strip was brilliant with flashing neons. I felt like an arriving rajah.

"After checking in at the conference motel, I had dinner in the coffee shop and then found an easy chair in the lobby and read the *Yuma Sun*. It didn't take long. Not much happens in Yuma. Although the lobby was crowded, I didn't see anyone I knew. I had a Raymond Chandler with me and was about to turn in and read in bed, when I saw a woman enter the lobby with several men. They were in the midst of a conversation."

"They paused near me, talking and laughing. The woman was the center of interest. She was small and dark with black hair braided around her head, and an enchanting smile and infectious laugh. Her teeth were the whiter for the darkness of her skin. She had a trim figure with slim legs. My whole being responded to her so instantly that I nearly got up and introduced myself. I had never felt such a powerful attraction."

"What was she wearing?" Claudia asked.

Graham laughed "Something green, dark green, don't ask me what. I'm aware of a woman's clothes only when they're wrong. I was immobilized—just sat and stared. Who was she? The motel's hostess? She seemed to belong there. After she and the men had moved on, I got up and went to the desk and asked the clerk who was the woman in green. At first he didn't know who I meant, and then when I described her, he said, Why, that's Miss Aalto. I was incredulous. You don't mean Pipa Aalto, the archaeologist? I thought she was a much older woman. I don't know how old she is, the clerk said, but that's her. She's beautiful, I said. You'd better believe it, he exclaimed, and she was born right here in Yuma. But she works at the museum in Flagstaff, I said. That may be, the clerk said, but we claim her as ours. There was both admiration and possession in his voice. Do you know her work?" Graham asked Claudia.

"On the cliff-dwellers of the upper Gila?" she asked. "I read it when I was interviewing Dr. Bryan. He said it was a brilliant demonstration of fieldwork, the more so for having been carried out by a very young woman. She didn't appear to have continued her research."

"Only scattered things on the Flagstaff collections."

"Is she still there?"

"No, not for many years."

Claudia paused, then asked, "Was *she* the witch?"

"She was the witch's daughter."

"Oh, how strange! Is she still living?"

Graham slowly shook his head. They stared silently into the fire. Finally he went again to the door and opened it. "Come see. It's snowing harder."

They stood in the doorway, breathing the bitter air, sweet with chimney smoke. The wind had gone down. "With your staying," Graham said, "it doesn't matter whether they plow it or not."

"They'd better. I'll have to go down for some clothes. I'm going to make us some sandwiches now. You can eat later if you aren't hungry."

"You're a healthy girl."

"I like to cook and I like to eat. I like everything around a house except washing dishes."

"It's the one thing I'm good at."

When Claudia returned with the sandwiches and more coffee, Graham asked. "Are you sure you want me to continue?"

"I know that you need to. I'm fine. Do you mind my asking questions? I'm apt to forget we're not recording."

"Ask me when it doesn't make sense. I don't attach any significance to dreams, but that night I dreamed an angel came and sat on the edge of my bed and laid her hand on my forehead. She didn't speak, just rested her hand there, and it was like a gentle wave of feeling, of healing, like a warm shower. I woke up aglow as if there were a sun in my belly."

"That was your solar plexus," Claudia exclaimed. "I had it happen to me once. It was when I conceived my son. That's how I knew I had. It's why I feel there's something special about him—that the angel was there."

⚘

The next morning there was an opening session and then my talk came before lunch. I thought they'd never get to me. I couldn't see her in the audience. Then when I finally was introduced and before I could begin speaking, I saw her at the back, standing in the door and looking for an empty seat. I spotted one down front and pointed to it. She came swiftly down the aisle. I'd noticed the night before how lightly she moved. I waited for her

to be seated, and then she gave that *flashing smile and said, "Thank you,*
Dr. Graham, you may begin." I couldn't help joining in the laughter. It
was obvious that everyone adored her.

I've never spoken better than I did that morning, God knows how many
years ago. It was all to her. Knowing that she was a native Yuman and that
I too was almost one, created a bond between us, although she didn't know
at the time that I had been born on the other side of the river. It was as
though I had written the talk for her alone. Her eyes never left me.

When I had finished, I hoped she would come to the platform and we
would meet. She didn't. She disappeared. I don't know where she went.
Then when nearly everyone had left, I saw her at the back, about to leave.
I jumped down off the platform and called "Miss Aalto, don't go. I want to
meet you." She turned and almost ran down the aisle toward me, came close
and laid her cheek against mine. "Yes," was all she said, "Oh yes!" And be-
fore I could say a word, she ran back up the aisle and out the door.

By the time I had gathered my wits and joined the crowd in the patio,
she was gone. Nor was she at the lunch. No one seemed to know where she
was. I was beside myself with desire.

"Do you mean physical?" Claudia asked.
"No, nor was it intellectual."
"She sounds artful to me. She knew you'd follow and find her."
"She was primitive rather than artful."
"What was she wearing?"
Graham laughed. "I don't remember. I was dazzled."
"I'd like to be a dazzler," Claudia said, ruefully. "Did you find
her?"

She found me. The afternoon was free and people were gathering for local
tours—to the historical museum and the territorial prison, and one to the
Army Proving Ground—it was a big tank-training area—to see a show of
paintings by servicemen and their wives. I had given up hope of finding her
and was joining the group to the Army post, when suddenly there she was.
She took my arm and before I could answer, she led me out of the amused
throng, through the patio to the parking lot and her car—an old pickup

truck. *"It's as beat up as I am,"* she apologized, wrenching open the jammed door for me to get in.

"Where are you taking me?" I asked.

"Nowhere special. We can talk here without being disturbed by our admirers."

"Do you know we've never been introduced? Are you really the *Pipa Aalto?"*

"There is no other," she said. *"What did you expect?"*

"Someone older and grayer."

"But I am old and beginning to gray, can't you see?"

"I can't see behind your smile."

"You say lovely things."

"You are *lovely. Why did you run away this morning?"*

"I was afraid."

"Of me?"

"Of what you made me feel."

"Isn't feeling good?"

"I thought I'd lost the power to feel," she said. *"When I found that I hadn't, I ran for my life. What you said about Palma moved me most of all. No one ever speaks of him, nor has even heard of him here in Yuma."*

"He was a great Indian. I learned that from Bolton. Palma would have spared Father Garcés."

"His blood is in my veins."

"What do you mean?"

"I am descended from Salvador Palma on my mother's side."

"So that's where your coloring comes from!"

"More Hispano than Indian; and on my father's side not at all. He was from another race."

"Aalto? Or is that your married name?"

"It was my father's name," she explained. *"I have never married."*

"Why not? You are beautiful."

"Too independent. I won't be domesticated."

"What nationality was your father?"

"He was a Finn. The form of my body comes from him, although my mother is not fat the way old mestizas usually are. She named me Pipa."

"I know that it means The People and that you were born here. So was I—almost."

"But you are a Californian."

"Barely. I was born over yonder across the river."

"How could you have been? There was nothing over there." She smiled. "There still isn't anything worth very much."

"Drive me across and I'll show you where. They haven't put up a plaque yet, but then I'm only forty. How old are you?"

"Older than you are."

"Not very much."

"Enough. Why were you so long in coming?"

"You were never here when I did."

"I hate it here."

"Why?"

"Because of my mother."

"What's wrong with her?"

"She's a bruja," Pipa said.

"You're joking."

"I wish I were. Have you come to free me? I sensed it this morning when you were speaking. I watched your hand turning the pages. Let me feel your grip. Good. You are strong. You'll have to be if you are going to hold me."

✦

Graham rose then, shook down the fire and put on an oak backlog, then spoke again.

✦

She was so forthright. I gave up trying to understand her and let myself be carried by her earnestness. We drove across the bridge and up the west bank to where I had been only twenty-four hours before. There was no one in the pool and so we parked there and I told her the story of my birth. When I said that my father's name was Samuel C. Graham, her fingers dug into my arm. "Why did it have to be you?" she cried. "You of all people!"

"I don't know what you mean," I said. "Tell me who you are."

"I'm the witch's daughter," she almost screamed, "that's who I am. You'll be sorry if I tell you who we are. Let's go back. I've had enough for now."

"Don't you want to go on to Imperial?" I asked her.

"Did he build that too?" she said bitterly.

"He died soon after Laguna was built."

"I know," she said, "I know."

I didn't know what to make of her. She turned around and drove back

193

down river. Before we reached the highway she took a dirt road that led to a plaza near the river. She drew up in front of a shack and a mob of mewing cats gathered. The door opened and a woman emerged. She was tall and heavy with hair cut like a man's, wearing blue jeans and a dirty shirt. She came to Pipa's side of the truck. "This is Carl," Pipa said. The woman nodded, her eyes on Pipa. "For the cats, do you hear," Pipa said, handing her some money. "Si," the woman agreed, laughing grossly, "por los gatos." Pipa drove away through the deep dust. "That's not your mother?" I half asked.

"My god no!" she exclaimed. "That's Delores Wolf."

"Who's she?"

"She was a promising researcher who couldn't keep her hands off the girls."

"Off you?" I asked.

"I was too quick for her," Pipa said. "We lived together for a while as graduate students until she came after me. She raped the young wife of the head of the department. Bit off her nipples. She had to disappear into Mexico for a year. She could never return to campus."

"Did she ever hurt you?" I asked Pipa.

"I never let her get any farther than her hand on my bare leg — once. We were driving home from a meeting when she pulled over on a dark street and grabbed me. I talked her out of it. I locked my bedroom door that night and then moved out. She was stronger than most men."

"She looks like she still is. That was more than cat money you gave her."

"I help her some."

"Why?"

"I have to be kind to someone. I've been cruel to so many."

"Women?"

"Men. I should hate you."

"What do you mean?"

"I'll tell you soon enough."

🙎

Again Graham got up and looked out. "You could never have gotten out tonight."

"Are you all right?" Claudia asked.

"If I stop now and then, it's because I've never tried to put it together this way."

"I don't know what to make of her."

"At first it was as though I'd met my other half."

Well, we drove back across the bridge and to the plaza on the prison hill. In front of the church is a conventional statue of Father Garcés blessing the Indians. We parked there and I told her more of my dream of a memorial to Garcés that would include Anza and Palma. She told me about her father—that he was a famous bridge builder who came to Yuma around the turn of the century for his health. From that first talk, I learned that Pipa Aalto was a woman of violent changes; gentle one moment, then explosively passionate. I also understood why she had never married. No one could have held her. In the beginning I thought I could. I was wrong.

"It must have been that mixture of races in her," Claudia observed.

"It was her mother. I'll come to her, the bruja."

Pipa and I were talking quietly there on the hill, looking down on the river, when she burst out with, "Dams and bridges damn and cross us. Goddamn them!" She wouldn't explain what she meant. "I'll tell you tonight," was all she would say. "You're coming to the dinner, aren't you?" she asked.

"Will you be there?"

"I'll be at the head table with the governor."

"Isn't he the speaker?"

"I wrote his speech. If you'll come, I'll have a place for you at our table."

She did indeed, between her and Governor John Clayton. I took to him, as I told you, with the first handshake. He was a big rangy man, wearing a tailored whipcord suit and polished boots, a dark red silk shirt and a silver bola. He was all man. I liked him.

"I'm sorry to have missed your talk," the governor said to me. "I flew down from Phoenix and have to go back after the square dancing. Miss Aalto has told me you made a magnificent presentation. What are you working on now?"

195

"A book on reclamation in the west."

"I recall reading a chapter from it in our state journal. Be fair to Arizona is all I ask, sir."

"I'm not a typical Californian," I protested. "I was born here on the river."

"On the wrong side," Pipa scorned.

"Has she told you she's going to be on my staff for a year? She's going to help us get the Great Dam bill through Congress."

"You couldn't have a more beautiful lobbyist," I said.

"It's my brains not my beauty he's hiring," Pipa objected.

"Both," the governor said. "Then I want her to finish her doctor's degree."

"Nonsense!" Pipa said. "Who would examine me?"

"Why didn't you finish it?" I asked when the governor had turned to the program chairman on his other side.

"Quarreled with my department chairman. I had no respect for him."

"And told him so?"

"Publicly!"

"Why haven't you published more?" I asked.

"Too busy running the museum. The director was often away. Besides there's too much worthless material being published. Why add to it?"

"You should have a better opinion of yourself," I chided her. "Your Gila monograph led me to think of you as a wise and learned woman."

"Old and gray, you said."

"I take that back. You seem to be very close to Governor Clayton."

"We were in school together. I wanted to marry him. I was young and foolish then."

"Why didn't you?"

"His mother wouldn't let him. They were ricos. He was already politically ambitious. His father was chief justice of the state supreme court, and I was a pobrecita from Yuma. I know I should finish the degree. I'll never be director without it."

"Do you still love him?"

"The girl in me does, the woman does not."

"Are you his . . . ?"

"Research assistant!" she interrupted with a smile.

"Miss Aalto tells me you were in school together," I said to the governor when he turned my way again.

"She used to watch me play polo. We had a magnificent team. We went

196

east once to play West Point. They played on turf. It was the first time our horses had ever seen grass. We couldn't keep them from browsing." His laugh filled the room. "If you think this girl is pretty now, you should have seen her then! When she came to the games, even the horses turned to look. She's still the most beautiful woman in Arizona and always will be." He struck the table with his fist until the glasses jumped and people turned. "That, sir, is an official proclamation, given under my hand if not seal!"

Pipa laughed in delight as the governor was introduced and rose to speak. I listened to his voice and her words—a brief account of Arizona's agricultural development brought about by the water from the Gila and the Colorado. And I watched her watching him.

"I *can* tell you what she wore that night," Graham said to Claudia. "It was a short-sleeved black dress and a squash blossom necklace. Her hair was drawn back. There were silver drops in her earlobes. She was very beautiful. I felt myself going over the falls."

At the end of the talk, as we rose from dinner, the governor said, "Pipa has told me of your plan for a fountain to the martyrdom. Are you ever in Phoenix? Come and tell me about it. The state might help."

"Thank you, governor," I said. "I'll try to get over one of these days. I'll need help in the funding, although I've been encouraged by the archbishop. I know the sculptor I want. And I haven't told her, but Miss Aalto is going to pose for the river goddess."

"I'll have to buy a new bathing suit," she laughed.

"Are you coming to the square dancing?" the governor asked me.

"No," Pipa answered, "he's going for a walk with me."

"You'll miss the greatest caller in the West," the governor warned.

"We won't be able to get out of hearing," she teased. "Wait for me. I'll need a wrap."

"She returned wearing a flame-colored poncho. Again she steered me through the crowd and beyond the lighted patio to the edge of an arroyo on the far side of the parking lot. The air was cold, the sky diamonded with stars. We could hear the sounds of fiddle and accordion, the governor's deep

voice, and the growl of the Diesel rigs on their way to and from the coast.
An owl swooshed low over us.

"Now are you going to tell me," I said, "all those things you've been hint-
ing at?"

"Hold me first," she said. "Here, put your hands under the poncho. Feel
how strong I am."

Ah, but she was! And radiant and warm. I drew her close. I was trembling. She lifted her face to be kissed. When I finally drew away, we were
both breathing hard.

"I'm yours," she said. "I knew I would be from the first sight of you last
night, reading that dreadful newspaper."

"How did you know who I was?"

"They pointed you out."

"I saw you."

"Did you want me?"

"I was too dazzled."

"Don't you now?"

"Why are you in a hurry?"

"How do I know if we'll ever meet again?"

"Mind before body," I said. "You must tell me who you are."

"I'm afraid to. You might not want me then."

"I'll take the chance."

"You're only the second man who ever said no to me."

"Let's sit in my car and talk."

"You are a very stubborn man."

"I'm not saying no—only saying wait."

Claudia rose from the couch and stood with her back to the fire.
"Did she want you to make love to her then and there?"

"She'd always had what she wanted when she wanted it. She
was utterly primitive, and also at odds with herself."

"Did she answer your questions?"

"Finally. She wasn't used to being refused. She had power, not
just magnetism, and projected it like a laser. She once told me that
when she entered a room, the men went down like tenpins—all but
the one who seemed to her the most desirable. Him she would back
against the wall until he was hers."

"That's witchcraft," Claudia commented.

"It was hard to resist her. She was so desirable—her smile, her laugh, her small musical voice. I remember the governor telling me, when I asked him how effective a lobbyist he thought she would be. Don't be misled by that voice of hers, he said. I've seen her dominate an audience of the meanest legislators north of the Gila. Here, get comfortable again. Let me tuck you in. It's getting very cold outside."

"That's a beautiful blanket."

"It's one she gave me. A Navajo cowboy gave it to her. His mother wove it, she told me."

Yes, she answered my questions, there on the back seat of the car. By the time we returned to the motel, it was late and the dance was over, the bar had closed and everything was dark.

She told me her father had built many bridges in Scandinavia and northern Europe. Then one of his most original constructions, the prototype of a new kind of suspension bridge, collapsed in a gale with the loss of many lives. It was over the harbor in Mälmo, Sweden. The tragedy broke him. He developed T.B. and then vanished, turning up later in Yuma. Pipa's mother, Artemesia Escalante, was a nurse in the local hospital. She brought him back from near death. They were married and lived in a little house he built beyond the confluence of the Gila and the Colorado.

It was there that Salvador Palma was last recorded in history, some time in the 1780s. Not long after Pipa was born, her father died and was laid to rest in the old Yuman burying ground above the confluence. When my father came to help carry out the Bureau's project for Laguna Dam, it was evident that the rising water would inundate the cemetery. There was agitation against it led by Pipa's mother, now Artemesia Aalto. She begged them not to build the dam, not only because it would drown the grave of her husband, but also because it threatened the ancient Yuman way of flood farming. From time immemorial their staple foods of squash and melons were raised in the silt brought down in the spring floods. When it rose, the river was sometimes half a mile wide. Her appeals were fruitless. She tried to knife my father. They locked her up. She escaped and attempted to blow up the dam. She was declared insane. Pipa didn't remember who took care of her while her mother was being held. When she was finally released and after my father had died, her mother developed her latent powers of clair-voyance. She became a bruja and earned enough to keep her and Pipa. The people came to her for love potions or maledictions or whatever. She was both feared and respected.

※

Claudia shuddered and drew the blanket closer. "I had no idea such things really happened. Dr. Baylor never made them more than academic."

※

You can imagine how I felt as her story unfolded. She was ambivalent as she told it. One minute she was in my arms begging me to make love to her, and then she was like ice, cursing me as the son of the man who drowned her father. I finally persuaded her to go to bed and I went to mine.

I couldn't sleep though. The night was still, with only the occasional sound of a Diesel, shifting up through the gears until it hummed away in the distance. What I had learned about my father was unreal, whereas Pipa Aalto was real, was now—all the feel and fragrance of her skin and hair, all the magic of one small woman who had detonated me. I lay there sensing what it would be like to make love to her, wondering if I had been right to make her wait. It was getting light when I finally slept.

※

"You said her mother was still alive," Claudia said. "Did you meet her?"

"I did. Although Pipa was convinced that I had been sent to break her mother's hold on her, she also feared that the bruja would bring harm to me."

"Weren't you fearful?" Claudia asked.

※

I was also full of power. We went the next afternoon to an adobe in the bar-rio, surrounded by wild tobacco trees in flower. As we walked up the steps to the screened porch, a hummingbird divebombed us. Pipa was trembling.

200

"Who is it?" a faint voice called as we opened the door.

"It's Pipa," her daughter said. I followed her in, and in the center of the room I saw a tiny gray-haired woman sitting in a black leather chair. "Mi madre," Pipa said, "this is Carl." I went closer and looked down on a blade-thin face, out of which bead-black eyes stared at me. I held her gaze, feeling both dread and power. Our eyes fought, and then she asked, "Why have you come back? I killed you once. Do I have to kill you again?" "Mi madre," Pipa pleaded, "this is Carl Graham." "I know you, Sam Graham," the bruja said in a voice like the rustle of dry leaves. She reached between the folds of her gray woolen robe and I saw her hand begin to rub a blue shell that hung from a silver necklace. Suddenly I felt power flow from her and hit my chest like a blow. I knew I must break her hold on the shell. It was not hard. She was weak. She must have been very old.

She was thin and wrinkled, but not ugly. Pipa got her coloring from her, but her beauty must have come from her father. I kneeled in front of the mother, grasping the shell in my hand, and said, "Old woman, I have come for your daughter, I have come to free her from your spell. Go back to your people. Your power has gone, your time has passed. The power is now in me, in Pipa and me."

"You shall not have her," the witch whispered. "No one has ever had her but me. I shall take her with me into the willows. There Palma shall have her. Palma will bless us and there will be no dams on the river." Whereupon I slipped the necklace over her head, and as I did so, her silky hair crackled with electrical force. I felt my hand tingle. The current ran up my arm and died out. I dropped the necklace on the floor.

All this time Pipa was standing with her back to the bare wall, arms at her sides, her face an agonized mask. I stood over the mother with my hand on her head. Her power was gone. She began to keen in a paper-thin voice: "I begged him not to. The river meant life to the people since the dawn of the world. The oracle said not to let the river be stopped in its flow. It would mean the end of the world. On my knees I begged him not to. He called me a crazy Indian and thrust me aside. The water rose and drowned all who slept there—Palma and Paavo and the others, los pobrecitos."

"Go to Paavo," I said to her, my hand still resting on her head. She smelled of wool and herbs. "We will bring you beans and squash and sweet melons. You will feast with him and Palma in the willows by the river." "Yes," she said eagerly, "I shall take Pipa with me and we will feast and sleep in the willows, I with Paavo, she with Palma. Palma is young and strong and tireless. Palma shall be the first to have Pipa." At that point Artemesia

Aalto buried her face in her hands and rocked to the sound of the silver bracelets on her thin wrists.

We stole away and I led Pipa to the car as the hummingbird swooped again. She lay back, drained and nearly lifeless. I found a bar, and in a dim booth at the back I ordered whiskey for us both. She downed hers and gasped for breath. "Now you know," she said. "You have seen the power she has held over me."

"I broke it," I said. "Did you hear her hair crackle when I was slipping off the necklace?"

"It is a power that paralyzes." Pipa said faintly. "You heard what she said about your father. How did *he die?"*

"I only know what my mother told me. He died from heart failure. It doesn't seem likely. She said he was strong as a bull."

"She thinks you are your father. You must go away. She has great power. No one has ever proved stronger."

"She is crazy," I said. "Can she be committed to the state hospital?"

"My mother?" Pipa exclaimed. "Do you believe she is really mad?"

"She is not a good mother. What did she mean by Palma being the first to have you? You have had men."

"I used to keep a notched stick," Pipa said bitterly, "until I lost count."

"The governor?"

"I told you never."

"Could you now if you wanted him?"

"I don't want him."

"Others?" I pressed her.

"Occasionally an old friend or another. They don't know that I don't feel anything. I haven't for years. I'm a good pretender. It became meaningless, like shaking hands. Then when you were speaking yesterday, I felt feeling return. It was like a desert spring, dry for years, that begins to flow again. I knew that we must make love."

"Were you in love with your wife?" Claudia asked.

"I was devoted, affectionate, habituated—everything but faithful. I came closer to fulfillment with Pipa than with anyone else. There has been no one since to approach her."

202

Graham paused, then said, "It's getting late. Shall we stop for the night? You must be tired."

"I couldn't sleep," Claudia replied. "It's pretty scary."

"It gets worse. Can you take it?"

"I think I can. I feel secure with you."

"Get comfortable then and I'll try to make sense of what happened."

❦

After the closing session Pipa planned to return to Phoenix on the Sunset. It was due in Yuma at two in the morning. We checked her bag at the station and then sat in my car and talked. It poured out of us both. We seemed to have known each other forever.

"You've convinced me that waiting is nice," Pipa said when we agreed to meet in December at a water conference in Los Angeles.

"I'll take you to meet Hodge, the great ethnologist. He's still alive and active in his nineties. If we have time, we'll go see the limestone statue of Father Garcés in Bakersfield, then go on farther to meet my sculptor friend, the one I want to do the memorial. His name is Lars Hansen. He works at a quarry in the Sierra foothills. He's a Swede I met when I was trailing Garcés. We became friends. You'll like him. Aren't Swedes and Finns kinfolk?"

"Finns and Lapps," Pipa laughed. "Let's walk. I'll show you my hometown. You showed me yours, such as it is."

Her voice had grown tender. She seemed girlish although she was well over forty. We strolled arm in arm through the arcaded center of Yuma under the flashing neons, looking in store windows, avoiding occasional drunks, and talking with common tongue of history, archaeology, flood and drought, and of love and death, at once earnest and carefree, lavishing ourselves in an effort to recover those years before fate at last brought us together.

Later we stood at the railing half way across the bridge and looked down at the river on its final run to the Gulf. "How can I tell you who I am," Pipa said, "when I am no longer who I was? I grew up so fast and so much kept happening to me. I was nubile at ten, a woman at twelve, a mistress at fourteen. My mother kept a boarding house then, and the men were always moving through. She encouraged me to be promiscuous."

"Did she have men?" I asked Pipa.

"She hated men. She used me to punish them."

"What saved you?"

"It was my mind, my father's mind. A Russian first perceived it in the wild girl I was. He was a hydrographer come to measure the river's flow. He was a boarder. I used to come in late from working in a dance hall and find him arranging the day's data. I seduced him. He was a good lover." Pipa laughed. "He never stopped working, even while we were making love. So I helped him with his work. Imagine, he got me aroused over the dynamics of languid and turbulent flow! He convinced my mother that I should go the university and study science. Only when she saw that it would increase my earning capacity did she agree. We moved for the years that it took. It was so unlikely—dance-hall girl gets her B.S. at nineteen, her M.S. a year later. The trouble was that I was never sure which I was— dancer or scholar—and there was always a line of men waiting their turn. I liked to see them fight over me."

Her voice lowered. "I remember when I put up my hair for the first time. I must have been about twelve. It was at a fandango. A fight broke out between an Indian and an Anglo."

"Over you?" I asked her.

"I was wild with excitement."

"Who won?"

"The Indian. He had a knife."

"What happened?"

"He carried me to a pickup and threw me in the back."

"And then?"

"One guess. It was the first time for me. I liked it."

"Did he keep you?"

"He would have, but the sheriffs came and pulled him off and locked him up. They said he was a Ute on the run from the law. The Anglo died. They hanged the Indian."

I was both frightened and aroused. I asked her if she had really never wanted to marry and settle down. "Only that once," she replied. "Then Jack's mother broke it up. So I hurt him by hurting others. I went on the warpath for scalps. My mother punished me whenever she saw I was getting serious with a man."

"How?" I asked.

"By her silence. She would go for days without speaking. Once she went for several weeks. I couldn't bear it. And yet somehow I grew stronger and finally I got the upper hand. The move to Flagstaff was the turning point.

I forbade her to come there and I rarely came back here. I value strength above all."

"You are strong," I told her.

"I bend," she said, "but don't try to break me."

"Would you marry me?"

She pulled free. "Are you crazy? You know you can't. Isn't your wife also a Catholic?"

"Yes," I admitted.

"And so you can't and I won't. But I will be yours in all other ways."

Thus the evening passed as we stood there on neutral ground my arm around her waist, her head on my shoulder, while the Diesels rolled by lit with green and red and orange running-lights. Occasionally a driver would blast his air horn and I would wave. It had all happened in twenty-four hours and there I was asking her to marry me!

Toward midnight we wandered back to the Arizona side, and in the waiting room kept watch for the Sunset. Toward two o'clock the telegraph began to click and the eastbound Limited was called for Phoenix, Tucson, El Paso, San Antonio, Houston, and New Orleans. I carried Pipa's bag to the platform. The night had turned cold. Few were there to board.

Then we heard the engine's horn and the roll of wheels as the train rumbled over the railroad bridge. The swinging headlight flashed, and the long train of Pullmans entered the station and stopped with a sigh of relaxing airbrakes.

I kissed her until it was she who broke free. I handed her up to the Negro porter. She waved and was gone. The train gathered speed. I waited until its red lights had vanished. The silence was broken by the horning engine, fading from sound.

Graham fell silent and sat staring into the fire that had burned low. He saw that Claudia was asleep. How young she looked! Her breathing was quiet and regular, her hair gleamed in the firelight. He touched it softly, then tucked the blanket around her. He went outdoors for another back-log that would burn through the night. The snow was falling steadily, the air sweet with smoke. The wind had risen. It was very cold. He suddenly felt tired. He put up the firescreen and went to bed.

Graham awoke early and went out on the deck. The storm had

passed over, leaving a white forest under a blue sky. The valley of the San Pedro was still shrouded.

Claudia was asleep. He put on water for coffee, then built up the fire. When he returned with an armful of wood, she was awake. "How did you sleep?" he asked.

"Yuk! In my clothes. Why didn't you wake me up?"

"I'd worked too hard to put you to sleep."

"What did I miss?"

"I don't know when you dropped off. I put her on the train to Phoenix and then drove back to Los Angeles. I could do without sleep in those days."

"It's obvious I can't! Give me five minutes in the bathroom and I'll join you. Is it still snowing?"

"The storm passed over."

They drank their coffee sitting on the hearth, the open fire between them.

"You're my first overnight guest," Graham said.

"Am I a nuisance?"

"An ornament."

"I should brush my hair. Do you realize these clothes are all my worldly goods this morning?"

"I'll drive you down as soon as they come through with the plow." Graham hesitated, then added, "And back, if you'll stay."

"Are you sure I won't be in your way?"

"I'd like to have had a daughter like you. Would your parents let me adopt you?"

"I'd rather be your mother. You need buttons sewn on. When did you last clean house?"

"I don't remember."

"If I could go to my cubicle, I'd bring back some work."

"We could market too," Graham said. "We didn't provide for beyond Christmas Day."

"Will you be having company? Someone like the president or the governor?"

Graham smiled. "That's the beauty of it here. No one can find me unless I want them to. Do you want to hear more about her?"

"Was she really like that?"

"You can see why I never married again. I had to find a new way."

"Oh but you did!"

"I'll tell you the rest when we come back up."

By noon the snow plow had reached the clearing and they learned that the road down the mountain was passable only for cars with chains. Graham and Claudia drove to the city and did their errands. Upon returning he stopped at the point where chains were required.

"I'll do my side," Claudia volunteered.

"You'll get dirty."

"So what?"

When Graham had finished his side, he came around and squatted beside Claudia in the slush. "You're as strong as I am," he said.

"Not really. That last link took all I had."

"Wash your hands in the snow. See how warm it feels?"

"I'm very happy," Claudia said.

"Is that a tear?" Graham asked.

"A melted snowflake."

"Why are you crying?"

"Have you forgotten how foolish a woman can be?"

"Here, dry your hands on this rag."

They remained squatting beside the rear wheel, aware that in the incongruous setting they had come closer. Graham took her hand and turned it palm outward. "You'll live a long time," he said. "I won't live to see the end of your life."

Before she could reply, the car in back of them honked to remind them they were blocking the lane. "Take me to your lair," she said, "before I shed another tear."

Back at the cabin they did chores and then bundled up on the deck and watched the light change on the Galiuros. "The road will ice tonight," Graham said, "then even with chains it's dangerous. What were you doing in the kitchen?"

"I hope you still like turkey."

"Are you ready to hear some more?"

"First let me turn down the oven."

"We could go in by the fire. Or I'll bring out another blanket."

"Let's stay out as long as we can," Claudia said. "Those mountains were blue. Now they're purple."

"The locals call them the Glories."

207

Our moment of truth came at the December meeting. Pipa arrived the night before the conference opened. My wife was at Palm Springs recuperating from the flu. A housekeeper was with the boys. I called Pipa's room from the lobby. I found her door ajar. She was standing across the room, arms at her sides the way she'd stood when we were at her mother's, only this time her face was smiling. Don't ask me what she was wearing. I found her mouth with mine. Finally she broke away and said, "Rest." When she sat on the edge of the bed and stroked my forehead, I remembered my dream.

She slowly unbraided her hair and brushed it out. It came to her waist, crow's wing black and glossy. I couldn't see any gray. She let her clothes fall at her feet. Her body was pure gold. When she was naked I took her gently by the hair and waist and drew her down and under me. The bedside radio was playing La Paloma Azul.

We were well matched. The conference was demanding, however, and we had no time alone. It was late the next night before we got to bed and we were dead tired and soon fell asleep.

The next morning I said to Pipa, "We've got a choice: stay in bed till noon or meet Hodge." She rolled out of bed and was dressing before I could grab her. She was like trying to hold a trout in your bare hands.

So we called on Frederick Webb Hodge at the Southwest Museum. I had phoned him that I was bringing Pipa Aalto to meet him, and he greeted her graciously.

"I've long wanted to meet you," he said, "ever since I read your work on the upper Gilans. Until Dr. Graham prepared me, I expected a much older scholar."

"Gracias, señor," Pipa smiled. "It is I who have looked forward to meeting you."

"I first saw the upper Gila in the 1880s," the old ethnologist said, "when we came over the trail of Pattie and Kearny. There were still beavers and bears. I failed to see the dwellings you described. May I ask what first drew your attention to them?"

Pipa smiled. "I was with a cowboy. We were looking for a place to be alone."

We all laughed. "I too was in a hurry," Hodge said. "We were making for the Salt River Valley and the newly unearthed canals of the Hohokam. They were great water engineers. I knew Dr. Graham's father," he con-

tinued. "He was in Reclamation when I was in Ethnology. Did you know that it was he who built Laguna Dam?"

I held my breath. There was a pause before Pipa answered sweetly, "I do know. My mother also knew Dr. Graham's father." I gave her a grateful look.

"Dr. Graham tells me that you have Yuman blood in a line all the way back to Salvador Palma," Hodge remarked.

"My people were never subjugated," Pipa said proudly. "If the river were still unrestrained, they would be the contented people they once were."

Hodge's weathered face gazed beyond us as he continued to muse. "That man Palma certainly lived a charmed life. Arrillaga tells of how a Spanish soldier shot at him three times at close range, and each time the pistol misfired."

"My parents dwelled beyond the Gila confluence," Pipa said, "near where history last accounts for Palma."

"When I was at the Heye," Hodge continued, "we were offered what was said to be Palma's galloon'd hat—the one he wore when Anza presented him to the Viceroy. It seemed unlikely that it would have survived."

Thus we continued to talk as we strolled around the great hall of the museum, filled with a display of baskets, pottery, and blankets.

"What is your position on the Great Dam project?" Hodge asked Pipa. "It appears to me that it will threaten the Rainbow Bridge."

"It will destroy it by undermining," she said angrily. "My position is ambivalent now that I am on Governor Clayton's staff. We need the water and the power for our crops and cities, yet we also need the bridge for our souls."

"That is well said," Hodge observed. "Have you been there recently?"

"It was long ago—with another of my cowboys."

We laughed as Hodge continued, "Is it not true that the area near where Palma was last said to have been living is now submerged?"

Once again I held my breath until Pipa replied. "That is true—ever since 1909."

"Can't you persuade your governor to give more attention to our archaeological sites?" Hodge asked Pipa. "The Army Corps of Engineers is ruthless in their work. I keep appealing to Washington."

"I hope I can convince Governor Clayton to look at the state from my viewpoint as an archaeologist," Pipa said, "as well as from his as a politician."

"Are you succeeding?"

"I don't know yet. In their lust for power, Arizona and California have

209

come closer than I ever dreamed possible. I am having to become accustomed to speaking for both in our arguments for the Great Dam legislation."

I told Hodge that we were on our way to Bakersfield to see the statue of Garcés and that we were then going on past Madera to see a sculptor friend whom I wanted to design a memorial to Garcés, Anza and Palma, and that I hoped to persuade the diocese to help fund it. As we left, Hodge offered to make a personal contribution. Pipa embraced him in parting.

As we crossed the Tehachapis the weather turned cold and we needed the car's heater. We were on a high plateau of fulfillment, our bodies at ease, our minds engaged. So active was Pipa's mind that I believe she preferred talking to making love.

As we began the descent to the San Joaquin valley, I recalled my work on Garcés. Pipa wanted to hear about Bolton. He was a great teacher I told her, as long as you were working on his ideas. What I learned from him was the importance of persistence and stamina and of primary sources whether in the archives or on the trails. Bolton didn't care for style. Fancy writing, he called it. He was blunt, self-centered, and a nonstop talker. Unless you were a good listener, you didn't survive.

"I wish we could have done our fieldwork together," Pipa said. "Mine was with Cummings and Douglass, and I had one summer with Kidder at Pecos."

"And with the cowboys," I reminded her. "What became of them?"

"It was I who rode away into the sunset," she said. "Men never got used to my way of leaving them. I always wanted more than feeling. I wanted meaning. And strength. If I have any philosophy, it is never complain, never explain."

"How do you account for her not having continued with research on other cliff dwellers?" Claudia asked.

"I suppose it was what she first told me. She became so involved in the Flagstaff operation. The director was in the field much of the time and it fell to Pipa to keep the place running. Yet she was passed over twice when a new director was named. Her not having the doctorate was the nominal reason. I believe there were other reasons. She could be savagely divisive."

Pipa was amazed by the extent of the San Joaquin. As we came down the Grapevine grade, we saw snow on Bear Mountain while in the northeast the white ramparts of the Sierra Nevada were discernible. "It's all new to me," Pipa said. "If I ever came to California, it was to San Francisco. One summer my mother and I drove all the way to the Columbia. We camped and picked blueberries. The bears had the same idea. It was one of our few happy times."

We finally came to the Garcés statue in the traffic circle at Bakersfield—a sixteen-foot limestone carving, stylized in garb and mien so as to bring into conjunction the fortitude and the humility of the Franciscan. After gaining the center we walked around the monument while the traffic encircled us.

"Garcés was more Indian then Spaniard," I told Pipa. "That's why Palma loved him. The trouble wasn't the priest's fault. The colonists were to blame. They turned their horses into the Indians' fields and trampled their crops. If Captain Anza had not been ordered to the Comanche frontier, the massacre would never have occurred."

"Tell me about the statue," Pipa said. "Did your friend carve it?"

"It was done by a sculptor named Palo-Kangas. He was on the WPA fine arts project. I had a clerical job with it because I could type. PhD's were worthless in the Depression. I checked in the limestone block when it arrived in the harbor from a quarry in southern Indiana. They flatboated it down the Ohio and Mississippi to New Orleans, then shipped it through the canal to San Pedro. I had done my work on Garcés then, and so when the statue was dedicated, the Archbishop asked me to attend the ceremony. Bolton was the main speaker. My idea for a memorial fountain in Yuma goes back to that day."

I told Pipa that Palo-Kangas would have made a beautiful fountain, but that he had died some time in the 1940s and that was why I wanted to talk with Lars Hansen about it. I also said that she would love him as I did, that he was a creative man of strength and passion.

We stayed the night in Tulare, then pressed on early next morning through miles of bare orchards. Grapes had been cut back, peaches pruned, while the bareness of the fig trees had turned their branches to purply white. The damp air was acrid with smoke from the burning of prunings and weed-grown ditches. Crows made their raucous flight over fields and orchards. The walls of the Sierra rose to heaven. Pipa was enthralled.

Beyond Madera a gravelled road left the highway and began to climb through stubble land on which cattle were grazing. Drought-stunted oaks were the first sign of elevation, then the sight of the mountains was lost as we threaded the foothills. Now the oaks grew denser and the first granite appeared—blunted graygreen outcrops among the darker trees.

At last we saw the quarry, cut into the side of a granite dome. During the century that it had been worked, the quarry had supplied the stone for most of California's public buildings. While on the trail of the Franciscan priest I had come on Lars Hansen, working at the quarry and quitting whenever he had enough to live on long enough to complete a work of his own.

As a youth he had been apprenticed to his fellow Swede, Carl Milles. One summer Hansen persuaded me to drive to St. Louis to see Milles's masterpiece, the enormous fountain, "The Meeting of the Waters" that marked the conjunction of the two great rivers. Coming to it on a windy afternoon, we walked around the fountain while Hansen discoursed on each Triton and Nereid, and of the central figures of man and woman approaching each other in restrained ecstasy.

I remember how exalted Hansen was, speaking with strong accent and nearly downing me with thumps on the back. As we grew drenched with spray, we peeled to our shorts. When darkness fell we ate dinner in the Union Station and headed west, taking turns driving and sleeping.

When we reached the quarry works, I listened for Hansen's whereabouts. In a moment was heard the sound of hammer and chisel, a rhythmic ringing that led to the sculptor's house-trailer, pickup truck, and stoneyard.

He was working with his back to us, golden-bodied with blonde hair, facing a block of gray granite. I laid my hand on his sweaty back and felt its heat and strength. He turned, jerked off his goggles and peered out from the forest of his beard. He dropped his tools and shouted "Graham!" as he crushed me in his grip. His sweat was goat strong.

I broke loose and said, "This is Pipa."

Hansen looked her over, lifted her high off her feet, then put her down and roared, "Hello Pipa!"

We all laughed in the crazy joy of meeting. Then Pipa touched the stone and asked, "What is it?"

"What is it?" Hansen shouted. "It's my answer to the welders, that's what it is. It's also hell on my chisels."

"What will it be if they hold out?" I asked.

"An eagle, can't you see? It's for the mall in the county seat. I like birds. I'm in my bird period. I don't know when to stop. I work for a week and sleep for a week, still on my feet. And I hate visitors." He poked me. "Unless they bring Pipas. Have you got another Pipa?"

"There is no other," she and I laughed in unison, and then Pipa said "Carl says you are Swedish."

"What are you?"

"My father was Finnish. He built bridges."

"I never heard of a Finn named Pipa," Hansen said.

"My mother named me Pipa. She is a mestiza."

"A what?" Hansen demanded.

"Indian and Mexican. She is also a bruja."

"A what?" Hansen again demanded.

"That's Spanish for witch," I explained.

"Good," Hansen exulted. "I'll make her a broomstick."

"What was your father's name?" Hansen asked her.

"Aalto," she said. "Paavo Aalto."

Hansen peered down at her. "Paavo Aalto? The bridge builder?" He paused. "Was he the one whose . . . ?"

"Yes, he was," Pipa said in a low voice.

"I'm from Mälmo," Hansen said softly. "My grandparents were on the bridge that day."

There was a long silence while no one seemed to breathe. "Oh," Pipa finally whispered, then more loudly, "I'm from Yuma. My father too was drowned." Then fiercely, "I'm a savage, do you hear?" Tears filled her eyes.

"I hear you," Hansen said, embracing her. "I'm one too."

The tension eased, then Hansen said, "Let me wash up and put on a shirt and I'll show you the old quarry."

Hansen emerged from his trailer, washed clean of stone dust, still wearing only his shorts. "Sorry," he said, "no clean shirts." He led us through scrub oak and manzanita over a spill of fractured granite to the edge of a deep pit in the side of the dome. It held a pool of water and as we approached, swallows darted from their nests on the walls and soared and swooped, skimmed and soared.

"This was the original quarry," Hansen explained. "They abandoned it when they began to use electrolysis. Blasting was too wasteful. You saw the spills. Now they burn the blocks free, then grapple them out. This way they don't lose as much stone. Now it's our springfed reservoir."

"I love water when it's this clean," Pipa said.

"Graham wrote me you were both born on the Colorado River," Hansen said.

"He was born on the wrong side, poor man."

"She's worried that Arizona is not getting its share of water," I said.

213

"I'm on your side," Hansen told her. "California's got too many people and they all wash too much. I don't believe in wasting water."

We sat on the edge of the pool with Hansen between us, watching the swallows. "Look!" Hansen pointed to a larger hovering bird. "Watch!" Suddenly the bird folded its wings and fell like a stone. The swallows scattered while the bird rose with a swallow in its talons. I saw Pipa lay her hand on Hansen's arm.

"It's a falcon," he said. "They strike only birds, especially swallows. Let's go have our lunch."

We ate at a little café store that served the quarry workers and their families. We shared a bottle of red wine from a Madera winery. The obvious sympathy between Pipa and Hansen troubled me. When he asked about her work, she voiced concern for Rainbow Bridge. "Have you been there?" she asked. "No, but I'd like to go," he replied. "Carl told me you never leave here," she said. "I could be persuaded," was his answer. "It's not granite," she said. "It's Navajo sandstone that changes with the light. Can you ride a horse?" "I can ride period," Hansen exulted, filling the room with his voice.

When Pipa went to the rest room, Hansen seized my arm. "Tell her to stop looking at me. She could burn granite with those eyes."

I felt helpless. We walked back to his stoneyard. Pipa stood close to the granite block, pressing her body against it and feeling the roughness with her hand. "What are you doing to it?" she asked softly.

Hansen led her hand to a smooth place. "I'm rubbing it," he said. "When I'm through, the whole stone will shine like this, see? The rubbing does it." He kept his hand on hers, pushing it back and forth on the stone.

I watched from behind them. His body was twice the size of hers. The smell of his sweat was now mingled with the smell of the wine we had drunk. "Carl wants you to make his fountain," Pipa said to Hansen. "Will you make it for me too?" "If you will pose for it," Hansen replied. "I'm not Milles though." "I don't care who you are," Pipa said, "you're a man."

She pushed against him. I saw his body tighten and swell. My mouth was dry, my chest constricted. "Let me see your house," Pipa whispered. She went ahead, pulled open the door and entered. Hansen followed and closed the door behind him.

✿

214

"My God!" Claudia cried. "What did you do?"

"What could I do?" Graham answered. "I was trembling with anger and, also, God help me, with excitement and dread."

I managed to follow them and jerk open the door. Hansen was up against the wall facing me, his face agonized. Pipa was standing against him, her legs apart, her hands grasping his buttocks. Hansen saw me. "For Christ's sake," he gasped, "take her away!"

Pipa turned. Her face was beast-like. I grabbed her and kicked open the door and dragged her out. "Get in, you bitch," I commanded, thrusting her into the back seat of my car and slamming the door. I re-entered the trailer. Hansen was sitting on the edge of the cot, breathing hard. His shorts lay at his feet. "She did it," he said.

"I know," I said, "I'll take her away."

I drove off with Pipa lying on the back seat. All the way back to Madera she lay there in silence, nor did I speak. It was dark when I checked into a motel. She stood in the middle of the room, arms at her sides her face blank. "What are you going to do to me?" she asked. "Undress and find out," I said, Garment by garment she took off her clothes, folded and hung them up, then stood naked before me, her face still a mask. "Take down your hair," I ordered. She unbraided it and let it fall.

I took her by the hair and forced her to her knees. I seized her throat in my hands. She did not resist. I choked off her breath until her face grew even darker, then sank my fingers in her shoulders and jerked her to her feet. She was limp. "If you ever do that again," I said, "I'll kill you."

She stiffened and clung to me and moaned. "Kill me now and get it over with. This is how she made me be. Now you know. I am no good. Please kill me now."

"I love you," I said. "I'll help you be good."

"Please help me," she begged.

I broke then and she undressed me as before, and we fell on the bed and made love. We went crazy. I don't know how long it was, but later I realized that she was asleep beneath me. I stretched out at her side and pulled the sheet over us.

In the morning we made love gently. Later she watched while I shaved. Neither spoke. We showered and dressed and went out for breakfast. After the first cup of coffee she asked, "What becomes of us?" "I don't know," I said.

215

"You nearly choked me to death. Why did you stop?" "I wanted you," I said. "I've never been made love to like that," she said. "Was it hate?" I thought a moment, then said, "Beyond hate. Tell me why you did it. I'll not punish you any more." "You won't have to," Pipa said. "I must know why you did it." "Habit," was her answer. "Every virile male was a challenge." She smiled wantonly. "The Swede was easy." "Were you punishing him for his speaking of your father?" I asked her. "He would have killed me afterward. He knew me for what I was." "What?" "What you called me — a bitch." Her voice was scornful. "You're hard on yourself," I said. "You're kind," she answered.

"Will you still want me?" "More than ever," I said, "but it scares me." "It won't again," Pipa said, "I promise you."

♒

Graham stopped then. Claudia remained silent, then when he did not resume, she said, "Rest awhile, you must be tired. Let me bring you some wine before I get supper on the table."

When she returned, Graham took her hand. "I'm glad you're here."

"Did she ever do that again?"

"No, she was faithful to the end — almost to the end. I made the mistake of telling my wife about Pipa — not about Hansen though."

"What was her reaction?"

"She slapped me with all her might. It nearly blinded me. I left home then and rented a small houseboat on the lake above Imperial Dam. Pipa came weekends. She had moved her mother to a nursing home in Phoenix. *Three at the River Crossing* was rising in me. Pipa had brought me to a boil. The book came with a rush. I wanted to divorce and marry her. She refused. She sent me back to home and campus. She refused to be domesticated, even by me."

"Strange, isn't it?" Claudia mused, "how some do and some don't. Did you see Hansen again?"

♒

We were better friends than ever. We'd been through the fire together. I persuaded the art committee at State to consider the purchase of one of his pieces for the atrium of a new Life Sciences Building. He arrived with it in

216

his pickup, the stone shrouded by a tarpaulin. What the hell is it? I puzzled when he uncovered an abstract sculpture of creamy stone.

"Don't you know travertine when you see it?" he growled. "I've had the piece for years since I was with Milles in Michigan."

I ran my hands over the stone, a larger part of it overhanging a smaller section. "Can't you see it?" Hansen said. "Remember there at the quarry, the falcon and the swallow?"

"Still in your damned bird period," I said. "If you'll label it at least the ornithologists will like it. God knows about the others." It was actually very beautiful.

"What they'll like," Hansen said, "Is my having been Milles's protégé. Your academics don't like things for themselves."

We avoided speaking of Pipa until we had left the sculpture for committee viewing. In an off-campus restaurant drink and food eased us. Hansen laid his rough hand on mine and applied pressure, then asked in a voice heard throughout the room, "Did you?"

"Did I what?"

"He grinned. "Did you take care of her?"

We laughed. "Yes," I said, "I surely did."

"Can you hold her?"

"Can you hold quicksilver?"

"Have you seen her?"

"She's been in Washington."

"Does your wife know?"

"Yes, and she's angry, and even more so about my talk of leaving the University."

"I'll be angrier if you don't," Hansen said. "Is the mother still alive?"

"Pipa doesn't think she has long to live."

"Be careful," Hansen warned me, "at least until the University decides to buy that piece of mine. I'll need you to bull it through."

"Men are better friends to each other than women are," Claudia commented.

"They are more secure."

"We'd better go in and eat," she said. "I'm getting cold."

Claudia served a casserole and salad by the fire. They shared another bottle of Mountain Red.

"I could never compete with such a woman," Claudia said, "either with mind or body."

"You'll never have to. She was one of a kind."

"Did you really want to marry her?"

"She raised me to a new level of awareness and energy. My channels were free and flowing. My wife said I was crazy, that it was a physical attraction that would burn out."

"Did you worry about that?"

"I never had the chance, it all happened so fast. I was fortunate to have had her—and to have lost her."

"Couldn't you have rebuild your marriage?"

"It was blown to bits."

"What became of your wife after the divorce?"

"She married again, a faculty widower with two little girls."

"Is she still living?"

"As far as I know."

"And your boys?"

"They've done well, both in foreign service—one in the State Department, the other in banking. We keep in touch." Graham paused. "Do you realize what you and I are doing?"

"What?"

"Living together."

Claudia laughed. "I like it."

"What would your father say?"

"He'd be speechless."

"Will you bring the children some time?"

"If you'll let me. I'll do the dishes now."

"Let me. You bring in some more wood."

When they were settled again with glasses of port, Claudia asked, "When did you see her next?"

❦

It was at Chicago in March—a Congressional subcommittee hearing on the Great Dam bill. When at the last he was unable to attend, Governor Clayton sent Pipa to give the testimony she had prepared for him. She called me and I flew east on a midnight plane. I reached the Palmer House in time to shave and shower and find the room where the hearing was being presided over by an elderly New England senator.

218

From my seat at the back I saw Pipa in one of the front rows. She appeared to be the only woman present except for the steno reporter. The morning was taken up with statements by spokesmen from the Metropolitan Water District of Southern California, the power companies of both there and Arizona, and the Colorado River growers association.

They all agreed on one thing: there was less water and more need. Hunger for power was also insatiable. The Californians maintained that the basic law of the Southwest was first come, first served, and that there would not be enough water to support the population Arizona was luring by such means as its glamorous highways magazine. Nor would there be enough power generated by the Great Dam to pump water from river level to Phoenix and even higher to Tucson and also provide for Southern California's increasing population and industrial growth. Therefore California must retain its prior rights to the water and power, even though its watershed contributes nothing to the Colorado River. These were the old familiar claims, and I dozed through most of the morning.

When the hearing adjourned for lunch, Pipa came up the aisle, her face stern. When she saw me her look grew tender and she slipped into the seat beside me. "You came! O you came!" she exclaimed.

"You are beautiful in red," I told her.

"Do you like it? I got it yesterday at Marshall Field's. Your Californians are a bad lot. Don't they know history? No culture in the Southwest has ever lasted more than a few centuries. Los Angeles is no different."

"Is that what you are going to tell them?"

"He made me tone down his testimony."

"When will you be called?"

"Probably not until late this afternoon."

"Is there a hearing tonight?"

"No, but I'll have to dine with our people. I'll come as soon as I can. Where are you staying?"

"Here in 1412."

Although it was not until late in the afternoon that Pipa was called, the room came to attention when she took the stand in her tailored suit, dark-skinned, her black hair drawn back, and wearing gold drops in her earlobes. She read in a low voice that was clearly audible in the hushed room.

I had moved down front and to the side from where I could watch the audience watching her. The committee's chief counsel had impressed me earlier by his powerful build and confident manner. He spoke like a Southerner. As the afternoon passed he paid less attention to the testimony,

219

but now that Pipa was speaking, I saw him lean forward and stare at her. She held the room in a kind of electric calm, and I recalled the governor's description of her "little girl's voice." It was full of music.

Her testimony placed the long struggle between the states for the river in the longer struggle of man to survive in an unfriendly land. I was startled to hear a quotation from my own work. Her argument was reasoned and dispassionate and enhanced by her beauty and the sweetness of her voice. The room had become her captive.

When she had finished reading, she turned to the chairman and said, "Mr. Senator, may I add a few words of my own to those of Governor Clayton?"

"Indeed you may," he replied.

Pipa hestitated, then spoke again in a still softer voice, yet with precise and audible enunciation. "It has been a long day, gentlemen, and I know you share my weariness. You have heard much testimony, including my governor's which I was privileged to give—testimony which indicates the conflicting needs of the inhabitants of this ancient land. I should like to speak, if you will bear with me, of the older needs of a people whose descendants still dwell on the river.

"I am one of them, a native Arizonan, born on the eastern bank of the Río Colorado near its union with the Río Gila. From my mother I received the blood of the people whose river it once was, the Indians known as Quechans or Yumas. They were never subdued by Apache, Spaniard, or Mexican invaders. They were a proud people who claimed what was theirs by immemorial ownership, a people willing and able to fight for what was theirs. For unrecorded centuries the spring overflow of the river meant life to these people. In its silt their foods were grown—squash and beans and melons—while from reeds and willows they wove articles of raiment and other usages."

At that point Pipa paused and looked inquiringly at the chairman. He nodded gravely. The room seemed suspended on a single held breath. Again she spoke, and in an even softer voice. "Now the dams of an alien people have ended those lifegiving overflows and diverted the water to distant lands. The source of our life and well-being has been dammed and drained off by and for people who have never seen nor ever will see the river, by a people to whom water is merely something that flows from a faucet, by a people who waste far more than they use. To my people and to me, Mr. Senator, this is sinful, for to us desert people water is the most sacred of the elements."

Again she paused and her eyes searched the room and found mine. I could hear my heart listening. She spoke again in a faraway voice that somehow filled the room. "I have a friend, a Californian born on the other side of the river. His dream is of an historical fountain on the river at Yuma which would also be a shrine to the sacredness of water. Although as an Arizonan I am in a sense his enemy, I am also his friend and I share his dream." She stopped then and the room waited for her to resume. "I can add no facts to those I have submitted for Governor Clayton. I can only ask, Mr. Senator and gentlemen, that you consider this problem and these conflicting needs as more than facts, as more than economics and the hydraulics of languid and turbulent flow. I ask you to think of them also as a matter of religion, and to think of water, as I do, as an element of equal sacredness with air."

Her voice dwindled almost to a whisper and yet was still audible because of the precision with which she spoke. The entire room had leaned forward and heard her say in conclusion, "There is a god who dwells in the sky and to him most of you pray. Yet there are also gods who dwell in the river; they are the gods to whom I and my people pray. These gods must be appeased if they are not to turn against us. Drought could come again as it did in the thirteenth century when it lasted for thirty years and brought to an end the predominant culture. California could not survive such a drought. Even the creosote bush would die.

"I have spoken for my governor and for that part of me that is loyal to him and to our commonwealth, and I ask you to bear witness to the respect in which I hold him and the land of which we are the present inhabitants. With your permission, Mr. Senator, an older and more primitive part of me has spoken for my people who have no one else to speak for them. I have sought also to speak for our gods, theirs and mine, for those river gods who in the end will speak for themselves. I thank you for hearing my words."

Like a red feather she went to her seat. There was a long silence, and then a collective sigh as the room drew breath. At last the chairman spoke, with grave courtesy and in a tired voice. "We have heard your words, Miss Aalto, and I assure you that we have also heard more than your words. We have heard your people and your gods speaking through you. In all my years in the Senate I have never before heard such words. We are deeply moved. Their claim will be considered, I assure you." He rapped with his gavel. "Gentlemen, Miss Aalto, the hearing is adjourned."

The room rose in noisy relief. I waited at the side as an approving crowd surrounded Pipa. Then I saw the chief counsel push through to her,

221

dwarfing her by his size. Although I could not hear what he said when he reached her side, I saw her stare and then nod her head. My heart beat wildly and I felt sick. As the room cleared I stood against the wall as she went out with him, not looking my way.

My anguish was deeper than jealousy. I went to my room for overcoat, hat and gloves, and made my way to the lakefront. The cold was bitter. The traffic in the streets and on the sidewalks, the lights of cars and signs and the swarming people were hell itself. I walked far down the lake and back. Later I ate a sandwich and drank milk and coffee at a snack bar, then returned to my room and waited for her to call or come. The hours passed. I was tormented by the vision of her body arching to his thrusts. I hammered the bed with my fists. At last I dozed.

Some time in the night I was awakened by a knock. I went to the door. It was Pipa. We embraced silently. "Are you all right?" she finally whispered.

"I thought you'd never come."

"Do you still want me?"

My heart sank. "You have been with him?"

She laughed softly. "Yes and no. I've been good, very good, the goodest I've ever been in all my wicked life." She locked the door. "Get undressed. You shouldn't sleep in your clothes."

That time none of our clothes were folded or hung up.

Only when the afterglow had faded did she speak. "He said he could be of help to Arizona if . . . "

"If what?"

"If I'd take him as a lover."

"Was that what he said to you after the hearing?"

"He said if I'd have dinner with him, he would provide me with information of value."

"And so?"

"And so I went to dinner with him."

"Where?"

"To the Blackhawk restaurant. It's near here on Randolph. We had scotch and soda—he the scotch and I the soda—and then he got down to business."

"What happened?"

"He didn't waste words."

"What did he say?"

"He said, 'Jesus, I'd love to fuck you!' "

"What did you say?"

"I said. Thank you, sir, but I'm well taken care of."

"What did he say to that?"

"He said, The lucky bastard!" Pipa laughed. "That's you, darling."

"Were you tempted?"

"I would have been a year ago, if only to see if he were as good as he made himself out to be. The big ones often aren't."

"What took you so long?"

"Poor dear, I ate two dinners I was so hungry."

"Did you go to his room?"

"I came to yours. Couldn't you hear me running down the hall?"

"Did you plan those last remarks?"

"They just came. Knowing you were there was part of it. He'll kill me when he reads the transcript. I'm finding it hard to believe in any more dams. How long will it take them to silt up?"

"Ask your mother."

"She grows weaker."

"I took her in my arms. "One more?" I asked her.

"O darling, I'm so tired."

And with that she fell asleep. I awoke in the night, pulled the drapes and looked out. It was snowing like it was here last night. Her sleeping face was a girl's, an angel's.

Claudia stood up then and said, "Let me stretch and get a bit of fresh air." She opened the door and soon closed it. "You were right. It's very cold."

We awoke to a white world. The desk reported blizzard conditions. I called the airline. Midway was closed, all flights cancelled. When Pipa emerged from the shower, I told her. "Good," she said, "we can live here till it clears."

"I've got to be back in California," I told her. "I'll call the Santa Fe and see if we can get space on the Chief tonight." Our luck held. I got the last bedroom.

It was noon before we went down for lunch. Afterward we managed to reach the Art Institute where we spent the afternoon. She loved a painting *in tempera by Andrew Wyeth of a reedy riverbank, its sandy texture infinitely real. "Would he come and paint our riverbank?" Pipa wondered. "It reminds me of your words about the river gods," I told her.*

And so we wandered from room to room, pausing and commenting on what held us, and letting our words go beyond pictures and sculptures back over our lives that had finally merged. We saw many lovely things: Monet's Gare St. Lazare and Blue Boat, Seurat's Grande Jatte, a virile Rodin bronze, and Mestrovic's woodcarving of the Deposition. Through the windows we could see the falling snow.

At closing time we were lucky to get a taxi to the hotel where we picked up our bags and went on to Dearborn Station. There in the buffet we were served by an elderly Fred Harvey waitress in starched cap and apron. We ate side by side on the leather banquette, our backs to the gilt mirrors and murals of the lands served by the Santa Fe.

When the Chief was called for Kansas City, La Junta, Albuquerque, Flagstaff and Los Angeles, we found our Pullman, Toroweap, and then walked to the head of the train just as the red and gold Diesel coupled with the mail car. The engineer, capped and gloved, looked down on us from his throne.

"What's the weather ahead?" I asked.

"Snow."

"Keep warm," Pipa called up to him.

The engineer smiled at last.

When the train had cleared the station and yards and was running fast through the suburbs, we lay in the lower berth with the shade up and looked out on the driving snow, the headlights of cars at crossing gates, and the glow of curtained windows. To the sound of wheels over the rail points and the incessant homing of the engine, we finally slept.

I was awakened in the night by the train's stopping. The Diesel blasted imperiously, then began to move again, slowly and smoothly, a master's hand on the throttle. I raised the shade and looked out. We were on a long bridge with broken ice below. I gathered Pipa in my arms. "Wake up," I said, "we're crossing it."

"I'm asleep," she protested.

"Wake up," I insisted, "it's the Mississippi."

She pressed her face against the cold glass. "Wrong river," she sighed and fell back.

All the next day we stayed in our bedroom and had meals sent in. Pipa worked on her summary of the hearing, I on my Yuma Crossing book. In

224

Albuquerque we walked the length of the platform, our breaths frosty in the clear air. Along the Navajo reservation were scattered hogans and huddled sheep, women in purple velvet skirts, and pickup trucks loaded with whole families. On a siding at Ribera we waited for the eastbound Chief. Now the red earth was greened with piñon and juniper.

We had lost time and it was late at night when we reached Flagstaff. The snow was deep. Pipa had left her car at the station. We scraped the windows free, fired up, then shopped for breakfast at an all-night grocery and drove to her apartment in the pines near the museum.

She switched on lamp and furnace. I saw a floor rug of gray and red, and monk's cloth drapes with a sunburst pattern in red. Couch bed, easy chair, desk and chair, bookshelves. A black and white photograph of Rainbow Bridge, a color photo of Roosevelt Dam spilling over. Walk-in closet with a few clothes on hangers. A chest of drawers. Bath and kitchen.

"You see all my worldly goods," Pipa said, "and still too many. I gave the museum my pots and baskets. One picture's enough. You can have the one of the dam, damn you!"

"Where's the mirror?" I asked in the morning when I went to shave.

"I don't need a mirror to tell me I'm not as beautiful as I used to be." She stretched out on the bed. "At least my legs still are." She rose and began to dress. "I'll drive you to Phoenix and you can fly back from there. I have a tiny apartment near the capitol. When can you get away again?"

"There's a Bureau meeting at Albuquerque in September I'd like to cover. Can you come to that?"

"If I'm alive. I'm afraid to face him. I'm beginning to realize I'm the wrong one for him. He demands blind loyalty. He won't recognize that he and his party in power are tenants not owners."

"How can I help?"

"I'll be all right when the time comes. If the weather were clear I'd like us to see the dam site and the canyon before it's flooded. We could sleep on the shoulder of Navajo Mountain and then make the bridge on horseback. Instead it's down off the Rim."

We ate breakfast and set out. When we had descended through the red rock country into the Verde Valley, the weather was warmer. We saw the river's course lined with silver gray cottonwoods, and the west walled by Mingus Mountain.

"I might settle here when she's gone" Pipa said. "It's handy to museum and capitol. It's not as hot as Yuma nor as cold as Flagstaff and there are ruins everywhere. How are you on the end of a shovel?"

225

"I'm still tied to campus, though Hansen is doing his best to cut the cord." It was the first time his name had been mentioned.

"You've seen him?"

I told her about his sculpture of the falcon and swallow.

"Did he talk about what I . . . about . . . " she hesitated.

"He asked me if I'd taken care of you," I replied.

"What did you tell him?"

"I said I had."

"That you'd punished me?"

"No, I didn't. That I love you. We also talked about the fountain, about your posing for him."

Pipa gave me a sidelong smile, slightly wanton. "We'd better let him do it from a photograph," she said, then added, "I've one of me as a girl — naked — Edward Weston took it."

We parted at the Phoenix airport and I was back in California in another hour.

"So she wanted to settle in the Verde Valley!" Claudia said when Graham came in with more wood, "Will she haunt me?"

"Her ghost is at the river crossing. Mine will be there too. Are you tired? Shall we call it a night?"

"I won't be able to sleep until I know how it ended."

Graham put a log on the fire and resumed his tale.

Spring came and then summer before we met again. My reclamation book brought a letter from Governor Clayton, inviting me to visit him. Pipa met me at the airport. "It's been a long time," she said. "I was afraid we'd come apart."

I was shocked by how much older she looked. "You're tired," I said to her.

"It's the heat," she replied. "You'd think a Yuma girl could take Phoenix. Give me Helsinki!"

"What does he want, do you know?" I asked.

"He wouldn't tell me. Something came up suddenly this morning, otherwise he was planning to meet you himself."

"Does he know about us?"

226

"Who knows what a politician knows?"

When we reached the copper-domed capitol, I said to Pipa, "It's more than the heat. What is it?"

"I've had to commit her. She began running away from the nursing home. They'd pick her up and call me from the police station and I'd have to take her back and spend the night by her bed."

"I don't understand your devotion to her. You keep saying you wish she would die."

"You should know by now how ambivalent I am about everything."

"Even me?"

"Even you, Californian!" Her voice was scornful, and then she added, "Man I love."

The governor received me in his sumptuous office with its flags of nation and state and portraits of former governors. I thanked him for sending Pipa to meet me and also for having expedited her mother's commitment to the state hospital.

"I'm worried about the girl," he said. "She's always had this love-hate relationship with her mother. I hope the old woman's death will end it. Have you ever met her?"

"Once. She scared me."

"All of Yuma was relieved when Pipa brought her up here."

"I was shocked to see how Pipa has aged."

"If and when we get the bill through, I want her to go back for the degree. I can arrange for a leave with pay."

"Why is it so important to you?" I asked the governor.

"I see a more lucrative future for her if she is Doctor Aalto, although I must admit, her needs are spartan. I hope you will influence her. She is devoted to you, as you must know. Where would you be at your university, my friend, if you were plain Mister Graham?"

"I recognize the mystique of the PhD," I said, "and also the mystique of Miss Aalto. She'd have it even if she were an eighth grade dropout."

"I trust you haven't forgotten my proclamation that night. She'll be Miss Arizona to the grave."

I kept waiting for the governor to reach the point of his invitation. "Has your leave ended?" he finally asked.

"I go back in the fall," I said. "I've got to decide whether it's to be administration or research and writing. They want me to be the executive dean."

"I suppose it pays well."

"Very well."

*"Don't make any decision until we've had a chance to talk again. I hope
to have something of interest to you on this side of the river. I expected to
be able to do so today, but I have had an urgent call from Washington and
have to be there for an early morning hearing. I tried to reach you but you
had already left. I hope it hasn't been too much of an inconvenience. If you
will sign this voucher—all five copies, please—I'll have a check for you while
you wait. You will see that I have added an honorarium. I trust you will
find Pipa an acceptable deputy."* The governor seized my hand and ushered
me out. I found Pipa waiting in the archives reading room.

"He just broke my hand," I said. "And I still don't know what he wanted.
Is he always this opaque? Now he's off to Washington. You don't have to
go too, do you?"

"He expected me to," Pipa said, "but when I pointed out that you needed
an escort, he agreed to take only his chief counsel. He should have been
there all week. He's depended too much on me. The hospital just called. She
keeps asking for me. Will you come with me?"

The sun was at zenith, the furnace heat nearly unbearable. As we drove
through the humid city we talked about what would happen if the rivers
ran dry as they had before in prolonged drought. The ground water would
soon be sucked up, the people drift away and the tall buildings stand empty.
"Probably a good thing," Pipa said.

We found the hospital grounds under flood irrigation, date palms and
bitter orange trees standing in pools of water, while black birds splashed and
preened and Inca doves cooed incessantly. White-gowned patients with
grounds privileges wandered about or sat in the shade.

Her mother was confined in a ward behind double-locked doors. We saw
her standing in a corner. "She's gone catatonic," the technician said as she
led us across the room peopled with disturbed women of all ages. The air
stunk of sweat and drugs and urine. Two old women were quarreling pitifully. Others sat alone and rocked or mumbled or hummed.

There was no recognition in the bruja's eyes as she stared at me. Her face
was thinner than I remembered it, her eyes like bits of obsidian.

"Mi madre," Pipa pleaded, "won't you speak to me?"

The old woman kept staring at me, and as she regathered her white
gown, I saw the blue shell hanging from the chain around her neck. Her
hands quickly drew the gown over it.

"Sit down," Pipa said, pulling up a chair. "You are wobbling."

Her mother obeyed, although she would not speak nor look up.

After a futile wait Pipa began to cry and I led her away. "Why won't she die?" she burst out when we reached the car. "Why must she always punish me?"

"She knows I'm not Sam Graham. She calls you to punish you. Stop going and she will die."

"Don't reason with me." Pipa cried. "Just tell me you love me."

"I most unreasonably do. Do you love me?"

"Oh, but I do! You're the one I've been waiting for all my life, the one who is giving voice to the river and the crossing."

"To our homeland," I said.

As we drove back to the capitol a windstorm enveloped us in a cloud of sand. Daylight grew dim. Cars turned on their headlights. "A horrible place," Pipa said. "Why did I ever leave the Rim?"

That night I read her a chapter from the river crossing book. "Yes," she said, "Oh yes!"

"That's what you've done for me," I told her. "Can you still get away in September?"

"Not for more than overnight unless she gets better—or dies. They say it can't be much longer."

We met as planned at Albuquerque, even though the Bureau meeting was postponed. My plane landed in wind and rain, hers also was late. By then the wind had dropped, the rain slackened, and the clouds opened to show blue sky over the Sandias. Pipa came down the steps wearing a white tailored suit, a turquoise scarf at her throat. She ran to my arms, oblivious of the jostling passengers.

"Are you all right?" she asked.

"I'm fine," I said. "What about you? Was your flight as rough as ours?"

"I was sick."

We rested in the lobby. I looked at her sombre face. "How is she?" I asked.

Pipa gripped my hand. "She's dead."

"When did she die?"

"I can't remember. Was it day before yesterday?"

"Why didn't you call me?"

"All I could do was come to you. We flew her to Yuma in the governor's plane. He was wonderful."

"You buried her there?"

"By the river near the willows."

"Like I said."

229

"I persuaded a priest to say a mass for her." Pipa smiled weakly. "It helped that I'd once had him before he became a priest."

"Can you eat something?"

"Poor dear, you must be starved."

When a strolling guitarist came to our table in the dining room, Pipa asked him in Spanish to play Los Colores. It was her father's favorite, her mother once told her.

Food and wine revived her. As her face relaxed, she looked like a girl again. She was wearing the blue shell and silver chain. I reached out, then drew back. "Must you wear it?" I asked.

"She asked me to. I couldn't refuse her last wish."

"I don't like it," I said. "Where is the one you wore that night?"

"The squash blossom? I don't wear it any more."

"Why not?"

"It means that the wearer is marriageable. That night I thought perhaps I was. I was wrong."

"Would you if I were free?"

"It's the same old answer. I'm not made for marriage."

"I don't understand you."

"Men never have."

We ate in silence, then she asked. "Where are we going?"

"Where do you want to go?"

"Where it's cool."

"The Gila wilderness?"

"Too hot getting there. Let's go up river."

When we reached our motel, I backed her to the bed.

It was not until afterward that we undressed. She fell asleep at once.

The morning was clear and we took the river road north through Bernalillo, the mountains on either side: Sandias, Jémez and Sangre de Cristos. After lunch at La Fonda in Santa Fe, we entered the cathedral and sat in a back pew as worshippers came and knelt and went. A mass for the dead began. The coffin was carried in to the altar. An old woman in black threw herself sobbing on the coffin. Her family lifted her up and led her back to the front pew. Pipa's lips moved with the Latin. The bell tolled. I crossed myself and knelt.

"May I?" Pipa whispered. She knelt and we prayed together.

"Do you go to confession?" she whispered.

"Not since we met."

"Maybe you should—for us both. I haven't gone since I was a girl." She smiled. "They grew tired of hearing me."

Beyond the city where the river enters the gorge, we stopped by a rickety suspension bridge and walked out on the swaying structure. A bluebird lit on the rusty cable, then flew away. "Good omen," I said.

We watched the river coming toward us, rounding the bend and riffling into rapids, then flowing smoothly beneath us where we sat on the planks and dangled our legs. Although the stream was diminished after the summer takeoff for irrigation, it was still a great river, bearing life to the lands all the way to the Gulf.

As we watched the swallows skim and soar, I said, "You have not told me how she died."

"I didn't want to. It took a long time, I helped lay her out and dress her in her gray robe. I washed it first. Then I went with her in his plane and saw them dig the grave and remove the stones and cover her with earth."

"None of that is bad."

"I haven't told you. She died cursing."

"My father?"

"She cursed you both. It was awful—a gabble of words and sounds. I nearly died. Then she cursed us. I prayed for her to die."

"Did they dig a deep grave?"

"So deep the coffin looked lost."

We stood up and kissed while the bridge swayed and the river ran on beneath us. We walked back to the shore and made our way along the bank through the willows to a nest of dry grass. There we lay down together. Afterward we looked up through the foliage to the cliffs of the gorge, ochre and amethyst, spilling down to the road in a tumult of fractured rock. There was silver sage among the willows. Our bodies crushed it and released the acrid fragrance.

"Mi madre," Pipa murmured. "Artemesia Aalto."

"Artemesia tridentata," I said, "good for what ails you."

"Hold me," she cried, "and never let me go."

❦

Graham paused when he saw a tear on Claudia's cheek. He took her hand. "Don't cry. We're all right."

❦

Beyond Taos we drove to the pueblo and on a log over the creek we sat and ate ripe plums. I remember how minnows tore at the pits as they sank through the clear water. "There's been no violence here for a hundred years," I mused. "I wish there could be peace between our states. Now the Metropolitan Water District is lobbying against the San Juan scheme that would divert water into the Rio Grande basin. They claim it is water that would otherwise reach the Colorado and be California's. If the barbecue had been on the other side of the river, I'd be your fellow Arizonan."

"You came too late," Pipa said. "How can I go on working for a project that will drown what I love?"

We unfolded the road map and charted our course into the Sangres. Thunderheads were forming as we drove toward Questa and we saw long tiger-stripes of lightning slash across the sky.

"I'm not used to being reconciled with anyone." Pipa said. "All my life I have fought with friend and foe alike. He was angry when he read the transcript of the Chicago hearing. Stop pretending to be an Indian, he said, you are not even a half-breed."

"Could you have him now?" I asked her.

"Power has corrupted him. Don't let it happen to you."

"What should I do with my life?"

"What you're doing—fieldwork and writing. That's why I believe in you."

"Her belief was what I needed," Graham said to Claudia. "She gave me belief beyond myself. I have never lost it."

Beyond Questa a gravelled road followed a tributary deep into the Sangres. Vacationers had left. Where the canyon narrowed and the road ended, we came upon a year-round camp-store serving fishers and skiers. There we rented a housekeeping cabin from whose porch we looked up to the shoulder of Mt. Wheeler. There were perennial snowbanks above timberline.

Our life was so idyllic that I abandoned my plan to follow the Rio Grande to the South Fork and thence over Wolf Creek Pass to the headwaters of the San Juan. Later, I said to Pipa when she questioned me, it will be a reason to meet in the spring. "If we could only winter here," she said, pointing to

232

the snow on Wheeler. "It would be very deep. I could lie down and let death come. They say it is painless."

"Why are you so morbid?"

"I thought her death would free me."

"Give it time."

"How can I go on living after we leave here?"

My answer was to carry her in to the creaky bed. Later we heard the roll of thunder and the rattle of hail on the sheet-iron roof.

At the store we bought a slab of sirloin and each night cut steaks for broiling. After supper we read by lamplight to the flutter of dying moths, then stood on the porch, heard the water on the stones and breathed the incense of streambed. The sky was swarming with stars, the earth seemed to be dissolving beneath us. Each morning before daybreak a thrush sang. Each morning I roused her to hear our bird of dawning. Her lips sought mine as she drew me down to her.

On our last day we walked over a trail to the Blue Lake of the Taoseños. By the water's edge we ate our bread and cheese and drank snowmelt, then lay on the needled ground and dozed. We were high in the Canadian lifezone of blue spruce and quaking aspen. The first freezing nights had colored their leaves. We were alone, anonymous and at peace, never to go higher.

That night we sat in the car and listened to a radio concert from Denver, crackling with static. They played the Grieg concerto. So bemused were we that the old warhorse sounded new. Pipa protested when it ended and I opened the car door. In bed she cried for the first time. Later I heard her talking in her sleep. I leaned on my elbow and listened. Her voice was a whisper from faraway.

In the morning she was withdrawn, her face blank. On the long drive down the little river to the big river and beyond, she remained silent. In exasperation I finally pulled to the side of the road and exclaimed. "Why punish me? Do you think you're your mother?"

"Christ in heaven! Can't you see that I don't know who I am?"

I sought to comfort her. She regained control as we drove on to Albuquerque and the heat of late summer. "I'll always hate it," she said as we boarded our flight to Phoenix.

"You should have been born on the cool side of the river," I said, "the way I was."

"On an island," she replied, "then there would be no river between. Only river around."

Our flight was through towering thundercaps. Pipa lay back while the

233

plane lurched and dropped and rose and kept flying. I held her hand. There was no more to say.

We slept that night in her apartment. I watched her undress, marveling at her unblemished body. When she was naked save for the necklace, she lay down beside me and we fell asleep.

In the night I awoke and felt for her. She was not in the bed. I heard her in the bathroom. Was she ill? I was not used to her getting up before morning. I raised on my elbow and listened. There was a clicking sound and then she came toward the bed, walking stiffly as though asleep. She sat on the edge of the bed and groped for my hand. I felt cold metal against my wrist. I jerked away and rolled off the other side of the bed.

"What are you doing? I demanded.

She answered in a hollow voice, "She told me to."

"Who told you to what?"

"She told me to kill Sam Graham—that he had come back to torment her."

I stood over her and shouted, "Wrong Graham, do you hear?" I seized her by the shoulders and shook her. "Pipa, wake up! I'm Carl." Her eyes were blank. "Give me what's in your hand," I commanded. She held out her hand and I took the razor blade and flung it across the room. Then I shook her even more violently until she fell limply across the bed.

I laid her with her head on the pillow and slipped the necklace off and put it in the pocket of my coat. Then I covered her with the sheet. For the rest of the night I dozed in a chair beside the bed.

I awoke early and made coffee. When I brought her a cup in bed, she asked, "Was it a nightmare?"

"No," I said, "it wasn't."

She cried out in anguish. The coffee spilled and burned my leg. "Where is it?" she asked, feeling for the necklace.

"I have it and I'm keeping it."

We were silent. For the first time I was afraid. "What shall I do?" she finally asked.

"I don't know. I've never loved a witch's daughter."

"Don't joke," she said, then added, "you'll be afraid to sleep with me."

I made fresh coffee and we drank it in silence, propped side by side in bed.

"What are you going to do?" she asked.

"I don't know."

"I saw them shovel the earth over her," Pipa said. "Tell me, is there something that survives? You believe there is, don't you?"

234

"I did."

"I heard her as plainly as I hear you now. Tell me you love me."

"I don't know how not to."

"Do you have a gun?" Pipa asked.

"Not here. Why?"

"I remember her once saying never kill an owl — that her life and the owl's life were linked — that an owl's death would be fatal for her."

"What are you telling me?"

"Find an owl and kill it."

"I used to hunt with a sling," I said.

"I don't care what you use."

"I'll shave now."

While shaving I came to a decision. "I'm going to fly back that way," I told Pipa, "and find her grave."

She drove me to the airport where I ordered a rental car for my arrival in Yuma.

Summer's hold on the river town had not relaxed. As the DC-3 began its bucking descent to the Marine base airfield, I looked down on long fields of grain in the stages of green and gold. Far up the Gila dark groves of oranges and grapefruit marked the course of the tributary. Below the dams the Colorado lazed its way to the Gulf. Beyond the river lay the Algodones dunes. This was our homeland.

I found the graveyard in the barrio, hedged by white oleanders in flower. As I sought the grave of Artemesia Aalto, I felt both fear and confidence. Was she not dead and I alive? At last I found it in a far corner, the fresh earth bearing a headboard with her name and dates of birth and death. Until then I had been soaked with sweat. Now I was suddenly dry and shivering. What should I do?

As I rested by the oleanders, my eye fell upon the heap of stones left by the gravediggers. Then I knew what to do. One by one I carried the stones to her grave, covered the mound and built a wall around it. As I toiled I made a prayer against evil, saying it over and over in an obsessive litany. By the time I had carried all the stones, I was again dripping with sweat and exhausted.

※

Claudia reached for Graham's hand and held it. He rested his voice, then resumed.

THE EVENING REDNESS

I leaned against my wall of stones and when I rested I took the necklace from my pocket and I said, "Old woman, your magic is now my magic, your girl is now my girl. Go to Paavo. Go to Palma and tell him he will be honored. If you should try to escape again, I will dig up your bones and throw them to the dogs that run the barrio. Do you hear me, witch, do you hear me? May God damn you to hell if you ever come back and haunt us!" Then I stood spraddle-legged and pissed on her grave. I watched the last drops soak away among the stones and be lost.

I made my way to the car and rested until I had stopped trembling and the sweat had dried. My hands were raw and bleeding. I hardly knew where I was or what I had done. I only knew that I had freed us.

I went to the motel where Pipa and I had first met, washed my hands and face in warm water, then drove across the bridge and up river. At the turnoff to the plaza where Pipa had taken me to the cat woman's shack, I saw the same woman at the group of mail boxes. She did not look up nor did I slow down. When I came to Laguna Dam I looked for the boys in the pool. No one was there. The heat was unmerciful. Dust devils were spinning around me.

When I reached Imperial Dam I parked in the shade of the cottonwoods and walked out on the barrier. Again I gazed past the desilting basins and bobbing birds and stands of arrow-weed and tules to the blue mountains, shimmering in the heat. There in the blazing light I heard the water sluicing through the gates with a muffled roar. The spray was cool on my face, and I prayed, "O father dear, come and help me hold my girl. Why must the old sorrow be visited on us? Hear me, father, and help me, I pray to you and to our Lord Jesus Christ."

I took the necklace from my pocket and laid it on the cement. With my heel I ground the blue shell to bits. With my hands I tore the silver links apart and cast the wreckage as far as I could. It seemed to hang a moment against the sky, then it fell and was lost in the turbulent flow.

Pipa and I did not meet for months, although we corresponded nearly every week. Her letters were typed now, more professional than personal, as she responded to my work and wrote me of hers. Her precise typing and the flowing lines of the loving postscript she always added in her own hand could not conceal her agony of divided loyalty as she continued to serve a government whose policy she no longer believed in. Most of the winter she was in Washington with the state's delegation. Her ambivalence grew more painful. I'm afraid to meet again, she wrote as spring came. It would not be kind to burden you with my troubles and yet I long to see you, wrong-side-of-the-river boy. The snow up there must still be deep. Can we go again when the aspens begin to tremble?

Lars Hansen came to campus for the dedication of his sculpture. He wore corduroys, moccasins, and a turtleneck sweater. His skin was golden and his hair now hung to his shoulders. After a ceremony in the atrium marked by his charmingly tongue-tied response, we strolled through the art museum.

"What junk!" he scorned. "I'm glad my birds are roosting outdoors. Look at that bicycle rack! I could enter it at the County Fair as 'Parallel Tubular Concept, Number Three' and win the blue ribbon."

I laughed and he asked, "Who was that little guy who spoke?"

"That's our librarian. He's got a collection of dirty books in his office. When he wants something special from faculty or administration, he lets them borrow. He knows that academic man would rather look than do."

"I like to do both," Hansen smiled. "Have you seen her?"

"Not since she tried to kill me."

"You said what?" Hansen shouted.

I told him what had happened and what I had done afterward. "If you'll buy the granite," he said, "I'll haul over a chunk she'll never be able to get out from under." Hansen laid his hand on my arm and grinned. "Pissing on her grave was a nice touch."

"It was the best I could do. After all, I'm only an amateur exorcist."

"Are you still hot to marry her?" Hansen asked.

"She hates marriage and children."

"Hates what she's never had."

I left Lars Hansen, envying him his singleness and his freedom.

※

"What became of him?" Claudia asked.

"He set out to cross the Sierra in winter on skis and was never seen again. An avalanche probably got him. His bones are up there somewhere. That's what he would have wanted. I'll take you to see

237

his falcon and swallow, if you like. When I think of his being dead for twenty years, then I know I'm old."

Claudia reached again for Graham's hand. "What became of her?"

I'll tell you. We met a last time in Albuquerque. It was in April. Dust had hidden the Sandias. This time she walked toward me. Her face looked old.

"I came," was all she said as I took her in my arms.

We ate dinner in Old Town. Her lips were thin. I fought against seeing her mother's face.

"I can't take it any more," she said after ordering a second drink. "I told him I'm going back to the museum. It's been horrible in Washington. Your people and ours are sleeping together."

"And so are we," I thought.

"No one believes in anything any more."

"What's happened to the bill?"

"It passed both houses and is on the president's desk. I was with Clayton and our delegation when we waited on the president."

"What do you think he will do?"

"He gave no indication," Pipa said. "Afterward at lunch I got tight and said to the governor, I hope he vetoes it. He would have hit me if I had been a man."

"Is this your final revenge on him?"

"I hate living in two pieces. Can't you put me back together? You did once."

"Do you still love me?" I asked her.

"I'm not the girl you knew."

"What are you going to do?"

"Have another drink."

"We're going to eat and then we're going to bed."

At the motel Pipa backed me to the bed before I could undress. "You've never been like this," I said.

"Do you want to go home?"

"I've lost the way."

"You should have stayed on your side of the river."

"Get hold of yourself," I said to her. "You'll feel better in the morning."

"Who am I?" Her voice rose. "You must tell me. I've got to know. I can't go on living like this."

When I tried to calm her, she grew even more disturbed. "I should never have left Flagstaff," she cried. "I think we'd better separate."

"Not until we've made love again."

"What if I don't want to?"

"I'll make you like it," I shouted. But I couldn't.

We felt better in the morning as again we took the river road north. The clouds were gathering early, the sky was blue between the billows. For a last time we were bonded by landscape as we followed the Río Grande toward its source.

Pipa spoke of the winter in Washington. "You think I'm wicked? Let me tell you what they wanted me to do the night before the House hearing." I waited for her to speak. "They asked me to go to dinner with the spokesman for the conservationists and get him drunk, then take him to bed and keep him there until the hearing was over."

"Did you?"

Pipa smiled wanly. "Don't think I wasn't tempted! He's a wonderful man, all mind and muscle and voice."

"What did you say to the governor?"

"I told him our contract was for my mind, not my body. The bill passed in spite of the various efforts to save the canyon and the bridge. That's when I told him I'd had enough."

Beyond Española the road rejoined the river, then passed the cherry orchards in new leaf and entered the gorge that bears it into Colorado and its source in the San Juan Rockies. When we came to the suspension bridge, I pulled up by the willows. "They were yellowing then," I said, "now they are green."

"No use," Pipa said, "I've yellowed."

After the river had emerged from the gorge I paused again for the view over the Taos plain, gray-green with artemesia, clear to the Sangre de Cristos.

"Can we stay here tonight?" Pipa asked.

"We need to make Alamosa and then the pass tomorrow. I made a rendezvous with the project engineer. It would be too far to drive if we stayed here tonight."

When we had left Taos and reached the little tributary at Questa, Pipa grasped the wheel. "Turn here," she begged, "Pipa wants to play in the snow."

"Don't say that," I warned her.

"Then take me where his bridges are—the ones that never failed. Why can't I be his daughter?"

As we drove into Colorado she began to muse on her past. "It was beautiful there that summer," she said. "The ruins had never been disturbed for ages. I was so excited he had to remind me what we had come for. He was my first cowboy. I don't remember his name. His legs were so hairy he didn't need chaps. He toughened me on a packtrip to Georgetown. They mined for copper there. It was Apache country. Mimbreño Apaches. Mangas Coloradas was their chief. There was a little graveyard gone to ruin. I thought what a beautiful place to sleep. He laid me on a grave. I imagined he was Mangas. I looked up at a hawk looking down on us. It was a big redtail."

And so her mind wandered back as I listened silently.

Nearing Alamosa we saw the sand dunes at the base of the Sangres and in the west the faint line of the San Juans. In town we found a motel on the lake formed by a weir on the river, and after dinner we sat on the porch and watched children sailing their little boats.

"You talked in your sleep once," I said to Pipa. "I could barely make out what you were saying."

"What did I say?"

"I think what you said was that we would have had a beautiful child."

Pipa laughed scornfully. "That proves I'm crazy!"

Next morning we pressed on up the San Luis valley, following the river as the mountains closed in. Near the South Fork I stopped at a bridge and we saw the stream running high with snowmelt and roiling with flotsam.

We stood at the railing, and Pipa said, "I can hardly bear to see such beautiful water."

"It is truly El Río Bravo del Norte."

"Tell me, is there a way to escape from her?"

"You know she's dead," I said.

"But I'm not."

"See how the water makes a golden track in the sunlight."

"Will you follow me if I go?"

"I want to live."

"Pity me who wants to die."

We turned at the South Fork and began to climb to Wolf Creek Pass. As the canyon narrowed, the water fell in thunder, pounding over the rocks to union with the great river. I stopped again and we stood by the bank.

240

"No dam on this one!" I shouted above the roar. We kissed long and hard, our faces wet with spray. I felt her come to life.

"Remember what you said," she cried, "that night when you kissed me for the first time?"

"What did I say?"

"That we were two rivers of parallel blood that had come together."

On and up we climbed into aspen and fir. Nearing the summit the road was walled by snowbanks. At the Continental Divide a narrow track of decomposed granite led to a treeless knoll posted with warnings against lightning. Although the sky was clear, we did not tarry. Now we saw the runoff melting in a network of seep and trickle, coalescing to form the San Juan.

At an overlook below the pass I found the diversion yard and the superintendent's shack. "Wait for me," I said to Pipa, "and don't play in the snow."

"I'll be good," she promised.

I must have been gone for a couple of hours. I returned with a heavy carton. "Duplicates he had made for me," I exulted.

"Must you always leave me?" she asked.

"You're beautiful when you're sad," I told her.

"Do my bones show?" she asked. "I feel bare."

"I realized later," Graham told Claudia, "that this was a turning point. I should have held her and comforted her. Instead I talked on and on about my own work."

Pipa finally interrupted me, and said, "I wish I could believe the way you do. I did once. The last time was that summer in the Gila wilderness. Did I ever tell you about it? I was only a girl. I felt bare then like I do now, naked and bare, beyond vulnerability. It was as if I had escaped from my skin. Do you ever feel that way? Or was it at the bridge? His name was Serafino. He was part Navajo. He taught me to rope. I taught him to make love. I was twelve when I learned. It was in the back of a pickup or was it in the willows? I don't remember. My mother taught him. His name was Palma, Salvador Palma. That wasn't his real name. That was the name Captain Anza gave him. He was my big brother."

241

Pipa's voice trailed away. "Mi Carlo," she whispered, "teach me to believe again so I won't have to die."

"Why do you say that?"

"Because I'm her daughter and she says I have to. Can't we stay here? Just us, two rivers in one. Can't we?"

"We can, darling, we can," I lied.

"Did you put your ear to the grave?" Pipa asked. "Was she quiet? Was there an owl in the oleanders? I told you to kill one. You said you would with your sling."

"There were only doves."

"Did you use all the stones? Were they heavy?"

"Some I could hardly lift. My hands were bleeding."

"Poor boy, Pipa will bathe them. If you had asked her, I know what her answer would have been."

"What?"

"The one Carmen got from the cards. La mort, toujours la mort. *She used to sing it. She learned it from my father. He was civilized. Why can't I be?"*

I could only say that I loved her, although I knew that I had lost her. As I held her I looked beyond and below a thousand feet to where the first meander of the San Juan looped across the meadow.

"We could follow it all the way to the Colorado," I said, "if we only had the time." Pipa freed herself and looked down, then lay back with closed eyes. "No time," she said, "only these minutes flowing like water. You are a medicine man, can't you stop them?"

I released the brake and we coasted the switchbacks down to the meadow. There by the young river we ate our bread and cheese and drank the icy water, then lay on the bank. Our feelings had ebbed away. When the air grew cold, we packed up and followed the San Juan into Pagosa Springs. "It's late," I said, "we'd better stay here."

"It's so ugly," Pipa said. "What's ahead?"

"Chama, Tierra Amarilla—villages with no motels."

"And beyond?"

"Española."

"How far?"

"Another hundred miles."

"We'd not make it until long after dark. We'd better stay here."

We drove slowly along the main street of Pagosa Springs, its sidewalks thronged with ranchers and Indians. A fight broke out ahead and spilled into the street. A man was knocked to his knees, then kicked into the gutter. I braked hard. The crowd scattered as a sheriff's car with wailing siren cut in from behind and two deputies waded in with swinging clubs.

"I wish we were back in New Mexico," I said.

In the next block we saw two coupling dogs. "Stop!" Pipa cried. "I want to watch." She slid over on the seat and grasped my arm.

"To hell with it," I said. "We'll do our own."

"Like them?"

We came to a motel on the edge of a meadow that sloped to the river. An encampment was forming along the river bank. "A trading fair," the manager explained as we were registering. "Utes and Jicarillas. They come every spring to trade and all that goes with it. I hope their drums won't keep you awake."

"Do they dance?" Pipa asked eagerly.

"Do they dance! Holy Christmas! Don't go over after dark. It gets rough. Be sure your door's bolted. Some try to find an open room."

"To sleep it off?" Pipa pressed.

The manager grinned lewdly. "Lady," he said, "Don't ask."

"Do we make love or eat?" I asked after we had gained our room. "Impossible choice."

"I'll flip a coin. Heads we eat, tails we make love."

I flipped a quarter and the coin fell head up. And so we washed and drove back to the café recommended by the manager. Pipa was silent.

"You're tired," I said. "We should have turned in."

"Of course I'm tired," she flared. "Tired of it all. I don't give a damn who gets the water."

When the waiter came she ordered a double whiskey. "Just one," I warned her.

"It's what you're doing with the water," she said. "Drowning all the wild places."

"You're the one who's lobbying for the bill."

"It's wrong, do you hear, wrong."

I laid my hands on her arm as her voice grew shrill and men turned to stare.

"I've about decided to leave the university at the end of this year." I said. "I took the deanship for only a year."

"Then what?"

"The M.W.D. wants me to write their history."

"A company history? Is that your ambition?"

"It would pay well. I'd have more time of my own. We could be together more."

"What if I don't want to be with a company historian—with that kind of company's historian."

"A man has to make a living."

"So do pimps!"

"Why don't you use a knife?" I said angrily. "It's cleaner."

"I'm glad it hurts. I'm tired of being the one who gets hurt."

"I had a letter from your governor."

"Why haven't you told me?"

"Afraid it would anger you."

"You're all alike, you academics. Cowards, all of you."

"Take it easy. People are staring."

"Let them. What did he write you about?"

"Remember when he asked me to come over and then was called to Washington? He wants to know if I'd be interested in a position with the state."

"Doing what?"

"As a kind of historian archivist, first to organize his office archives. He likes what I've done and am doing."

Pipa's lip was trembling. "What did you answer?"

"I wanted to talk with you first. It's along the line of what you said I should be doing."

"Hardly!"

"It would bring us together on your side of the river."

"We should have kept the river between us. First you take our water, now you take our work."

"What should I do? What are you going to do?"

"I don't give a damn what you do. I'm going to work for that conservation man. He said he wanted me if I ever saw the light. I've seen it."

"I don't understand you."

"You've never seen my dark side."

"At the quarry?"

"That was only my body. This is all of me."

We ate in silence, and then I asked, "What are you staring at?"

"Those men in back of you."

I turned and saw in the next booth two Indians in Anglo clothes. One was an old hawk; the other, facing us, was young and bold, eating with fierce relish.

"The two chiefs," the waitress said in reply to Pipa's question. *"They're having a pow-wow before the fair opens tomorrow."*

"Which is which?" Pipa asked.

"The old one's the Apache. The young Ute's the new chief. They say he killed the old chief in a fight with knives."

Pipa kept staring. Although I had turned back and could not see him, I knew that the Ute was returning her stare. It was like it had been at the quarry.

The Indian finished eating and as they passed our booth, the Ute looked down at Pipa. She returned his stare.

"We should have gone on to Española," I said. Pipa did not answer.

By the time we had returned to the motel, darkness had fallen and fires were burning in the encampment. We heard drumming and saw figures moving in the firelight. The meadow was running with loose dogs. A stallion trumpeted and was challenged by another. It was a bedlam of men's shouts and women's laughter, rising to screams.

Pipa was bemused. I felt paralyzed. And yet when she dragged me on her in the way she wished, I thrust fiercely until she collapsed under me.

The drumming had grown urgent. *"Don't let me go!"* she said as we lay panting. We got up off the floor and lay on the bed.

I must have fallen asleep. When I awakened in the night and felt for Pipa, she was not there. I went to the bathroom. Not there. Her jeans and blouse were gone. My heart was pounding. My mouth was dry.

I opened the door. Across the meadow in the firelight dancers were leaping and stomping while above the pounding drums came the roar of an aroused people, pierced by shouts and screams and wild laughter.

I tried to stop trembling as I pulled on pants and shirt and shoes. I started across the meadow, stepping around couples locked in intercourse. Halfway across I puked. I lay on the grass until I could summon strength to crawl back and lie on the bed.

Daylight came. Pipa had not returned. I found her asleep on the grass beside the locked car. I carried her in and laid her on the bed. While she clung to me, I removed her torn clothes and washed her with a warm cloth. Her body was bruised, her mouth bloodied, her hair tangled. I covered her with the sheet.

Pipa slept until noon while I sat beside the bed and organized the carton of San Juan material, pausing to gaze on her face, angelic in the sleep into which she had escaped again. When she moaned and stirred, I touched her cool forehead.

At last she awakened, showered and dressed. Neither of us spoke. We drove to Chama and stopped for something to eat. We were hungry. Then we sat in the car. I took her hand.

"Don't be good to me," she said.

"I don't know what else to be."

"I told you not to let me go. It was the drums."

"They put me to sleep."

"I'm glad you didn't try to follow me."

"I started to and then I was sick and turned back."

"You knew where I'd gone?"

"I saw it start."

"Why didn't you stop me?"

I managed a smile. "He was bigger than Lars Hansen."

Pipa gave a strange laugh and said, "Just the way it began. In the back of a pickup with a crazy Indian."

"What's it going to do to us?"

"Don't you know there's nothing left of us? I don't mean just because of him. After all, what's another fuck between Indians?"

Down the colored valley of the Chama we drove to the Río Grande. Beyond Española and Santa Fe we took the river road that led through Bernalillo. The Río Grande was flowing full with the spring runoff; its cottonwoods had put out their new leaves. Along the embankment lay fields of alfalfa in purple flower, orchards of blossoming apples and almonds, and plastered adobes painted purple and pink. Chickens and dogs and children wandered loose.

"Why couldn't our river have been like this?" Pipa asked. "Go back to the highway," she cried, "I can't bear it."

We were silent the rest of the way to the airport. I turned in the car and we sat at the counter in the coffee shop, awaiting our flights, due at the same time, mine a TWA Constellation to Los Angeles, hers a Frontier DC-3 to Gallup, Winslow, and Flagstaff.

At the same instant our eyes saw the headline in the morning's Albuquerque Journal: PRESIDENT SIGNS GREAT DAM BILL. Her fingers dug into my arm. My hand found hers. She shook her head and her lips moved wordlessly. A tear ran down her cheek. I reached out for it.

Our flights were called. She left her coffee untouched. We went outdoors. The wind had risen and the Sandias were lost behind blowing sand. My flight was in from Kansas City, the passengers debarking. Hers had not

246

yet reached the gate. We stood together at the TWA check-in. I held her. She felt lifeless.

"So you're giving me the gate," I joked badly.

Pipa didn't answer. Then she seized me and whispered fiercely "Will you remember your river girl?"

I touched her cheek with my lips.

Pipa tried to speak again and no words came. She shoved me through the open gate. I walked to the plane and mounted the steps. It would have been useless to look back. Tears had nearly blinded me.

I found the last window seat. I wiped my eyes and blew my nose and looked out. Her plane had reached the gate for its brief stop, one engine still spinning the propeller. I saw her come through the gate and walk toward her plane, carrying her flight bag and holding her hair in the wind. As her skirt blew above her knees, she tried to hold it down with her hand.

Now the Constellation revved up with a roar, shuddered and began to move. I was as powerless to hold it as I was to hold that small, strong, and fated woman.

I saw her approach her plane when suddenly she threw away her bag and dashed headlong toward the spinning propeller of the DC-3. My mouth gave a soundless shout as the moving Constellation cut off my view. The big plane lumbered to the head of the runway, gathered speed and was airborne over the river. I tried to yell at the pilot to turn around and go back, but I was frozen with horror.

❦

Neither Graham nor Claudia spoke as they stared into the fire, now burned low. The only sounds were from the cabin's beams and boards cracking in the cold. At last Claudia sat on the floor beside him and rested her head on his knee. Graham touched her hair and it sparked softly. "What are you thinking?" he asked.

"How brave she was—and how you must have loved her."

"I felt I had to redeem her death. I sought to fulfill the things she saw in me. That's why my life went the way it did. Now you know. There are no more doors to open."

"It's almost too much," Claudia whispered.

"You see why I couldn't tell it to the machine?"

"I am glad you could tell me."

"Now you're the only one who knows. The governor died ten

years ago. He was flying in to the strip at Chinle in a snowstorm and crashed. We had become close friends."

"You told him?"

"I got the first plane back to Phoenix and told him the whole story. We flew that night to Albuquerque in his plane and back the next day to Yuma with her body. There we buried her beside her mother."

"Were the stones still there?"

"Just as I had piled them. He said to me, now you've got to come. He was right. I never went home nor back to State. It was a clean break. I wonder sometimes why I didn't die from the pain. It was the Lord's will that I live and work."

"Thank God!" Claudia murmured.

"I couldn't have made it without Jack Clayton and Lars Hansen. I spent a month at the quarry, drawing strength from Hansen's strength. He worked on a model of the fountain. I took him that photograph of Pipa, and he had the daughter of one of the quarrymen pose for him."

"Was the fountain ever done?"

"It was and cast in bronze, and the governor paid for it all. It's there in Yuma. Her name is on the base. We'll go see it. I moved to Phoenix and became a Friend. It was as far as I could get from a faith I no longer had. Since then everything has been of her and for her. In that sense she is not dead."

"Did her mother ever return?"

"There was no need to."

"I'm thankful that you lived."

There was a long silence, broken only by the soft snapping of the fire, while Graham's hand continued to caress her hair. Finally Claudia spoke. "I've been remembering what Yeats wrote to a young woman he loved when he was old. Do you want to know what it was?"

Graham's heart beat faster. "Yes, I do. Tell me."

"Yeats wrote her about what to him was the supreme experience of life—one possible only to the young."

"What was it?" Graham asked.

"He said that it was to share profound thought and then to touch."

Graham's hand came to rest. "You are telling me?" he half asked.

248

Claudia's reply was nearly inaudible. "That fifty-two and a half is young."

Graham leaned down and framed her upturned face with his hands. Their first kiss was tender and deep.

Claudia rose at last and excused herself. Graham opened the door and looked out on the white ground and dark trees. Chunks of snow were falling from overladen branches. He took a deep breath and bolted the door, backlogged the fire and put up the screen, then resumed his seat on the hearth.

In a moment Claudia returned in a robe, barefooted, and stood before him. Her face was loving. Graham rose.

"Let me see you," he said gently.

She let her robe fall open.

He reached timidly and touched her cheek. "Dia," he said, "you're beautiful."

"Am I?" Her voice was shy yet sure.

"Very."

Claudia put her arms around him. "Oh my dear, you are trembling."

Graham held her close. "So are you."

EL MORRO

EL MORRO

1.

Paso por aqui ǧ!
ǰu de la R.ua.
y y ǰu de Vr̲
bam Año de 1)o9

After the blowing dust came an even fiercer wind that brought thunder and lightning. As flares and swords and flashes filled the sky, his passenger asked, "Hadn't you better pull off the road until it's over?"

Stone did not reply. His strength was needed to hold the wheel as rain now drove in sheets against the side of the vehicle. Despite its weight, the car was unsteady and the road ahead was obscured by the rain.

"Please," she begged. "Please stop. I'm frightened."

"Brace yourself," he said bluntly. "We'll be through it any minute."

She did not speak again.

He was right. As suddenly as it had broken over them, the storm blew away to the west leaving calm air and clear sky.

"I'm sorry," she said. "I panicked."

Stone smiled and drove on until they reached the all-night gas station on the mesa above the Black Canyon of the Agua Fria. He pulled into the parking lot and they entered the coffee shop patronized by truck drivers.

As Stone relaxed over coffee in a corner booth, he watched his passenger as she went toward the rest room. It was his first close look since her plane had arrived at the Phoenix airport. The flight had been delayed by the dust storm which had forced it to circle for an hour. He had gotten under way fast in the hope of beating the electrical storm he knew would follow.

When she returned carrying her coat, she had removed the scarf that had covered her head, and he saw over her full brown-eyed face a heavy mane of dark red curly hair that fell to her shoulders.

Stone could not help staring. "You'd take the blue ribbon at the State Fair!" he exclaimed

She gave him a faint shocked smile. "I'm glad you know good stock when you see it."

His face reddened. "We don't see hair like that around here."

Her smile softened. "It's common where I come from."

"Where is that?"

"The north of England. You even see it on our menfolk. I'm sorry I behaved badly. I was frightened. I've never seen such weather. Now that it's over, it was glorious!"

"There's no danger as long as you don't let go the wheel."

"Doesn't it ever strike the car?"

"The car's a natural ground. The strikes pass on through. You must be tired."

"I'm so tired I don't know I am! I've been up about twenty hours since we left London. It's kind of you to come in place of the Secretary. I was determined to make the trip even though he had to cancel. I'm afraid I don't know much about you."

"Nor I about you," Stone confessed.

"Didn't he tell you anything about me?"

"Not much. He called yesterday morning to say he was taking off for Rio de Janeiro to represent the President at a conference."

"He also telephoned Daddy. He told him that your knowledge of the Southwest far exceeds his—and furthermore that you have an impeccable character."

Stone laughed. "That's a hell of a recommendation! What I am is his brightest errand boy."

"You sound put upon. Aren't you with the Park Service?"

254

"I'm in charge of ranger training for the Southwest region."

"And also an archaeologist?"

"I meant to be one but never finished my degree."

"What a pity. Daddy knew the Secretary when Daddy was our ambassador to Washington. If you would stop staring at my hair, we might get acquainted."

Again his face reddened. "Sorry. I'm also going to have to get used to your accent."

"Is it that bad?" she demanded.

"It's on a new wave length. You must be hungry."

"I am! What does one order?"

"Coffee is all I'm having. I had a sandwich waiting for your plane to arrive."

She studied the menu. "How is the mesquite-broiled charburger?"

"The truckers' dream of gourmet food!"

"What *did* the Secretary tell you about me?"

"That your father is Sir Tor Bay, the Minister of Transport, and that your husband, Professor Williams, is a distinguished archaeologist. And that I am to spare nothing to see to your safety and comfort."

She laughed. "So chivalry did not die with Lassiter!"

"You read Zane Grey?"

"What do you expect? Dickens? Do you know my husband's work on Roman Britain?"

"My work has all been on the Southwest." He paused. "Why didn't he come with you?"

She hesitated and their eyes met for the first time. "He's not able to travel. I've come for him."

"Are you an archaeologist?" Stone asked.

"Heavens no! I was a music student he captured to keep him warm in the field. I use my own name: Arla Bay."

"It sounds medieval."

"It was originally Baystrom. They were Shetlanders from way back."

"Do you realize that two weeks is not long enough for everything the Secretary said you want to see?"

"I suppose not. We're not used to your distances. I thought Phoenix was a suburb of Los Angeles."

255

"It is in everything but distance!"

"I have priorities among those sites. What would you be doing otherwise?"

"Retiring."

"You're not that old."

"Older than I look."

"And I, sir," she said grimly, "am younger than I look."

"I'll have two weeks to add to my twenty-five years' service. I've had enough. I'm not happy with what's happening to the West— the way the power interests are moving in."

"It's happening everywhere," she said. "North Sea oil threatens our old ways. Daddy and my husband are at odds over it."

"Does your husband know that only I will be guiding you?" Stone asked.

"He does," she answered carefully. "I insisted there not be a group. I despise group travel."

"He won't be worried about you?"

"He trusts me. Will your wife be worried?"

"I'm not married," Stone said.

They were silent, and then she said, "You must help me with this sandwich. It's enormous. By the way, where are we?"

"Between Phoenix and Flagstaff, in Yavapai County."

"Aren't we due at the Grand Canyon?"

"We were, but your plane was late, and then the storm slowed us. We'll stay in Sedona and reach the South Rim tomorrow. If you hadn't wanted to see the Grand Canyon, Albuquerque would have been the best place to arrive. It's nearer most of the sites you want to visit. Phoenix is the worst place to enter the Southwest."

"Is it always dusty and hot?"

"Only twelve months of the year. It will get cooler as we head north and east."

"I hope I brought the proper clothes," she said. "They told me it would be hot everywhere."

"Not that suit you're wearing."

"My dear sir, this is my travelling ensemble."

"We'll talk about clothes in the morning."

"My top priorities after the Grand Canyon are Chaco Canyon and El Morro. My husband wants a report on Chaco and I want to see El Morro."

"Do you know that the latter has no particular archaeological significance?"

"I told you I'm not an archaeologist. Call it a woman's whim. My husband says I am very whimsical. Daddy calls me capricious." She smiled. "What I really am is stubborn."

"Like our canyon mules? Well, you're the boss and we'll go where you want to go as long as we have time. We should hit the road. Sedona's another hour. I've reserved rooms at the Red Cliffs motel. I think you'll find it comfortable."

"All I want is hot water and a good bed."

When they had regained the car, Arla exclaimed, "What is the monster? I couldn't see it for dust when we arrived."

"It's a Ranger the Secretary had outfitted for his own use. It sleeps two on air mattresses when he brings his wife." Then Stone quickly added, "We'll be staying in motels, in case you wonder."

"It dwarfs our Land Rover!"

"It's actually a glorified truck. We'll need it before we're done."

They stood for a moment while she looked up at the sky. The only sounds were of cars and trucks passing at high speed on the interstate highway.

"I've never seen this many stars since North Africa," she said. "I feel remote. Did we land by mistake on another planet?"

"You'll be back on earth in the morning," Stone answered as he eased the Ranger into the northbound lane.

She fell asleep at once.

In the morning Arla found Stone reading the paper in the lobby. "Why didn't you call me?" she demanded.

"You needed the sleep."

"Don't treat me like a nanny."

"I was told to look after you, and I don't want the Secretary to take away my gold stars. Are you hungry?"

"Starved again. Have you breakfasted?"

"I'll have another cup of coffee with you."

When they were served on the terrace facing the cliffs, Arla said, "It was thoughtful of you to have them painted in my honor."

Stone smiled. "They're actually a John Wayne set—they'll be gone next week."

"Do you know him?"

"Not favorably since I had a run-in with him."

"My goodness, what over?"

"The way his Hollywood crew was fouling up Monument Valley."

"Good for you!"

"He complained to the Secretary."

"What did *he* do?"

"Apologized to Wayne and complimented me."

"Good for him!"

"That's why I'd never go into politics," Stone said.

"Am I dressed for the wide open spaces?" she asked.

Stone looked at her slacks and pullover and coat sweater. "Nice for town," he observed, "but you'll need warmer things where we're headed. Summer is over except in the low desert."

"What *should* I wear? I didn't bring much else—and only one evening gown."

"Those sandals won't do. You'll need desert boots, whipcord pants and a couple of Pendletons. Also a down jacket. The coat you carried will do. Also this morning's scarf. I like purple, although yesterday's green did more for your hair."

Arla laughed. "Such gallantry, Nanny Stone! Where could I find such an outfit in this wilderness?"

"At Babbitts' general store in Flagstaff. You'll be surprised. There's nothing they don't carry—even Yardley's lavender, I'm told. We're only an hour from there. We'll make the South Rim by late afternoon. First though I want to show you a site not on your list."

"Tuzigoot?" she ventured. "We read about it."

"You're close. One that has no more archaeological significance than El Morro."

"Why do you want me to see it?"

Stone smiled. "I'd like to say hello to the ranger."

Arla laughed. "So this is going to be your trip as well as mine! Good. Give me five minutes." As she left, she said over her shoulder, "I'm used to bossy men!"

Stone drove southeast through the low piñon-juniper forest along the base of the red cliffs to where a gravelled road led to a low mesa. At a green Park Service building they were greeted by the young ranger.

"We'll take a look at the Well," Stone said, "then go down to the creek. We haven't time for the Castle."

"You've got it all to yourself," the ranger said. "Few come this early."

"Not getting lonesome?"

"Suits me fine."

"He's one of our new trainees," Stone explained as he led Arla up a steep trail which suddenly levelled off and they looked down on a wide round pond, banked in a limestone bowl edged with tules and a vestigial cliff dwelling. A few black coots were cruising over the surface. From somewhere near, a quail was calling.

They stood looking, then Arla exclaimed, "How lonely and beautiful! I do prefer places to people."

"It's called Montezuma Well," Stone explained, "although there were never any Aztecs up this far. It has no special significance in either history or archaeology."

"It must mean something special to you."

"It does, ever since I first came as a high school student on a field trip to the Grand Canyon."

"I don't see an inlet."

"The water comes from a subterranean spring."

"Does it remain at this level?" she asked.

"Three hundred years ago the first Spaniards described it as you see it now. To me it is a symbol of constancy. Even in the driest period, the level never drops—something not true of water elsewhere in the Southwest."

"I do appreciate this guided tour," Arla said.

Stone paused. Was she mocking him?

"Where is the outlet?" she asked.

Stone smiled. "Come and I'll show you."

He led her down another trail to a creek below the limestone bowl, then along a vine-grown path past leaning sycamores to where the stream narrowed to a rockbound channel ending at the cliff's base.

"Here," Stone said, "here it drains just enough to match what flows in. A perfect system of hydraulics." He kneeled and cupped his hands, dipped, then held them toward Arla. "Drink!"

"Oh!" she exclaimed. "It's cold." She wiped her mouth with her sleeve.

"*Muy fresca*, the Spanish say."

She softly echoed the words, then said, "I saw where some is diverted—for irrigation?"

"The early Indians were the first to use it for their corn and squash."

"We saw that in North Africa—using water from the oases."

"Before we leave, we'll fill our canteens," Stone paused. "I think of it as water from the underworld, from Persephone's Well."

"That's a nice touch, Professor Stone. I suppose you read Greek."

"No, but my mother did."

Arla smiled. "Do you bring all your visitors here?"

He shook his head.

"Why did you bring me?" she persisted.

Stone did not answer at first, then said, "Perhaps it's wanting to show you something that's special to me. I don't suppose it means much to you, coming from a wet land. As well as a symbol of constancy, I see it as one of survival, a measurement of our future. If it fails, we fail. The land was not meant for many people. Now it's getting crowded."

Arla laughed. "Until you've seen London, you don't know what crowding is."

They walked downcreek to where the Ranger was parked. After filling the canteens and chatting with the ranger, they regained the highway. The view west was over the Verde Valley to a wall of blue mountains.

"How far are they?" Arla asked.

"Twenty miles."

"I could reach out and touch them."

"You're looking through crystal air."

"What is that dark line in the valley?"

"Cottonwoods along the river. Two weeks ago it would have been a golden line. It's a cold valley when summer goes. The Verde is one of our few constant rivers."

"I thought all rivers were constant."

"We won't see another one until we reach the San Juan."

"Not the Colorado?"

"We won't see it from the South Rim. It's too deep down."

They continued to gaze at the panorama, then Arla said, "Is this what the prophets meant by 'world without end?' "

"Visitors either like it or don't. No in between."

"I don't know if what I feel is liking. It calls for a new vocabulary."

The road climbed toward the ponderosa forest of the Coconino plateau and the first cliffs of the Mogollon Rim, the great escarpment that divides the state. Arla remained silent, then nearing Flagstaff she said, "I feel more at home up here. These pines and peaks are like the high parts of Wales and Scotland. They are our Northwest."

"And our Southwest is Mexico's Northwest. I suppose the two poles and the equator are the only absolutes."

In the railroad and lumbering settlement of Flagstaff, gateway to the Grand Canyon and Glen Canyon dam, Stone drove to the Babbitt Brothers' general store. For a hundred years that family dynasty has ruled the north, trading to Anglos and Indians in towns and on reservation posts. This was the mother store, selling everything from handkerchiefs to harvesters.

As they entered, Arla breathed deeply. "Cloth and leather smell the same everywhere. I love it, although a secondhand shop would do me as well."

"What you're wearing didn't come from a thrift shop," Stone said.

"Daddy spoils me," Arla admitted. "My mother died when I was born. I was their only child, and he raised me. Even after I married, Daddy insists on buying my clothes."

"What does your husband say to that?" Stone asked.

"He's relieved. He doesn't care about such things as clothes and money."

"A woman's lucky to have two such providers."

Arla sighed. "Sometimes it's a bit too much."

"I know about ambivalence," Stone said as they walked through the store in search of women's western wear. "If I thought I could have an impact, I'd stay on in the Service, although the doctor tells me I'll live longer if I retire now. You can charge whatever you want. The Secretary would regard it as a legitimate expense."

261

"That's most kind of him," Arla said, "but I have plenty of money. My husband gave me a belt and Daddy filled it with your bank notes."

"What if Babbitt Brothers want to trade?" Stone asked. "Did you bring any wool or turquoise?"

"You do have a sense of humor!" she laughed.

Stone left her to make her selection. When he returned and gathered up the parcels, he asked, "Didn't you have to have anything altered?"

"Mine, sir," she said indignantly, "is the ideal figure—which you would have known if you hadn't spent your time staring at my hair."

"It's your scarf that takes my eye!"

After lunch at Granny's Kitchen, Stone drew up at the railroad crossing on the Grand Canyon road for an eastbound freight—a long train drawn by six thundering blue and yellow diesels.

Arla's eyes were shining. "I wish Daddy could see this!"

"Does he like trains?"

"Rather!"

"Does England still have good train service? Passenger, I mean. Freight is all we have left."

"We're too poor to have as many autos as you have. Even the Queen couldn't afford a Ranger!"

As they drove through the forest toward the South Rim, Stone pondered his charge. Was she really the spoiled darling she seemed to want him to believe, or was it her English sense of humor? Why had she come alone? What was she seeking? He was relieved that she was not talkative.

"Look," he pointed out. "There's the first of the Sacred Mountains."

"What is the golden band near their summit?"

"Aspens. If we had time, I'd show you why they're called quaking aspens."

"So you lecture in botany! You and my husband would get along. He's always lecturing me about gorse and lichens and spores. To me flowers are things to press in a book. I promised to bring him some."

"I believe I'd like your husband better than your father."

262

"I feel the same way! You and I are going to get along, aren't we?"

"Did you wonder?"

"Of course. I took as much of a chance as you did. Does my accent bother you?"

"I might come to like it."

"Is that Texan you tease me with?"

"TV western."

"I'll trade you a lesson in Lancashire," Arla said.

The day was ending when they reached the canyon. Stone drew up in front of El Tovar, the old resort hotel on the South Rim.

"What a beautiful building!" Arla exclaimed.

"I though you would prefer it to one of the modern motels."

"I adore anything made of wood and stone."

"What you're seeing is Douglas fir and Coconino sandstone."

"These chimneys must have enormous fireplaces."

"They take whole trees!" Stone said.

As they entered the high-ceilinged lobby, Arla remarked, "It smells like our clothes closet."

"That's Utah cedar. We call it juniper."

"How long can we stay?"

"A couple of nights—no more."

While Stone was registering, the manager came from his office and greeted them. "Sorry you didn't make it yesterday."

"Does that mean we have to eat cold roast beef?" Stone asked. "No Yorkshire pudding. Miss Bay is from Lancashire."

The manager bowed. "Perhaps she would prefer our Rocky Mountain trout. Caught it myself this morning."

Arla smiled. "You seem to know each other."

"Mr. Wheaton is a wise man," Stone explained. "Wise enough not to be a park ranger."

"Someone has to do the work," the manager said. "I trust Miss Bay will find things comfortable."

"Are you too tired for a walk along the rim?" Stone asked as he saw her to her room on the floor above. "Sundown and sunrise are the best times to see the canyon."

"I'd love it."

"Meet me downstairs when you've washed up. Wear your new jacket. The minute the sun goes, it turns cold."

263

They joined the visitor throng along the rim walk, then made their way to a less crowded viewpoint and sat on the low rock wall. The canyon was filling with shadows and smoky colors though the buttes and spires were still in golden light.

Arla was silent until Stone asked if she had brought a camera, then she said, "Why compete with those postcards in the lobby? I promised my menfolk to send back a stream of them. I'm dazed by it all—your red cliffs and now this."

"Well?" Stone asked, as darkness deepened, "What do you make of it?"

"I told you I'll need a new vocabulary. Is it another of your film sets? Are there always this many people?"

"Even more in summer. Now they're flying them in from Las Vegas—foreign tourists now that the exchange favors them. It's crazy. In and out in twenty-four hours."

"When did you first come?" Arla asked.

"As a boy with my folks."

"How wide is it?"

"A dozen miles."

"Are there trails down?"

"From both rims. Those lights are at the lodge on the North Rim—two hundred miles around by car. It's higher, which means it's snowed in from October to May. Even in the summer, it's not crowded."

"Do you work there too?" Arla asked.

"One winter soon after I joined the Service, I maintained the lodge and cabins. I had an Indian helper—a Ute. There were only the two of us."

"Wasn't it lonely?"

"I wanted to be alone."

She did not question him.

Night was closing in. The color had faded from walls and spires, and the far lights began to sparkle as the canyon deepened in gloom and finally vanished.

Arla stood up and began to step over the low wall and look down. Stone seized her arm. "Careful. People have fallen over here. It's a long way to the first ledge."

They made their way back to El Tovar, her arm still in his. When

264

they reached the lobby, Arla looked in on the great dining hall. "What a beautiful room! Are we dining here?"

"If you'd like. There is a coffee shop less fancy."

"What if I feel fancy?"

"Then we'll eat here. In an hour from now? I'll reserve a table."

"Shall I dress?" Arla asked.

"Most people don't."

"Do I have to be like most people?"

Stone reddened. "Of course not. All I have though is a fresh uniform."

"Do you always wear a uniform?"

"Does it make you feel you are in custody? It will help us along the way. Would you rather eat alone?"

"Don't be silly. You're really quite handsome."

Stone blushed again. "I got the new one in Phoenix for the trip."

"I'll wager, too, you didn't have to have it altered!"

When they remet, Stone observed, "Lucky for me it's the same head of hair, otherwise I wouldn't have known you! And you weren't joking about the evening gown!"

"Do you like it?" Arla was wearing a long dark green sleeveless dress, her hair done up with a gold comb. She smiled. "I got it in London for the trip."

"Unaltered!"

She squeezed his hand. "I'm beginning to feel civilized again. And will you kindly stop blushing, Ranger Stone."

They were greeted by the maître d'. "Would madame prefer a table nearer the fire?"

"Thank you. I want to see the whole tree Mr. Stone says you burn."

Admiring glances followed them to their table. Great pine logs were blazing in the wide stone fireplace.

"I want you to meet Miss Bay from overseas," Stone said as the maître d' seated her.

"*Enchanté, mademoiselle,*" he bowed.

"*Mais je suis anglaise.*"

"*Je sais bien.*"

"Jeff likes to practice his French," Stone explained.

"I learned French in Lausanne," Arla said, "which is why Parisians scorn my accent."

"She speaks good English for a foreigner," Stone observed.

"My friend has promised to teach me T.V. western," Arla laughed, "In turn for my help with his sense of humor."

"What do you recommend, Jeff?" Stone asked. "How is the filet of buffalo?"

"But excellent! And will mademoiselle have a cocktail? I know my friend never touches strong drink."

"I'd like wine with my dinner," she replied.

"But certainly. I'll have the card brought at once."

"Please order for me," Arla asked Stone when their waiter brought menu and wine list. "I'll choose the wine."

He proceeded to order Sonoran shrimp cocktails, the trout, and potato balls with green beans *amandine*.

"Perfect!" she approved and ordered a bottle of true Chablis. "All this and the Grand Canyon too!" she toasted with their first glass. "I'm glad you ordered the fish. That's something we don't have at home, although our Scotch salmon can be very tasty. Since rationing ended, beef has become so common. Most of it comes from Australia."

"I haven't lived this high since the Secretary was here," Stone said. "This room scares off most tourists. You like to tease, don't you."

"You're doing better. We northerners are more like Americans than Londoners are. Down south their veins flow with weak cold tea. North of Humber ours flow with strong hot tea. If you must know, I was born a wee bit south of Humber. Where were you born?"

"In a mining camp at the junction of the Gila and the San Pedro. That is to say, in the midst of nowhere!"

"What on earth were your parents doing there?"

"My father was a metallurgist with the mines. He and my mother were Philadelphians of English stock—west of England I'm glad to say!"

"Gold mines?"

"Copper. Although my father came to Arizona for his health, it was death he found and not from T.B. Copper killed him—a blight that eventually kills everything it touches. My mother too. She did not live long after his death."

"Until you've seen our Midlands, you don't know what blight is."

"Is your last name French?" Stone asked.

"Heavens no! I told you it was originally Baystrom. My grandfather was a Shetlander who ran away as a lad and washed up on the Yorkshire coast. He married a local girl and prospered in the Grimsby fisheries. Their son, my father, left fishing for engineering. He, too, prospered, married a Lancashire woman and rose to own the works at Derby and later at Crewe where the L.M.S. locomotives are built. That's one of our main lines. They're all nationalized now. You've heard of the Flying Scotsman? The overnight train between London and Edinburgh? Daddy's works built the locomotives that draw it. One bears his name on a brass plate. They did that when he was knighted. Once he arranged for me to ride in the cab on the run from Newcastle to Berwick. I couldn't hear for a day afterward."

As Arla grew animated from the wine and food and fire and telling of her antecedents, Stone felt rising trepidation at the prospect of two weeks with this woman, intelligent, responsive, and beautiful. He was not used to feeling inadequate. He let the waiter fill his glass, took a long swallow, and ventured, "Did your father marry again?"

"He did indeed and has regretted it ever since! I think he did it to get even when I eloped with Glyn. Poor dear, it served him jolly well right!"

"I never knew the English were so impulsive."

"Stiff upper lip, eh? Not so! We're descended from Beowulf!"

Stone laughed. "I told you Tor and Arla Bay sound medieval."

"You mean primitive!"

"Is your husband English?"

"Can't you tell from his name? Pure Welsh, and like all of them, a charmer."

"Where did you meet?"

"In Switzerland. Our school was skiing at Gstaad and so was Glyn. I took a fall in a snowbank and he pulled me out. That was it for both of us."

"Are you the same age?"

"He's older. How old do you think I am?"

Stone hesitated, then ventured, "Mid-thirties?"

"Not too far off. I was a headstrong girl. Glyn settled me. He was leading a restoration team on Hadrian's Wall—the great wall that crosses the north of Britain. I gave up music to marry him and he's been my life ever since."

"Do you have children?"

Arla shook her head. Stone saw tears in her eyes. "I'm all right," she said. "I mustn't carry on so. Please fill my glass. It will either steady me or I'll fall apart."

"Is your husband ill? Is that why he didn't come with you?"

Arla emptied her glass and said defiantly, "Worse than ill."

"You mean he was in an accident?"

"Yes. He lost both of his legs."

Stone was stunned to silence, then exclaimed, "O my God! I'm sorry. I didn't know."

"How could you? Please, I don't want to talk about it. I'm beginning to feel the strangeness of being here, both civilized and not civilized, and so far from home."

"I've upset you."

"It's not you. It's everything but you. You are very kind, and I appreciate it, believe me I do."

"Thank you, ma'am."

"Please don't call me ma'am."

"Yes, Miss Bay."

"I don't like that either. Call me Arla, will you? I'll feel more at home if you will. Why not talk about *your* marriage?"

"That was so long ago I've forgotten it. Did your father ever forgive you for eloping?"

"But not for giving up music. He wanted me to be a singer. My mother sang, beautifully they said. It's our finest art in the north. I don't suppose you've heard of Kathleen Ferrier? She was pure Lancashire and England's greatest. She died of cancer at the peak of her career. My husband sings. All the Welsh do. He and I sing together when we're happy. We used to, I mean. Perhaps I'll study again. It depends. Since the accident, I've been too distracted. Maybe it's too late. I'm too old. I'm glad you let me dress. It reassures me. That canyon was beginning to frighten me. I began to feel like jumping." Arla paused. "Am I talking too much?"

"I'm a good listener," Stone said quietly. "I know what you mean about the canyon. Some people take one look and want to run. I heard one say, 'What if it should open wider and swallow us?' Another feared something would come up in the night and drag her down."

Arla smiled. "It doesn't affect me *that* much! It's just that I never imagined it like it is. Everything at home is on a smaller, more human scale."

Stone rose. "We'd better call it a night. It's been a full day for you."

"I'll sleep. I'm relaxed now. You've been good to hear my troubles. What will we do tomorrow?"

"We'll decide at breakfast."

In the morning Stone challenged her with, "That's still another scarf! How many did you bring?"

"Enough to last, I trust. Where were you?" Arla asked. "I was on the rim for sunrise."

"Unaccustomed as I am to high living, I overslept."

"That's not how the West was won."

"I like your new outfit," Stone said.

"I told you I have an accommodating figure. It's lucky for I don't sew."

"Can you cook?"

"In an emergency. We've always had help."

"Where do you live?"

"In Corbridge up the River Tyne from Newcastle — a constant river and a lovely one. We live at the eastern end of the Wall."

"What do you want to do today? I've made no plans."

"Prepare for a shock," Arla said. "I want to leave."

"Are you that scared?"

"Not by the canyon. By the people. I was nearly pushed over the edge by a troop of Japanese with cameras. What about the North Rim? Can we go there? You said it would not be crowded."

"If you like. I'll drive around and be there when you arrive by muleback."

"No you won't! I'll go with you. That long drive sounds lovely. It will settle me, I know. I'm sorry I was distraught last night. Can you book for us at the lodge?"

"No problem, if you're sure you want to leave."

"I told you Daddy says I'm capricious."

Stone bowed formally. "This is your trip, Miss Bay—I mean Miss Arla."

"Can't it be our trip?" she asked.

"Are you ready to leave?" he said bluntly, ignoring her plea.

"Give me time to address these cards." Her voice was now cool. "You probably wish you'd never agreed to this trip."

His tone was flat. "I had no choice."

They were silent as they left the South Rim on the road that ran east near the edge, past occasional viewpoints, then diverged to meet the gorge of the Little Colorado.

Stone took an unmarked turnoff and steered among rocks and cactus to the edge. Arla was apprehensive.

"Where have you brought me?"

"To a different kind of South Rim," Stone said softly. "All rim and no people."

They got out and he led her to the brink.

"Hold my arm," he cautioned.

She peered over the edge, then shrank back. "Don't let me go! How far down is it?"

"A thousand feet and sheer."

"Is that white the river?"

"That's sand. There's water only after a thaw in the mountains or a summer flash flood."

Arla was silent. Stone looked closely. "You aren't crying, are you?"

She shook her head. "I'm all right."

"Are you sure?"

"You knew what I needed. People were smothering me. Is there a way down?"

"Only by roping—or jumping. You can enter the gorge only where it begins upstream near Cameron. Then there's no getting out until it reaches the big Colorado."

"How far is that?"

"Fifty miles. If you're in the gorge and the river rises, you've had it."

"Have you ever followed it to the confluence?"

"Once."

"Don't let go of me. I might jump."

270

"Don't worry, I've got you. The danger is from sudden wind gusts. Soon after I joined the Service, a Navajo shepherd was blown over at this very point. His people asked us to go down and bury him before the river rose. There had been a thaw. We had to hurry."

"Didn't they want a proper burial?"

"They believe it should be where death occurs."

"Wouldn't the body have been swept away in any case?"

"We wedged him in a crevice above water line."

"We?" she asked.

"Two of us roped down."

"Wasn't that dangerous?"

"Danger doesn't mean much when you're young."

"Poor old man!" she murmured.

They returned to the car and he said, "Look there in the east. You can see the Painted Desert. We'll skirt it this afternoon."

"You choose strange things to show me—that Well and now this gorge. Are you telling me something?"

"I have the feeling I won't be seeing these places again," Stone answered.

She knew that he would not respond to questioning.

They drove on to Cameron where they met the highway to the North Rim turnoff. The trading post was thronged with Navajos and travellers. Arla was wide-eyed while Stone bought food for their ice chest. After filling a thermos jug with coffee, they settled in the coffee shop to look at the map.

"If we had time and the river was running," Stone said, "we'd detour to see the Grand Falls. They are as high as Niagara."

"We read about them in the material the Embassy sent. Since the accident I read aloud to him on exploration and archaeology, though mostly things on the Near East and North Africa where the Romans were. We'd planned to return on holiday to Leptis Magnae."

"What all did you read on this country?"

"He preferred the government survey reports—liked their matter-of-fact style. He found the personal narratives overwritten and untrustworthy—things like that wild trapper Pattie's. One of the first books was one I chanced on in our town library. God knows how it got there! Although he found it too flowery, it did provoke

271

his interest in the Anasazi and their mysterious exodus and it led to the high priority we have for Chaco Canyon. It's really his wish, although I share his curiosity. The same book led to my wanting to see El Morro. Those two are the musts."

"What was the book?" Stone asked.

"One by a writer named Mary Austin—her *Land of Journeys' Ending*. You must know it."

Stone smiled. "I have a copy—one the author gave me."

"You knew her?" Arla asked.

"I was the ranger at El Morro when she came on a field trip."

"Small world! What do you think of it?"

"I'm like your husband. I found it too imaginative and overwritten. That was twenty-five years ago. I'd probably like it even less now."

"Be careful what you say!" Arla warned. "I intend to read some out loud to you. I brought it in my duffel bag. What was she like?"

"Big around the bottom! I had to boost her up a ladder or she would have never made the top."

"My dear sir, top not bottom writes book!"

Stone grinned. "I grant you she had brains, although she talked so much I never had a chance to give my lecture on the monument."

"Good for her!"

"I prefer a woman who listens."

"Nonsense!" Arla scorned.

"I'll admit I learned things from her about the land—ways of seeing it that had not occurred to me. I was young then and able to learn, even from a woman I didn't particularly take to. I have come to like people less and less—another reason for retiring early. This work breeds cynics. I heard a tourist say this morning while waiting for you to come down, 'Man,' he said to a fellow tourist, 'If they'd let us bring our guns, I'd've had me an eagle!' I wanted to shoot him."

"Good for you! Will we see eagles? Those were crows soaring over the canyon."

"I promise you a golden eagle before journey's end. We're entering their habitat. Incidentally, I was also stationed at Chaco Canyon."

"I can see Fate at work!"

The road now ran toward the river crossing for a hundred miles through sandstone country bordered by the chromatic desert, a land barren of trees and scattered with blue-roofed hogans and isolated stands where Navajo womenfolk were selling their handiwork.

Stone drew up for Arla to see their offerings. She was enthralled by their solemn manner. After looking at moccasins, turquoise-and-silver jewelry, and wool rugs, she bought a dozen strands of cedar beads for a dollar each.

"Beats Cartier!" she exulted, then asked, "Don't they ever speak?"

"They figure their work speaks for them."

"Oh but it does!" Arla exclaimed.

"Does your husband have money of his own?"

"Only his government grant, and that ended after the accident. Now he has his government insurance—a pittance—although with what Daddy settled on me, we get along quite nicely. I don't need much.

"What do you spend it on other than postcards and cedar beads?"

"These clothes you made me buy—and I'm glad you did. They're beginning to feel better the farther north we go. Oh and cravats for him that he never wears." She wiped her cheek.

"I'm sorry. I know it's none of my business."

"I shouldn't be so teary. Things move me so—things like a Navajo woman selling cedar beads out here in the wilderness. The deeper we go, the farther I feel from the earth. Don't you ever feel that way?"

"Occasionally I have feelings," Stone admitted drily.

"I do know that men and women feel differently. I'm afraid I'm going to be a problem for you." Again she wiped her cheek.

"There's kleenex in the glove compartment," Stone offered.

Arla felt among maps and tools and rags, then exclaimed, "Money! Oh, a golden coin!" She looked at it closely. "No, it's a medal," then read aloud, "*The Carnegie Medal . . . greater love hath no man than this, that a man lay down his life for a friend.*" She paused, then cried, "But that's *your* name engraved there!"

Stone grabbed the medal from her and threw it back, slammed the lid and drove on, looking straight ahead.

Arla bit her lip. They rode in silence until she ventured, "I'm sorry. I was so surprised."

When he did not answer, she added, "Was it for what happened there at the gorge?"

"No," he said, "it was not."

She gave up, and they drove on for miles without speaking.

After crossing the Colorado on the high bridge at Marble Canyon, Stone continued on along the base of the Vermillion Cliffs, past great battlements where lone hogans and colored cottonwoods lit the canyon mouths.

"This is silly," Arla finally said, "but I can't stand our not speaking. Please forgive me if I offended you. It startled me so I couldn't help reading it. Please, you *must* understand."

"Okay. I'm sorry I was short with you. It's something I toss in there when I have a lot of driving to do—a kind of good luck token."

"We all need a talisman. I'm afraid I lost mine. Yours is very beautiful and I'm sure even more meaningful." She knew it was not the time to question him.

"Could you drive this rig if you had to?" Stone asked.

"I drove our Land Rover. They're not that different. I'd have to remember to drive on the right-hand side. Back home I bicycle everywhere, unless it's in to Newcastle. Oh but these cliffs are glorious! They dwarf those at Sedona. I've never seen anything so unblemished."

"It's still virgin country. Let's hope the Navajos can keep it that way, although they're learning greed from us. The pressures on them are mounting from oil and uranium interests, not to speak of coal. See that dark line ahead? That's the Kaibab plateau where we're heading. Watch it grow and take shape."

Their road had now begun an almost imperceptible climb toward the dark highland over which clouds were beginning to mass.

"That's the weather front I heard was heading our way," Stone explained. "It could be the first Pacific storm of the year."

"Does it mean snow?" she asked.

"Probably only rain this early. It will be cold though and poor visibility, worse luck. Now you'll know why I took you to Babbitts'."

By the time they had gained the plateau, the conifer and aspen forest was shrouded in mist. Stone turned on the heater.

274

"The canyon will be filled to the rim with clouds," he said, "and most of the visitors will have left."

"You sound glad," she said.

"It's time I retired when I no longer like people."

"Please don't include me. I'll behave!"

After stopping for coffee and a snack from their ice chest at Jacobs Lake, another hour passed before they reached the North Rim. The few cars met were heading out along the dirt road lined with barely visible golden aspens.

The old lodge was another weathered building of wood and stone. A few hardy souls were playing cards in the lounge, drawn up to a fire of juniper logs. Through the windows that usually afforded a view of the canyon, only clouds were to be seen.

"There's still daylight," Stone said after registering. "How about a walk along the rim? You'll need your coat and gloves."

Stone led her down a rocky trail to a flat place on a rim jutout from where the nearest pines and firs could be seen rising through the rain mist. A crow flew to a farther tree. Even its caw was muted.

"No eagles in this weather," Stone observed. "Nothing hunts when it's this thick." He gripped her arm. "Listen!" Up from below came a distant roar. "Can you hear it?"

She nodded. "What is it?"

"Rapids. That's where river runners get a bath. Are you warm enough?"

She gathered her coat tighter. "Shetland tweed. Only bearskin is warmer."

"Do you ever go there?"

"Not since the accident. They're our farthest north. There are still Baystroms in Lerwick, all very poor. Daddy helps them. North Sea oil is ending the old ways. All the young people are leaving."

"So there's doom everywhere! I'm sorry the weather's so bad."

"I loved the drive, and now this. We could be the last people on earth. How long has the river been running?"

"Geologists say millions of years. Beyond a point, time is meaningless. It cut its way down to where it now is. The strata get harder the deeper it goes. If it reaches the fiery heart, the world will end in steam!"

"Lovely! That sound makes me think of *Dover Beach*."

"Where is that?"

"I mean the poem—one about the sound of water over stones."

"I haven't read any poetry since I was in school."

"Do you like music?"

"Both ears are tin," Stone confessed.

Arla squeezed his arm. "There are some things more important than music and poetry, but don't ask me what they are. Although we have historical antiquity, you have something older—geological antiquity." She shivered. "And more lasting."

"You're cold."

"More than cold. It's a remoteness I've felt since I arrived. Let me hold your arm."

"You're feeling the power of the canyon," Stone said. "Sensitive people feel it the most."

"Don't you feel it?" Arla asked.

"Differently. A reassurance that the world of canyon and desert can be depended on when all else fails."

"I had no idea, even from Mary Austin, of its power."

"It will diminish as we leave here."

"I couldn't bear being alone," Arla said.

"Aren't you too sensitive?"

"Merely a woman," she said. "Haven't you known any?"

"From a safe distance," Stone said.

They stood shrouded in the dripping cloud, hearing only the far roar of the river. Arla had not relaxed her grip on his arm.

"Let's go back," she finally said, "I've had enough."

The dining room was nearly empty. Stone sensed her mood and they ate in silence.

"I confess I'm disoriented," she said as they parted to go to their rooms. "We've come such a distance from that beautiful meal on the other rim. I need to get lost in sleep. I'll be my talkative self in the morning. I hope you can stand another day of me."

"I'll meet it as it comes. I'm not too hopeful that it will clear."

276

2.

el castillo paso por aquí año de 1620 de las adelanta qu mes la

Stone's fears were right. The wet cloud still smothered the plateau. They set out before the dining room had opened and backtracked to Jacobs Lake for breakfast.

"We can get out of it," Stone showed her on the map, "by heading into Utah, then east to Glen Canyon. The front is moving southeast away from us. Okay?"

"Whither thou goest," Arla said. "I'm completely *déraciné*."

The road dropped fast through piñon and juniper to grasslands without horizon. No cars were seen for miles. Entering Utah they met a band of pronghorn antelope that froze, stared, then turned white rumps and bounded away.

"This could be the veldt," Arla said. "No buffalos? Or polygamists? I know from reading Zane Grey that we are in their domain. Are you a Mormon?"

"No, why do you ask?"

"There's something Old Testamentish about you. You seem older than fifty, although you do show traces of a sense of humor."

"I've been trying to hide it!" Stone said.

"You must find me hopeless giddy."

"I thought the English were more like you say I am."

"Not this Lancashire girl married to a Welshman!"

"Have you known Americans?" he asked.

"Mostly archaeologists—Harvard and Princeton types."

"No wild westerners?"

"Only in novels and films."

"The sleep did you good."

"Bring on another day, sir. I can cope."

Beyond the town of Fredonia the highway entered Utah, and

then at Kanab, another isolated Mormon stronghold, it turned east for a hundred miles toward the river-crossing at Glen Canyon dam.

Again the road was lonely. Stone drove at high speed while Arla let the rush of wind and the colored landscape soothe her insecurity. Nothing was what she had anticipated. Stone also puzzled her. What lay behind his formal exterior?

At the river crossing he asked, "Do you want to see the turbines that generate the power?"

"Not especially, but they would interest Daddy. I don't suppose there are postcards."

"There should be. They are works of art provided you don't know what's at the other end of the line."

"What do you mean?" she asked.

"I mean the cities that live by electrical power—Phoenix, Las Vegas, Los Angeles, all vulnerable, all ignorant of their dependence on water and turbines and a few miles of copper wire. Still, they're worth seeing."

The elevator dropped them deep into the massive concrete dam where a walkway bordered a range of gleaming turbines spinning with an organ-hum. Across the walk, high windows looked down on the green water as it resumed its flow toward the Grand Canyon.

"So this is what the Grady Gang wants to dynamite!" Arla marvelled.

"You've read Dan Grady?"

"Glyn loves him. I preferred his *Alone*. Do you know him?"

"He was in and out of the Service, first as a park ranger, and then when his books earned enough to support him, as a summer fire watcher. He wrote a sexy novel about the North Rim. He gave me a copy but I haven't read it yet."

"You seem to have a number of unread books."

"I prefer life at first-hand."

"I did too until it came too close. Have you been tempted to join his Gang?"

"I admire their guts, but I've been disciplined too long. I'll always be loyal to the Service as long as it has leaders like the Secretary."

"Could they blow this up?" Arla asked.

"Not with dynamite!" Stone scorned. "It would take an atomic bomb to destroy it—or Time that will silt it up in the end."

278

"I'm glad you insisted I see it," Arla said when they had regained the Ranger and drank coffee from the thermos jug. "We built cathedrals, you build dams."

"Still it's wrong to interfere with the river's flow, monitoring it to the needs of distant users. The lower river has been killed, turned into a chain of stagnant lakes."

"Can't you Park people do anything about it?"

"We're hamstrung by the politicians who are influenced by the power interest and their lobbyists. One of our congressmen proposed to cantilever a church out over the South Rim. He said the Grand Canyon needed somewhere for people to worship. Another suggested leasing it to Walt Disney. Imagine Disney's Grand Canyon World!"

"Did you oppose him?"

"One Dan Grady is enough. Not that I'm a coward. Just conservative."

Arla shook her head. "It makes our Wall seem like child's play with blocks."

"I should have been like my father. This would have thrilled him. I'm more like my mother."

"Two parents are always a problem!" Arla said.

Beyond the construction camp of Page they came to the tall stacks of the steam generating plant. Gray smoke was drifting toward the southeast where the receding weather front darkened the horizon.

"Would you like to visit it?" Stone asked her. "Your father might be interested in a report."

"I'll report from a distance, thank you! What lies ahead?"

"Deep Navajo country—Shonto, Betatakin, and Kayenta where we'll be tonight. Also Monument Valley."

"How far is Kayenta?"

"Another hundred miles."

"Let's carry on, although I do want to see Betatakin. It's in her book. I warn you, I'm going to read to you whether you like it or not."

As they drove east Stone began to speak softly. "It was not enough to use just water power. They had to build that monster that feeds on coal. You see what it's doing to the sky."

"Where do they get the coal?"

"Near Kayenta. It's stripped from the Black Mesa and hauled here on an electric railway built for the purpose."

"That would interest Daddy!"

"Tomorrow I'll show you how they bring it down and load the cars." Stone pointed to a landmark on the northeastern horizon. "That's Navajo Mountain coming up—another of the Sacred Peaks. Rainbow Bridge is on its far side."

"You've been there," Arla half asked.

"Not since the rising water threatened it."

"Didn't *that* tempt you to join Dan Grady?"

"I told you I'm not an activist. I've been too many years in government harness. We'll see an even bigger monster in New Mexico. The hunger for power is insatiable."

"You have strong feelings, stronger than you show."

"Don't report me to the Secretary! Seeing that dam and this plant always provokes me."

"Glyn taught me to take the long view. We have survived so much destruction, wave after wave scouring our island. What you are seeing is only the first wave to break over the West."

"What does he say about our surviving an atomic war?"

"Only if there's slime left in the sea."

They saw Navajo Mountain grow larger, change shape and dwindle as they bore southeast. At the turnoff to Shonto the road worsened and he shifted into four-wheel drive. The road snaked in and out of dry arroyos and finally dropped into a deeper canyon with thinly leaved cottonwoods along a flowing stream and a smoke-plumed rock trading-post.

"It won't be like the one at Cameron," he told her. "This is the real thing."

He drew up in front of the low building and they entered. The air was stifling from a wood stove and blue with layers of tobacco smoke. There was a stink of raw wool. A wrinkled Navajo behind the counter spoke rapidly and Arla was astonished to hear Stone reply in the same tongue. Several lounging young Navajos showed no interest as they continued to smoke. Stone bought a bag of piñon nuts, and exchanged a few more words with the expressionless old man. As they left, he spoke rapidly to the loungers. They grinned without looking up.

After they set out again, Arla demanded, "What did you say to them?"

"That my daughter is shopping for a velvet wedding dress."

"You didn't!"

"They're great jokers—at someone else's expense," Stone said.

"You don't do too badly yourself. How did you know I want a dress of green and purple velvet—like the one the old woman was wearing where I bought the beads."

"I saw you admiring her. We'll get you some velvet at Chinle and you can make your own. It's time you learned to sew. Things are cheaper there—it's a big post that used to be run by old Lorenzo Hubbell. Now the Navajos run it."

"Where did you learn their language?"

"At Chaco. I was there after El Morro. It's not as hard as it sounds."

"My husband has tried to teach me Welsh. French is my limit."

"I had to learn it or leave, and I wanted to stay."

"How far is it to Chaco?" she asked.

"Two hundred miles."

"One hundred seems to be your standard unit of measurement," Arla laughed, "and your distances get greater and greater. North Africa is like that, back from the coast."

As they started up the east bank of the arroyo, Stone warned her, "Tighten your belt and hold on."

While she clung to the doorhandle to keep from being thrown about, Stone maneuvered the Ranger around and over rock slides as the road shrank to a shelf.

He stayed in compound low gear, barely maintaining headway as they lurched onto the mesa. There he halted and they shared a beer.

"You're sweating," she observed.

"Keeping your momentum and not hurrying does it."

"Keeping your nerve helps!"

The road was still rough though no longer perilous. After a dozen miles through piñon-juniper woodland and deep red sandstone dust, they eased up to the headquarters at Betatakin from where the Navajo National Monument is administered. While Stone visited with the rangers, Arla shopped at the Navajos' jewelry display.

281

"Presents for the family," she said when he rejoined her. "What a gorgeous place! I adore the people. Such dignity! Our shopkeepers are so beastly obsequious when they see you have money and such bastards when they see you don't."

"I'm glad you respond to them. In some ways they are my people. Now we have a choice of two walks. One is up Tsegi Canyon to a point below the cave. That takes a couple of hours. The other is only half a mile to a viewpoint opposite the dwellings. It will be deserted there. Everyone's gone on the longer walk. Which is it?"

"To where there's no one!"

With bread and cheese in Stone's backpack, they took the shorter trail along which the vegetation was discreetly identified. Arla was delighted as Stone assumed the role of ranger-naturalist. A bluejay flew along with them, scolding for crumbs. At a gap in the scrub oak, Stone pointed toward the northwest. "There's our friend again."

"Navajo Mountain," she marveled, "like a blue cloud. How far is it?"

"A hundred miles."

She laughed. "Will I ever see Rainbow Bridge?"

"Next trip."

"Be careful, I might just!"

They ate at the viewpoint across the deep narrow canyon from the restorations in the red-gold cliff. Far below them a stir of air rustled the tipmost leaves of cottonwoods and aspens, still thinly leafed with gold. Muted voices rose from the canyon trail. The bluejay kept scolding until quieted with crumbs.

"It's quite perfect," Arla sighed. "That Grand Canyon was a bit too much, and also I felt so diminished by distance when we came down off the plateau. It must be like that on the moon."

"We'll return to civilization before we're through. You'll like Santa Fe."

"I feel we are in civilization here. Something happened that's lasting. What does Betatakin mean?"

"They say it means House in the Canyon Wall."

"And Tsegi?"

"That depends on which Navajo you ask. Some say Rock Canyon, others Canyon of Ghosts. Chelly (Shay) is how the Spaniards pronounced it. We'll be there tomorrow."

"It's strange yet natural. I feel secure here. Did people live in that huge cave or is it one of your sets for tourists?"

Stone laughed. "My dear Miss Arla, people really lived there in a hundred apartments."

"How long ago? No, don't tell me. Space by the hundreds, time by the thousands, right?"

He looked closely at her. "Is that a tear? I thought you were happy."

"Don't you know a woman can be happy and sad at the same time? I know I'm too emotional. Just like my Mum, Daddy says. The Lancashire strain, he calls it. It's the way I felt when we were working on the Wall: that they were dead and we were alive and there was a gulf between us more impassable than any wall. That canyon is our wall and there's no way across, no way back. We took the wrong trail."

"You feel things deeply."

"Aren't all women emotional?" Arla asked.

"I'm no authority."

"I'm not as simple as I seem. I shall read you something tonight that says it better than I can—something she wrote about this place. It's what made me want to come to Betatakin."

"I warn you I get sleepy after supper!"

As they walked back up the steep trail, Arla stopped to pick up a feather.

"Blue feather *muy buena*," he observed, "black feather *muy mala*."

When they registered at the Holiday Inn at Kayenta, managed by Navajos, Arla said, "I'd like you to request adjoining rooms." And when he looked puzzled, she added, "Don't misunderstand. I'll feel more secure."

"This is not Apache country," Stone laughed.

"I feel ambivalent, both at home and alien and always on the edge of the unknown. Yet today has been magical."

Stone spoke in Navajo to the desk clerk who replied rapidly.

"What were you saying?" Arla demanded as they unloaded the Ranger.

"More about women's fashions."

"You make fun of me," Arla protested.

"You're not the only one who can tease."

"Where is my velvet?"

"At Chinle I told you, at the trader's boutique."

Arla laughed and slammed her door.

That night was their first Indian meal. The dining room was peopled mostly by Navajo matrons, maidens and girl children, wearing purple-and-green velvet and white dresses, and adorned with silver and turquoise jewelry, the four generations eating with silent relish.

"Is it a special occasion?" Arla asked.

"The grandmother's birthday," Stone explained. "Navajos don't talk at table. Afterward there's no stopping them."

After they finished, she said, "I still intend to read to you. The lobby is too noisy. Would it be improper to ask you *chez moi* for a prose nightcap?"

"We're far from those who make the rules. I warned you though, I get sleepy after I've eaten."

"Give me five minutes and I'll call you."

Stone found her in robe and slippers, her hair down over her shoulders like a ruddy mane. She was holding the book by Mary Austin.

"This is what brought me here. This one book." She saw his hesitant look. "Don't worry, I have no designs on you other than as a listener. I wanted to be comfortable. Do you mind? My head aches after I wear my hair up all day." She opened the book. "Let me read you why I wanted to go to Betatakin. Here is what she wrote about it." She began softly, *Walking there, one of these wide-open summer days, when there comes a sudden silence, and in the midst of silence a stir, look where you walk. Always, incredibly, there lingers about these places where once man, some trace that the human sense responds to, never so sensitively as where it has lain mellowing through a thousand years of sun and silence.*"

Arla paused, and when Stone remained silent she added, "Can you see why the book moved me so, reading it there where we're lucky to have one month of sun out of twelve? No wonder the Romans returned to Italy! I wondered are there really such places— ones that have mellowed through a thousand years of sun and silence. Now I know there are. Will it be the same at El Morro?"

Stone stood up. "It won't have changed. Few people go there

284

even in summer. All I can promise is another day, a good breakfast and an early start."

"Have I bored you?" Arla asked.

"No."

"Where will we be tomorrow night?"

"At Chinle, at the mouth of Cañon de Chelly."

"What does Chinle mean?"

"Where water flows from the canyon. How many bolts of velvet will you need? Not as many as a Navajo matron."

"How discerning of you, Mr. Stone."

"The desk says cooler weather by the weekend, possibly rain."

"Where will we be by then?" she asked.

"Santa Fe, barring trouble."

"Trouble?"

"Apaches. We'll skirt their reservation after we leave Chelly."

"Please be serious. And sit down for one more paragraph. It is her definition of the land we're seeing. Now listen. *By land, I mean all those things common to a given region, the flow of prevailing winds, the succession of vegetal cover, the legend of ancient life; and the scene, above everything the magnificently shaped and colored scene.* Isn't that how it is?"

"More poetical than our literature describes it!" Stone said drily.

"How would *you* describe it?"

"I wouldn't. I'd show it."

Arla laughed. "You win."

Stone rose again. "If anything frightens you, call me. You'll have to shout though."

"Good night, Mr. Stone," Arla said cooly.

Early next morning he backtracked to where coal from Black Mesa came down in chunks on an endless belt that dumped into a silo. Between its high legs the train from the power plant entered at snail's pace, pulled by an electric engine that crept forward as each car was loaded through a chute beneath the silo. By the time the last car was full and the train on its way back to Page, an empty train had arrived to take its place. It was a cunning system.

From their vantage point in the Ranger, Stone and Arla watched the cycle revolve with banging and rattling, whistles and bells and an occasional trainman's curse. Eventually Black Mesa would be levelled and the Hopis on the far side have an unobstructed view of the mountain sacred to their ancient Navajo enemy.

Stone began to speak, almost to himself. "I didn't object when they dammed the river in Boulder Canyon. Students then didn't get excited about such things. After all, no water was lost, merely passed through the turbines and penstocks and released to flow on to the Gulf. Fiat Lux, says the Lord, and why shouldn't His people have light and power even though they dwell far away and know not from whence it came? Then when they flooded Glen Canyon, I began to question. I was older then and had seen what cheap power had done to the air in and around the cities. Finally when oil and coal began to be used as fuels and the desert sky darkened, I balked. My orientation lectures changed. That brought a letter of concern from the Secretary when he got a complaint from one of our congressmen. That triggered my plan to retire early." Stone paused, then raised his voice, "Had enough?"

Arla shook her head. "I'll never have enough when you are moved. Then it wasn't just your health."

"I'd gladly die in harness if I were doing what I believe in. No, I've had enough of being hypocritical. Yet I'm just not made to join the Grady gang as much as I admire their guts." He paused again. "We've got a long drive ahead of us and we haven't seen Monument Valley. What do you say?"

"I don't want to see merely beautiful landscapes. I want to see where people lived and died, like at Betatakin. And I can do without Mr. Wayne's autograph, thank you!"

Stone laughed "Welcome to my side! So it's on to Chinle and ten bolts of purple velvet!"

And so they resumed their journey on a seemingly endless road toward an unattainable horizon, passing striding matrons in brilliant garb and pickup trucks packed with entire families; in and out of dry arroyos marked by cottonwoods and trading posts; and everywhere the solitary hogans of a people who in the end might prove the most enduring of all.

Later Stone slowed to a crawl for a flock of sheep that filled the road, shepherded by two passive Navajos on horseback and one active dog. They found themselves in a dusty tumult of bells, bleating, and barking. He came to a stop abreast of the riders. They stared until he spoke in Navajo. Then they grinned but did not answer.

286

"What did you say this time?" Arla demanded when they had resumed speed. "Go in beauty?"

"I said that dog doesn't need you two lazy bastards!"

Arla reached for his hand on the wheel.

As he maintained speed, she lay back and dozed, to wake and doze again. Navajo Mountain had long since disappeared behind them. Now and then she roused and read from her book while he listened, barely hearing the sense, until these words fixed his attention:

" . . . *and to many people grass is as indispensable an index of fertility in the earth as long hair is of femininity in a woman.*"

"That I can understand," he said.

She smiled. "There's more. *In arid regions where the period of growth is confined to the short season of maximum rainfall, the processes of foliation and floration are pushed almost to explosion; followed by a long quiescence in which life merely persists.*"

He remembered her hair on the pillow and his wish to touch it — touch it and nothing more.

"That makes sense," Stone said. "What I don't understand is how just a book could bring you all this way."

"It's not just a book. It's a visionary way of seeing a particular land in relation to all life on earth."

"I'm not a visionary." Stone protested.

"You are and won't recognize it. You are too rigid. You need to let your imagination go. I think it's your uniform that inhibits you."

Stone smiled. "Could be."

"She makes what I'm seeing wider and deeper," Arla continued, "although the strangeness of it all still troubles me, so different from our green little overcrowded island, all known and secure and safe. The people here seem alien with no sense of community. How silently they ate together! Yet I respond to it, could even come to hunger for it. I can understand why you have never left. I think the power comes from the far distances as well as from the deep canyons."

As the landscape flashed by, Stone pondered his role in her mission. There was no one in his experience to relate her to, admittedly spoiled and wealthy, capricious and a tease, beautiful in evening dress and also in whipcords and gum-soled desert boots, a wine-red shirt and purple scarf restraining her heavy hair; a woman schooled

287

in Switzerland who had ridden in the cab of the Flying Scotsman and worked alongside her husband on the Roman Wall; a north of England woman with even more northern blood in her veins, a woman out of Beowulf she said. Was there a Grendel for him to slay? He smiled at the fantasy into which his mind had wandered.

Nearing Chinle the valley widened and grew fertile. Although the tribal seat lay southeast at Window Rock, here was the heart of Navajoland and their ancient canyon retreat. Stone drew up at a roadside monument for Arla to read of the death there in a plane crash of Governor John Clayton.

"He was a friend of the tribe," he explained, "and also of the land, although he helped lobby through the last great dam. What I learned from him was not to expect absolute consistency in anyone, least of all in myself."

The trading post at Chinle carried a wide variety of goods. "Like an Army PX," Stone observed. "One of these days they'll start carrying mobile hogans! If I'd been born earlier, I'd have been a trader."

"At Shonto?"

"Or Shiprock."

"How did you survive this long in government service?"

"My sterling character, what else?"

"So I've met his model for Lassiter!" she teased.

Her good humor endured as she wandered through the store. Stone finally had to tear her away, laden with more presents for her people and the bolts of velvet she was determined to buy.

"What are you going to do with it?" Stone asked. "You don't sew."

"Do you really want to know? I shall have Givenchy make the gown for my next court appearance! Then tell these traders they can boast 'By Appointment to Her Majesty the Queen'!"

Stone drove to the lodge among cottonwoods at the mouth of Cañon de Chelly. "Get washed up," he said. "Leave your boots on and bring your coat. We're going for another sundown walk."

"Yes, my Lord," Arla murmured as they went again to connecting rooms.

"Not too tired?" he asked.

"Just dazzled. It's been a day of days."

"There'll be more," he promised.

288

The sun was low at their backs when they reached a deserted viewpoint on the south rim of the canyon. As he led her along the narrow trail, she said, "Keep holding my arm. Since you told me about that shepherd, I dream of falling."

Suddenly the canyon appeared beneath them—a wide deep opening with meager cornfields and fruit trees, a few hogans, sheep and horses. At the end of the day the walls were radiant with golden light.

"We're just in time," Stone said.

"It's not another film set?"

"Sit here on the edge and we'll watch it grow dark."

Stone felt her gripping his arm and turning, saw that she was again tearful. "Ladies don't cry," he muttered, offering his handkerchief.

"Damn you, William Stone! A woman can cry when she needs to."

"What's there to cry for?"

"If you don't know, I can't tell you."

"It has to be seen at this hour. We'll have a jeep tomorrow to ourselves. The regular tour is by charabanc. Are you okay?"

"As much as I'll ever be. It's different from Betatakin. Are they still excavating sites?

"They'll never finish. It was a big community, bigger than Mesa Verde, and more fertile though smaller than Chaco. Water determines size in the Southwest, then and now. This is one place where the living and the dead dwell peacefully together. Only Navajos can live in the canyon, although it is administered by us as a national monument. Are you warm enough?"

Arla squeezed his arm in answer as they heard a woman's voice from below calling to someone on the rim who answered.

She tightened her grip. "Listen! An antiphonal. Is it an evening prayer?"

Stone chuckled. "She's telling him what to bring home for dinner!"

"I'll have to believe you. How far down is it?"

"Not like that gorge. A few hundred feet."

"Isn't it dangerous without a railing?"

"The Navajos won't permit one. They only tolerate us for the revenue visitors bring them."

They fell silent as the darkness deepened. Then Arla asked, "Was that an eagle that flew by?"

"An owl hunting his dinner."

"Thank you for the beautiful timing. I feel secure with you."

"Why shouldn't you?" he asked.

"Men aren't always what they seem. I know how disciplined you are; and also that you reveal so little of yourself."

"What do you want to see?"

"I sense things deeply hidden from everyone."

"Is that wrong?" Stone asked.

"I don't mean that."

"Aren't we all hiding something?"

"Not my husband. He's transparent."

"You love him, don't you."

"We took vows and we've kept them. Did you take vows?"

"Once," Stone said.

"Did you keep them?"

"I did."

"Did she?"

"No," he said.

Arla was silent, then asked, "Why haven't you married again?"

"Does a man have to have a woman to prove he's a man?"

"Not necessarily," Arla admitted.

"You want me to tell you about my marriage, don't you."

"Wasn't it what made you what you are?"

"As well as curious, whimsical and capricious, you are also perceptive."

Arla laughed. "Don't tell me if you don't want to. I know I'm being cheeky, but it is a quiet place to talk, free from interruption. Were you stationed here?"

"No, but I've been here many times. There's a strong pull."

"I feel it the way I did at Betatakin."

"You're easy to be with. I was skeptical about the assignment, even resented it."

"You didn't conceal it very well!" Arla said.

"I still can't conceive of your coming all this way for a book, least of all for *that* book! And alone."

"I've not been alone. Her book is *my* talisman."

290

Stone shook his head. "Are you sure you're warm enough? You don't want to return to the lodge?"

"It's not cold like the North Rim," she reminded him.

"Not getting hungry?"

"I can wait."

"Are you over your tears?" Stone persisted.

"Completely."

The sound of a sheep bell came from below, then a chattering cry, followed by the barking of a dog.

"What is it?" Arla whispered.

"Coyotes."

"A pack of them?"

"Only one with several voices," Stone explained.

The night grew quiet again. A few lights came on in the canyon. Then Stone began to speak softly as he had at the base of Black Mesa.

"I've never talked about my marriage," he began. "I was hurt by it."

"Don't let a foolish woman's curiosity cause you pain." Her voice was tender. "Sometimes talking is the best way to be free of it."

"I don't know if I can. Are you sure you're not hungry?"

"Being here means more to me than food," she replied.

Stone began again. "It goes way back. I married during my graduate year at the university—a Mexican girl from a wealthy ranching family in Sonora. She was younger than I and in rebellion against her upbringing. She'd been in a convent. She had a good mind and wanted to be a soil chemist and go back and inherit and manage the ranch. Her body got in the way. It was stronger than her mind. She was very beautiful and that was her fatality, and mine. After we married she told me she required six meals a day, three of food and three of love. Our first year was a feast for us both, then my studies began to suffer. I scraped through the M.A. and was not encouraged to go on for the doctorate. I entered the Park Service and went to train at the South Rim. I made the mistake of taking her with me. The work and long hours took my strength and time. I was away a lot, learning the canyon and my job. I couldn't keep providing the other three meals so she got them elsewhere. It was my fault, not providing for her as I had vowed to do. I came home late one night and found her in bed with the boss of the mule string."

291

Arla gripped his hand. "What did you do?"

"Nothing," Stone said. "Your lower-class Mexican is a gentleman even in a situation like that. He begged my pardon, took his clothes, and backed out."

"Didn't you punish him?"

Stone laughed. "We needed him! And the truth is I was relieved. I had come to realize I'd made a mistake. I wasn't meant for that kind of marriage. Even though she swore she would be faithful, I said I'd had enough. When I began to pack to move out, she threw on a robe and ran out screaming bloody murder. You could have heard her on the North Rim. I took off after her. She was running along the rim walk where you and I walked; and there where we sat on the low wall, just as I was about to catch her, she dove over the edge."

"Oh my God! What did you do?"

"Just stood there frozen, listening to the rock slide she'd started. People came. They'd heard her screaming. We could see that she was caught on something part way down. She was whimpering and calling my name. Then she must have fainted. They brought a powerful light and we saw that she was caught on the branches of a dead pine. We'd been intending to uproot it and let it go on down at least to the first ledge. Somehow she and the slide hadn't taken it down. She'd gotten heavy. I suspected she was pregnant."

"What did you do?" Arla asked.

Stone sighed. "The wrong thing. I told them to get all the rope they could find, and over the edge I went, expecting every move to be my last, the rim was so unstable. She was whimpering again and I kept hoping the tree would break loose and take her with it. I kept inching my way down. There were some bushes to cling to. As I got closer I saw that a dead branch had impaled her through the leg above the knee. Her hair had also caught and helped hold her." Stone paused. "Her hair was long and black as night, though not as thick as yours." Arla silently kept his hand.

"They let down the rope," Stone resumed, "and when I reached her—she had fainted again—I got a sling around her. I was gambling that when they began to pull her up, the branch would break off with her still impaled on it. That's what happened. I held on to the trunk as she rose, loosing more rocks that came down on me."

"God was surely looking after you!"

292

"He misunderstood my prayer! When at last the rope came back down, I got it around myself, then I must have passed out for I don't remember anything until the hospital in Flagstaff. I had a dislocated shoulder and a hundred cuts and bruises. They said the tree went down as they pulled me up. I remember giving it a kick as I swung free."

"How long were you in hospital?" Arla asked.

"A couple of weeks maybe. They moved me to a better hospital in Phoenix. The tetanus shots nearly killed me. I'd also strained my heart, on top of a congenital defect they discovered. They said that I should avoid extreme excitement if I wanted to stay alive. So after work at El Morro and Chaco, I took a training center job and eventually came to be in charge. Then you came along."

Arla asked, "What became of her?"

Stone laughed softly. "She rode off into the sunset with the mule string boss. We hated to lose him. They said she'd always walk with a limp."

"You'd think she'd have miscarried."

"Too tough."

"Are you still married to her?"

"I heard she returned to Mexico and divorced me for desertion. If she had a child, I hope it was not mine."

"Did they know she had jumped?" Arla asked.

"I said she had fainted and fallen over the edge."

"So that was how the medal came!"

"The Secretary himself brought it. The Old Curmudgeon, we called him. There's never been another like him."

Night had closed down, the canyon was invisible, the lights gone out. Arla kept his hand as they walked back to the lodge. The cafeteria had closed. They ate in the kitchen with the Navajo dishwasher.

Arla remained quiet while Stone and the Indian carried on an expressionless conversation in the latter's tongue. She did not ask Stone what they said.

Stone was late for breakfast. He found Arla writing postcards in the lobby.

"Sorry," he said. "I overslept again. Have you eaten?"

"I waited for you." Her face was concerned. "You look like you hadn't slept at all."

"It took a while."

"I slept poorly. That dream of falling again."

Coffee and food revived Stone. "I'm okay, but we'd better take the charabanc."

"That means you're not okay."

"I'll feel better as my mind settles. That was a lot of talking I did. Poor girl!"

"I asked for it." Arla smiled and took his hand.

"Tom the driver is the guide. He was born here. He was one of the Navajo team that devised the code the Japs could never crack. He knows more about the canyon than anyone. You'll sit up front with him."

"But you'll come too."

"I'm not that tired."

Arla waited for fresh coffee, then said, "I too lay awake thinking about what you told me."

"I'll feel better for having gotten it all out—and for the first time."

"It's not healthy to keep things bottled up so long. Are you really alone in the world?"

"I have a dog," Stone admitted.

Arla laughed. "Why didn't you tell me? What kind?"

"Believe it or not, a Shetland sheepdog."

"How strange! Where is he now?"

"She's boarded with the vet who's always cared for her. He's near the airport in Albuquerque from where you'll leave. Her name is Sheltie. Should I change it to Bay?"

"Why didn't you bring her?"

"The Secretary thought you might be a cat lover."

Again she laughed. "But I love dogs. I have two Airedales— mother and son. Is yours purebred?"

"The vet says she is."

"What color coat?"

"Tri-color. She has the two coats, the softer inner and the rough outer."

"I had one as a child, although she was really a border collie. Where did you get her?"

"I found her along the highway west of Albuquerque, matted and covered with ticks and with a broken leg. She'd probably been abused and run away and been hit by a car. That was four years ago.

She's five or six now. I'll check on her as we go through Albuquerque on the way to El Morro."

"That will be nice. I keep thinking about your being alone. If you have no people, who will inherit your things?"

"What things? I keep a bare apartment at the South Rim. Sheltie's my only valuable possession and I'll outlive her. An annuity left by my parents ends with my death. I give the income from it to the Defenders of Wildlife. My needs are few."

"I envy you. We are sinking under the weight of our things." She paused. "Will you leave me something to remember you by?"

"My old postcards? Visitors sometimes write to me when they get back home."

"I'm serious. Will you leave me your medal?"

"That? You're joking."

"It will mean so much to me after last night."

"If you really want it, I'll add a codicil to my will. There's Tom driving up. Get your jacket and a scarf I haven't seen. The afternoon will be windy. I called Albuquerque. Another front is not far behind us. I'll meet you in ten minutes."

Arla took her place next to the driver, while Stone sat on one of the benches filled with visitors and their camera equipment.

Tom proved an entertaining guide, employing a mixture of English, Spanish and Navajo. As they drove deeper into the winding canyon, stopping to take pictures of restorations, Stone could hear Arla's high-pitched laughter as Tom outdid himself for her benefit.

"I adore him," she said to Stone at one of the stops. "My accent puzzles him."

"I told him you are Queen Victoria's great granddaughter."

"What did he say to that whopper?"

"That his grandmother grows the best peaches in the canyon."

"I want to pick some!"

"Too late. Apples and pears are in now."

They stopped at noon beneath a working site part way up the canyon wall. Box lunches provided their meal. Stone left Arla with the others and went to talk with a group of Navajos cleaning out a runoff channel at the base of the cliff. The sound of her laughter assured him she was at ease.

As they reboarded he said, "You've gone native!"

Her eyes where shining. "I love it here. Can we stay a few days?"

"And forget Chaco? We're due there tomorrow night."

"Glyn would never forgive me."

"It's not like this."

"I've seen photographs," she said.

"Photographs don't lie—they just don't tell the truth. We'll get an early start. The wind is rising. Tomorrow will probably be wet. The winter rains are early this year."

After they set out again deeper into the canyon, the sand began to blow. Tom wheeled the charabanc around and headed back to the lodge.

"Gotta get the hell out," he explained. "Wind make Cañon de Chelly all the same Cañon del Muerto. *Es muy malo.* Too goddamn many tourists."

As they backtracked down the sandy streambed, a fox ran across in front of the car, chased by a dog of mixed breed. While the little red creature ran smoothly near the ground, the yapping cur kicked up sand as it was outdistanced. The fox reached the talus slope and disappeared among the rocks. The dog lay down panting while the visitors cheered.

At the lodge over tea in the cafeteria, Arla complained, "Why can't they boil the water and heat the pot?"

"Poor girl, why don't you drink coffee like a good American? Too bad we had to return. Tom usually stays out until sundown. You liked what you saw."

"It's fabulous. My two pets would have gone up after that fox."

"They'd never have caught him. Brother Fox can climb the walls if he has to."

"Was this the model for the Garden of Eden? If I could choose another time and place to live, it would be here a thousand years ago, with Betatakin for holidays! There can't be much difference between the way the Anasazi lived and those who live here today."

"The basics never change: food, shelter, sex. I was thinking as I lay awake last night, Mary Austin wasn't wrong about everything. A woman's hair is truly the essence of femininity."

Arla smiled. "Thank you, sir. You were right, I needed my scarf."

"You surely did bring one for each day."

"Is it going to rain?"

"By tonight at the latest. The wind from the west means rain. The grass needs it."

"Do you want to hear a poem about wind and rain from the west?" She began softly, " 'O western wind, when wilt thou blow that the small rain down can rain? Christ, that my love were in my arms and I in my bed again!' "

"Who wrote it?" Stone asked.

"No one knows. It's very old."

"I said the basics don't change."

"At home we long for sun," Arla said.

"We never get enough rain."

"What's scarce is precious!"

Arla stepped outdoors, then returned and asked, "What's that bitter smell in the air?"

"Rain on the creosote. Good, it's begun."

3.

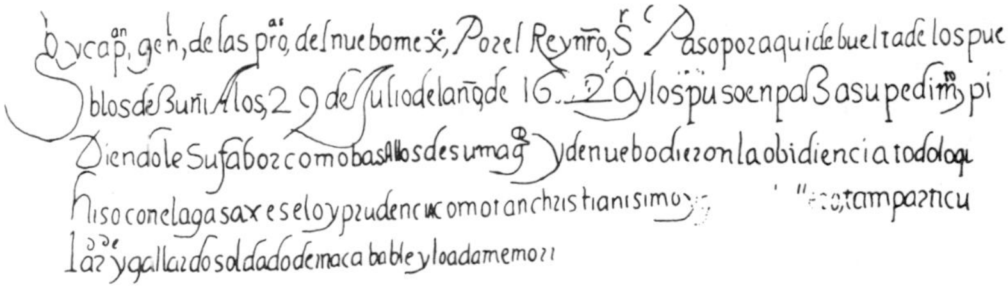

Rain was still falling next morning when, after coffee in the kitchen before the cafeteria opened, they took the north rim road, angling east to Lukuchukai and over the Chuskas into New Mexico. The gravelled road was crowned for drainage and Stone drove fast, the big tires singing on the wet surface, the windshield sweeps working rhythmically. The Ranger was warm from the heater.

Arla was watchful at first, worried by such speed in wet weather, until she acknowledged the authority with which he drove. Then she lay back and let her mind range over their journey. After what he had told her the night before, she recognized that he was not the man who had seemed matter of fact and formal.

After they had come down out of Washington Pass and were

resuming speed north on U.S. 666, Stone pulled onto the shoulder. "It should be about here," he said.

"What is it?" she asked drowsily.

"Put on your coat and get out. Look ahead on your left."

Arla peered into the light rain, then cried, "What is it?"

"Another of the Sacred Mountains. Shiprock!"

"We read about it. The mist makes it even more mysterious. Do you understand their religion, their legends?"

"No, but I recognize the sacredness of their mountains. Better guides than a man nailed to a cross."

"What you are showing me gives her book the depth reading alone doesn't give it."

As they peered at the great basalt formation that appeared and vanished in the shifting veils, beads of moisture gathered on hair that had escaped her scarf. This day's was autumn-colored. He wanted to touch her hair and tell her how beautiful it was in the rain. He did not.

"You have a gift for what you show me," Arla said when they had resumed their journey. "You must have been an extraordinary leader for those coming along. What will you do in retirement? How can you leave all this?"

"I won't know until I've tried," Stone admitted. "Perhaps some travelling."

"You and my husband would hit it off. Have you ever been abroad?"

"I've never crossed the Pecos. What I've been showing you is only what I wanted to see, perhaps for the last time.

In another hour, approaching Farmington on the San Juan, they came to the other great new power plant, its topmost stacks invisible as were the pinnacles of Shiprock.

"They shut down when the ceiling is low," Stone explained, "otherwise everything would die from the fumes. As it is, things are dying anyhow from what killed my parents."

"Where do they get their coal?" Arla asked.

"From a nearby open pit mine. The Navajos fought against it. They said if we keep digging, the earth will open and swallow us. They believe the earth suffers pain."

"Do you?" Arla asked.

"Could be."

"They were ignored of course."

"They were too disorganized. The younger ones who would profit from long leases prevailed over the elders."

In Farmington, Stone headed for a restaurant whose buffet, he told Arla, served the best food in the Southwest.

"Meet here at the phone booth," he said as she went to wash up. "I have a call to make."

Although the luncheon hour was nearly past, the buffet was still a gourmet's dream of roast and cold meats, fowl, fish, cheeses, salads and sweets, all presided over by a chef of great height and girth.

"Travelling salesmen avoid thin chefs," Stone observed. "People come from far to eat here. I used to come weekends when I was at Chaco. Sometimes I'd go on to Mesa Verde."

"Will we go there?" Arla asked.

"Not if we make Acoma and El Morro. They're in the opposite direction."

"These well-fed men remind me of the Northern Hotel in Manchester!"

"You're seeing Texans come to rape the Indians."

"Mary Austin must be spinning in her grave."

She's lucky to have died when she did. Our technology means that mountains are no longer safe from the bulldozers."

"She predicted that her ghost would return to haunt us," Arla remarked.

"Someone must speak for each generation. We have Abbey, DeVoto, Stegner, and now Dan Grady. Earlier, Major Powell and John Muir raised their voices against our waste of the land."

"You're going to be a spokesman in spite of yourself!"

"I have no voice for public speech nor am I a writer." Stone insisted.

"You're still a young man. You shouldn't just disappear."

"I called Chaco. Tomorrow should be dry."

"Will we come back here tonight? I read there are no accommodations there."

"There will be for you—on a cot in the restroom off the museum lobby."

"Where will you sleep?" she asked.

"In the Ranger." Stone stood up. "We must get moving. The road is poor and there will be standing water."

After they had turned south, Arla read again from the book about the land ahead, prose that mingled meaning and music in a description of mesas with sandstone walls knobbed with granite and basalt, and tongued with darker forest on the peaks which thinned out in scattered piñon and juniper.

This forsaken landscape was leading to the great rift of Chaco Canyon, a widening gash once grassed, woody and watered, and now ravaged by the elements into a wasteland with no signs of life, not even a hogan, trading post or tree.

She paused and said, "It was after reading this next passage that my husband said. 'Go and see if it's true.' "

Then these words: "*Down on the floor of the cañon, or mounting occasionally to the sandstone rim, concentrated within the space of a score of city blocks, are to be found the traces of a culture era that, in many of its aspects, rivaled the organization and artifacts of ancient Crete.*"

Arla closed the book. "I needed to get away even if it meant running from what I could no longer face. I wanted to see El Morro, to see if it is as magical as she said it is. *Here I shall haunt*, she wrote. Do you believe that one's ghost returns to a beloved place?"

Stone shook his head.

"I know I'm romantic and emotional and everything else," she continued. "Even he gets cross with me. He's all thought and I'm all feeling. He says that's the polarity that makes a marriage. Perhaps what happened to him is meant to test me." She paused. "What a lonely road this is!"

"It's an area with no public appeal, although they are beginning to file uranium claims. In this weather there won't be anyone at the canyon. I don't know why it moved Mary Austin so. Betatakin and Chelly I can understand, but not Chaco. It's been dead for centuries. Yet it was what I needed when I was there. I wonder what kind of book Grady would have written if he'd been stationed here?"

As they kept angling southwest, they saw the dwindled rain now pooled along the shoulders of the rough road. Arla lowered her window and breathed deeply. "There's that smell again. I'll call it Creosote No. 5."

Darkness had fallen when they reached the descent into the heart of Chaco Canyon. Stone eased the heavy vehicle down the steep curving road and across the wash, now running with a shallow flow, then entered the widening rift and drove toward the lights of the headquarters building. There they were welcomed by the young superintendent, Quinn, another of Stone's trainees.

"My apologies for our facilities or lack of same," he said to Arla. "My wife keeps having babies until our mobile is overflowing. As for Mr. Stone, he wouldn't want a bed even if we had one to offer."

"The Service has gone soft," Stone growled. "Mobile homes!"

"The museum is warm," Quinn said. "We burn an oil heater in this weather for the mummies."

"He's a joker, isn't he," Arla said after they had supper with the family and found her quarters in the small museum.

"Not really. Chaco is said to be haunted. Not by Mary Austin though—by the Anasazi. It was hard to keep Navajo workers. Cañon de los Muertos, they called it."

"That must have made it difficult for you."

"I liked the remoteness and the few archaeologists who were here. Visitors soon left when they found nothing spectacular. I got along with the Navajos and would have been glad to stay indefinitely. Yet it seemed advisable to take the job at the South Rim. Will you excuse me if I visit with the ranger? Leave your door unlocked and I'll tuck you in."

"Where *will* you sleep?"

"I'll bring my bag in and sleep on the floor."

"Please do. It's spooky here."

It was midnight when he returned. He opened her door softly. She was asleep with the light on, the book fallen from her grasp, her hair like banked fire on the pillow. He snapped off the light, shut the door and made up his pad on the floor outside. Sleep came quickly.

He was awakened by the light flashing on. Arla, fully dressed, stood by the wall switch.

"Time to get up," she laughed. "If you're going on my tour."

Stone rubbed his eyes. "Score! Give me time to shave and I'll join you."

"It's a gorgeous display," she said as they walked over for breakfast with the family. "Wait until I tell Glyn about the mummies!"

"Do you know you fell asleep with the lights on?"

"When did you come in?" she asked.

"Late."

301

"I must have been more tired than I realized. This morning I looked at the displays while you went on snoring."

"The best pieces went to the Smithsonian," he explained.

At breakfast Stone marvelled at Arla's way with the children while he talked shop with the ranger. Afterward they set out in a monument jeep, first to the ruins down canyon, then back to Pueblo Bonito. The rain had passed over and the landscape was clear for miles around.

"I want you to see Bonito," Stone said," as the sun rises above the mesa, just as you saw Chelly at sunset. There'll be no one there. A tour from Farmington won't arrive until late morning. They're from Flagstaff en route to the river pueblos."

He pulled into the parking area and led Arla by a trail to the back of the great pueblo. They stopped at the base of the towering redrock mesa next to a long curving high wall made of many layers of unmortared stones of various size and thickness. The quiet was absolute except for an occasional piercingly sweet birdsong.

"This is what he wanted me to see," she said at last. "Masonry of delicate counterpoint and flow like music or lace. Is it the original wall or has it been restored?"

"All that was done was stabilize it," Stone said. "An Italian mason supervised the Navajos. It was mostly done by the time I came. My job was interpretation. You see how unstable the cliff is, always a threat to the wall. The Anasazi built it too close to the mesa. See that slide there? When it fell, it took out part of the wall. It still hasn't been cleared. Doing so might trigger an even bigger slide. We lost two Navajos when the rock came down."

Arla gripped his arm. "What do you mean?"

"They were buried under it, buried alive. By the time we got to them, they were dead."

Her comment puzzled him. "They were lucky," she whispered.

"No more work that season," he continued. "The crew took off and never came back. Come, I'll show you the interior."

She was silent as he led her through the rooms of the pueblo, stooping through doorways that led to the great kivas.

"You can see what small people they were," he said.

"I could tell that from the mummies." She stopped. "I need to sit down."

"Don't you feel well?" He sensed that something was troubling her.

She shook her head. "Go on talking while I rest here. I'll be all right."

She got up and they continued through the rooms while Stone resumed his talk.

"Bones and pots, a few bead and shell necklaces, empty architecture and masonry—that's all they left. Everything else was scoured away. They did what we are doing—used up their resources until they had to move on, probably to the valley of the Rio Grande where there was water."

"I know," Arla said quickly. "She described Chaco as once fertile."

"A thousand years ago this canyon was grassy and wooded. They kept cutting the timber farther and farther away from their dwellings. Stone was for the kivas and apartments of the priests. The ordinary people built with wood. Once they had destroyed the fabric that held the soil, rain did the rest. An unusual rain cycle probably lasted for several decades and in the end, the canyon was scoured of all life, including their own. Only rock was left, and rock means life only to lichens and such."

Stone was again puzzled by her remark. "Rock also takes life."

"Do you want to sit and rest again? No? What do you make of it all?" he asked as they followed the long wall back to where they had first stood.

"It's not what I expected, even after our reading—but then nothing has been since I arrived. How long ago was that? A thousand years did you say? This is a new world, almost another planet, or have we gone back in time as she did? Her prose makes it more vital than it is. That's what language can do."

"It can also show the effects of too much imagination!"

Arla continued to muse. "Now it is sterile like a moonscape. And frightening. Those mummies last night—I felt them approaching, I called for her ghost, but there were only mummies after me." Her voice grew agitated. "I feel disoriented! Where have you brought me?"

Stone was alarmed when she burst into uncontrolled sobbing. "What is it?" he demanded, seizing her arm. "There's nothing dangerous here. What's happened to upset you so?"

Arla shook her head. "There's something horribly dead still here."

"Aren't you over-reacting?" Stone asked sternly.

"It's not like the South Rim. There was too much life there. Here there's too little. Actually none. It's dead, I tell you. I can't stay. I want to leave. Take me away, I beg of you."

"What will you tell your husband?"

"He knows me all too well. Your telling me about those Navajos triggered it. Can't we go somewhere and have coffee?"

"We can drive up on the mesa," Stone said calmly. "There's a rock trail we widened into a jeep track."

"I'm afraid something terrible will happen if we don't leave here right now."

Stone led her back to the jeep, and after a rough climb in compound low, they gained the top. There they parked high above Pueblo Bonito, now lit by the sun at their backs.

"You'd never know it had rained," Stone observed, "the earth drinks it so fast." And when she did not respond he added, "I'll be quiet if you'd rather just look."

"I'll get ahold of myself. Coffee helps. And I feel safe up here."

"Perhaps I should have heeded your wish to stay at Cañon de Chelly."

"I had to come, but can't we go on now? I've seen enough."

"I'm not as understanding as your husband." Stone said.

"I know I'm irrational in your eyes. This place is wrong for me. Now I know why she called her chapter 'Cities that Died.' I felt it last night. I heard a coyote, crying like a lost soul. At those other places there were voices that said the living and the dead can live together at peace. Here the dead don't want to be disturbed. They resent us and will drive us out by whatever means, including rock slides. That's why we must leave before something happens to us."

"You could be right. When we lost those workers, the tribe said that it was because we had provoked the dead. The Navajos wanted to close down the monument for good."

"What did you do when they left?"

"I stayed to look after things. I was the only one the tribe would talk with."

"How did you manage that?" she asked.

"By not talking. By sitting and smoking and listening."

"I could never just sit and listen. Glyn and I never stop talking. Of course I do all the crying!" Arla paused. "You have never asked about his accident."

"So that's what's troubling you! It wasn't my place to ask."

"You don't have a woman's curiosity. I need to talk. It's my turn. Is there plenty of kleenex? I'm so flighty. How can you stand it?"

"As you say, coffee helps."

She began softly. "Rock killed your Navajos. Rock only crippled Glyn. I know I shouldn't say it, but death would have been more merciful." She began to cry.

"There's more coffee and kleenex and no one to interrupt."

She seized his hand. "I'll be all right if I can talk. He came up to King's College in Newcastle with a Ministry of Works team to tackle the Wall—the one built by Hadrian in the first century. Didn't I tell you about it at El Tovar? That it was built to keep the Picts and the Scots from raping the English girls? He was already known for his work on Roman Britain. I had been postgraduate in music at Newcastle, and was also busy repulsing the Picts and the Scots. In Switzerland the natives were even more obnoxious. That was when my Lassiter came along. I was beginning to feel smothered by Daddy, and Glyn saved me from him too. He's like you, a field worker, a teacher."

"What did you learn from him?" Stone asked.

"Wonderful things. How to handle a pick and shovel, how to mix mortar and trowel it. I'm out of shape now. Too heavy." She smiled wanly. "All's left is my hair! I saw how life had persisted along the Wall—along the site where it ran. Most of the stones are gone—carried away to build houses and barns. Restoration has been undertaken only in a few places to show people how it once was."

"Did his accident happen there?"

"Pour me another drop and I'll tell you. It was my fault, not his. We were with the team west of Corbridge, rebuilding a gateway fort—actually a watch tower—making another of the strong points for sightseers. It's getting like your South Rim—trippers with transistors tuned to the soccer matches. Glyn was directing the placement of two great stones for the arch. They were being lowered by a tractor derrick, swinging them high over where he stood below. I was on a ladder where I could keep them from swinging out too far. As I reached out, I lost my balance and crashed into the tractor.

305

When the driver sought to break my fall, he accidentally released the control lever, and the stones came down on Glyn and pinned his legs. They were very heavy. The operator panicked and ran for help. No one could restart the engine. Men finally came from Corbridge and lifted the stones. A doctor had brought morphine. They rushed him to hospital in Newcastle. It was too late. Circulation had gone. Gangrene set in. They had to amputate both legs above the knees. His whole nervous system was disrupted. Daddy had the best doctors in Europe. Clinics in London and Zurich couldn't help him." She began to cry. "It was my fault," she sobbed, "all my fault."

Stone gripped her arm. "Don't say that. It was one of those crazy accidents."

"Now he's lost his will to live, and I've lost my hold on myself. You've seen how shaky I am. That's why the doctors urged me to come. Part of me knows it's running away, yet he said I must go and bring back a report on what we are looking down on. And now I want to leave. We will leave, won't we?"

"Whatever you want," Stone assured her.

"I should be more like you, like him. I'm so insecure. Losing my Mum, and Daddy being so domineering have made me this way, the doctors say. Now all I can think of is to get away before something happens to us. Talking has helped. Thank you for letting me. Will they post him that literature I saw at the museum?"

"That and more," Stone said.

"Where will we go from here?"

"East and south—Cuba, Gracia, Española. Even make Santa Fe tonight, if we start now."

"Can we stay there? You must be tired and I'm exhausted. Yet I must see El Morro."

"You will. It's only a hundred fifty miles from Santa Fe."

Arla thought a moment, then asked, "Isn't Gracia where the painter Hester Crane lives?"

Stone was astonished. "Do you know her work?"

"Daddy has one of her paintings. I promised him I'd call on her if we came anywhere near Gracia. You must know her. You seem to know everyone."

Stone smiled. "She came once when I was here."

"Did you like her?"

"Do you like an artifact? Even then she was an old woman, a beautiful old woman. Now she must be nearly a hundred!"

"Do you like her paintings?"

"Too violent for my taste. She sees only the land's violence. I see its quietness."

"That's harder to paint. It's that latent violence that frightens me."

"You get used to it if you stay. When you were reading yesterday, I realized that although Mary Austin may have been a violent woman, she was also a quiet writer."

"So you were listening! Can we call on Hester Crane?"

"We'd have to phone ahead. They say her place is set with traps for uninvited callers."

"Will you ring through to her?" Arla asked.

"If you want me to."

"Wouldn't you like to see her again?"

"Not especially, but this is your trip."

"*Our* trip! Am I hopeless?"

"Women have rights men don't have."

"I don't want to trade on them."

Stone paused, then said, "If I had known what a—how shall I say it?—what a puzzling woman you are, I'd have asked the Secretary to give you another guide."

"You're fed up, aren't you."

"You continue to puzzle me," Stone admitted.

"You must have known other puzzlers."

"They never got inside my walls!"

Arla smiled. "Perhaps you needed to be invaded."

"Be that as it may, bid your farewell to Pueblo Bonito. We'll go back and give Quinn a bit of puzzlement."

"What will you tell him?" she asked.

"That we're leaving."

"Is that all?"

"The rest is between you and me," Stone said.

Arla gripped his hand.

4.

paso poraqi.el p m'sasa laxpa

Pedro de
mon byo

Stone and Arla returned to headquarters, repacked their gear, and while she wrote postcards to her husband and father, he informed the ranger that a tight schedule compelled them to push on. Arla added her thanks to him and his wife, hugged the children, and so they left Chaco Canyon. Across the dry wash he stopped at the top of the hill for a last look.

After a long silence, Arla asked, "Did you tell him what a spoiled darling I am?"

"I did not, although it's true! You leave having seen Bonito as other visitors never see it. Was it enough to satisfy your husband?"

"I'll tell him what a strange place it was to sleep. I've probably read too much, yet I believe that without life around them, the dead are beyond resurrection. That's why his work on the Wall was so meaningful. Life there has never died out. When Rome packed up and the Wall was breached, the locals used the stones to build for a new life. They still do it although it is forbidden. That made his work so important—to save what's left before all is lost. He has a favorite Wall poem. A poet named Auden wrote it for him when they were at Oxford, said it would cheer him in foul weather."

"I've now figured out why you puzzle me so," Stone said.

"Why?"

"The way your thoughts and feelings merge so that I can't tell one from the other."

"Isn't that what makes the whole person?" she asked.

"I've never thought about it before."

Stone took the road to the southeast, driving fast on a surface hardpacked by the rain. When he began to speak again, she could barely hear his voice for the wind through the partly opened window

"Sometimes," he mused, "I think I'd like to end my days at Chelly. You've expressed what I've always felt there, that life and death can be compatible."

"Do you mean be stationed there?"

"No, I mean after retirement."

"Would they allow you to live in the canyon?"

"Since Chaco, they've accepted me."

"And live as Lassiter did after he rolled the stone?" Arla asked.

He smiled. "I mean live alone."

What came next? he wondered as the miles flashed by and Arla dozed. Would she go on abruptly leaving places she had wanted to see? Would even El Morro hold her?

Upon reaching the paved highway to Cuba, he pulled up at another roadside marker. She opened her eyes.

"The Continental Divide," he said. "The point where the waters part."

"How do they know which way to flow?" she asked. "How do *we* know when we come to our divide?"

Stone shook his head. "I'll stop in Cuba and telephone Hester Crane if you still want me to."

"Is Gracia far from there?"

"Another hour."

He drew up in front of a Circle K in the small lumbering settlement. When he returned, he was smiling.

"What?" she demanded.

"She said don't bother to bring another woman, even if she is the Queen's god-daughter. I wasn't sure she'd remember me."

"Don't they all?"

"Not when they're that old! If you'll buy some sandwich makings, I'll get the thermos refilled and we'll picnic along the way. It's a good road through the National Forest."

The road proved enchanted for Arla, reminding her again of her northwest—wave after wave of dark forest with clear meadows and solitary ranches, the sheep still in pasture before winter drove them to the lower lands. Where they stopped to picnic, Arla gathered a bouquet of late-blooming flowers—penstemons and asters—and also pressed a few between the pages of *The Land of Journeys' Ending*.

"I feel so much better since we left Chaco," she said as they were packing up.

309

"You needed food and drink," he said sternly.

"And to talk. That helped me, as it did you the other night. I'm sorry I panicked. I promise not to again—today!" She took his hand.

"Time to saddle up," he said, starting the engine.

The afternoon was waning when they reached the ancient village of Gracia, high on the western slope of the Chama Valley. Here the aged painter lived in seclusion, having long since left her husband to make her own career, growing old and rich as her paintings achieved fame and corresponding price. Now she was beset by the importuners who enjoy reflected esteem.

"That's why I've never come to see her," Stone explained as they reached the door and he pulled the bell rope. "When you've lived that long, you deserve privacy."

"You didn't really tell her anything absurd about me?" Arla half asked.

Before he could answer, the door was opened by Hester Crane herself. "I must say you've been a long time getting here," she challenged Stone. "I was about to have tea without you." Her weathered face relaxed in a sad smile as she led them into an old-fashioned parlor where the table was set.

"You dress sensibly—for an Englishwoman," Crane said, scrutinizing Arla. "Now don't tell me you're one of those odd ones who never drinks tea."

"I was weaned on it and love it when it's properly brewed, as I see yours is."

That brought a faint smile to the painter's finely wrinkled face. "I trust you like it strong with milk and sugar," she said, adding both. "What are you doing with those flowers? Are they from my garden?"

"Indeed they are not!" Arla replied sweetly. "I picked them for you along the way."

"Dawdling, eh? So that's what took you so long to get here. Stone!" Crane commanded, "Find a vase and get them in water." Then softly to Arla, "My favorite colors. How did you know?"

"My father owns one of your paintings in scarlet and purple."

"He does, does he! What did he pay for it?"

"He didn't buy it. It was a gift to him when he was our Ambassador to Washington. Your Secretary of State gave it to him when he returned to London."

310

"Well, that's rather a nice pedigree," the old woman conceded. "I don': remember it though, I've painted so many pictures. That's what comes from living forever." She grinned craftily. "How did you capture him? I never could. I was once as beautiful as you. You don't believe me? See here."

On a table by the fireplace was a book of photographs of Hester Crane, taken years ago—nudes and close-ups of her face and hands.

She turned the pages as Arla stared.

Stone returned with the flowers in a Mason jar.

"How awful!" Hester Crane said, grabbing it from him.

"It's all I could find," he apologized, then joined them in looking at the photographs.

"Well," the painter finally demanded of Stone, "which one of us gets the apple?"

"That's not fair!" Arla protested. "Mr. Stone has never really seen me."

Hester Crane looked her up and down. "You're not bad," she admitted. "Those pants do something for you. Where did you get that outfit?"

"I took her to the trading post in Flagstaff," Stone explained.

"I'd paint her hair if I could decide what color it is. Do you fool with it?"

"I do not!" Arla said indignantly.

"All right, Stone," Hester Crane said slyly, "make up your mind. Which one of us gets it?"

"Bring me an apple and a knife," he said. "Don't think I don't know my Greek mythology—learned it at my mother's knee."

Hester Crane walked deliberately to the kitchen and returned with apple and knife and waited. Stone proceeded to cut the apple precisely in two, then gave half to her and half to Arla.

"Bravo!" the old woman beamed. "See what a jewel you have? Come from Chaco, have you? Is it still as monochromatic as ever? Nothing there worth painting."

"I love your work," Arla said. "Our home was dark, like England most always is. Your painting lit up the room where my father hung it. I wish I could afford one for my husband."

"Married, are you? Where is he? Does he know you're running around the country with Stone?"

"My husband is ill," Arla said simply. "He knows what good hands I'm in."

"Hands and arms, no doubt. He's ill, is he?" Hester Crane opened a portfolio and rummaged through a batch of watercolors until she found one of red and orange rocks. "Here, take it to him. What's his name? Glyn Williams? A Welshman, eh!" She grinned. "They're good, aren't they." She signed the painting to him, then demanded, "Where are you two sleeping tonight? I can't put you up."

"Don't worry," Arla said demurely. "We have sleeping bags and air mattresses."

"I'm sure you'll keep warm at your age." Hester Crane hugged Arla and kissed Stone on the lips. "If you'd come back, I might do a pastel of you together."

They drove through the village to the highway before Arla spoke. "If I could be like her, I'd gladly grow old. As for you, sir, you are a naughty man."

"What did I do?"

"You let her think we are lovers."

"You're the one who talked about our sleeping equipment," he protested. "Perhaps I should have told her about our connecting rooms."

Arla laughed. "At least she feels as I do about Chaco Canyon."

"She seemed to like it when she was there."

"What she liked was you."

"Do you know you have a valuable painting?"

"Of course I do. Daddy had his appraised for insurance. Where *are* we sleeping tonight?"

"We can make Santa Fe now. I'll stop in Española and phone ahead for rooms at La Fonda. They have the only bathtubs in New Mexico in which I can stretch my legs."

"Do you know a writer in Santa Fe named Maria MacPherson? She wrote a book about her childhood on a ranch where her playhouse was an Indian ruin. A friend sent me a copy when she heard I was going to be in New Mexico. It seems the MacPhersons came from Scotland in the nineteenth century."

Stone smiled. "I've known her for years."

"I should have known! Does she still live there?"

"I'm sure she does. In a hacienda on the edge of town."

"She sounds well off."

"She married an inventor who sold his patents to General Electric. He was a widower. She had never married. Her father's ranch was in the mountains near Santa Fe. By the time Maria had grown up, their property was condemned for a highway. It went right through the place where she had played. When her father lost what he got for it by speculating in oil stocks and Maria was left nearly penniless, she opened a tea room in Santa Fe for the upper crust and became a noted hostess. Then along came the widower and carried her off. They built the big house and did a lot of travelling to the western parks and monuments. That's when I came to know them. He died a few years ago. She seemed lonely the last time I saw her."

"Is she a recluse like Hester Crane? I'm sure she'd welcome a visit from you, but what about me?"

"She'd welcome anyone I'd bring. I mean, I know she'd welcome you."

"Her book reminded me of Mary Webb. Have you read *Precious Bane?*"

"I haven't even read Maria's."

"How old is she?"

"Seventy maybe."

Beyond the Chama cliffs, Stone took a cutoff around Española that threaded hills and arroyos through land that sloped to the Rio Grande.

"Los Alamos is up there," Stone pointed as they neared the river." And Bandelier. San Ildefonso pueblo is at the foot of the mesa. One makes pots, the other makes bombs."

He drew up at the river crossing between the old and new bridge, alongside the tracks of the abandoned narrow-gauge railroad. The river was running high from summer rains up near the source.

"At last a real river!" Arla marvelled.

They walked out on the old bridge and looked down on the urgent water. "It reminds me of a childhood poem," she said, and quoted, "Dark brown is the river, golden is the sand; it flows along forever, with trees on either hand.' "

"Did you write it?" Stone asked naïvely.

313

"Ask that Scot! I brought her book with me. Would she autograph it, do you suppose? Remind me to take it, if we call on her. I'm not as remembering as you."

"I dream of a forgetful retirement," Stone said.

"You don't really mean Cañon de Chelly, do you?"

"More like Santa Fe. I have other friends there. Maria learned a lot from her husband about the environment, although he was an unlikely person. After making his fortune from electric power, he became an ardent conservationist."

"I know you'll think me frivolous, but what should I wear when we call on her? She sounds like a grande dame."

"She's old shoe. Wear what you have on now. You saw how you impressed Hester Crane."

"I'm getting tired of this outfit—pants and boots and itchy shirts. I'll tell her my coutourier is Babbitts of Flagstaff. That should impress her." Arla hesitated. "Has she courted you?"

"Not that I was aware of."

"That doesn't mean she hasn't. You seem to know a lot about her."

"That because I'm a good listener," Stone said.

"How ludicrous! You've done nothing but lecture me ever since I arrived."

"I know how attractive I am—to older women."

Arla laughed. "I feel so much better. This has turned out to be the best day of all, after leaving the canyon and meeting that amazing old woman and her burning cliffs."

Darkness had come by the time they descended the last long hill through the low piñon forest to the lights of Santa Fe.

"But it's not much of a city," Arla protested as they threaded the narrow winding streets that led to the plaza and La Fonda. "Is it really the capital of New Mexico?"

"Since the year 1609. It's the most civilized city in the U.S.A. No heavy industry, no high-rise buildings, no big airport. Lack of a good water supply has kept it from the uncontrolled growth of Albuquerque and Phoenix. The railroad's having bypassed it also helped."

"Daddy wouldn't appreciate that!" she observed. "I must call him from here to ask about Glyn." She paused. "I've feared to find out."

314

"Are you worried?"

"Of course, although he has been stable recently. He is at the clinic in London while I'm away, where Daddy can keep an eye on him. His lack of will is what holds him back. He seems to be letting go. He was so active, I could hardly keep up with him. Talking did me good, didn't it."

"The whole trip has been good medicine."

"Not to mention Ranger-Doctor Stone."

After registering at the inn and taking a short rest, they met in the lobby, hungry from the long day of meager nourishment. Arla had changed into the suit she had been wearing on arrival in Phoenix.

"Did you call your father?" Stone asked.

"I woke him up! It's four in the morning there. Glyn keeps asking when I'm coming back."

"Should you return now?"

"Daddy said not to. It will be only a few more days. And yet I can't help feeling guilty. How long can we stay here?"

"That depends on what else you want to do. If we see both Acoma and El Morro, that means eliminating most everything else, unless you want to spend the days in driving. And there's Maria MacPherson. Do you really want to meet her?"

"I'll tell you my priorities: Santa Fe and MacPherson, Acoma and El Morro."

"Okay, you're the boss."

After dinner they crossed the street to the nearly deserted plaza. Arla breathed deeply. "What is that fragrance? I smelled it in Gracia and then coming into town."

"Piñon smoke. That's the wood they burn for cooking and heating."

"What a charming square! The crossed walks, iron benches, bandstand and monument and the old-fashioned illuminators. It's old world—shops shuttered and the people gone to their homes."

"It's the right rhythm for life," Stone agreed.

As they walked back to the inn, a rising wind swept away the dry leaves.

"What an ugly church!" Arla said of the neighboring cathedral as they paused at the entrance to La Fonda. "That's French provincial of the worst sort. What on earth is *it* doing here?"

"The archbishop who built it was a homesick Frenchman."

315

When Stone telephoned Maria MacPherson, they were invited to lunch the next day.

Arla was excited as they approached the adobe hacienda, its doors and windows trimmed in blue, and set among piñons, fruit and nut trees. They passed through an arched entry and across a flagstone patio to a massive wooden door with silver studs and handle. Stone pulled on the rope. A bell clanged from deep within.

The door was opened by Maria MacPherson. "Stony!" she cried, embracing him, then backed off to inspect Arla. "My God, a woman in pants and boots! I thought you were bringing an English lady."

"She *was* one when she arrived," he laughed.

"He made me buy these," Arla spoke up, "and insisted I wear them today. He said you wouldn't be formal."

"You see how right he was," Maria laughed. She was wearing baggy gray woolen pants, a flame-colored poncho and leather sandals on her bare brown feet. Her face was deeply lined and tanned, her gray hair tied in a short pony tail with a tartan ribbon. "So they trusted you to this *mal hombre*!" she exclaimed, holding out her hand and then hugging Arla. "You wait here, Stony, while I show her around. The English don't see houses like this. It's a mess though. My help's grown lazy since Frank died."

Stone watched Maria depart with Arla in tow. What would Arla make of her? he wondered, this Scotswoman born in New Mexico. He browsed among the magazines in the great living room, its Mexican tile floor strewn with Navajo weaving and opening onto another larger patio centered with a jetting fountain.

When the women returned, Maria declared, "She'll do."

"Do what?" Stone asked innocently.

"Do things her own way, of course."

"The way you did with Frank, eh?"

"You mind your business and leave her to me."

"I do have business at the Service office. I'll be back for lunch."

"Lunch? Did I invite you to lunch? Well, you'd better get yourself something in town. She tells me she dislikes cooking as much as I do. We'll eat badly for sure. That was for his benefit," she said when Stone had left. "Now you and I can have a good talk. I'm glad you kept your own name. I won't tell you what Frank's was, it was so awful. He was nice though. I miss him." She stared at Arla and asked, "Are you in love with Stony? He'd make an even worse hus-

band than Frank. What do you talk about with him? I never could
get him to say much. For that matter, Frank and I never said very
much to each other."

"What held you together?" Arla asked.

"The land. We didn't need to talk about that. Each knew what the
other was feeling. Did he tell you how Frank and I met?"

"Only that he came along and carried you off."

Maria laughed. "Exactly! He swore I'd put something in his tea
to enchant him. He followed me into the kitchen where Elena was
washing up. 'Are you married?' he asked. No, I said, and I don't intend to be. 'Then change your mind,' he said, 'for I'm going to
marry you.' And by God, he did, a month later. The fandango in
the plaza lasted until daybreak."

"Was he older than you?" Arla asked.

"Quite a bit, and with grown children. Do you have children?"

"No, and now I never will. I must be near the change although
I'm only forty-one. I'm always on the verge of tears. I'm afraid I've
been a problem for Mr. Stone."

"He told me your husband is ill."

"Worse than that. He lost both legs in an accident." She paused.
"I caused it. It was my fault."

"See here, woman," Maria said sternly. "You can't go on feeling
guilty for the rest of your life."

"I can't help it."

"Do you love him?"

"More than ever. We too had a romantic beginning, I've never
wanted anyone else. Were you a faithful wife?"

"I once fell from grace for a fool of a poet who got me to writing.
That's when I wrote my book. He said you'd like me to sign your
copy. Did you buy it in town?"

"I did not," Arla said indignantly. "I brought it from London, although I had no idea I'd be meeting you. Did you have an affair with
the poet?"

"You're from the north of England, Stony told me, so you know
how we northerners are. He wanted me to run away."

"Did you?" Arla asked.

"Frank wouldn't let me. He threatened to rope and tie me in the
corral. I learned that all writers are liars, and that poets lie the
most."

"What happened to him?"

"He died of a broken heart and was resurrected—by another woman, of course." Maria drew back and looked at Arla, then smiled. "I must say I take to you at first sight—an improper English-woman gallivanting around the country with that woman-hater. Most unlikely! Are you going to be hungry? Can you wait until tea? What part of the north are you from?"

"Lancashire. I also have Yorkshire and Shetland blood. I told him I'm British mongrel."

"No wonder we hit it off. But I'm really New Mexican. Born here and plan to die here."

"Have you ever been to Scotland?"

"Frank insisted that at least I see the country of my ancestors. Once was enough. Too small a scale. You'll find that's true when you go back, the feeling of being hemmed in."

"I know what you mean. Oh the distances we've come!"

"Do you like it?"

"I didn't care much for Arizona until Betatakin and Cañon de Chelly. My husband insisted I see Chaco Canyon. It frightened me. I panicked. Then we called on Hester Crane and things got better, and now you. You are kind to let us intrude this way."

"I wanted to know what you two are up to."

"I'm not sure myself," Arla laughed. "Nothing has been what I expected, least of all Ranger Stone. And Santa Fe is so old-world. That dear plaza!"

"We're an island in a rising sea. He said you are obsessed by Mary Austin—even sleep with her wretched book."

Arla laughed. "What was she like?"

"A dreadful woman I was very fond of. She made good sugar cookies. I'd take tea with her—bad tea—for her cookies."

"Was she hard to get along with?"

"Impossible! Demanding, dogmatic, and mostly wrong."

"Why don't you like her book?" Arla ventured.

"Why should I? It's bad geography, bad history, bad Spanish, bad everything! Do you want to see where she lived? It's across the way, now a gallery of bad art. There's nothing left of hers. Everyone is a painter these days. At least she had sense enough not to paint." Maria paused. "I was jealous of her. She came late and took posses-sion in the name of the King of Spain and Mary Austin, I came early

318

and took it for granted. I was young then and let her bully me. If she came now, I'd do her in and put her bad prose on her gravestone."

Again Maria stopped for breath. "We seem like old friends. Do you feel it? Strange, isn't it. Not really. There *are* instant affinities. You've heard of Indian blood brothers. I think we're blood sisters. Has Stony told you of his life? I know he had an unfortunate early marriage and that some kind of heart trouble made him give up field work. He may have a bad heart but it's not a stone heart. Do you know that stones are beautiful?"

Arla hesitated, then spoke carefully, "Yes, I know."

"I wrote a poem about river stones," Maria continued. "Would you like to hear it? We used to gather stones for mosaic walks like the ones you see in Portugal. I'll show you some we made. We took a last trip over our honeymoon trail. I was so excited. For the first time he was unresponsive. I was cross when he didn't rise to my level of feeling. A month later he was dead. I realized later that he had a premonition and was trying to keep it from me. When he was dying he seemed to want to tell me something. By then only his eyes could talk." Maria stopped and demanded, "Why are you crying?"

"I can't help it," Arla said.

Maria embraced her. "Go ahead and cry. It's the only way we have. Let's take a walk. I told you there's nothing left of Mary's over there. They sold her letters and manuscripts to some library in California. I would have burned the lot. Let's walk in the orchard. It's beautiful at this time of year."

They strolled between the rows. "The leaves fall early at this elevation," Maria explained. "My trees are mostly apples, pears and almonds."

"What are those?" Arla asked, pointing to golden fruit on the boughs of a small bare tree.

"Persimmons. Have you ever eaten one?"

"Once in Lausanne. My mouth was puckery for a week."

"That's because it was green. These are ripe. Here, try this one." Maria reached up, jerked off a fruit and pulled out the capstem, then split the fruit and handed it to Arla. "Dead ripe. Let it slip down."

"It's so sweet!" Arla cried.

319

"We used to walk here," Maria said, lowering her voice. "He loved me to pick one for him. He'd suck it down." She laughed. "It excited him."

Arla smiled. "Figs excited Glyn. 'Fica, fica!' he would cry."

"I'd miss it if Frank had been younger when he died. He'd cooled off by then, and now the fire in me has died down." Maria spoke even more softly. "How long since you've made love?"

"Too long."

"Don't you miss it?"

"Of course."

"Haven't you had anyone, like one of the doctors?"

"No, but I could have," Arla admitted.

"What about Stony? Aren't you tempted with him? All those nights under the desert stars."

"Not Mr. Stone. Besides, it's rained a lot."

"He's a man," Maria said grimly.

"I probably shouldn't tell you this," Arla hesitated. "I found a way without breaking my vows."

"Aren't we blood sisters? That means no secrets. I have no vows to break, but there's no man I'd want to touch me. Tell me. I might need it when the moon's full."

Arla laughed and again they embraced. They found a bench in the orchard and she began softly, "It started a few months, maybe half a year after his accident. I always went in to Newcastle on Saturday mornings to have my hair washed. I can never get the soap out of it."

"Wherever did you get that crowning glory?" Maria asked enviously.

"Daddy said it came from Mummy. I know it looks ghastly now. Well, I always had the same girl, Lily, then when she left I had Elizabeth, an Irish girl from Cork. She had marvelous hands, even stronger than Glyn's. She had short grey hair, blue eyes and rose petal skin. You know those Irish girls! When she first touched my hair and it crackled, I knew something was going to happen. I began to tremble inside. The first thing she said was 'Oh Madame, your hair is alive!' All the others had ever said was how thick it was. What do you mean? I asked her. 'Most hair is dead,' she said, 'yours is alive.' She began gently, then worked deeper until I began to

320

tremble, couldn't keep from it. 'There, there, Madame,' she said, 'lie back and let me work. I always stimulate the scalp before I wash."

Arla paused while Maria remained silent, then resumed. "So I would lie back and let her have her way. And she would say, matter of fact, 'See how lovely it feels?' Oh but it did! Her fingers kept digging deeper and harder until I could feel them throughout my entire body. When I realized what she was doing, I both fought it and wanted it. As it came nearer, it was all I could do to keep from arching up under the sheet. Her hands held me down. Oh she was strong but gentle! Finally I had to let go. She quickly covered my mouth with her hand to keep me from screaming."

Arla burst into tears. Maria embraced her. They clung together trembling until Arla calmed herself and spoke "Elizabeth would say. 'There now, Madame, sit up and I'll wash your hair and dry it and you'll go home a new lady.' And I did, every Saturday morning, week after week."

"Did you see her elsewhere?"

"Oh never!"

"Wasn't she a lesbian?"

"I suppose so. Maybe not. Perhaps she felt my buried desire that led her to do what she did."

"Or your hair!" Maria laughed.

"I asked her once, 'Elizabeth, do you have other ladies with live hair?' "

"No, Madame,' she assured me, 'only you.' You know how the classes are in England. If we had been of the same class, we might have become lovers. I craved it so."

"She probably did too. When it comes down to it, don't we all? You do have glorious hair. Dare I touch it?"

They both laughed and embraced again.

"How long does it take to get to Newcastle?" Maria asked.

"No use. She went home to Cork and I've done without."

Maria hugged her. "You've made my day."

"That persimmon must have loosed my tongue!"

"Has Stony tried to make love to you?"

"Certainly not!"

"He isn't queer, is he, like so many of your countrymen?"

"I'm sure he's not."

"Haven't you been tempted?" Maria persisted.

321

"Not so far."

"What does the man read?"

"Government reports, he says. He said you'd given him your book, but he hasn't gotten around to reading it."

"I'll ask for it back! Does he like music? He told me you were a musician before you married."

"I studied voice. He says his ears are tin."

"What are you doing tomorrow night?" Maria demanded.

"He hasn't said."

"How long will you be in Santa Fe?"

"Not long. My flight leaves Albuquerque in a few days and I'm determined to visit Acoma and El Morro."

"Then you'll be near Enchanted Mesa. Have him take you up on it. Frank took me there once. I wrote a poem about climbing it. Listen to me, dear girl. I have two tickets to a dinner and concert tomorrow night. A visiting chamber music group with a tenor soloist is in town and they're giving two song cycles by English composers. Your cup of tea if any music is. I want you to take him."

"I'd love it, but I can't speak for him. I've missed music. My husband was always too busy, although we sing together. I sometimes went alone to concerts in Newcastle, and in London on visits to Daddy. Music sounds best when shared. I had no idea you had such things here."

Maria sniffed. "You'll find, my dear, that culture came early to New Mexico, in fact while that man Shakespeare was alive."

When Stone returned he found them settled with high tea by a piñon fire. Maria promptly announced, "I've got news for you, Stony. You and she are stepping out tomorrow night. Don't tell me you've made other plans."

"What have you done?" Stone demanded.

"I have tickets to a benefit dinner and concert for the opera. I want you to take her."

"Why don't the two of you go?" he protested. "I'm not musical."

"It's time you began. You like to eat, don't you? They'll feed you well at the Palace. I'll see that you have interesting tablemates."

"I can't go in this uniform. Besides, I'm planning an all-day drive tomorrow."

"To Bandelier?"

"I'll tell you when we're back."

"See that you get back in time for the dinner. And listen to me, William Stone, you and Frank were the same size. The closets are still full of his clothes. Come along. You too, dear girl, we'll get this man properly dressed. I don't know why he wears that uniform everywhere. I suppose it gives him a feeling of power. Ridiculous! As for you Arla Bay, I know that the English never travel even into the wilds without a proper wardrobe."

"I love dressing!" Arla admitted.

They found the closets and bureau drawers packed with suits, shirts, ties, shoes, socks, and even a cape and overcoat, all hand-tailored. Stone's resistance collapsed as the delighted women fitted him for the formal evening.

As they returned to La Fonda with the clothes in tooled leather cases, Arla lay back with eyes closed.

"Tired?" Stone asked.

"Overwhelmed."

"You need a drink," he said, leading her to the bar. "What do you make of Maria?" he asked.

"We got along beautifully, even though we don't agree about Mary Austin."

"What are your wishes for tonight?"

"Simple and few: bathe and go to bed and read."

"No dinner?"

"Not after that tea! Please eat for us both."

"Do you mean it?"

"I need to be alone. I loved being with her. It was as if we'd known each other forever. Her book made her real even before we met."

"Is talking all you did?"

"We walked in the orchard and I had my first ripe persimmon."

"Did she talk about me?" Stone asked.

"She wanted to know if I thought you are a homosexual."

"She did, did she?! Do you?"

"Of course I don't! And I told her so. I've wondered though why you have stayed alone so long."

"It has been a long time," Stone admitted.

"In your position you must have had many opportunities. Have you . . . ?" Arla did not finish.

323

"No, I haven't. I didn't want to get hurt again. The doctors told me to avoid that kind of excitement. When I was a young man, intercourse aroused me to violence. I hurt my wife more than once although apparently she liked it. Sometimes I was sick afterward. After what happened at South Rim, the doctors said I had what they called an aneurism and that I must be careful." Stone paused. "I suppose it boils down to fear. I wanted to live."

"That's not a natural life for a man like you."

"I know it isn't, yet we all have restrictions on our lives. I have learned to live with mine. I hope you can."

"O God," Arla cried, "why does life do these things to us?"

Stone rose. "We'd better leave ourselves out of it."

"What are you going to do tonight?" Arla asked as they parted in the hall.

"Hang up these clothes. Have something to eat, then take a walk around the plaza. Sure you won't join me?"

"I've had enough for one day. What time are we leaving in the morning? And where are you taking me?"

"Meet for breakfast at seven."

"You didn't answer me. Where are we going?"

"*Buenas noches, señora.*"

"Have it your way. *Bonne nuit, mon ami!*"

After she closed the door, Arla murmured, "I almost said *mon amour*, as I do to Glyn!"

The morning was clear and cold as they drove north. Arla was watchful and quiet while the landscape, walled by mountains, opened before them. At Española a gravelled road threaded the foothills to the east along a rising creek lined with cottonwoods still showing a thin gold leafage. Behind their roadside stands, Hispanos offered apples and pears and red chiles in garlands or powdered in bags. The day warmed as the sun rose from behind the high wall of the snow-capped Sangre de Cristo range.

"When are you going to tell me where we're going?" Arla demanded.

"We're here," was his reply. He smiled. "We've been here all morning."

"It is utterly different from Arizona. Why is that?"

"Because people have lived here for five hundred years and left their cultural humus. That's not true west of the Rio Grande."

"Maria and I talked about how old-world it is. That's why I feel so much at home."

"The river is the answer. Water is why the Anasazi came and stayed and why the Spaniards followed."

"Tonight should be lovely. Are you reconciled to being bullied by the two of us?"

"What chance did I have? Do you know those tickets cost her a hundred dollars apiece? I still think the two of you should go."

"Do you mean you'd rather not go?"

"I didn't say that!" he protested.

"I know it will be nice, and I'll be happy to dress again. I can't go completely native."

The road kept to the narrowing creek as the triple peaks of Truchas soared above them. Stone stopped at the sanctuary of Chimayó and a woodcarver's shop in Córdova, then at a weaver's in Truchas village. At the highest point he paused for a view across river to the Jemez mountains.

"Did Maria talk about her father's losing the ranch?" Stone asked.

"Only that she never goes back. She said the book was her way of coming to terms with it."

"We could still go to Bandelier. It's over there where you can see Los Alamos."

"How could America have done that to the world?"

"They say it was to keep others from doing it first."

"Now everyone will perish. What have you up your sleeve? I keep waiting for it, Mr. Magician. Is this what you call Indian Summer?"

"What do you call it?"

"The Little Summer of St. Martin. Ours comes later. Yesterday in the orchard I remembered an old Lancashire song. I sang it for Maria. Do you want to hear it?" And without waiting for his answer, Arla softly sang, " 'Apples be ripe, nuts be brown, petticoats up, and trowsers down.' "

"You should see a Navajo woman in a hurry!" Stone laughed. "Are you wearing your Chinle velvet tonight?"

"You'd better not dare me!"

325

The road dropped off the Truchas hogback, passed through Trampas village with its ancient Spanish church, then climbed again to a ridge above the settlement where Stone drew off the road and said, "Now we're *really* here. You've been patient. Come, I'll show you."

Arla followed him down a steep rocky path to a little creek crossed by a trestle where a flow of water was carried over in hollowed-out logs. He took her hand and led her along a single-plank walk alongside the flume. Halfway across he said, "Kneel with me." Cupping water in his hands he held it for her to drink.

She buried her face and drank, then cried, "*Muy fresca!*"

"Good girl!" Stone applauded. "And colder than Persephone's Well. This is snow melt."

After he had taken a drink, they stood up and he led her by the hand back along the plank.

"You're trembling," he said when they reached the bank.

"But you're not," she murmured.

"It's a woman's skin that trembles," he observed. "With a man it's his guts."

They stood close for a long moment, then Arla gently withdrew and said, "Now I know why you brought me here and to that well. They are shrines for you, aren't they. To you water means what sun means to me. Water and fire."

"I hadn't thought of it that way."

"It's not a matter of thinking, Mr. Ranger, but of feeling. There's so much feeling you keep locked up inside you."

"You're the first to know it." Then matter of fact, "That flume is called a *canoa*. They hollowed it out of old cottonwoods to bring water to the villagers and their fields. I once asked them how old it is. 'Who knows?' the patriarch said. 'My grandfather told me his father helped make it.' "

The road led into the Peñasco valley, crossed a larger creek and then switchbacked up the forested slope of a spur of the Sangres. As they gained altitude, isolated aspen groves stood out among the conifers. He stopped at the summit of the pass for a view over the lower ranges, breaking in dark waves of green in which the aspens burned like signal fires. Farthest and highest rose Mt. Wheeler, lordly crown of New Mexico.

They gazed silently over the immense panorama, then Arla asked, "What are you thinking?"

"That this won't last forever. In another century it will have been lost to lumbering, mining and all that goes with greed. The continent was once this virgin. The Indians lacked only the technology to destroy it as we are doing. Maybe they would have been wiser, but I doubt it."

"I learned from Glyn," Arla said, "that history is cyclic. Who can count the waves that have washed over Britain? The Romans had centers like Santa Fe. Where are they now? Buried and forgotten, except for those that have been unearthed. That's how Glyn began. You don't realize how little you have known of destruction."

"What's ahead?" Stone asked sombrely.

"More of the same—building up and tearing down and burying under. We have it to look back on. You have it to look forward to."

"If I thought I could help slow it, I'd stay on."

Stone let off the brake and they coasted down to Talpa, Ranchos de Taos, and Taos itself. Except for the backwall of mountains, Arla did not like Taos, its congestion of cars, crowded plaza and commercialized pueblo. He agreed to her offer to buy bread and cheese and fill the thermos for a picnic on the way back to Santa Fe.

They stopped along the river after entering the gorge where the cliffs came down in a tumult of fractured rock, ochre and amethyst. The dark water was swift and wide and cold as Arla learned when she dipped to wash her face.

"*Es fresca?*" he asked.

"*Frescissima!*" she cried.

"Snow melt from the Rockies."

"Come and see our River Tyne and the Highland streams."

"Come back and I'll take you where this river rises," Stone promised.

Where the Rio Grande left the gorge and the valley widened to accommodate the river pueblos, they passed more orchards where the natives were selling apples and cherries at roadside stands. Now cottonwoods reappeared, belting the river with gold as far as the eye could see.

"You've an hour to dress," he said when they reached La Fonda. "Meet in the lobby at five-thirty and bring your coat. It will be cold later."

327

"Don't forget to wear your tuxedo," she warned as they parted.
"Not too tired?"

"I'll be a new woman. You'll see."

"That's not Chinle velvet," Stone said when they met again.

"It's all I brought. How handsome you are! I'm glad you're not foolish about wearing someone else's things."

"I've never worn a dead man's clothes."

Arla's face clouded. "Please don't say that."

Stone took her hand. "Forgive me."

"Should I have left him?" she asked.

"Did you phone again?"

"Is it awful of me not wanting to know?"

"You'll be home in a few days."

"That's part of my trouble," Arla said.

They walked silently across the plaza and as they neared the restaurant Stone said, "That's a silver comb in your hair. The one at El Tovar was gold."

Arla took his arm. "Betatakin!"

They entered the Palace and joined the crowd at the long bar where Stone was greeted by old acquaintances. Maria MacPherson had place-carded their table where they were welcomed by a Hispano woman of middle age with fine black hair to her shoulders, wearing a blood-red gown.

"Stony!" she cried, embracing him. "Do you remember my son Juan? He's grown since you last saw him. I'm Jennie LaPorte," she said to Arla.

"This is Arla Bay," Stone managed to say.

"Maria told me what a nice visit you had. Did you like her?"

"Very much," Arla replied.

"Who is this handsome man who resembles William Stone?"

He smiled. "I had it made in London."

"Next stop Hollywood!" Jennie laughed and said to Arla, "We knew Stony at Grand Canyon. Are you an archaeologist?"

"My husband is. He is Glyn Williams. Perhaps you know his work on Roman Britain."

"I'm sure Maurice did. He was an archaeologist before he became a writer."

328

"I read *Rainbow Man* as a girl in Switzerland and loved it," Arla said.

"That's sweet of you to say so, but he did grow annoyed by people who knew only his first book. He was a nice man, wasn't he, Stony."

"The best friend the Park Service ever had, and of the tribes too."

"The house has become too big for Juan and me. I disposed of his books and papers and they left a big empty space."

"Why don't you and Maria move in together?" Stone asked. "She said the same thing about her place."

"We're too old and independent. When Juan goes east to school, I'll have to do something."

During dinner they talked of the trip Stone and Arla were taking, Juan playing his part in the conversation.

"Do you have children?" Jennie asked Arla.

"We kept putting it off and now it's too late. May I ask, are you Spanish?"

"And French. I was born near here."

"At a place I should have shown you today," Stone said to Arla, "even more remote than those we saw."

"Where did you grow up?" Jennie asked Arla.

"In the north of England near Manchester. My grandfather was a Shetlander who took himself a Yorkshire wife—by force, no doubt. His son took a Lancashire wife, or from what he says, she took him. She died at my birth. I bear her name—her hair and temper too, Daddy says. He builds railway locomotives."

"Her father is Sir Tor Bay," Stone explained. "The Queen's Minister of Transport."

"What a marvelous name!" Jennie exclaimed. "With a name like that he should be Prime Minister."

"I'm sure he could be if he wanted to," Arla said, "but trains are his true love."

"After his daughter," Stone added.

"Mr. Stone had been learning how to treat spoiled children!" Arla laughed.

"With those clothes who knows where he'll end!" Jennie glanced at the tables around them, then asked Arla, "What do you make of Santa Fe's finest?"

329

"It's a lovely gathering, although we're now all so alike it could be almost anywhere."

"Your shows are funnier than ours," Juan said. "My favorite is the Goon Show."

"Miss Bay is learning western talk so she can be on T.V. when she gets back home," Stone volunteered.

"The man claims he's speaking Navajo," Arla said, "when he makes those strange sounds."

Jennie grimaced. "He and Maurice simply murdered that language—Apache too."

"I know some Hopi," Juan volunteered.

"The bad words," his mother said, then asked Arla, "What have you liked most on your trip?"

Arla thought a moment, then said, "Persephone's Well where it empties into the creek."

"She means Montezuma Well," Stone explained, "the one in the Verde Valley."

"And the *canoa* at Trampas," Arla continued. She smiled at Stone. "Am I doing all right?"

"We went to places I wanted to see again," Stone explained.

"Not the Grand Canyon?" Jennie asked.

"I would have loved the North Rim if I could have seen it!"

"At least we heard the river," Stone said. "The canyon was full of rainclouds."

"What Mr. Stone really likes," Arla teased, "are the power plants we saw."

He muttered something in Navajo and Jennie laughed. "Maria said you've just come from Chaco. Did you like it?"

"It frightened me. But then we called on Hester Crane, and now Maria MacPherson has been wonderfully reassuring." Arla turned to Juan. "Do you like music?"

"I like drums," the boy replied. "I have a whole room full of them. Why don't you come home with me and I'll drum for you. Mother and Mr. Stone can go to the concert."

"Alas, I'm in his custody."

"I'll go with you, Juan," Stone said, "and they can go to the concert."

"This has got to stop!" Jennie laughed, "or we'll be late."

"*Que lástima!*" Juan sighed.

330

While Stone and Juan visited with familiar Santa Feans, the women retrieved their wraps.

"I've been waiting to tell you," Arla said, "how lovely your hair is."

"I know that women my age, unless they're *brujas*, shouldn't wear their hair this long, but mine is too silky to do up. Besides, if I did, no one would know me."

"Your husband must have loved it."

"He used to say that he married me for my hair."

"You were happy, weren't you."

"He had what makes a woman happy."

"So did mine until . . . "

"I know," Jennie interrupted softly. "Maria told me."

"Now all I have is my two Airedales."

"May I tell you what he said in Navajo?"

"Please do," Arla said.

"He said the name they gave you is Woman Whose Head is on Fire."

"Let's hope I'm not that hot-headed!"

Jennie reached out. "May I touch it? Oh, it's so thick! It must be awful to wash."

Arla smiled. "It does take special handling."

The concert was given in a chapel seating only a few hundred. There were no reserved seats, and the four sat together in a cushioned pew. The song cycles featured players from the opera orchestra and a local tenor who had achieved recognition in the East. The program opened with "On Wenlock Edge," Vaughan Williams's setting of poems from *A Shropshire Lad*. After the intermission this was to be followed by Benjamin Britten's "Les Illuminations" to poems by Rimbaud. The audience was rapt.

At the intermission the sounds of visiting filled the foyer. Everyone knew Jennie and Juan and many knew Stone. Arla disappeared and did not return until the music was ready to resume.

"Are you all right?" Stone whispered as she slid in beside him. She squeezed his hand. "Jennie said you are the most beautiful woman here," he added.

"Ssh, she is!"

331

Arla kept his hand as the concert resumed. Again the audience was transfixed.

"There is a reception for the musicians and the singer," Jennie said afterward. "Will you join Juan and me?"

Stone looked at Arla who replied, "Would it be terribly rude to refuse? I'm afraid I've reached the saturation point." She turned to Stone. "Leave me at the hotel and you go."

"I'm sorry," he said. "That would violate the Secretary's directive."

"Please go. I'll be all right."

"But I won't! Do excuse us, Jennie. We've a long day tomorrow, to Acoma and back to Gallup for the night, and then El Morro the next day."

"At least you'll let us drive you back to La Fonda."

"I know I'm hopelessly ill-mannered," Arla said, "but I do want one last walk on the plaza."

Jennie embraced her. "I love it too. You'll come back, won't you. Remember what Kit Carson said: 'Those who have heard the bells and smelled the piñon smoke and loved the women of Santa Fe will always return."

"What a lovely prospect!" Arla said, kissing Jennie and hugging Juan.

"Please come back," Juan said, "and I'll drum for you."

Stone and Arla crossed the deserted plaza. The cold air was sweet with the smoke from a thousand fires. Leaves rattled under foot. Her arm remained linked with his. Neither spoke until Arla asked, "Did my holding your hand embarrass you?"

"It seemed natural. I've never been to a concert before, nor any-where with such a fair lady."

"I needed something to hold on to. The music made me feel as if I were about to leave my body. Have you ever felt that way?" She continued before he could answer. "I'm so troubled about every-thing. I don't want to let go of your arm."

"You don't have to," he said softly.

When they entered the warm smoky lobby, Arla asked, "Will you stand me an Irish coffee?"

"I'll join you. It's been quite an evening."

As they lingered over their drinks in the nearly empty bar, Arla finally asked, "Well?"

When Stone did not respond, she persisted, "Did you like it?"

"I liked your liking it," he ventured.

She smiled. "You're not entirely hopeless. Maria told me she once grew cross with her husband when he didn't match her feelings, and will regret it to the end of her life."

"I must be like him," Stone said, "emotionally retarded. I did like being there and seeing people I know. I told you what Jennie said about you."

"And you heard what I said about her. Lucky man, with the two of us on your arm! I'm glad you didn't go with them. I didn't want to be with strangers, nor do I want to be alone. May I have another drink?"

After it arrived, with another for him, Arla continued, "I need to talk, probably to cry. I haven't cried this whole day."

"I have a clean handkerchief—never ask me whose!"

"Maria said something nice about you. Do you want to hear it?"

"It had better be, after that crack of hers!"

"She's miffed at your not having been to see her. What she said was that, although your name is, your heart isn't!"

"What do you think?"

"I've had to learn what moves you."

"Places more than people. Weren't those your words?"

"Everything moves that crazy Welshman of mine. You are more the typical Englishman. And you deserved a better marriage. It left your feelings crippled. Do you mind if I babble?"

"Better your tongue than your eyes!"

"Did you wonder why I disappeared at the interval?" she asked.

"I figured you had to go to the restroom."

"Those songs undid me. They are favorites of Glyn's. He was born in Shropshire on the border with Wales, at Ludlow. The poet Housman is buried there. We go back to see Glyn's people."

"What is Wenlock Edge?"

"A wooded hill near the village Much Wenlock. We do have odd place names."

"No odder than Betatakin."

"I could hardly bear to hear those songs without him. Please sir, one more drink?"

"If I don't have to join you."

"You don't have anywhere to drive."

"I will tomorrow."

"I'm already drunk from the music. Please tell me you liked it."

"I liked the songs in English," Stone conceded.

"The French songs *are* obscure, I'll admit, even when you know the language. Not the final one, though—*Départ*. Rimbaud wrote it as his farewell to poetry. He was only eighteen. He used poetic shorthand for feelings most would take a whole book to express. And the music rose to the words. Britten composed it when he was departing—leaving England and all he loved. Give me your program and I'll translate it for you. I too departed—left my husband and now I'll be leaving you and your land that has taken such a hold on me. I should never have come!"

Arla began to cry. Stone deliberately unfolded his handkerchief. After she had regained her composure, she began to translate the verses.

"*Assez vu*—that's easy. It means 'Seen enough.' Next, *La vision s'est rencontrée à tous les airs*. I take that to mean 'An ever-present vision.' *Assez eu*. That's also easy. 'Had enough.' *Rumeurs des villes, le soir, et au soleil, et toujours*. That means 'Sounds of the city that go on night and day and forever.' Next, *Assez connu* means 'Known enough.' *Arrets de la vie*? That could mean 'Life commands.' Now it gets harder. *O rumeurs et visions*. Perhaps 'Those things that trouble your dreams.' Then the last line, *Départ dans l'affection et le bruit neufs*. What does that mean? I think he meant 'Go lovingly to the sounds of new music.' " She handed him his program. "Don't the Navajos say Go in Beauty?"

Stone rose and said, "It's our time to go. Drink up, it's your bedtime."

He helped her up and she said, "Don't forget, we're going to see your Sheltie tomorrow."

Arla took his arm and they walked carefully to the elevator. "I'm a wee bit drunk," she confessed at the end of the hall. "I think we'd better lock our doors tonight."

"Good night, Miss Arla," he replied. His mouth was dry.

Stone had trouble getting to sleep. He thought he heard her crying softly. Should he go to her? Was it only comforting that she needed? The tenderness of someone she trusted. Did he have that for her?

Early next morning they stopped at Maria MacPherson's to return the clothes.

"You needn't have," she chided him, and turning to Arla she asked, "Was he the beau of the ball?"

"He's in love with Jennie LaPorte," was her answer.

"What man isn't?" Stone asked.

"I didn't tell you," Maria said, "that she is dying of leukemia."

"Oh how awful!" Arla cried. "I'm glad you didn't. I couldn't have stood it. She's so beautiful, so lovely!"

"They're the ones that go first," Maria said. "We homely ones live forever. Was the concert nice?"

"Perfect. I had no idea Santa Fe was such a sophisticated place. I'm afraid we were rude in not going to the reception."

"We went back to La Fonda," Stone said, "and drank Irish coffee till past my bedtime."

Maria sniffed. "You could at least have made it Scotch! Stony, listen to me, I want you to come back with a trailer and take all of Frank's clothes. Why let the moths get them!"

"I don't need clothes. Before long I won't need this uniform."

"What do you intend to do, go around in a loin cloth?" Maria asked disgustedly. "Now listen to me, you two, I want this girl back, do you hear? I'll have the governor proclaim her a native daughter."

"How sweet of you!" Arla laughed. "Please write another book. Thank you for the lovely things you wrote in mine."

Tears flowed as they embraced and parted.

5.

[handwritten script]

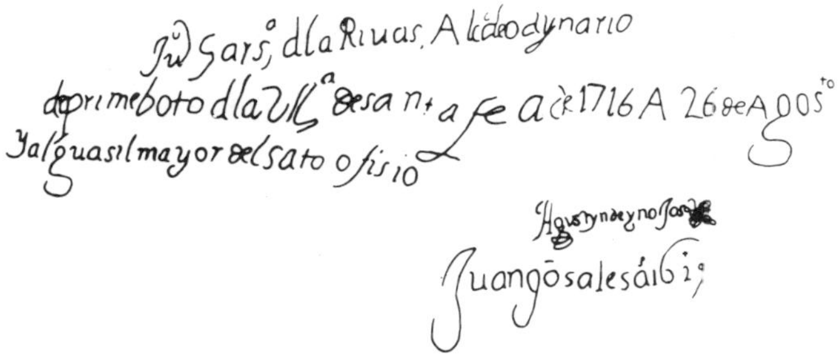

It was another Indian Summer day as Stone and Arla left the *bajada* for the river valley.

"Those canyons we saw seem so far away," she mused as they drove steadily south. "I love Santa Fe and all we saw yesterday. And I heard the cathedral bells ringing early mass. Perhaps I should bring him here for a change."

"And take him to Chaco?"

"I'd want you to take him. He must try to reconcile himself to fitted limbs. Loss of will is the worst of all. Perhaps it's too late to go anywhere. Daddy wants to take him to Zurich to a famous prosthetics clinic. Glyn refuses to have anything to do with Daddy. I'm caught in between."

"I wish I could help you," Stone said.

"You've given me magic to last a lifetime."

Stone stopped at the kennel in Albuquerque. Sheltie was wild with joy, barking, circling and jumping, until he managed to gather her in his arms. She began immediately to sniff Arla.

"She smells my two. What a lovely bitch!"

"My dog's not bitchy!" Stone protested.

Arla laughed. "We call female bitches. Only males are dogs."

"She sleeps with me."

"Why can't we take her with us?" she asked.

"Do you mean it?"

"Can we?"

"She'd love it."

And so they settled the happy animal on the seat between them and headed west for Acoma.

Beyond the river the highway vanished over the horizon. Stone pointed to a blue form in the northwest that grew and changed shape.

"Mt. Taylor. That's the last of the sacred peaks we'll see. There's a fire road to the top if we had the time. You can see the whole world from there."

"Had we but world enough and time!"

"You sound sad."

"I want to go home and I want to stay. I didn't tell Jennie LaPorte what I've liked the most of all: your distances. Day after day the Ranger has devoured them and now they've devoured me. Will there be many tourists at Acoma?"

"There never are, and even fewer at El Morro. They are off the beaten track. The Acomans have never exploited tourists the way Taos has. There's even less to exploit at El Morro—only landscape and history and some fading inscriptions."

"Will her ghost be there?"

Stone shook his head.

"Is it tomorrow we'll be there?" Arla asked.

"Unless you decide to end at Acoma."

"Never!"

"We'll stop in Grants and stock the ice chest. There's nothing at Acoma but Pepsi and candy bars. The Acomans want it that way."

"Are they unfriendly?"

"Indifferent. They know we won't be around much longer than the Spanish were."

"*Les jours s'en vont, je demeure.*" Arla murmured. "Jennie told me the Navajo name you gave me."

"I didn't give it to you."

"Who did?"

"Remember when we were registering at Kayenta and the desk clerk spoke in Navajo?"

"They would scalp her first! What is a *bruja*?"

"A witch."

"Jennie said only an old *bruja* would wear her hair that long. There are witches in the Highlands. Do you believe in them?"

"All women are dangerously perceptive."

"Their defense against predators!"

As they backtracked from Grants to the Acoma cutoff, Stone said, "Keep a lookout for it. It is like a crouching cougar."

"Like Shiprock?"

"Ready to spring not sail."

When suddenly the pueblo appeared, Arla exclaimed, "Do people actually live up there?"

"For a thousand years."

"Of course!" she laughed.

They came to the base of the rock from where a steep road led to the top. "That's something new," Stone remarked. "It used to be either the sand trail or the rock climb."

An Acoman in Levi's came toward them and pointed to where several cars were parked.

"Can't I drive up?" Stone asked.

The man continued to point.

Stone shrugged and said to Arla, "You see how they rate a government officer."

After locking Sheltie in the Ranger, they set out up the rough road. A crude sign led to a plastered-stone structure on a narrow lane of similar dwellings with grass growing on their flat dirt roofs. All else was rocky and bare except for a few potted geraniums on window ledges.

"They had to carry everything up by hand," Stone explained, "including the church of St. Stephen. It must have taken thousands of trips. They even carried trunks of whole pine trees for the *vigas* that hold up the roof. Now at least *they* can drive up."

A young Acoma woman bade them wait with a few other visitors until the guide returned for the next tour. No one spoke. There were no postcards for sale.

A silent half hour passed before the guide returned. She was another impassive young Acoma woman, wearing pants and shirt and no jewelry. The obedient band followed her to the huge adobe church that dominated the east end of the mesa. They filed into the nave which held only an altar and a few tin wall shrines with paper flowers. Arla quietly read aloud from the leaflet furnished by their guide who waited while her subdued charges wandered about the empty structure.

"It comes to life," Stone said, "only on their saint's day. Then it stinks of sweat and incense."

"What would a priest from Notre Dame make of it?" Arla wondered.

"He'd probably say how impoverished these aborigines are!"

As they trailed out after their guide, past the burial ground made of earth also carried up in baskets, they came to women seated on their doorsteps, selling the pottery for which the pueblo is famed. Arla's eye was taken by little black-and-white clay lizards. She bought several from an unsmiling old woman who wrapped each one in toilet paper.

"I love that pot," Arla pointed. "What is the bird on it?"

Stone addressed the woman in Navajo. She shook her head. Then he spoke in Spanish and she replied in that tongue. "She says it is a singing bird—*es un pájaro que cánta*."

"I'd never get it home unbroken. Let me buy it for you."

Stone shook his head. "A pot is the last thing I need!"

"Such dignity!" Arla marvelled as they descended the steep road. "I have never felt so humbled."

"Isolation has saved them. They had nothing we wanted and still don't, except what we need most if we only knew it."

"They will survive us, won't they," she half asked.

"By another thousand years."

"What *can* I give you to remember me by?"

"Do you think I'll need something?"

"Not really. I'm just being conventional."

Stone thought for a moment. "How about a lock of your hair?"

"You *are* getting sentimental."

"I'll recover when you've gone." he said gruffly.

Stone drove on to Enchanted Mesa, smaller and lower and of a blonder stone now honey-colored in the light of the western sun.

"This is what Fray Marcos saw at sundown," Stone observed, "and then returned to Mexico City and reported discovering the Golden Cities of Cibola. That brought the Coronado gang on the run."

"Have you climbed it?" Arla asked.

"Once."

"With a group?"

"No."

Stone left the road and steered among junipers to the foot of a talus slope.

"There's the way up," he pointed. "First a climb over the loose stuff, then rock steps to the ladder. There you'll find, if it's still there, a rope to haul yourself up by. I was younger then."

While Sheltie scrambled ahead and back again, they made their way to the steps in the soft stone and sat with their backs against the sun-warmed cliff. The land below sloped to the valley, now golden green with grama grass. Acoma lay to the south while in the north Mt. Taylor was dark blue against the paler sky. Two birds glided down to inspect the noisy dog who kept starting up rabbits, then returned to lie panting at their feet.

"At last your golden eagles," Stone said. "They mate for life. This cliff is probably their home." He paused. "Don't tell me you're crying!"

Arla accepted the handkerchief and wiped her tears. "No reason," she said, "absolutely no reason."

"That's when you cry the most."

"There *is* a reason only a woman would understand."

"Try Sheltie. She's very understanding."

"When must we start?" Arla asked.

"Soon. Gallup is another hundred miles. We'll snack now and have late dinner."

While Sheltie raced on ahead, they regained the Ranger and ate bread and cheese and fruit. Stone broke off a branch of juniper and handed it to Arla. "Bruise one of the berries and smell."

She did so, then exclaimed, "A martini!"

"I'll buy you one in Gallup—two if you promise not to cry. Those cedar beads you bought are the nut of that blue berry."

Arla and Sheltie slept most of the way to Gallup. As the highway ran toward the setting sun, Stone watched the blue mountain change shape, diminish, and finally disappear behind them. To the north, battlements of salmon-colored stone lined the road and railway, until the ammunition bunkers of Fort Wingate appeared, then the fort itself, including the original wooden buildings from the time of the Indian wars.

They reached Gallup with the darkness, and Arla had her first sight of drunken Indians lying alongside the road.

"Can't anything be done about it?" she asked.

"Something *is* done—they're gathered up every morning and sent out in a road gang to pay off their fines—and it starts all over. LaPorte's preface to the paperback of *Rainbow Man* cries out against what alcohol, autos and politicians have done to the Navajos since he first knew them."

They checked in at the station hotel, washed up, then met in the lobby for dinner.

"Where's my fifth of Gordon's?" Arla demanded.

"I said two martinis and no more!"

"Don't worry. I don't want to work on the road!"

After dinner they walked across the street to the Santa Fe station and watched a long freight easing on through to the east, drawn by a tandem of growling diesels that throttled up through growl to roar as the train cleared the yards, tailed by a faded red caboose.

"I'm going to turn in and read," Arla announced as they returned to the lobby.

"Last time to buy good jewelry."

"I could take one of those cravat clips to Glyn — that beauty in silver and turquoise and coral. May I get one for you?"

"I told you what I want."

"Tied with a red, white and blue ribbon? Let's sit here in the lobby for a few minutes. I can't believe I'll soon be back in England. Must we come back here tomorrow night?"

"If we spend the day at El Morro, Albuquerque will be too far to drive."

"Where will you go when I leave?"

"Back to the South Rim."

"And afterward?"

"I'll decide that when I come to it."

"I'll think of you in places we've been — Cañon de Chelly, Santa Fe."

Again they parted in the upper hall. Sheltie greeted Stone with her usual exuberance, then scratched at the door to Arla's room.

"What does she want?" she called.

"To see you."

"Can she sleep with me tonight?"

"That's up to her."

Arla opened the door and Sheltie ran and jumped on her bed.

"There goes my dog!" Stone laughed.

"I'll leave the door open a crack so she can go to you if she wants to."

And so they settled for the night to the roll and roar of the trains.

When Stone awoke before daylight, Sheltie was not on his bed. For a moment he wondered, then pushed open the connecting door. Arla was propped with pillows, reading by lamplight, his dog asleep at the foot of her bed.

"Good morning," she said. "Give me five minutes."

"I knew I'd lost my dog," Stone said.

"She prefers my smell."

"She's taken to you as never to anyone before."

"You're going to have to add another codicil!" Arla said.

"I planned to read her chapter to you," she said to Stone as they drove south and then east, "but I can't stop looking. I don't want to miss that first sight."

"I'll warn you when we're near."

"She wanted El Morro to be her last resting place."

"That would have taken an Act of Congress."

"Where *was* she buried?"

"Santa Fe fought a civil war before agreeing on a nearby site in the National Forest. Even that took some doing. Old Hodge was luckier. We scattered his ashes from one of our planes over a site he had dug near El Morro.

"Wasn't that breaking the law?"

"We invoked a higher law."

"Will you stop somewhere?" Arla asked. "I want to press a few more flowers for Glyn."

Stone drew off the road by a meadow among the pines, and waited while she picked red, blue and yellow blooms and laid them between the pages.

"I like to think this is what she did when she came this way," Arla said. "She wrote so beautifully about flowers."

"Last stop," Stone said, "we're nearly there."

"Last day," she echoed. "You planned it perfectly. I can never thank you enough for the care you've taken of me."

"Secretary's orders," he said bluntly.

They came to a dirt road that turned off to the monument. Stone drove slowly among the pines as Arla watched for the rock. "I see it!" at last she cried. "Stop!"

Beyond a low rise Inscription Rock towered above the tallest trees, its great promontory facing north like the prow of a ship.

"You see why the Spaniards called it The Headland," Stone observed.

"It's beautiful and noble and God knows what else."

"Is it what you imagined?"

She shook her head.

Stone drove on to the headquarters-museum building. The hour was still early. Only the superintendent's green pickup and one other car were there. The young ranger came out and introduced himself as Arnulfo Archuleta.

"I remember you, Arnie," Stone said. "How do you like it here?"

"Don't transfer me!"

"What if I want my old job back?"

"You're the boss!"

"This is Miss Bay, a guest of the Secretary."

"They have been calling from Washington to expect you any day. What would she like to see?"

"Ghostly evidences," Arla said.

"Beg pardon, miss?"

Stone laughed. "We'll do the inscriptions this morning and the long walk this afternoon. I'm told it's easier now."

"No more ladder. I hope you won't miss it."

"May I leave my dog with you?"

"Take her with you. Better keep her on leash though. There are a lot of squirrels."

"We're due back in Gallup tonight. Miss Bay leaves for England tomorrow afternoon."

"Will you do the honor of lunching with me? Nothing fancy. I shop at Safeway in town."

"Please, no green chile!" Arla warned.

For the rest of the morning Stone led her lingeringly around the north face of the rock, past the *tinaja* and its guardian pine where the early travellers stopped for water and to carve their name. They deciphered the inscriptions aloud, from the first one made in the soft stone by Don Juan de Oñate in 1605 upon his return from El Mar del Sur.

"How do you translate *Pasó por aquí?*" she asked Stone.

"*Came this way.*"

"Did she leave her mark?"

"I doubt it. If she did, she would have violated the President's

343

proclamation of December 6, 1906, that established the national monument. It warned all persons not to appropriate, excavate, deface, injure, or destroy said monument. What he didn't take into account was that all inscriptions are indifferent to presidential proclamations. The wind and the rain will win in the end. I required all visitors to recite that proclamation with me. Many inscriptions were lost before the government took charge. Now those who come here are mostly ones like you with respect for the past."

Although irked to be leashed and yet obedient, Sheltie was excited by the gray squirrels that scampered ahead. The sky was beginning to pile with clouds. Bluejays flashed among the pines. Arla was subdued, content to listen as Stone recalled his time at the monument.

At noon they returned to headquarters. Aided by the museum attendant, a Mormon woman from the nearby village of Ramah, Archuleta served enchiladas and frijoles, chopped lettuce and beer.

Stone grew more expansive than Arla had known him, recalling his time at the Rock. Their host listed the improvements that had been made and complained of his problems with report-hungry bureaucrats in Washington.

"Nothing has changed," Stone observed.

As they lingered over coffee, he continued to reminisce. "There was one couple I've not forgotten. The woman had black hair and eyes and light brown skin. I thought she was Hispano until she corrected me. *'Estoy Quechan'* she said. She was the only slim Yuma woman I've ever seen. There must have been much other blood in her. The man was Anglo, an academic type. They wanted their picture taken seated on the railing in front of the *tinaja*. Although they promised me one, I never got it. After I'd gone to Chaco, a book was forwarded to me. It was about desert rivers. The author had thanked me for his day at the Rock. I believe he was the man with the Yuma woman."

"Was it a good book?" Arla asked.

"It's one like Maria's I'm saving for retirement." He rose from the table. "We'll have a look at your steps, Arnie. Miss Bay also hopes to find an eagle feather."

"There's a pair nesting on the west face, but they're not moulting now."

"What's the weather out of Albuquerque?" Stone asked.

344

"Rain by tonight and clearing, with ground mist toward dawn. I'll have another report at five. We need the rain though. The fire hazard has been high."

"I'll check with you when we come back down. We should be starting for Gallup by then."

"I'm afraid you'll have a wet drive. I hope you'll approve of what I've done with the trail. It had gotten rough. I've also reposted it where people wandered off."

Bearing the book and a canteen of water, Stone and Arla set out. When they reached the rock-cut steps he said. "Here's where the ladder was. If she'd have been a pound heavier, I'd never have gotten her up."

"You're very naughty," Arla scolded.

Even with the steps and railings, it was a steep climb to the top where they rested. The trail led toward the southwest corner of the rock, past a box canyon that widened into a pine-ringed meadow.

"You see where the kiva was," Stone pointed out.

"She called it the dancing place. Let me read you her closing words. If we listen hard we might hear their drums."

"More likely thunder."

"*Here, at least, I shall haunt,*" Arla began softly. "*You of a hundred years from now, if when you visit the Rock, you see the cupped silken wings of the argemone burst and float apart when there is no wind; or if, when all around is still, a sudden stir in the short-leaved pines, or fresh eagle feathers blown upon the shrine, that will be I, making known in such fashion as I may the land's undying quality.*"

"I find it hard to reconcile what she wrote with the abrasive woman she was," Stone said.

"Isn't her book all that matters?" Arla asked.

Stone nodded and pointed to the southwest. "There's the weather front. It will take a couple of hours to reach us."

And so the afternoon passed as the man, woman and dog lingered over the long, wide rock, resting, reading, talking and gazing on the forest in which they were enislanded.

The trail led to the promontory from where their view was toward the Zuñi mountains that hid Mt. Taylor from sight. Through the pines they looked down on the road from Zuñi, and as they watched, a clang of sheep bells grew louder. Sheltie began to bristle and growl. Along the road came a small flock, accompanied by a man and dog. When the leaders lagged to graze, the followers built up pressure until they moved on and the flock flowed after. The shepherd trudged along in their wake, leaving the work to the dog.

"What would Sheltie do," Arla asked, "if I loosed her?"

"Take off! The dog would drive her away, the flock would scatter, and the shepherd have the law on us. The Zuñis and Acomas have passage rights between their reservations."

"What is an argemone?" she asked.

"A prickly poppy that blooms in early summer before the rains come."

"I'd like to have pressed one for Glyn."

"We'd better start down. That front has gained on us.

"I wish we could stay and watch it darken as we did at Cañon de Chelly."

"We'd get soaked," Stone said.

They made their way along the down-trail, past the inscriptions and the *tinaja*. "It will be full again by morning," Stone observed of the rain pool.

As they reached headquarters the first rain came in fine stinging drops. Archuleta greeted them. "I thought you'd left for Gallup until I saw where you'd moved the Ranger. Will you have something to eat before you leave?"

Before Stone could reply, Arla said, "Thank you, but I've food in our ice chest. You've been most kind."

As they went to the car she added, "I couldn't bear making small talk even with that nice young man. Our last time I want to be alone with Sheltie—and with you, sir."

Whereupon she proceeded to make martinis while Stone broke out two folding chairs. They sat back and toasted the day as the rain started to patter on the roof.

"I've two things to say," Arla began. "Are you listening? First, I'll not have you driving in this weather when you are as tired as I can see you are. Besides, I dislike Gallup even more than you do. I'll make us another drink before item two." When that was done, she continued, "Second, I intend to stay here tonight. I want to end at El Morro as, spiritually, she did. What do you say to that?"

Stone was slow in replying. "Two things, Miss Arla. First, you are even more assertive than she was, if such is possible. Second, there is nowhere to stay as there was at Chaco."

"What about the village?"

"There's nowhere in Ramah." Stone grew stern. "Please don't get balmy. I prefer your tears."

"They're all shed. So you think I'm assertive? Wait until I really want something."

"I suppose that's because you're from the north of England."

"Don't try to be amusing," she scorned.

"Where do you propose to sleep?" he countered.

Her reply stunned him. "Right here."

"What do you mean, right here?"

"I mean here where we are." She smiled. "I don't mean in these chairs. We do have sleeping bags, and you said there are air mattresses. Do you remember when I arrived how you bragged on your vehicle's roominess?"

Stone was silent, then asked, "What would Archuleta think?"

"Didn't you train him to respect authority? Tell him flat out we're staying. In this weather he'll understand." Her voice grew softer. "Now listen to me, William Stone, you and I have slept within sound of each other for nearly two weeks. Can't we sleep within touch our last night?"

Stone did not answer.

Arla said no more. The rain had increased and they could hear the rising wind in the pines.

When he had finished his drink, Stone donned slicker and rain hat and went outside. Arla waited. He was gone for what seemed a long while. She made herself another drink.

When he returned, she looked questioningly but did not speak.

"I checked the weather with Archuleta," he said. Still she waited. "I told him we'll be staying," he added softly.

Arla reached for his hand. Her lip was trembling. "Goddamn it," Stone said, "if you cry again, we start for Gallup rain or no rain."

She laughed wildly, then controlled herself and asked, "What did he say?"

"What did he say? He said 'Very good, sir.' "

Arla laughed delightedly. "Now I'll make you another drink, and then I'll prepare dinner. *Qu'est-ce que Monsieur desire? Faisan El Morro? Langouste Marie Austin?* No? Then how about a ham on rye?

347

Wups, sorry, *pas de moutarde! Comme boisson,* I can offer beer, milk, or coffee, but the gin's all gone. How about a straight juniper berry?"

Stone was content to watch Arla stirring about, then said, "He asked us to have coffee with him before we leave. I told him we'd be heading out by daylight."

And so in the dim glow of the dome light they made their last supper, while the rain drummed and the pines began to roar. When it grew colder, Arla donned her Shetland coat and Stone found a down-lined jacket among his gear.

Back they lingered over the way they had come, though now there was little to say. Later he fired up the engine, connected a pump and inflated the mattresses, then unrolled the sleeping bags.

"We are not sleeping in our clothes," Arla announced. "I'll take Sheltie out while you undress. Don't tarry though, we don't want to get soaked."

"Let me go out while you undress." Stone's mouth had gone dry.

Arla laughed. "I peel off so fast you wouldn't get a glimpse even if you tried."

When she returned, letting in a rush of cold and wet, Stone was zipped into his bag. Sheltie shook herself dry, then lay down between the two bags. Stone closed his eyes and listened to the sounds of Arla undressing.

"You may watch me brush my hair," she murmured. "Or shall I snap off the light?"

"Leave it on," he whispered.

He saw her hair fall below her shoulders. Auburn, she had called it, a rich dark red, and thick, thick. Rain drops flew as she shook her head. He heard her hair crackle and spark as she brushed it out. She had donned a blue nightgown. Now he began to tremble. He knew he had to have cold air. He zipped the bag part way down and freed his arms. "Too warm," he explained.

As she continued to brush her hair, Arla said, "Sheltie acted strangely when we were out. Did you hear her howl?"

"She probably smelled a lion. This is deer country. Are you warm enough? Your arms are bare."

"My gown is viyella—warmer than silk, cooler than wool."

"These bags are kapok." Stone said softly. "We'd roast if they were down."

"Will she be all right between us? Shall I spread my coat for her?"

"Good idea. I'll put my arms back in when I cool off."

The warmth had now permeated his body, soothing his tiredness and bringing an ineffable sense of well being. He realized that she had taken charge, and he was grateful for her determination and strength, relieved to be out of the storm and not driving back to Gallup. He continued to watch her with half-closed eyes. Her face was serene. The world had drawn back and left them alone.

"*Et voilà!*" she said at last, putting down the brush. She snapped off the light and slid into her bag, all but her arms.

"Now Sheltie's our connecting door," she said, taking Stone's hand. His heart began to beat faster as together they stroked the contented animal's fur.

"The rain will be over by morning," Stone said carefully. "We'll have no problem in making your flight."

"Daddy will meet me at Heathrow. Maybe he will bring Glyn." She fell silent. They continued to pet Sheltie. Then she whispered. "I must go, mustn't I."

"You want to go, don't you?" he asked.

"Yes and no. You know I love him, don't you."

"Yes, I know."

"And that I have kept my vows."

"I know you have." He paused. "You are a rare woman."

"Am I? Not too assertive?"

"Like no other I've ever known—or ever will."

"I know what a long day it has been for you, and on top of putting up with my crazy emotions for nearly two weeks now." She paused. "There's more I could say but I'm afraid to begin."

Stone could not control his trembling. He knew they were at the edge.

"We have come very close, haven't we," she whispered. "Can't we end in beauty?"

He knew her meaning and his heart raced out of control. His hand seized hers and her grip matched his. He let go and began to caress her arm up to her shoulder, bare and warm and strong.

"Do you want me to come to you?" he whispered.

"Do you want to come?"

"God, yes!"

She seized his hand and drew him. "Then come, please come!"

Stone managed to disengage his hand and stroked Sheltie, then choked, "My God, I can't. You know I can't. Nor can you. You know we can't."

Time stopped as they fell silent, abruptly withdrawn and disconnected. When he heard her crying, his hand found hers, now tenderly, and they lay slackly joined while the rain drummed insistently and the wind in the pines swelled like organ music.

Then he heard her whisper, "You have never felt my hair." In the darkness, she took his hand. "It's thick," she murmured. "You'll have to find your way down to the roots."

His fingers found her warm scalp and there moved secretly about. His body was now throbbing.

"Oh but that's lovely!" She whispered.

As he continued his massage, he heard her breath quicken with the rhythm of his rubbing.

"Harder," she urged, "you can't hurt me."

He bore down and spread his fingers, summoning his strength to fulfill her need. Sheltie sensed their excitement and began to bark until Stone withdrew his hand and calmed her. Arla was trembling violently.

"Please!" she begged, seizing his hand and pulling it back. "Don't stop now!"

Stone drew on all his strength in a deep rhythmic stroke, knowing that it was all that kept him from stripping her from her cocoon. He felt her body seeking to free itself.

The fire in him was now out of control. His body was about to burst and shatter. He knew his time of glory had come and he no longer cared. As with a scream hers came, so did he let go with a growling thrust that sought to break his bondage.

Their ecstasy endured while his hand stayed buried deep in her hair. Only when her shuddering had subsided and her breathing slowed, did his fingers unclench and withdraw, then tenderly trace the contours of her burning face. Their hands met again in Sheltie's fur as she licked them gratefully with her rough tongue. Slowly their sweetness ebbed and they slept.

Arla awoke later and listened. "Are you all right?" she called. When there was no answer, she spoke his name. He heard her voice from far away and tried to answer, and could not.

350

She persisted. "Do you hear me? You must hear me. If I come back . . . when I come back . . . will you be here?"

With a last agonizing effort, he managed to press her hand. She lay back content and slept.

Later when she awoke, the rain had stopped, and the wind had died. The pines were dripping on the roof. She felt cold air on her face, turned and saw his arm still out of his bag. She freed her arm, reached across Sheltie and managed to put his arm back in and close the bag. Sheltie licked her hand and whined. Arla petted her, closed herself in and slept again.

She was awakened by whimpering. Daylight had come. She turned her head and saw Sheltie licking Stone's face.

Arla freed her arm and touched his face. *What she felt and saw turned her to ice.*

She lay rigid, afraid to breathe. After what seemed forever, she freed herself and without looking again, she donned coat and slippers. "Come," she called to Sheltie, "we must go out."

The dog would not leave although she did not growl when Arla petted and coaxed her. "You must come with me," she cried. "No? Then I'll go and come back for you." Sheltie raised her head and licked Arla's hand and face.

She opened the door and stepped down into the cold wet grayness. A light shone in the headquarters building. She started toward it, then turned back and opened the glove compartment and felt until her fingers found what she sought. She put it in her coat pocket and stepped down again.

From out of the ground mist El Morro soared above her, golden against the morning sky. A crow flew cawing from the tall pine that grew by the *tinaja*.

The window was a lighthouse toward which Arla ran through the wet grass.

PORTRAIT OF MY FATHER

PORTRAIT OF MY FATHER

Many call it the city of light—*la ville de la lumière*. To me it is the river city. Water gives soul to a city—ocean, bay, lake or river water. From Sydney to San Francisco, Seattle and New York, Lisbon and Paris, moving water provides extra being to a city. Without endless laving, stagnation and corruption set in and death replaces life.

Born on the Potomac, raised on Pacific shores and schooled on the banks of the Seine, and employed in the river and sea ports of Europe, my health and long life came from nearness to living water. And so when faced with the task of completing the biography of my father whose final form had eluded me for nearly half a century, I came back to the city of my youth and there took a room in an old hotel overlooking the river, determined to bring the elements together in what might prove to be the last thing I wrote.

Only recently a long hidden cache of material appeared which altered the work's content and form. For the first time I discovered that it was in Paris in October 1908 that a meeting occurred between my father and a woman which profoundly affected his being and the rest of his life. In seeing him newly, I realized that what I was writing had to be thought anew. Suddenly I had a different man to write about. And so I returned to the river city to seek vestiges of the ambiance he had once savored years before. Before me was a month of freedom from all other demands.

Each morning after early breakfast in my room of café au lait, brioches, jam and butter, I walked along the quay to the Pont des Arts, thence across the river and back over the Pont du Carrousel, pausing in the middle of each bridge to watch the Seine go by on its way to the sea. River traffic was light that early—a house barge, a tug with a string of barges in tow making its labored way up river from

355

Rouen or Le Havre, a launch, canoe or kayak. Auto traffic along the quays was not yet aroused.

As well as quickening my blood, the walk enabled me to ponder the work ahead, while with me always was the beneficent presence of the city's great river poet and lines of his masterpiece *Le Pont Mirabeau*.

> *Sous le pont Mirabeau*
> *Coule la Seine et nos amours*
> *Faut-il qu'il m'en souvienne*
> *La joie venait toujours après la peine*

By the time I reached the corner café-restaurant where I was wont to work, I had thought out what came next, and the morning passed swiftly. I favored the leather banquette in a back corner beneath great wall mirrors. Generous tipping to *patron* and *garçon* made me especially welcome although I drank only café noir until before lunch. It was the perfect regimen for my nature and need, long conditioned to regular hours and steady work.

On this Sunday morning as I reached the middle of the Pont des Arts, I saw a woman there ahead of me, gazing down at the river. My first feeling was of annoyance. I wanted to be alone. When she looked up, I recognized her as a new guest at the hotel whom I had heard speaking English to another guest.

From instinct I said "Good morning. Aren't we both staying at the Voltaire?"

"I recognized you," she smiled. "I even know your name."

"You are ahead of me," I conceded. "Who told you it?"

"Monsieur Le Concièrge," she said sweetly.

"You must be a news correspondent," I said crossly. "I'm not giving any interviews."

"My goodness!" she exclaimed. "I didn't realize you are famous."

"I'm not."

"He warned me how fiercely you guard your privacy."

"I have only a month to get something done. I always walk alone."

"So do I," she countered, still sweetly. "It was you not I who spoke first."

"Touché," I conceded. "I hear from your speech that you are British and my ear also tells me from the North."

356

"Beyond the Tyne and the Tweed."

"Of course—with the richest speech of all who claim English as our mother tongue."

"Thank you, sir. So vast and various is your country that I have no clue to your native region."

"How could you when I'm a typical cross-breed American, born in the District of Columbia—Washington, that is—then raised in the Far West, schooled here in France and employed round about western Europe. I sometimes wonder who I am and how I sound. *Citoyen du monde*, you could call me, in the words of the man who built our hotel."

She laughed.

Without my knowing it, my intention to remain aloof had vanished as I heard myself asking, "What is your name?"

"Graeme—G-r-a-e-m-e. Margaret Cameron Graeme, called Meg. And you?"

"Family and friends call me Laurie."

"That's a proper Scottish name."

"It derives from the Norman French Laurent."

"I doubt there's a pure-bred Scot in Scotland. I haven't known many Americans, but those I have, have all been nice, more so than the English. Imagine an Englishman carrying on like this with a lone Scottish woman!"

"They *are* standoffish."

"Especially when they're trying not to be."

We continued to lean on the railing, watching the traffic passing beneath. A tug appeared with a grunt on its airhorn.

"That was for you," I said.

She laughed. "Are you here for a stay?"

"Until I get my work in hand."

"Our concièrge also told me you are a writer."

"Sees all, knows all, and apparently tells all. I'll have to speak to him."

"Too late!"

"Are you on holiday?"

"I'm in school every day."

"Language? You already speak good French."

"No, Art. I'm at the Beaux-Arts for life drawing."

"You are an artist?"

357

"Strictly amateur. I seek what's not found in Edinburgh and London."

"I too came for what's only here."

"What is it?"

"Freedom, acceptance, tolerance, Beauty and grace, good food and drink. And above all what you see there below us. *Sous ce pont coule la Seine.* I misquoted Apollinaire."

"Are you a poet?"

"Not guilty. That's a modern French poet whose work I love."

"I'm mostly ignorant of poetry, except the classics of Corneille, Racine and Ronsard. And of course our Bobbie and RLS."

"You've been here before?"

"It's my first time ever."

"Where did you learn French?"

"In convent school. My teacher was a French Sister. She was the most important person in all my life." She held out her hand. "I'll be getting along on my walk and let you get to work."

I thought of telling her that I never worked on Sunday, but instead we shook hands in the European manner and parted.

Such was our first meeting. I found it disturbing yet natural.

During the ensuing week we spoke only in passing at the hotel. Neither made any effort to continue our conversation on the bridge. From where I was working each morning at the café, I saw her coming to and from class in the Rue Jacob around the corner from the Ecole des Beaux Arts. I found myself watching for her, admiring her strong and graceful walk, her quietly elegant clothes and an obvious certainty about what she was doing. Each of us was absorbed in these daily routines, and yet I wondered what had brought her alone to Paris at an age neither young nor old. Her self sufficiency attracted me in spite of my resolve to avoid personal contacts.

Then on the following Sunday morning we met again at the same place and time. Was it an unconscious desire on my part to find out who she was? I felt glad when I saw her there ahead of me. Again she was dressed warmly in red and brown woolens, her black hair gathered under a red tam.

"Creatures of habit, aren't we," I remarked as I took her extended hand.

"There's no lack of bridges," she said. "Each could have his own."

"I prefer this one."

"So do I."

We were silent as tug appeared beneath us, laboring up stream with a string of laden coal barges. Then she said softly, still looking down at the water, "I came here to work and you seem to have the same purpose, although I don't see how you can get anything done in that noisy little café."

"In France," I replied, "a writer is always accorded his privacy, even in a café. In fact any kind of artist is shown respect. That is the difference between France and the rest of the world, and is why Paris has always been the creative capital of the world."

"The concièrge admires you. He calls you Monsieur L'Ecrivain. Are you really a writer or just passing the time?"

"Yes, I'm a real writer," I laughed. "Of sorts."

"Do you write books?"

"Yes, I write books—of sorts."

"What kind of books?"

"Books for students, for young readers—actually a whole series of them."

"They must be quite successful if you've written that many. What are they about?"

"The geography of various countries, mostly here in western Europe. Their success made it possible for me to retire before I was required to."

She frowned. "You make me ask all the questions. Retire from what?"

"Our Consular service. I have been a commercial attaché throughout Europe. My knowing maritime law meant that most of my posts were in river- and sea-ports—Lyon, Marseilles, Genoa, Barcelona, Lisbon. There were also long tours in Rouen and Le Havre. That's when I fell in love with the lower Seine. Water has always drawn me. I went to sea when still in my teens. Took a year out of school to work as a ship's musician."

"How romantic!"

"Everything's romantic when young. Now it's the river that made certain my coming back to Paris."

"To continue your series?"

"To write something entirely different and more difficult—something that's troubled me for years."

I was glad that she did not press me for more answers.

She hesitated, then ventured, "I'm honored to know a real writer."

"Have you never known one?"

"None that worked as hard as you do."

Again she fell silent as we continued to watch the river traffic. Then she spoke again. "When my husband was alive we moved in a restricted circle where any kind of writer was uncommon."

"Have you been widowed long?" I asked politely.

"For a year now." She paused. "A year that might have gone on forever if I hadn't come here."

"What did your husband do?"

"He was the professor of Canon Law in the university."

"Did you have children?"

"Two sons, grown now and far away. I'm very much alone. I go to bed early and sleep soundly. My coming here was a gamble for either a new life or no life." She frowned. "Do I sound desperate? I'm not, although sometimes I'm not sure *what* I am. Walking helps, that and drawing."

"Would you like to join me this morning?"

"Don't you prefer to walk alone?"

"You mean you do?"

She blushed for the first time. "I don't wish to intrude on your privacy. You keep very much to yourself, and I know you spend your mornings writing." She smiled. "He told me where you work."

I laughed. "I wondered how you knew I worked at the café. Well, he *is* paid to see and know all—and apparently tell all when asked."

She was indignant. "I did *not* ask him! And that's all that he told me."

I smiled. "I don't work on Sunday."

"Nor do I," she laughed.

"So let's walk through the Tuileries and back by the courtyard of the Louvre."

In the fall of the year the sycamores along the quay were in thin gold leaf. Throughout the Tuileries Gardens, beds of chrysanthemums were heavy with blooms. Nurses with prams were already on the move. A few old men and women pottered about among the flowers or dozed on the stone benches.

Although I am a strong walker, Meg matched my stride, until at last she said, "Let's rest."

"Too fast?"

"I want to let it soak in. It's glorious. I've seen it all in their paintings."

"You wear sensible shoes."

"I *am* sensible, can't you tell?"

"Some would say your coming alone to Paris was not sensible."

"Please don't be like those some. Back home they thought I was dotty. I *am* a trifle over thirty-five. Isn't that middle age?"

"Are you liking it here?"

"So much freer than anything I've ever known. I can stay only a month."

"Not too lonely?"

"It would be if I were younger and not working." She paused, then said, "You seem to be very much alone. Do you have a family?"

"I have a wife and two grown daughters in the States."

She hesitated before asking, "Were you here in Paris when you were young?"

"At different ages. Paris hasn't changed. The gray rain and then a blue day like this. The river means the most to me. I came back to see if it would sweep away the refuse on my banks."

"Is writing school books so difficult?"

"That's not what I'm writing." I did not explain and she did not ask more. We sat watching the scene around us. I stole a look at her profile. Her face was serene, somewhere between pretty and beautiful. I felt content in her company, different from anything I had anticipated. Still I meant to remain aloof until the book was written.

"In spring the hyacinth is my favorite," she said. "Then in autumn the 'mums." She continued almost to herself. "It is comforting that seasons have their own flowers." She crushed a chrysanthemum leaf and held it for me to smell. "Don't you love it, so voluptuous—everything Scots aren't supposed to be."

"Did you come to Paris for a Highland Fling?"

She ignored my bad pun. "I came to learn if I have any real talent—anything more than facility."

361

"How is it going?" I asked gently.

"Our teacher quotes his master. *Il faut toujours travailler*, Rodin said. Work, work, work, nothing but draw, draw, draw. He gives us only basic life drawing—knees, elbows, necks, all the ugly parts that make up a beautiful body. He says at the end he'll tell us if there's any hope." Then with her first show of feeling, "I should hate him, but I know he's right."

"Do you ever draw flowers?"

"I have, of course, but now it's only drawing from models. I wanted to see what I could do with the human form. Something frowned on in Edinburgh."

"Are you willing to submit to the discipline?"

"That's what I came for. Actually, my life has been one of submission." She smiled. "I'm still an apt pupil although beginning to feel a stir."

"What is your goal?"

Her jaw set. "I intend to realize the gift God gave me or die in the attempt." Her tone changed. "Scots are an earnest lot, aren't they."

"Paris will soften you. Shall we walk some more?" And before she could reply, I added, "If you breakfast as early as I do, you'll be hungry. Would you like to go on to the Cité and lunch at the restaurant across from the Palais de Justice? They do eggs to perfection, or do you eat porridge three times a day?"

"I thought I'd miss it. They would deport me if I tried to tell them how to make it."

We traversed the courtyard of the Louvre, past the bronzes of Rodin and Maillol and the Roman arch, then down river along the tree-lined Quai des Orfèvres.

"Look!" she exclaimed, "The leaves are translucent."

"Paris is usually gray in the fall. I work better then, content to remain indoors."

"Edinburgh's weather kills the soul. A day like this I feel reborn."

She changed with each turn of her mind, now open, now hidden, new to me who was not a green youth. I felt my earlier intentions dissolving.

Upon reaching the square of Notre Dame, I suggested we enter the cathedral.

"You are Catholic?"

362

"No, but I never pass without offering a silent prayer. Haven't you been here?"

"I've been nowhere except to school and back. My unBritish ways may lead you to think I'm not what they call *une personnage très sérieuse*."

"What a nice accent!"

"I told you I had a good teacher—one who was born and lived long in France."

"Then you are a Catholic."

"Not really, but that's too long a story."

An organ postlude was being played as we took seats in a pew at the back. The cathedral was peopled with sombrely clad worshippers. The great hall was reverberant with music and pungent with incense.

We stayed on as the congregation flowed up the nave in a black tide. Suddenly I felt a need to speak of what I was working on. The pressure had been building in me if only for a listener. Was that why we had met on the bridge?

"Now that you haven't asked," I began softly, "I'll tell you why I never go by here without entering. Are you starved?

"Not if you aren't. I am a good listener. My husband said that was what I did best. He was always well meaning, although he didn't encourage me seriously to draw and paint. My having come alone to Paris would shock him."

After a long silence while the organ died away, I began, "It was here that I last saw my mother. That was twenty years ago. I was then our commercial attaché in Le Havre and in Rouen, the latter also a busy port, up river from Le Havre. I'd take bicycle rides along the banks to Paris and down to Le Havre. Then my mother wrote me that she had terminal cancer and wanted us to say goodbye in Paris. Handsome royalties enabled me to bring her over on the *Queen Mary*. I took two weeks' leave. She loved the galleries, shops, parks, and the music. It was her only trip abroad. See Paris and die! she joked."

"On the day before she was to return home," I continued, "we came here on a Sunday morning; and after the mass and music, she began to talk to me as never before. My father had died when I was a boy of fifteen. As the youngest of three sons—my brothers died in middle age—I remained dear to her although we lived far apart.

363

In the beginning I had intended to enter foreign trade because of a gift for languages. The Depression diverted me into government service."

I paused. "Shall I go on?"

"Please do," she murmured.

"You could call us strangers, and yet . . . Can you understand my need?"

"I know the need. It's often easier to talk to a stranger." She quickly added. "I don't mean that. I saw you from the first as a kind person."

"Thank you," I said. "My mother and I were close in an impersonal way. Neither went below the surface. She had rarely spoken of my father since his death, and I was too busy with my own life ever to wonder about theirs. They seemed happy. There were no disagreements or quarrels, at least not vocal. I've since learned that silence is one of the most deadly ways of quarreling."

"How true," Meg said. "What did your father do?"

"He was a scientist, a horticulturist with the U.S. Department of Agriculture—actually a pomologist specializing in fruits—with everything concerning their growth, picking, packing, storing, shipping, and marketing. His name was G. for George Harold Powell. At first his work was in the peaches and plums of Georgia. That led him to wider field research that deeply influenced the California citrus industry. Millions of dollars were being lost from the decay of oranges and lemons in transit to the eastern markets. Although the railroad cars were refrigerated, a mold developed that meant the loss of part of every shipment representing millions of dollars. The growers and shippers had formed a big cooperative known as Sunkist—"

"Oh I know that. Today in Scotland the choicest oranges bear their stamp."

"When they asked the government for help, a team led by my father was sent in response. During several winters they conducted field and laboratory research. Cooperation of the growers was essential. Here my father demonstrated a natural gift for human relations. It was not easy for them to change their methods. He proved that careless picking and handling of the fruit resulted in skin punctures and bruises which led to the decay from the blue mold—*penicillium glaucum*. The results were published in 1908 in a seventy-nine page government bulletin that led to my father's being named the general manager of Sunkist. His salary straightway tripled—a blessing for his growing family's needs."

"I know very well what more money can do!" Meg observed.

"And so we moved to Southern California in 1911 and there I grew up in a free-ranging orange grove boyhood. After his sudden death at fifty we moved to San Francisco to be near my mother's brother and sister. She hoped that one of us boys would someday write the biography of my father's career as a scientist and administrator. My two older brothers seemed better qualified, but they died before doing it, and so I was her last hope. I promised her to do it." I stopped. "I didn't mean for this to turn into a lecture, and yet I wanted you to know the background and problems of writing his biography so many years after his death, for that's what I'm writing now—long after his death!"

"Why have you waited so long?" Meg asked.

"For many reasons, mostly selfish, and yet whenever I would gear up to do it—and I made several false starts, years apart, something kept me from pressing on. As it turned out, it proved better to have waited, as I'll explain. I no longer have the guilty feeling that hung over me for years."

"I'm not sure that I understand," Meg said.

"Nor am I that I can explain it."

We were silent and then I spoke again. "On that last Sunday morning after the cathedral had grown quiet, my mother asked, 'When are you going to write about your father?' "

"I've had to put it on the back burner. So many other things seemed more pressing. I'll get to it eventually, I promise you. My mother smiled wanly, 'I hoped you would do it while I . . . ' I'm sorry, I said, there's been so little time after my job and my writing. God knows I should have done it," I said to Meg, "but with what I know now, I am glad I waited. Now I can do justice to the whole man, not just to the public figure he came to be."

" 'We've never talked about your father,' my mother said, 'other than his public life.' "

"That's all I intend to write about, I told her—all that I have material for. I have everything in hand when I come to write it. You must have been proud of his accomplishments."

" 'I was,' my mother said quietly, 'and I know you will make a

365

fine book of it.' She hesitated. 'Now that I'm near the end and in this confessional place, I want to tell you, I must tell you something about his life that was not public.' And then sadly, 'About a part of his life in which I played no part, or if I did, not a helpful one.' "

I paused. "I had no idea what she was leading up to. 'You should know the complex man he was.' she continued. 'I admired him for what he did for the world. His other part I might have admired if I had understood it. We were too different for that to be, too alien— outwardly happy, inwardly strangers. He needed and appreciated the home I made for him. He loved you boys, especially you. You were his favorite. He would have been so proud of you. I don't say we were unhappy. We never had words between us. Perhaps we should have. Perhaps my very passivity left him unsatisfied. I suppose I was never deeply aroused by him—or by anything. Well, whatever, we just weren't for each other on any plane other than the domestic.'

"Again my mother fell silent, then continued softly. 'He was too much for me. Sexually, I mean. After we had you boys, I could never satisfy him. Even before, as he grew more physically demanding, I grew more spiritual.' She smiled wanly. 'Old story, isn't it! And when he found someone who *could* satisfy him on every level, he asked for his freedom. I realized later I should have granted the divorce, but alas I didn't. It seemed wrong. There were you boys. You were only five then. And his new career. We needed his salary for you boys' schooling. I was never an earner. And so I refused. His affair–if I may call it that, but I realize now it was far more—continued nearly to his death.' "

"Who was the other woman?" I asked after I managed to conceal my astonishment.

" 'She was a fellow government scientist, even more distinguished than your father. She was a chemist. The first woman Ph.D. from the University of Pennsylvania. He had only a Master of Science degree from Cornell. I think he was flattered by her in some ways superior intelligence.'

" 'Was she too in the Agriculture department?'

" 'In the Bureau of Animal Industry, in charge of its research laboratory dealing with public health, in Philadelphia. He was, as you know, in Plant Industry in Washington. Both were specialists in refrigeration, she in meats and poultry, he in fruits and vegetables!'

" 'Unlikely areas for romance.' I said to my mother."

" 'Again she smiled feebly. 'At first I thought it was only an infatuation that would burn out. That was part of my refusal to divorce him. It didn't. It began in 1908 and lasted over ten years.'

" 'Where did they first meet?' I asked my mother.

" 'In Paris. Strange isn't it that it's here I should be telling you of it. They were delegates to the First International Refrigeration Congress, sponsored by the French government. They had never met before even though in the same department. Their bureaux were separate. She was from an old Philadelphia family. Her name was Mary Engle Pennington—Dr. Pennington, if you please. At least he chose someone of good background. Do you want to hear the rest?'

" 'Yes,' I said, 'although I don't see how I can use it in what I plan to write.'

" 'Perhaps not,' my mother said, 'But I still want you to know.' "

I stopped then and said to Meg Graeme, "You must be starved."

"I recall your saying something about eggs?" she smiled. "I understand why being here led your mother to unburden," Meg said softly. "In that setting she must have felt very close to what awaited her. Certainly I do, yet I hope my end is not as near as hers was."

"For the remaining hours of her stay her spirit was almost gay." I continued, "It was a long needed unburdening, such as I now am feeling. We parted without tears. My only regret is that I didn't do it before she died. And yet it proved best that I waited until the whole story was clear—at least as clear as it will ever be."

"Was there more that she didn't tell you?"

"There was indeed, but for now let's see if those eggs are as good as I said they are."

"It can wait if there's more you want me to hear."

"Perhaps later."

We made our way across the square to the café-restaurant where we settled on the privet-hedged terrace for omelette aux champignons, cheese cake and coffee. We ate with silent relish. The scene enthralled Meg. The crowds were carefree, gay and yet sedate—Parisians of all ages on promenade in their Sunday finery. Inside the café older men and women ate, drank and talked, silently played chess or read the journals. Around us on the terrace were young families with small children.

"What sweet children," Meg said. "Well behaved and yet not beaten down."

"What you're seeing is the middle class, *la moyenne bourgeoisie*, at its best. The weekday scene here is different. Then the courts and government officers predominate, plus the cathedral crowd from 'round the world. Notre Dame may not be the most beautiful cathedral but it is the greatest in the public's heart."

With my having spoken freely of what I was writing, plus the food and coffee and Meg Graeme's sympathetic presence, I felt expansively well, with a renewed confidence in what I was doing to keep my promise of twenty years ago.

After we had finished, Meg asked, "I have been wondering why your mother waited so long to tell you."

"Perhaps she felt a need as her life ended to justify her refusing to free him."

"What did you think then? What do you think now? Was it the right thing?"

"My first thought was of pride in my father's manhood. I inherited his drive, his energy. I would have gone higher in State if I had not chosen to pursue my own writing with its lucrative rewards. Nor did I like the social demands of career advancement. I am more introverted than he was. That came from my mother, her love of poetry and music."

"What led you to become a writer?"

I laughed. "It was a publisher's advertisement in the overseas *New York Times*. They wanted someone with European experience and contacts to write a series of geographies for schools. I'd always had a passion for geography and had written many reports and briefs in the course of my work, *et voilà!* I have never understood the success of the series. It's earned so much money that I had to create an education trust to keep the government from taking it all in taxes." Again I laughed. "I suppose I'll be remembered for those books, not for myself."

"Why be remembered?" Meg asked. "Isn't that vanity?"

I shook my head and continued. "As it turned out, we boys never saw very much of our father, so wrapped up was he in his career in California which took him repeatedly to the Middle West and Eastern markets and to Washington where he lobbied Congress for higher tariffs on Italian lemons. He was an ideal lobbyist, magnetic

and persuasive. I have a tribute written after his death by a California lemon grower who remembered his kindness and wit and
leadership. In 1911 he made a second trip to Europe, again to the
lemon groves of Sicily where he had gone in 1908 before the opening of the Congress. During the war he served in Washington as
Hoover's right hand man in the Food Administration."

"How strange that he met the woman here in Paris! When did
he die? 1922? Goodness! That's when I was born!"

"Their having met here was another reason for my coming back.
The hotel where the American delegates stayed is still here. The
Chatham. The ambiance of Paris hasn't changed. Let's hope it never
does. I want it to permeate the book."

"But you told your mother you wouldn't be able to use what she
told you of his personal life."

"That's what I thought then. I didn't see how I could include
what there was only her word for. There was no other evidence.
Most of his contemporaries were dead. Then, only recently, letters
from him to my mother and a diary he kept in Europe in 1908, came
into my possession. When my mother died, I was out of the country. She wanted no service, only to be cremated and her ashes given
to the ocean. Her brother took care of that. He also settled her estate. It was willed to him and me—what the Depression had left of
it. My brothers had died. Her personal things, letters and other
effects, were left to me. I never had them forwarded, probably because I had no permanent base. Also I assumed she had told me all
there was to know about the woman and my father. I never
redeemed them from storage until I went to San Francisco earlier
this year to settle my uncle's estate. Among her things for me in
storage all those years was a packet of my father's letters written to
her from Italy, France, and Great Britain in the fall of 1908, telling
the details of his falling in love with Mary Engle Pennington."

"Your mother kept them?" Meg exclaimed. "Why didn't she give
them to you when she told you of Dr. Pennington?"

"Probably because I said then that I wouldn't use personal material in the career biography I planned to write. His pocket diary of
1908 held even more revealing details."

"She kept that too? They must have hurt terribly."

"I like to think she had finally come to recognize the whole man

369

he was, and was telling me to write what was, not what appeared to be."

"Your mother must have been a remarkable woman," Meg said.

"I see her in a new light," I admitted. "She was more than a betrayed wife. She too was a Cornell graduate, a member of Phi Beta Kappa, the top honor society. After their graduation in the class of 1895, he stayed on another year for the Master of Science degree, while she taught high school—Mathematics and Greek. I learned later from my Aunt Mabel, my father's only sister who survived him many years and who lived part of each year in Florence, that my mother had a nervous breakdown that year and had to leave school and come to live with her fiancé's parents. My aunt was then a schoolgirl and remembered her future sister-in-law as always being in tears. She told me she wished her favorite brother would not marry such a crybaby. My mother was apparently depressed from the death of her mother who died of t.b. during my mother's senior year at Cornell. She had been urgently called home and was at her mother's bedside when she died. She never forgot her mother's last words. As an orthodox Quaker, she said fiercely to her daughter, 'Gertie, don't let them make a Hicksite of thee,' and then in a failing whisper, 'Gertie, thee must learn patience.' "

"Was your mother impatient?" Meg asked.

"Always, although I must say she tried hard to heed her mother's charge. She did remain orthodox and died in her sleep, her brother told me, after she had gone a last time to Meeting."

I ordered more coffee for us both and continued, "They were married a year later and my mother settled down. It was a Quaker wedding where those present signed the wedding certificate—a parchment scroll in her father's hand. In most ways she made him a good wife, faithful, passive and never competitive, and a gracious hostess. Although she read Homer for pleasure, she never flaunted her learning, which was broader than his. She was able to relate to his friends and colleagues from Herbert Hoover on down."

"What was wrong between them?" Meg asked.

"His physical appetite which she could never satisfy, nor accomodate his drive for achievement and recognition. All of those were met by Mary Pennington."

"Does a man need two wives?"

"Some do."

"Did you?" Meg persisted, and quickly added, "Indiscreet, aren't I!"

I smiled. "Whose book is this, his or mine?"

"Why not both? Your mother's too. You seem cunningly joined, all three of you."

When I did not answer, Meg asked, "Did your father leave other evidence of his love for Mary Pennington?"

"Apparently not."

"Did she leave any?"

"All I found were her professional papers in the government archives—useless for my purpose. Theirs was a discreet affair. At that time it had to be."

"Did you ever meet her?" Meg asked.

"Only once." I stopped. "I'm afraid I'm swamping you. If you can stand it, I'll tell you more in due time." I smiled. "That means more Sunday walks."

"What you tell me is fascinating. Have you decided on what kind of book it will be?"

"It still troubles me how to deal with what I know of his private life; and yet what I do know of his public life is not enough. How did he remain integrated? How did he manage to function when pulled by conflicting desires? They were what helped cause his early death. There is also another matter to resolve, one so deeply hidden as perhaps never to emerge. That's why I have been seeking help from the fluvial sibyll."

She smiled. "Are you serious?"

"Rivers have their gods—and goddesses."

"So that's why you stop on the bridge each morning. Have you had an answer?"

"Not yet. All I hear are echoing lines of Apollinaire:

> *Sous le Pont Mirabeau*
> *Coule la Siene*
> *Et nos amours.*

Do you know his poetry?"

"I'm afraid not. My teachers were very conservative."

"Apollinaire is not radical. No Frenchman is ever truly radical, regardless of his rhetoric. I'm beset by doubts that I should tell all

371

in the book. Will I be condemned for revealing him, my own father, as having feet of clay?"

"Your dilemma is moral rather than technical. Those are always the hardest to resolve."

"I've talked enough," I said. "Once it began to flow, there seemed no stopping it."

Again she smiled. "May we go back through the Louvre? There is an exhibition of Renaissance master drawings our teacher is taking us to see later in the week. I'd like a preview."

"One more coffee and we'll go."

"Those letters must have hurt your mother terribly. I can't imagine a husband writing that way to his wife. Did he mean to hurt her?"

"Perhaps it was an unconscious wish to shock her into freeing him. He came to know that she didn't have what he needed to fulfill himself. That first trip abroad stripped him bare, laid him open to the beauties of France and Italy. He responded so passionately to people, to art and nature. For the first time he saw who he was and what he needed. Meeting that woman in Paris, a woman such as he had never known—one both intellectual and sensual—brought it all together. His letters were written despite what he thought he had always been. He exploded into them."

"How strange! And that she kept them until her death. Did your mother talk about this with you?"

"Not in as many words. I don't think she knew *what* she was telling me. Hers was a need to travel light on the last voyage. So much remains hidden that we never tell even ourselves."

"I'm growing tired of being hidden and silent." Meg declared. "That's why I'm here. I wonder why your mother would have left them to you, if it were not for you to use them."

"My father was primitive in his drives. She came to know too late that she should have married a gentler man."

"Then she would never have borne you! How can I help you other than to listen? My husband wrote two books on church and canon law, and I read proof for him, but not for sense. It was all so terribly dry. Tell me, would you like to go to the Louvre? You haven't said."

I rose. "On one condition, that I show *you* a painting there that puzzles me."

Around the corner from the café we came on the weekly Bird Market—a colorful swarm of sellers and buyers amidst cages and perches of birds of all feathers, hues, songs, and cries: larks and linnets, long-tailed, high crested tropicals with brilliant plumage and downcast raptors, their sky fallen. Meg was enthralled as we worked our way through the good-natured crowd, then gasped, "I'm glad I escaped my cage."

"Is that what your life has been?"

"Scots are restricted by everything including themselves—there on their rocky end of the island, fit only for men and sheep. From here it's hard to imagine the meagerness of it all. And to make it worse, an inhibiting religion. My escape to this freedom and abundance, this light and color—you can't imagine what it's like for me!"

"That's exactly what my father felt on coming to Paris—he who had been a Quaker farmboy. Not a poor boy, mind you—his father was a prosperous Hudson River Valley apple grower whose prize crop of Cox's Orange Pippins was shipped in sawdust-packed barrels via Covent Garden to London's best tables."

Meg laughed. "Alongside the Scotch Presbyterian, your Quaker is a libertine! Are you a Quaker?"

"Birthright if not practicing, although my wants are simple and few. I grew up with my grandmother's sampler on the wall:

> Old wood to burn
> Old wine to drink
> Old books to read
> Old friends to trust.

"And I remember them singing the Old Shaker spiritual 'Tis the gift to be simple, the gift to be free, 'tis the gift to come down where we ought to be.' "

"Scotland has always driven out its creative sons," Meg said sadly. "A tree needs dirt not rock for growth. I had to find dirt for my roots." She paused in our walk and added, "Today is the deepest down they have reached." She took my hand. "I'm grateful for this companionship." I pressed her hand silently.

As we continued along the Quai des Orfèvres, Meg asked, "Did the goldsmiths settle here because of the trees?"

"River and trees were here before men—and will be here after."

The Louvre held a sluggish Sunday throng through which we

made our way toward the Raphael drawings, then couldn't get close enough to view them. The crowd was more pushy and less good-natured than the one at the Bird Market.

"It will be better on Tuesday," Meg said, "By then the tide will have ebbed."

"It's the tourists that make the trouble. The Salle Delacroix won't be crowded."

"Is he a favorite of yours?"

"Only one picture," I said.

"Now you're puzzling me!"

The Delacroix room was pulsing and glowing with the life and color of his men, women and wild animals. I led her to a painting that hung in a corner—his self-portrait in a green jacket, painted in the prime of middle age, passionately rendered in every detail of hair, face, and cloth.

Meg looked hard, then said, "You'll have to tell me what I'm *not* seeing."

We crossed the hall to a bench from where we could see the portrait through gaps between viewers.

"I was on my way back to Washington for re-posting," I began. "I had met a French woman in the Dordogne. She returned to Paris. I wanted to see her before I left. She had warned me that it wouldn't be the same. I didn't believe her, that the passionate woman I had known in the country was now a discreet urban matron. She gave me a rendezvous here in the Louvre in this very gallery. Delacroix was her favorite. She led me to this self portrait. I too stared at it and was puzzled. What did she mean for me to see? After my unknowing look, she seized my arm and said fiercely, 'Be like him, dost hear, be like him!' That was all she said. We parted in the courtyard. We never met again.

We went back for another look at the portrait. "What *did* she mean?" I asked Meg.

"Perhaps for you to be strong and honest and also a bit wild. Isn't that what he saw when he looked in the mirror?"

"It's true," I admitted, "I'd been full of self-pity and disappointment at not finding the woman I had known. Was it her way of chiding me? I learned from his journal that he never stopped painting. He loved nature and women and music—and painting above all. That self portrait was left to his servant, Jenny Le Guillou. She be-

374

queathed it to the Louvre. There's his portrait of her, old and beautiful. 'Be like him?' How can we be other than we are?"

Meg took my hand. "You've given me too much for one day."

We walked back across the Pont des Arts and before returning to the hotel, I showed her the secluded Place Furstenburg where Delacroix had his studio, now a museum.

"Another day," she protested when I suggested we enter. "I can't absorb any more."

"You must see the square at night when these old-fashioned illuminators are lit."

"I've not wanted to go out alone at night," she demurred.

"It's safe enough in this quarter," I assured her.

"It's not the night. It's the being alone." She hesitated. "I want to hear more about your book."

"I'm finishing his formative years—his parents, his apple orchard origins—so unlike my orange grove boyhood—a hundred miles up the Hudson River from New York. His father founded the state agricultural extension service in New York state. His mother too did social work in the reform of the state's prisons. Both were zealous Quaker educators and reformers. My grandfather's sister, my great-aunt Elizabeth—the family called her Aunt Lizzie—was a noted Abolitionist, joined with Garrison and Emerson and her brother Aaron in the work to free the slaves. She became a beloved educator at Swarthmore, the Quaker college." I paused for breath. "Then came my father's five years at Cornell, studying under Liberty Hyde Bailey, the greatest horticulturist of his time, one who had a profound influence on my father. Bailey lived to nearly a hundred, twice as long as my father. I hate to think of his dying at only fifty."

We had reached the hotel. "Do you really want to hear more?"

"Indeed I do." She smiled and added. "In due course."

"I didn't mean to swamp you. I didn't realize I was so pent up. Someone must have sent you. I have more to do until I reach 1908. Then how deal with what detonated him? Does it make him greater or lesser to reveal the whole man? Until now the world has no idea of who he truly was."

"I told you I can only listen," Meg said. She smiled. "Yet given the chance I might just have something to say."

"Is it what my mother intended?" I continued, ignoring her gentle reproof. "I wish I could talk to her now. When I could, I didn't know what I learned only after her death. Why *didn't* she give me those letters and that diary when she first talked to me? Can you stand another torrent?"

I paused when I saw how tired Meg was, "Next Sunday?"

She smiled and we parted, no longer the strangers who had set out that morning on a Sunday walk.

By midweek I needed a break. I had brought photographed items to annotate, and was weary of the labor. I knew that I wanted to see Meg Graeme again if only as a listener. My mind kept turning the material over and over, seeking the form to give it.

On Thursday morning I encountered her in the lift. "There's a recital tonight in Salle Gaveau—violin-piano sonatas played by a Russian woman and her French accompanist. Would you like to go if I can get tickets? It's at five o'clock. We could dine afterward."

"I'm as ignorant of music as of poetry," she said frankly.

"But you like to hear it?"

"Of course I do. I'd like to go. We play more than bagpipes, you know." She smiled. "I once played with the university orchestra. It was in Haydn's Military symphony."

"What did you play?"

"The triangle," she replied.

We laughed.

When we set out on foot for the recital, we wore coats and stout shoes as rain was expected by evening. We took the wide gravelled path paralleling the Champs Elysées, walking briskly as the dead leaves swirled and crackled underfoot.

Halfway to the Arc de Triomphe, I suggested coffee at a pavilion café in a bosque of bare trees. When Meg removed her coat, I admired her suit of black and green wool.

"The Graeme tartan," she explained, "That was my father's Cameron I was wearing when we met that morning on the bridge. More red in it." She laughed. "The Graemes are a more subdued clan. That's what marriage did to me. Still I've a wide streak of Cameron left—and something more too." She looked at me earnestly, even pleadingly. "You've never asked about me—who I am. Your book must be terribly interesting—to you."

I laughed. "Poor girl, I'll give you three minutes."

Her eyes flared. "Don't try to intimidate me, sir. I'll tell you

376

whether you want to know or not: I'm only half Scot. The other quarter has the same scarlet thread as the Camerons, even redder, I'll have you know."

"I'm listening," I said placatingly, with no idea of what was coming from this woman seen for the first time.

"My mother was Italian," she began softly. "While on holiday when quite young, my father suffered an accident in Florence. He met my mother in hospital where she was volunteering as a nurse's aid. She was from an old Florentine family—the Alinaris. It was a mutual attraction like the one you have told me about. He brought her home—carried her off apparently—and they were married and I was born—too soon, I was told. Only a year after receiving his diploma in surgery, he and my mother were killed in a road accident at Thurso, a village in the very north of Scotland. I was too little ever to know them. Both families had disapproved of the marriage. Neither had any use for the child—for me. I was conceived out of holy wedlock—a love child if you will—and hence damned. They also blamed my mother for having lured their son to his death. She realized she had to get away to keep from being smothered. They were on their way to the Shetlands on holiday."

"Did they finally accept you?"

"Never. Malcolm, bless him, would not accept an invitation that did not include me."

"I'm glad to know the Scots aren't all bad."

"With more food and less religion," Meg said scornfully, "they might have become human. I blame the English. They stripped us bare, then drained the rest of their Empire, and now they are dying of anemia."

"I take it you don't care for them."

"Is there a word between dislike and hate? Yet it began with the Romans—my people. They built that wall to keep out the Scots and the Picts. So I guess we're all to blame for history, including our own."

I saw that she was crying softly. I took her hand and asked gently, "What became of you?"

"I was raised by the Sisters in convent. My father had taken my mother's faith, and so the church was really the last resort for me. There I had a good education, and miraculously an understanding of my native desire to draw and paint. One of the Sisters, bless her

377

memory, sensed my need. It was through the church that I met Malcolm, although he was not a Catholic. He was twenty years older than I and already the authority on his subject." Meg paused. "I must confess that I never truly loved him. He was a way of leaving what would have become a stifling environment. Was that wrong?"

"Who are we to judge? What of your sons?"

"Nature took its course. Malcolm really asked no more of me than that. I think I was a good wife and mother. Now they are grown and far away, one in New Zealand, the other in British Columbia. I told you Scots have to leave in order to prosper in body and soul."

"Your mother's people did not want to raise you?"

"They had disowned her when she eloped with my father. They were said to have been a proud fierce lot. I've never been to Italy. Perhaps Paris will be a stepping stone."

"Do you speak Italian?"

"Less well than French. I learned both in convent."

"You've done a good job of concealing all this from me."

Her laugh was wry. "I had to seize an opening."

"Sorry! Now I know where your black eyes and hair and white skin come from. I'm not flattering you when I say that the women of Florence—young and old—are the most beautiful in Europe."

"I have pictures of my mother. She was indeed beautiful. Were you ever posted to Florence?"

"No, but I went there on holiday when I left the Ecole de Commerce. Florence and Paris were my father's favorite places, after Taormina and Amalfi. He brought my mother lovely presents from Italy in silver and silk. There was a tiny goat—a ram—in solid silver to wear on a chain. Was it to remind her who he really was? To me he brought a silk handkerchief in brown and blue and red, and two little Renaissance pictures of cherubs and angels framed in carved olive wood. I still have them, although the handkerchief is long since gone. I gave it to my first high school sweetheart. I used to write her love letters, composed to the 'Meditation' from *Thais*, played on the family's Victrola." I laughed. "I don't know how they affected her, but I cried."

We had resumed walking while continuing to talk as we made our way through a network of avenues to Salle Gaveau. It was in

378

a neighborhood of large apartment dwellings on a street lined with bare elms. The leaves had drifted everywhere.

The program was a recognition of the Franco-Slavic players — sonatas by Debussy, Franck and Prokoviev. I held Meg's hand and felt her response.

During the interval we remained in our seats and talked.

"Like it?" I asked.

"Can't you tell? I like the audience too, so various they appear to be. Were your parents musical? I'll never know if mine were. I think they must have been, particularly my mother."

"My mother sang. She took the alto solos in choral groups. They sang 'Hiawatha's Wedding Feast.' She regretted not having had voice training. She was too accepting, always left behind as he forged ahead."

"She should have married a man like my Malcolm. Although he never pushed, he was a steady worker."

"Could you have kept up with my father?"

"Now I could!" She laughed. "Earlier? No. I was like your mother. I always put Malcolm and the boys first."

"Women should have their children in old age!"

"Was your father also musical?" Meg asked.

"He liked to dance. He and my mother waltzed together. The family got its first Victrola when we moved to California in 1911. They organized a dancing class. As a little boy my task was to wind it after each record and sharpen the fibre needle. I'd give concerts when they had company. My mother's favorite was Schubert's *Serenade*. My father liked Caruso."

"What did you like?"

"Lively things — The *Hungarian Rhapsodies* and *Carnival of the Animals*. I cried when my mother told me what the *Erl King* song was about. Later I took piano lessons and my middle brother taught me the saxophone and clarinet. I played jazz in high school and college. I was pretty good, they said."

The Russian sonata followed. Its savage rhythms brought the audience, us included, cheering to its feet. Meg's eyes were shining.

"I never saw a Scottish audience react like that," she marvelled as we donned our coats and went outdoors. A light rain was falling.

379

"I remember wanting to, but no one ever did. Malcolm would have been horrified."

"Too wet to walk," I said. "There's the Métro at the corner—the perfect shelter in storm."

"Storm?" Meg laughed. "We'd call it a mist."

"Where we're going is too far to walk."

She followed as I led her through three corresponding stations until at last we emerged in Montmartre at the foot of Sacré Coeur. Above us the great white marble basilica crowned the highest point in Paris.

"Oh!" Meg cried. "You *are* an impresario."

"You've never been here?"

"I told you how unworldy I am. Between convent and canon law my natural impulses were smothered. When Malcolm died and left me well off, my Latin blood began to rise and I determined to learn if I had any real gift for drawing. Friends predicted no good would come from my going off alone to Paris. When I told the sisters who remembered me, they were aghast, all but Sister Ursula." She laughed. "I reassure them with postcards of the churches, although that dearest sister is dead."

"First things first," I said, leading us into a bistro at the foot of the long staircase that ascended the mont. The air was rich with smells of food and tobacco smoke and sounds of contented eaters and talkers. Without word from me the *patronne* set before us a steaming tureen of rabbit stew, thick with carrots, leeks and what not; a basket of bread and a decanter of red wine. She then fastened bibs on us both. We tucked in as she urged us to eat well, and then withdrew to the zinc.

"Her husband is the cook," I explained. "He also raises the rabbits."

"It tastes like chicken."

"Sticks longer to the ribs."

"It's obvious they know you here. She doesn't tie everyone's bib. I heard you tell her your friend is a Scotchwoman."

"Did you hear what she said?"

"Yes, but tell me," she teased.

"*Qu'elle est belle!* she said. True too, although it's taken me a while to perceive it."

"Rain brings out my sparkle—and that last sonata."

380

"Happy?"

"Utterly."

I marvelled at what the walk and the music, the food and wine had done to change the passive even subdued woman Meg Graeme had first appeared to be.

"It was becoming a monologue," I admitted,"until you managed to tell me who you are. May I have the floor again?"

"I yield!"

"I've been simmering," I began, "ever since returning to Paris. Now I'm coming to a boil. It's coming clear what I must do. Will you be my listener a little longer?"

"Only if I may have a turn?"

"Say once a week?"

"If we meet only on Sunday, I'll never have a chance."

"I promise you. Now listen. Here's how I see him. First there's the public man in the crowd's gaze and then the private man known only to the two women. That makes one divided man. The public's man is one whole half, the private half is in two parts, one belonging to his wife, the other to Mistress Mary. You see how subdivided he was?"

"What part did you and your brothers have?"

"Not a large one. We had the most during summers before the war. They were older than I, then they went away to college without my ever having really known them. The oldest was the brightest. By the time he died at thirty-eight, he was internationally known as a horticulturist in the footsteps of his father and grandfather. Now one of his sons is carrying on the scientific tradition as a marine biologist. The other left a son with great talent as a violinist. They make up for my having had only daughters."

"Why were you your father's favorite?"

"I suppose because I was the unexpected who came five and six years after the others. I sense that we would have grown close. There was a strong genetic bond I felt even as a boy. When he returned from trips back East, he always brought me a packet of Peters Milk Chocolate. If he forgot to produce it, I'd remind him."

"That was cheeky," Meg observed.

"I would sit on his lap and strike the match to light his cigar. He was short and stocky, about five foot eight and 180 pounds—you'll have to convert that to stone—and solid, not fat. He gave off warmth like a stove. I couldn't stay on his lap for long. I'd get too hot, jump down and he'd try to grab me. He smelled good in addition to the fine Havanas he smoked. It was the cologne he used after shaving, and the smell of his skin, of the man himself, healthy and radiant. My mother's doctor told me after she died and I asked him what kind of a man he thought my father had been—mind you, he never knew him, only learned of him from my mother. He said, 'Your father was a bull of a man.' Hearing that evoked a memory of his coming from the bath as I was getting up to dress for school. I was waiting my turn in the bathroom; he had gotten out of the tub, naked and dripping, and was reaching for the towel. I handed it to him and before he could wrap himself in it, I saw the thick black hair like fur on his chest and belly, clear down to where his maleness hung low—an extraordinary sight for a boy to see for the first time. I was transfixed, until he laughed and said, 'Get that face washed and those teeth brushed or you'll be late.' I still remember the steamy air and the bittersweet smell of soap and bowel movement. A bull of a man? My God, yes! He was intensely physical, an outdoorsman, a tennis player and fisherman. I chased tennis balls for him when they went out of bounds; and caught softshell sandcrabs for bait and sold them to him for a penny apiece."

"You are fortunate to have such rich memories. I have none of my father or my mother. I can only imagine what they were like. Am I they? Didn't they fashion me from their inmost beings? Sister once assured me I was a blessed love child."

I continued in spite of her felt need also to talk and unburden. "Those summers before he went back to Washington and the work that was to drain his life were idyllic, at least for the boy I was, and I like to think also for my parents and brothers. They took a furnished cottage on the ocean front at Newport or a cabin in the mountains on Big Bear Lake. He would come for weekends and we would fish and swim, and I roamed into the headwaters of the bay where I anchored the rowboat and fished for sharks. He and my oldest brothers preferred surf fishing, standing side by side on the sand, casting and reeling in, silently intent on the catch which would make our evening meal along with salad and corn on the cob and ice cream, while I ran back and forth keeping them in bait."

"Did he pay attention to you?" Meg asked.

382

"He would give me a piggyback into shallow water, then dump me off. That's how he taught me not to fear the water."

"Did they ever punish you?"

"Not really. He never did. Mother would switch my bare legs or tell me to hold out my hand and then try to swat it with a ruler before I could snatch it away. Once when I was learning to drive the family car—it was a big Marmon—he let me back it out of the garage and dust it before he drove in to his office in Los Angeles. One morning as I was running it back and forth, I failed to stop in time. Into the tool bench I crashed. I got up my nerve and went in to the house where my parents were breakfasting—my brothers had gone off to high school—and I said, 'I creased the fenders.' "

" 'You what?' my father demanded."

"I ran into the tool bench and creased the fenders. Actually, I'd bashed them in. My father went out to see. I feared the worst."

"Did he punish you?"

"No, he was very calm. 'I know you didn't mean to,' he said, 'but after this you'd better just back it out and leave the driving to me. I was planning to have it repainted and they'll fix it then.' Was I relieved! After that he saw that I took driving lessons. I had my first license at fourteen. Those were idyllic years before the war came. Southern California was a pastoral land of groves and gardens, with no industry and not much traffic. Now it's all houses and cars and violent people. I never go back. What about Scotland?"

"It's still nice in many ways," Meg said, "if you can make do with little. They live better here in France."

"They know how to live on little. Even the poorest bring an art to living."

I poured more wine, then spoke again. "I want to give him the life he lost before he had fully lived it. Only that bull of a man, naked and dripping, could have achieved what he did as a public man. His virility propelled him too fast and not far enough. And to what? Oblivion. Now only I know what will resurrect him, and yet I have no model."

"Can you distinguish what the two women did for him? Weren't both necessary, though in different ways?"

"There is so little evidence. My mother's journals are maddening in what she didn't say. There is a unique entry that gives insight into the power of his presence. She wasn't alone—the boys, the

383

cook, friends, were there—when she wrote 'Harold is away and the house is so empty.' "

"Did he and Mary Pennington collaborate?"

"In refrigeration matters although there are no joint publications. Later when they had returned in 1908 and he was on a trip to California, he wrote my mother of a bold plan to merge the two bureaux—Plant and Animal—with him as director and Mary as his assistant. It might have won favor with the Secretary of Agriculture, but then California gleamed and he never returned to government service until during the war. What a couple they must have made! I imagine they slipped away during the Congress and had a rabbit stew in this very bistro. No, there was no time for that. He was up every day from six until midnight."

I settled the bill—*la petite note*—then asked Meg, "Can you climb those stairs after that enormous meal?"

"In Edinburgh this would be called a gentle rise!" she scoffed.

The rain had slackened. We toiled up the long flight to the summit and saw below us the glittering city amidst a far plain of smoking chimney pots.

On entering the church a great altar mural of the Christ greeted us with outstretched arms. Again we sat in an empty pew at the rear. The gloomy air was sweet with incense. There was no heat.

After a long silence Meg said, "Tell me about your meeting Mary Pennington."

"I was in New York on a visit to my Aunt Mabel. She'd inherited wealth from her society doctor husband and lived in suburban Riverdale in a spacious home whose lawn ran down to the Hudson. She had become acquainted with Miss Pennington during their work with Quaker Relief, leading to lasting friendship.

" 'Do you know about your father's friend, Dr. Pennington?' she asked me, and when I said that my mother had told me something about her, my aunt asked, 'Would you like to meet her? You're the only one of the boys she doesn't know.'

"And so I lunched with them at the Women's Republican Club. Mary Pennington was then about sixty, austere, mannish, with thin lips and hooded eyes behind steel-rimmed glasses. I looked in vain for the woman my father had wanted to give up everything for. Although my aunt sought to enliven it, the luncheon dragged. There was no communication between Dr. Pennington and me. When I spoke of my fondness for Paris, having just come from that Delacroix rendezvous at the Louvre, she cut me off with 'Paris has become a ghastly place—all noise and filth.' Imagine that from a New Yorker!"

"How extraordinary!" Meg murmured.

"I telephoned my aunt the next day," I continued, "to thank her. She was apologetic. All Dr. Pennington had to say after the lunch, she reported, was *He looks like his mother*. I don't know why she spoke of Paris as she did,' my aunt went on. 'She had always rhapsodized over it. I was sure you two would get on, having so much European background in common. I can't imagine why she took exception to your looking like your mother.' "

"Do you?" Meg asked.

"Yes, but I *am* like my father."

"Didn't your aunt know about her brother's relationship with Mary?"

"I don't think she knew how deep it was. Neither her brother nor her friend had apparently confided in her. I should have sought out Mary and asked her help in the biography I was planning, but at that time I didn't know what I came to know later—the extent of what she had meant to him and what she did for him that my mother was incapable of doing. Still, I don't believe she would have opened up. She had banished it all, years before. What she saw in me was the child she never had, borne by a woman who had denied her fulfillment. I can see now why she hated me."

I paused. "Yet I wish I had tried. She *was* a brilliant woman with an original mind, certainly the most unusual woman he ever met. I have read her obituaries in the professional journals where I also found pictures of her taken in later life. As far back as 1906 her research led to stricter enforcement of the U.S. Pure Food and Drug Act and to cleaning up tainted ice cream that was being sold to children in the Philadelphia black district. In some ways she was his coequal. I can only speculate on what they would have made of marriage. At sixty-five she retired from government service and established herself in New York as a refrigeration consultant. She became widely known in Europe and America. She lived on Riverside Drive in a penthouse apartment. Her rooftop garden was noted. I like to think it was a memorial to him. And you'll love this from one of the obituaries. When asked why she liked to knit when she was travelling by train, she said it was because it enabled her to keep her eyes lowered and thereby not give herself away."

Meg laughed. "Shouldn't there be more of her in the book?"

"I would have to invent it."

"Perhaps you should be writing a novel, not a biography."

"But I'm not a novelist. I've never written fiction, although my geographies are said to be highly readable. The known facts about him will be of interest to only a few historians, and yet there is so much more to the man. How integrate what I alone know with what the world knows? And how little even I know. Except for what my mother told me and the letters and diary she left me, his personal life is a blank." I paused. "Aren't you getting cold?"

"Not this northern girl!"

We remained silent as a few worshippers made their way down the aisle to kneel before the altar.

"No, I'm not cold," Meg said at last, "but I do need fresh air."

And so we left the church and strolled on the terrace at the top of the great staircase. The rain had passed over the city, and the sky's glitter was answered by the golden swarm of Paris, disappearing at the far horizon. A few worshippers were making their careful way down the steep flight as a smaller number toiled toward us.

"What a site for a temple—*sacré mont* indeed." Meg marvelled. "What power the church has to draw the flocks."

"Didn't the convent confirm your birthright faith?"

"I was a problem to them. Without Sister Ursula I don't know what could have become of me. When I left to be married, she counseled me never to abandon my gift. 'I too have hot blood,' she told me and for the first time. 'I was born in France, and I too was a nurse after I became a Dominican. There was freedom in the suffering of others. I was also a nurse here when they sent me to Scotland, until I became too old. They then had me teach physiology and anatomy in the convent.' She confirmed my secret vow to embrace what I sensed was a gift which would someday lead to a calling. My aesthetic nature responded to the beauty the church has brought to this sorry earth—cathedrals, music, processionals with gorgeous accoutrements. Theology and dogma meant nothing to me. I was insulated against them. I suppose that's what led to my flight to a

Protestant husband, and yet the bareness of Scottish Presbyterianism chilled me to the bone."

Again Meg paused. I did not interrupt her, sensing her need. "If I have met your need for a listener," she resumed, "so have you made it possible for me to experience a city closed to a lone woman, however adventurous." Again she paused as we continued to walk back and forth, arm in arm. "Thank you," she finally said, "for giving me a turn."

"I need to rest my voice," I joked. "You might not be cold, but I'm beginning to feel it. Let's go back to the bistro and have a café cognac. I'll even set us up with a Remy Martin."

"I've never had cognac. I'm game."

We picked our careful way down the shining steps to Au Sacré Mont. We were greeted by the *patronne* who led us to a table in a far corner. When I returned from the W.C. I heard Meg speaking French with the old woman who was laughing delightedly.

"What a jewel you have!" she said to me. "She says her mother was Italian. I know what that means, having been born in Nice. An artistic and flighty people. Her common sense must come from her father, although I know nothing of the Scots. I don't think I've ever encountered one before. She tells me she can't stand whisky. That cognac will be good for her. The Lord's favorite drink." While Meg continued to blush, the *patronne* rambled on. "She says if you'll bring her back with pencil and paper, she will draw my portrait— without wrinkles or any sign of my bad character." The old lady cackled. "That calls for one on the house and another for your having brought her. You haven't been back in a long while." She returned with glasses, coffee, and a bottle of Remy Martin, and we toasted all the countries including Scotland.

"What a person!" Meg exclaimed when we were alone. "How civilized!"

"That's France wherever you go. What an impact France and Italy had on him. Add the good Mary and off the deep end he went. Shall we stay and talk some more? The cognac calms my mind and limbers my tongue."

"You hardly need it!"

"Do you like it?"

"It's smoother than Scotch. When does she close?"

387

"Never before midnight. The faithful are always coming and going. I like your French. You'd soon pass for a native, although you're much too pretty."

"From something my mother told me," I began again, "my father and Mary might have been together again in 1911 during his second trip abroad, perhaps in Florence or in Paris, or only in Washington, although there is no evidence. From my mother's journal I know he wrote her letters and postcards from that second trip abroad, none of which survived. She cherished only those of 1908. They were in a little packet tied with a pink ribbon. It was after his return in 1911 that he asked for the divorce. That caused my mother's breakdown. She spent a month at a seaside resort near San Diego, she told me, and sought to compose her soul by walking on the beach, lying on the sand, and reading Edward Carpenter and Walt Whitman. She had given him a copy of *Leaves of Grass* at Christmas in 1904, and it was with her at Del Mar and bears her notes made then. She was in love with him up to that point. His asking for a divorce was surely a bombshell. There are photographs of them taken in California in the spring of 1906 when she was pregnant with me. How happy they and my brothers looked! He gave her many presents, listed in her journal. On her fortieth birthday in 1910 it was a color print by Franz Stuck, a German painter of the Decadent school—'Pan Asleep,' showing the man beast straddling a limb in the crotch of a tree, the goat god spread out in utter relaxation, his hairy, hooved legs hanging down. An odd gift. Was that picture and that little silver ram his way of telling her who he really was? Yet he also gave her two volumes of the Letters of your countryman Robert Louis Stevenson and a framed print of the Mona Lisa. I brought the Whitman with me. I see these gifts as clues to their natures."

"Theirs *was* a strange marriage." Meg observed.

I continued. "Most of his scientific books went to my oldest brother after my father's death. Others indicated interests not unrelated to the Pan—Nietzsche, Cellini's Memoirs, and two French novels, *The Red Lily* and *Mlle. de Maupin*. Who led him to read them? Not his Quaker friend—or *was* she a secret voluptuary?"

"When your mother went away to the seashore, you must have missed her."

"Children take things for granted."

"Who cared for you boys?"

"A housekeeper from Washington who walked with a crutch and was cross-eyed. The doctor prescribed port wine for my mother's depression. Miss Bussard developed a fondness for the bottles kept down cellar. I sneaked down to spy on her. Once I drained the dregs and threw up."

Meg laughed.

"When the war came, my father was called to Washington to take charge of the country's perishable foods in Hoover's Food Administration. He brought Dr. Pennington from Philadelphia to manage the refrigeration of meats and poultry, dairy products, fruits and vegetables. How did they avoid scandal! Probably too busy, and yet when on fire there is always time. After the war, he helped Hoover in relief work in Belgium, France and Italy and was decorated by those governments. During those years he was rarely home. Once he brought Mr. Hoover, who later sent me an autographed photograph. I hung it alongside Mary Pickford, Douglas Fairbanks and William S. Hart. That was ten years before Mr. Hoover became president. My father would have been the Secretary of Agriculture in his cabinet."

There were few customers this late to break the bistro's quiet.

"That war work," I began once again, "brought about his early death. What hair hadn't fallen had turned white. In a photograph of him then, it is terrible to see how ravaged he was. 'Not only by the war,' my mother told me. 'It was also her demands. When he finally came home to stay in 1919, he confessed that she had become insatiable. I urged him to go to Palm Springs for rest, even as he had sent me to Del Mar years before.' My mother smiled wanly. 'He did more than rest. He found a new friend, a Mrs. Brown.'

"That was in 1920 before Palm Springs became a fashionable resort," I explained to Meg. It was a desert oasis with one boarding house called the Desert Inn. Mrs. Brown was a painter staying there. She painted desert and mountain scenes. My mother told me he brought one home and hung it in his bedroom. I don't know anything about her except that she was with him when he died."

"There in the desert?" Meg asked.

"In Pasadena. He had returned to his position with Sunkist, although a couple of heart attacks had led him to slow down. He was then approached by the Republican state committee to run for the United States Senate. By then my father was said to be the most in-

389

fluential man in Southern California. Earlier he had declined the deanship of the university's College of Agriculture and also an appointment to the Board of Regents of the state university. Professor Liberty Hyde Bailey also wanted him to join him at Cornell in horticultural research. He too might have lived to be a hundred! A testimonial dinner was given by the Republicans at the fashionable Maryland Hotel in Pasadena. My mother said that Mrs. Brown was there that night with my father."

"Your mother wasn't with him?"

"Maybe she was ill? Mrs. Brown could have been a Republican committee member. During the meal, the chairman proposed a toast to my father as California's next Senator. His response was smilingly to say, 'I'll have to think about that.' He leaned forward with his head on the table. He never raised up nor could he be revived. It was a massive heart attack—a coronary thrombosis."

"Dear God," Meg murmured. "How awful for your mother!"

"There was no mention of Mrs. Brown in the paper the next morning. I don't know how my mother learned of her presence. I suspect the informer was a country lawyer my father had advanced to become rich and powerful. He looked like a bullfrog."

"There's always a Judas," Meg observed. "How did you learn of his death?"

"The next day was Sunday. I was away for the weekend with a schoolmate on a hiking trip to the family cabin in the mountains back of Pasadena. I got back that afternoon."

"Did your mother tell you?"

"She had gone into seclusion. Our cook told me."

"How did it affect you?"

"All I felt was that I would get attention at high school the next morning. The news of his death was on the front page."

"Was there a public funeral?" Meg asked. "He must have had masses of friends and associates, as well as family and relations."

"There was a big affair, somewhere between a public and a private funeral, although basically a Quaker service in the absence of ritual. I remember the flowers—the funeral chapel was overflowing, their scent stifling."

"Was it held at a Quaker meeting house?"

"The Orange Grove Meeting could never have held the people. His public connections could apparently not be denied attendance.

The service was led by a Friends minister, an old family friend from Philadelphia who spent her winters in Pasadena and Whittier. Her name was Mary Travilla—a Cornishwoman. We called her Cousin Mary. She was an impressive figure whose bulk was increased by a mass of snow-white hair piled high on her head. She was a kindly woman with a fine voice who thee'd and thou'd us to a fare-thee-well. I was always forgetting and being chided, 'Laurie, thee must keep the old tongue alive.' I remember her speaking of 'our dear Harold,' then falling silent until others rose and spoke of his service to others."

"Had she arranged for them to speak?" Meg asked.

"Oh no! It was spontaneous. Our Lithuanian cook and Japanese maid, and our gardener—he was from the Canary Islands—spoke of my father's kindness. He was loved by many."

"I can understand," Meg murmured.

"I have clearer memories of a public memorial held in Los Angeles. The talks were printed in a booklet. The secretaries of Commerce and Agriculture—Mr. Hoover and Mr. Wallace—came from Washington to speak, and there were local notables, including the president of the Sunkist cooperative—my father was the general manager. It was then that I first realized my father's national stature."

"It must have been good for your mother, she who had so much disappointment in the marriage."

"The following summer I worked as a ranch hand in the San Joaquin valley. My oldest brother was foreman of the Mexican labor force—he was bilingual. He had graduated from the university, like our father a horticulturist, and he got me a job irrigating rows of grapes in 120 degree heat. There was a girl named Tommy Chaplin. We used to raid the watermelon fields in the moonlight."

"How extraordinary!" Meg murmured. "Where was your father buried?"

"His parents took him back to the Quaker burial ground at Ghent in New York state where they were all born."

"When was the last time you saw him?"

"It was Friday afternoon the day before he died. I was leaving to spend the weekend at our cabin in Big Santa Anita canyon. My father drove me to the streetcar line where my chum was to meet me, and we were to ride to the end of the line from where the trail took off. My friend was late and the car had not yet come. As my father and I walked on the platform he abruptly asked, 'Has your mother talked to you about playing with yourself?' Yes, I admitted. 'What did she tell you?' That it leads to insanity. 'That's not true,' he said angrily, 'she shouldn't talk that way. Just don't overdo it,' And after we had reached the end of the platform and started back, he put his arm around me. 'Just remember, my boy,' he said softly, 'it's not the real thing.' I don't know what he would have gone on to tell me, but then my friend's mother dropped him off and the Sierra Madre car arrived. We scrambled aboard with our knapsacks and canteens. I leaned out and waved. My father waved back. That was the last time I saw him."

Meg took my hand.

"That was a strange parting, wasn't it?" I said. "Now the longer he is dead, the more living he becomes. I remember his big brown eyes and the warmth of him. I must resurrect him in this book. For years I kept postponing it. Perhaps I sensed there were things I did not know. There were. Now how should I use them? When my oldest brother died and I compiled a brief memoir, my mother asked, 'Now will you write the one of your father?' I haven't forgotten," I said.

"Did she forgive him?" Meg asked. "Or is that the right word?"

"I don't think she was bitter—only crushed by her own failure to meet his needs. She was a passive woman married to an aggressive man with enormous drive and appetite. Each married without knowing who the other was. How *can* we, when we're young? I remember her saying, 'If it is not freely given, I don't want it.' "

"Should she have freed him?"

"She believed that he needed the harbor she provided. Yet in the end both women lost him."

"Did your mother and Mary ever meet?"

"Upon his and Mary's return in 1908, he invited her and her niece who had been with her to their home in Washington. My mother's journal tells of several visits, one for overnight."

"What did she say about Mary?"

"Only a mere mention. There was another time they met when we were all back in California for the winter—he had completed his field work and was writing the report that led to his offer from the Sunkist cooperative. It was a lucrative move. His government sal-

392

ary was pitifully small. By the time he died in 1922, he had reached $25,000 a year, an enormous amount for then."

"What did they spend it on?" Meg asked.

"On us boys, entertaining, antique furniture, dozens of oriental rugs—a few of them have survived, including a gorgeous small prayer rug—silver, pictures, a big house, a cook, a maid, a gardener, an expensive automobile with my father's monogram on the doors. His tastes approached the sybaritic, a far cry from his Quaker origins. My mother also liked fine things, but she remained more simple. She out-lived him thirty-five years."

"Did Mary follow him to California?"

"She came only that once in 1909 as a consultant on the cooling of the freight cars in which fruit was shipped to the eastern markets. That was before electrical refrigeration. Cars were cooled by ice— great blocks of ice in bunkers at the end of each car. 'Reefers' they called the cars. They had to be re-iced at stops on the long journey to the eastern markets. My mother was back in Washington that year and his letters told her again in cruel detail of Mary's visit to Riverside and of how a visiting group of Florida citrus growers had assumed she was his wife. That was two years before he asked for the divorce. Did my mother see it coming? Probably not. She was naturally trusting."

"Most of us are." Meg murmured.

"The last time she and Mary met was a year after his death. Immediately after he died, my mother told me, she had a bitter letter from Mary, blaming her for his death. She never answered it and apparently destroyed it. His parents were wintering with them that year and my mother showed the letter to his mother. That must have been sad for my grandmother. A year later Mary arrived unannounced. She was in San Francisco for a scientific meeting. She came, my mother told me, to ask forgiveness for that letter. My mother then told her of Mrs. Brown, and it was she who comforted the disillusioned Mary."

"What a strange turn that was! Do you have any pictures of her?"

"Only the later I told you of, reproduced in journals at the time of her death. That was in 1952. She was eighty and a distinguished consultant to government and industry. She left a large estate to the niece. She had never married. My father was probably her only love. I wish I had a picture of her at thirty-six. By the time I met her,

her face had grown cold and cruel. She was a brilliant woman. Would she have made a good wife and mother? Probably not. Life took longer to kill her than it did him. She outlived him thirty years. My mother outlived them both."

"Good for her!" Meg said.

"Although I said that my mother was unable or unwilling to express her feelings either in speech or writing, yet she was capable of deep emotion whether or not it came to the surface."

"How do you know that?" Meg asked.

"She told me in that confessional talk that there had been one unfulfilled love in her life—for a family friend apparently happily married. She never named him and I didn't ask. After her death I came on a note in her copy of *Leaves of Grass*, the one she had given to her husband at Christmas in 1904—I wonder if he ever read it? In the margin next to one of the most passionate poems in the 'Calamus' section was pencilled in her hand: *February 1917*. I turned to that date in her journal and there read of a dinner they had given for another couple at the Los Angeles Athletic Club: 'I met him in the hall. He said he was going home to S.F. in the morning.' On October 2, 1919, she wrote, 'About five this evening a telegram came saying E.S. had passed away at eight o'clock this morning. I had understood he was getting better, but it was a mistake, I guess. Dear Friend! He had a wonderful faculty for friendship. I was very fond of him and he of me.' Turning back to June 24, these words: 'E.S. came out with Harold to dinner and to spend the night. He looks very tired and thinner.' Later she added in the margin: 'Last time I ever saw him.' "

"Oh, Laurie!" Meg exclaimed. "How quietly her heart broke! How did she tell of her husband's death?"

"She didn't, at least not at the time. Her last entry on December 13, 1921, not quite two months before his death, told of sewing accomplished and preparations for Christmas, then nothing until January 1, 1923, except for a single undated pencilled note, "G.H.P. died Feb. 18, 1922, Pasadena. Marcia P. born Mar 7, 1922, Berkeley.' That was their first grandchild, my oldest brother's daughter. On September 1936 my mother added a bold note in blue pencil on the half-blank page following the last 1921 entry, these strange words: '1922 no record for reasons not remembered.' Then her journal volume for 1924 is even more puzzling. At one end it opens with the stubs of twenty-five pages cut out with a razor or sharp knife. It is evident that the pages had borne writing in the purple ink she always used. What was it she wrote and when did she write it? Was it an effort to understand her marriage and its failure? And when did she cut out those pages? They are the only mutilation in the journal she kept for seventy years."

"It is curious that she wrote that much and then destroyed it. Her heart and mind must have been at war with each other."

"I had no idea of any of that going on in her. She seemed so calm and controlled."

"I am very like her," Meg said. "I mean I was!"

"Reading from the other end of the 1924 volume," I continued, "it opens with a list of his personal effects—clothes, jewelry, books and so forth—and how she disposed of them. His mother and father, brothers and sisters were all remembered with something; also Cousin Mary and his secretary Rhano Mabel MacCurdy."

"I like the MacCurdy tartan," Meg murmured. "What came to you and your brothers?"

"They could wear most of his clothes. I was too small. I got his Cornell class cane of briarwood with a silver 'C,' also his gold Eversharp pencil and stickpins. I still have them although they are out of fashion. And that desert water color that hung in his bedroom."

"Do you still have it?"

"It disappeared during my many moves. I still have one of his pictures my mother said was his favorite—a mezzotint of Rembrandt's portrait of his son Titus. The original is in London in the Wallace Collection. What is strange is that Mrs. Brown received one of the gifts made by my mother. She gave her his opal ring."

"Then they did know each other. That *is* strange."

When it neared midnight and after a fond parting we left the bistro. Again there were three transfers to reach St. Germain des Près. The station platforms were nearly deserted except for late travellers and the homeless sleeping on the backless benches and on the cement floor with only newspapers for cover.

"I don't like to see them," Meg said, "but at least they are out of the weather."

"It's noisier than London and cleaner than New York. They say Moscow beats them all."

395

"What's that characteristic smell?"

"Probably the high voltage current used to operate the trains."

"I prefer Paris's outdoor smell."

"That's coal smoke and Chanel."

Meg laughed. "We burn only coal. The English cut our forests for the Royal Navy. That was in the seventeenth century. They justify it by saying their ships kept the Spanish from taking Scotland."

"No Chanel?"

"None since our own poor Queen Mary went to her death."

As we parted in the hotel lobby I saw her questioning look. "You mean what next and when?"

She smiled. "Only if you can match tonight."

"What about a boat ride? Sunday is the last day before they are tied up until spring. We could take the *bateaumouche* down river to the last stop, have a country walk and lunch and be back by dark."

"Lovely."

"I'll play the strong silent man."

"I don't doubt your strength," Meg scoffed.

Sunday dawned clear, and we got an early start, walking down river to Pont Neuf, the nearest stopping point for the boats. In the middle of the bridge we leaned on the parapet to watch a tug, *Guêpe No. 4*, pulling a string of barges up river. The skipper's wife was hanging out a washing on a line stretched across the foredeck, clear of the exhaust smoke. Meg waved to the man at the wheel. He answered with a grunt on his air horn.

Meg gripped my arm. "What's the word from your sibyll?"

"I heard from her yesterday morning."

"And what did she say?"

"That I should leave the city and its distractions."

"Does that include me?" Meg teased.

"She said to go up river," I continued, "up near the source into the deep countryside over which the river deities rule. There will I hear the answer I seek."

Meg stared at me. "For heaven's sake, what *are* you telling me?"

I seized her arm. "Come along, there's our boat."

We rushed across to the Cité, and down the stone steps to the landing stage as the slim craft eased alongside.

"Will you be warm enough on deck?" I asked as we boarded.

"I have a cashmere next to my skin."

She was again wearing the Cameron tartan with its bright red threads, a dark blue beret and sturdy brown oxfords.

We found bench seats on the upper forward deck under the eye of the pilot. The boat pulled out swiftly and threaded its way downstream under bridge after bridge.

"I like the practical way you dress," I said.

"Haven't you ever known a practical woman?"

"My wife."

"Are you still married?"

"Oh yes."

"Where is she?"

"In Washington where we keep a home."

"Doesn't she travel with you?"

"She did when we were first married. We lived in Marseilles. Our first daughter was born in Montpellier where there is a fine maternity hospital. We had a country cottage there. Then when she was pregnant again, she wanted to go home. We moved to Washington. She and the girls stayed, I returned to another foreign post."

"What an unsettled life!"

"It suited us. My wife was a doctor's daughter, as you were, though with medicine not painting in her blood. She went back to school to get a hospital administrator degree. She was at the top of the class. She rose to have her own hospital. She is a very capable woman. When she found that she wanted children and a career, my part was over."

"What about the girls?"

"They spent time abroad with me when they were younger. I wanted them to learn languages."

"Your wife is younger than you are."

"Quite a bit."

"You Americans are an extraordinary people. I envy you."

"Our home is in the Georgetown area of the capital. She has a glass house for her plants in winter, and an aviary for her birds."

"Doesn't she miss you?"

"She's too busy, and also she came to recognize that a writer is solitary, even savage when working."

397

"My goodness! Am I in danger? I've disturbed your work habits."

"Not really. I never work on Sunday and that recital was in the evening. I'll be going back when I finish this book. We always have a family round-up at Christmas. Both daughters are now married with children. No, you haven't disturbed me. You found I needed a listener. I was at that point where I needed to organize and articulate my material. You've helped. Was your husband supportive?"

"As long as painting remained a hobby. He had a hatred of personal publicity, and yet he was always kind. Can we ask for more? His work did not deeply interest me."

"Did you have friends? Men friends?"

"Life in Edinburgh, especially in the university and church milieus, is strictly regulated."

"Did you feel you were missing something?"

Meg paused. "Not until after his death. Then I knew I had to get away." She smiled. "This was the first step. You have been kind to share your walks and your work with me. Also the music and the cathedrals and now this."

"Have you made friends in class?"

"They are mostly young people to whom I must seem very old."

The launch was indeed like a fly or water spider, darting through and around the river traffic, stopping at intervals to let off and take on passengers. The banks grew less industrialized, until at last we were in rural surroundings at the end of the line.

We walked beyond the village into bare fields and orchards. At a crossroads café we settled on the terrace with steaming café au lait, bread and butter. There were other Sunday morning walkers, old and young, families and lovers, and ones on bicycles heading into the deeper countryside.

"A morning like this," Meg said, "gives me a new appreciation of the Impressionists. I could see them all as we came down river, then in the village and now here. They painted what was at hand and with love, Monet most of all."

"Does it make you want to paint?"

"Oh yes! I've painted on holiday in the Highlands and the Isles, and once in the Shetlands with sheep for models. Scotland is so different from here, remote, cold, and unloving. It must be the Latin in me responding to light and air. It's a bit frightening."

398

"Will you go to Italy?"

"Not this time, although it's inevitable I go eventually. I have no ties there other than blood. I want to see the master drawings in the Uffizi, the greatest of all such collections. What about your sibyll? Will you heed her?" I did not answer at once while we watched the scene, then I said, "I need to decide on how to use those letters he wrote her. I want you to hear them."

"Where will you go?" Meg persisted. "Do you know?"

"I do—to Vézelay—a remote village in northwest Burgundy, the site of a Romanesque church—the Basilique de la Madeleine. I bicycled there when I was posted to Lyon and stayed at the Cheval Blanc. Vézelay is in idyllic countryside—on the western slope of the Langres plateau from which all water flows to the Atlantic either by the Seine or the Loire. It's the nearest to where she said to go—up near the source."

"You do know your geography."

"What's more basic?"

"Does Vézelay lie on the upper Seine?"

"Between the Yonne, the Seine, and the Aube, the three streams that merge and take the name of the largest. It's on a hill, with a view to the ends of the earth. Eastward beyond the watershed, all waters flows to the Mediterranean by the Rhone. The Langres plateau is a great limestone sponge that stores the water. All the streams on either side rise from perennial springs."

"When do you plan on going?" Meg asked.

"Tomorrow."

"Will you come back to Paris?" Her voice was soft.

"Not for long."

"How far is it?"

"A hundred fifty miles."

"By bicycle?"

"I'll go by train and bus." I took a breath, then asked, "Would you like to go with me?"

"Isn't that too far for a day?" she countered.

"Much too far."

Meg set down her cup and stared at me. "What do you mean?"

"Just what I said."

She shook her head, then rose and went inside. I ordered more coffee, and waited.

When she resumed her seat after what seemed a long time, she said quietly, "You are joking."

"No."

"But . . . "

"But what?"

"Just everything. You're married. I'm in class." She began to cry.

"Don't cry," I said, taking her hand.

"You've upset me so."

"Should I apologize for offending your Scottish soul?"

"I have another half, you know." She paused. "You've shocked it—in another way—and more deeply."

I felt my heart quicken. "What do you mean?"

"I'm afraid to tell you," she whispered.

"What?" I persisted. "Tell me."

Her voice was soft. "You've spoken to the other me."

My heart slowed. I said no more, nor did she. We drank our coffee, then I said, "There's a wood beyond here. Let's make a bonfire of leaves, then come back for lunch."

I paid our bill, took matches from the *patron*, and we set out.

After a brisk walk we reached the bosque of bare oaks. The ground was drifted with dead leaves. Meg helped make a little pile and I set it afire. We squatted by it and warmed our hands. A crow rose from the tree overhead and flew away cawing.

Still I waited. Meg began to speak. "We went once to a sacred wood in Yorkshire near Fountains Abbey where the Druids had a shrine under a huge oak. It is said to be the oldest in Britain." She smiled. "I wanted to climb it, but it was much too big, even for the boys."

"You have good memories," I said.

"I haven't been an unhappy person. And I was always seeing the world as something to paint."

"Do you still?"

"Even more vividly."

We lingered over the fire, then walked farther into the countryside. Neither spoke again.

Back at the café, roast lamb and white beans appeased our hunger, with apples and grapes for dessert.

"I've never done anything like that," Meg said at last.

"Perhaps no one ever asked you."

400

She smiled. "You *are* a knowing man!"

I took her hand. "Listen to me. I have grown to like your company, Meg Graeme. It happened so fast. Suddenly we were not strangers. I don't want to give you up even for a week."

"Did you plan it this way?"

"Until you asked me if I had heard from the sybill, it was the farthest from my thoughts."

"Do you mean share the same room—and bed?"

"The White Horse is a small hotel. Guests need to room together."

Meg laughed. "I don't know how you could be more impossible than you are!"

"Persuasive, I hope."

"Can such swift intimacy be good?" she countered. "We have been together so few times."

"We won't know till we try."

"I am not as experienced as you are."

"You bore two children, surely not by immaculate conception."

Again she laughed. "Malcolm was no lover. I'm afraid I don't know my capabilities."

"Although I've never won any awards, I *am* noted for my kindness to animals." Then seriously, "We do like each other, don't we? And from that first day on the bridge. You recognize the attraction, don't you?"

"I do."

"Remember those lines of Apollinaire?" I continued. "*Sous le Pont Mirabeau coule la Seine et nos amours. Faut-il qu'il m'en souvienne la joie venait toujours après la peine.*"

"I've had more pain than joy," she said softly.

"Does adultery trouble you?" I asked.

"The Scottish me? Yes. The Italian me? I don't know. I have never tried. May I sleep on it? Do you have to leave tomorrow?"

"No, I can wait."

On the return trip we sat again on the foredeck, seeing the sun's last light on the darkening city. We held hands and did not talk. Although we were moving against the current, now another river was bearing us.

Night had fallen when we disembarked at Pont Neuf. We walked back along the Boulevard St. Germain, then to the river, again

401

through the Place Furstenburg. The old electroliers were glowing softly.

"Oh!" Meg exclaimed. "How beautiful."

"It was the quietness he needed to paint those wild pictures."

"Are you determined to be like him?"

I stopped and faced her. "Yes, I am. I want more than Sunday walks. And I'm tired of talking, you'll be glad to know."

She did not answer.

We returned to the hotel in stride, her arm in mine.

I passed a restless night. I had not thought of us as lovers. Now I could think of nothing else. The window was showing light when I fell asleep.

After late breakfast and my walk, I worked as usual at the corner café, arranging material to take to Vézelay.

Toward noon I looked up as Meg approached my table. I rose and we shook hands. My eyes questioned her.

"Have you changed your mind?" she asked.

I took her hands. "It's all I thought of all night."

Her face reddened. "I too," she confessed.

We laughed.

"When will we go?" she asked.

"I changed my reservation until tomorrow. There's an *express* from Gare de Lyon at nine that will get us to Auxerre at noon, then the bus leaves for Avallon and Dijon via Vézelay—and every last village, hamlet and crossroad en route. We'll get there in time to see the basilica before dark."

"How organized you are! What clothes shall I wear?"

"Wool pants and shirt, jacket, walking shoes, warm coat."

"Will I need a dress?"

"It's only a country inn."

"You know I'm used to dressing for dinner."

"Bring one," I conceded. "Was your teacher understanding?"

"He made me promise to bring back some bucolic sketches."

"I'll model for you."

"As Pan?" She laughed. "Pan Awake!"

We embraced and parted.

It was a clear cool day when we taxied to the station. Now on the verge of the unforeseen and uncertain, we were content to sit silently in the empty first-class compartment, holding hands and watching the colored woods and smoke-plumed villages flash by. Occasional hunters with gun and dog were part of the Breughelesque landscape. Between stops the train ran fast with a yelping of its whistle.

In Auxerre there was barely time for ham and cheese sandwiches and milk in the Buffet de la Gare before crossing the square to where our bus was loading. The country folk were on their way back to their villages after a morning of selling and buying, and the top of the bus was piled with their belongings, including trussed up fowl and a baby goat that bleated pitifully. The good natured crowd was dominated by the driver who was everywhere at once, warning that his bus never failed to leave on schedule and the devil would surely take the hindmost.

Although Meg and I were obvious foreigners, my ability to enter the badinage, albeit in an accent far from rural, gave us leeway in reaching to the back of the crowded bus.

"It will ride rougher over the back wheels," I explained, "but we won't have people climbing over us at the stops. What do you make of it all? Do you like it?"

"Oh but I do!" Her eyes were shining as they were after the Prokofiev sonata. "Is that French I'm hearing?"

"That's the Burgundian patois."

"It sounds like they have a sore throat."

"Next to Meridionale, Burgundian is the worst of all spoken French. If we'd had time, I'd have shown you the cathedral. It has powerful Gothic sculptures depicting the fate that befalls sinners."

"I've heard about such things," Meg admitted.

"I'm the sinner, not you, and to this point only in mind."

"The church makes no distinction between mind and body," Meg said primly.

"Did your husband interpret church law in strict orthodoxy?" I asked.

"The strictest of strict. I hope he won't inhibit me."

I took her hand. We were squeezed together on the back seat, and I could feel her warmth even through our wool clothes.

"There's the cathedral of St. Etienne," I pointed out the window. "I used to bicycle here from Lyon. It dominates the town from miles around. On our way back I hope we can visit the cathedral. There's

403

a strange story about it and the town by Walter Pater. Have you read him?"

"Only his Renaissance studies," Meg said. "Sister Ursula led me to him. I shall never forget his essays on Leonardo and Botticelli."

"His Auxerre story," I continued, "is about a local boy named Denys who grew up to be a kind of Pied Piper. He incited the townspeople to such sensual excesses that they finally turned on him, hunted him through the streets and tore him to pieces. That story was what first led me to Auxerre. I wonder if my father ever read it? Somehow that picture of Pan he gave my mother is connected in my mind with the Pater story and with my father's sensual awakening in Paris with Mary Pennington, and also that last burst of feeling with Mrs. Brown. It's very strange and I'm not sure what part to give it in his story."

With a final blast at last minute boarders, the driver pulled out with a grinding of gears, crossed the Yonne on an ancient stone bridge and we were soon in open country. The road was narrow and smooth, winding and hilly, with stops every few miles. Meg left her hand in mine as we watched the landscape unroll. More hunters were seen, and shocked corn and corded firewood. Each stop was the same. Like a monkey the driver leaped atop the bus and threw down their belongings to departing passengers, then stowed the pieces hoisted up by boarders. We remained on to retain our seats, until at one stop we got out to stretch.

"We are near Alésia," I remarked. "There's a hilltop statue there to Vercingetorix, the last of the Gallic chieftains to resist the Romans. He and his Gauls were starved out by Julius Caesar and his legions. Thereafter all Gaul was Roman and finally French."

"What happened to him?"

"He was taken to Rome in chains, paraded through the streets in Caesar's Triumph, then put to death. The P.L.M. passes near there en route Paris-Lyon. I always saluted him."

Toward four o'clock, Vézelay appeared in the southeast, its stone dwellings crowning the ridged hill in the midst of checkerboard fields and woods. As the hill grew larger, the buildings took form. We began to climb the narrow road that spined the hill.

I called to the driver to let us off at the Cheval Blanc, a short distance below the public square where the bus stopped before going on to Avallon and Dijon.

As he handed down our bags, the driver asked me, "*On est bien la-dedans?*"

"*Mais oui. On mange bien, très bien, mais vous savez, nous ne venons pas seulement pour cet espèce de nourriture.*"

The driver slapped his thigh. "*D'accord! Votre femme, est-elle Russe?*"

"*Ecossaise.*"

"*Tiens. Mais elle est belle quand même.*" He gave me a knowing look. "*Alors, bon répas.*"

On up the hill the bus lurched in low gear, leaving a swirling cloud of fumes.

When Meg demanded that I translate our repartee, she said severely, "I'm beginning to realize what a wicked man you are!" Before I could reply, the *patron* was greeting us, recognizing me from earlier visits. "I've given you our best room with an extra table and chair—and a strong, comfortable bed."

"Perfection as usual," I acknowledged.

"Let's head up the hill," I said as we went to our room, "without changing our clothes. We can make the church before dark."

And so off we went to the public square, one side of which was formed by the great basilica.

"There's the café," I pointed out, "where I can work in the morning while you are sketching."

"There'll be no lack of subjects. I too will be glad to have a break from routine."

"Shall we keep the afternoons for walks?"

"Perfect!"

The Basilique de la Madeleine was built of the creamy golden limestone which gave the nearby Côte-d'Or its name. The sculptured façade and narthex were peopled with saints and sinners, angels and devils, all conveying powerful warnings to a credulous people. We entered open space of luminosity unlike the jewelled gloom of Gothic cathedrals. The window glass was clear and the walls a creamy pink, so that even though night was nearing, the nave was still lit by daylight.

"We'll return in full daylight," I said, "to see the sculptured pilasters. Here is the apogee of French Romanesque, although the choir is Gothic. There's nothing like it in France. If you're not too weary, let's see the esplanade behind the church."

We walked to the ramparts from which the hill dropped steeply to bare fields below. The area was bordered with leafbare chestnut trees in which crows were raucously settling for the night. Neither of us spoke. Meg held tightly to my arm as we returned to our hotel, walking fast downhill in stride.

At last we were alone in our room with double bed and bath and tall windows that opened on a balcony. We stepped outside. Up and down the hill lights were showing. Woodsmoke drifted up to us, and we heard the sound of children at play before being called to supper.

"Do you approve?" I asked.

"It's a lovely dream."

"Take a bath? A liedown? Are you hungry?"

"Let me collect myself."

"I'll take a bath while you rest."

Meg stood close and put her cheek to mine for the first time. "Thank you for the beautiful day."

"I want it to be the way you want it."

We embraced and I went to take my bath.

When I came out, wearing a dressing gown, Meg was stretched on the bed in a dark red robe, her hair below her shoulders. I stared.

"Well," she said softly. "Do you like me?"

I drew the easy chair next to the bed and took her hand, leaned and kissed her cheek.

"Rested?" I asked.

"I'll be hungry. Did you leave hot water for me?"

I nodded. Meg whispered, "Shall we wait?"

Again I touched her cheek. "Napoleon said an army fights best on a full stomach."

She laughed and went for her bath.

She wore a handknit peasant dress and a shawl as we went down to the small dining room. Rust-colored chrysanthemums were on our table.

"You think of everything," she said.

"Only of you now," I said.

I ordered pan-fried river fish. They came with tiny potatoes and green beans.

"We're not great drinkers either of us," I said, "but tonight is spe-

406

cial. We're near Chablis and the most fragrant of the white Burgundies."

When the waiter uncorked and poured the wine, the flowery sweetness filled our nostrils. I touched glasses.

"I've surely taken the high road from Scotland," Meg said as we lingered over the meal with a café noir. "I'm not tipsy am I? How does one tell?"

"Is it a nice feeling?"

"It makes me bold enough to ask, why did you want me to come with you?"

"I wanted more of what we were beginning to know."

"Is that all?"

"Truthfully, I never thought of you then as the desirable woman I now see that you are."

"You told your wife that you needed to be alone when you were working."

"I *was* alone, working and content, and then suddenly you were there. Don't you recognize life's inevitabilities?"

"I've not had your experience."

"I'd reached a point where I needed a listener to help me."

"You've had helpers?"

"Some."

"Women?"

"Not that many. I've not had time."

"What happens when your need has been met?"

"We go our ways," I said softly.

Meg was silent, then said, "I understand what you are telling me. I accept it, I think, yet it saddens me. Or is it the wine?"

I took her hand. "Are you sorry you came?"

"I'm feeling pain and joy so that I don't know which is which. What was it your poet said about them?"

I recalled the lines.

> *Faut-il qu'il m'en souvienne*
> *La joie venait toujours après la peine*

"Isn't it sometimes the other way around?" she asked.

"Now there's only joy ahead. Shall we get a breath of air? You'll need your shawl."

Again we toiled up the hill to the square. The shops were shut-

tered and dark, all but the café where we could see chess players at a table. The night was quiet. There was sweet woodsmoke in
the air.

"No, not sorry," Meg mused. "And grateful not to be alone."

"I too."

"It's nice when needs meet as ours have."

We grew cold as we returned to the inn. The bowl of flowers was
in our room.

We undressed back to back and donned robes. Then Meg turned
and let hers fall. "I insist you see who I am before you turn out the
light."

I was dazzled by the whiteness of her body and the blackness of
her hair, and moved by the sweetness of her gesture. "*Ah, quelle est
belle!*" I murmured.

"What are you hiding?" she teased.

I let my robe fall.

"What a wonderful suntan!" she said.

"I spent the summer in swimming trunks."

I threw back the blanket and Meg slipped under the top sheet.

"You may now put out the light and open the window," she said.
"You like fresh air, don't you? The French seem to fear it."

I lay down beside her and drew the sheet over us. She was trembling. "This is as far as I can lead us," she whispered.

I put my arms around her. "Do you want to wait?"

"For what?"

"To make love."

"Would you rather talk for a while?" she asked.

"My mouth is too dry," I said.

"For kissing?"

I found her mouth with mine.

When I awoke at daybreak, Meg was asleep, tangled hair fram-
ing her peaceful face. I drew a quiet tub and thought about the work
ahead. I was deeply relaxed.

When I returned to the bedroom, she was reading in the *Leaves
of Grass* I had brought with me. She silently reached out her arms.

"You smell good!"

I kissed her again. "Not as good as you. Sleep well?"

"Like a babe. I'm afraid I'm out of practice."

"Sleeping?"

"Doing what we did."

"Once learned never forgotten."

"Was it nice for you?"

"Lovely."

She smiled and sat up. "Lessons over?"

"Another tonight."

Meg looked at me closely. "You want to go to work, don't you."

"I *am* a man of regular habits," I admitted.

She sighed. "So was Malcolm. Well, what's on our schedule?"

"I've decided to work at that table in the back garden instead of the café. Too noisy up there. Would you like to draw in the church?"

"I suppose so."

"Come back toward noon and we'll lunch here and then take a long walk."

While she bathed, I rang for breakfast and we lay in bed and ate and talked about my work.

"Your sibyll gave you good advice," Meg concluded.

"Do you like it here?"

"You were very gentle."

"You are beautiful—before, during and after."

"Not too old?"

"You'll never be. It's the Latin in you."

"No one ever sought it out."

"You've broken my block. Now it will flow."

"Where is the river from here?"

"The Seine is to the north, the Yonne is closer to the south. Both are too far to walk. Vézelay lies in their embrace, even as we do. Those are his letters and diary there on the table. I'll read to you tonight."

"How long will we stay? I shouldn't miss too many sessions of class."

"Let's see how it goes."

Meg began to dress. "I thought Malcolm was well organized," she said, shaking her head.

"I had to learn to be."

"You say your wife has been supportive."

"Both found in marriage what was needed."

409

"I suppose I found what was best for me. For Malcolm too. I think. I didn't want very much after what I'd been used to. Now I don't know what comes next. Edinburgh is no place for a professor's widow with Bohemian leanings."

"Italy?"

"I told you I have no connections other than cousins I don't even know exist. Will I be in the way here?"

"Why do you say that?"

"You're new to me seen up this close."

"What do you mean?" I asked.

"You shut out everything but what engages you."

"Isn't that how to get things done?"

"Yesterday you made me feel I was your world." Her voice lowered. "Especially last night. I nearly died from your intensity. Now I'm keeping you from your work."

"Isn't this how Delacroix worked?"

"Was he married?"

"He never married."

"Was he homosexual?"

"Apparently not. He had mistresses."

"Between pictures."

"I suppose so."

"Isn't that the way your life should have gone?"

"That's for genius. I have talent and industry. Genius is the power to focus both and raise them to a new level."

Meg sighed. "What I have is even lower than talent—mere facility."

"Meg, listen to me. You *have* genius—the genius for companionship. I have never felt so companioned. It makes me eager to work."

I held and kissed her. She struggled free, laughing. "Oh you're impossible."

She gathered her sketch book and pencils in a lightweight backpack and we went downstairs.

"I'll meet you at the café toward noon," I said, "and we'll lunch there if we like the *specialité de la maison*. Otherwise back here. Got your wristwatch? Make it high noon."

After seeing her off up the hill, I settled in at the garden table. The day was cool and I was grateful for a long-sleeved pullover.

410

When I put aside the morning's work and walked up the steep hill before noon, I found Meg seated on the café's terrace, reading the Whitman.

"I'm glad you came," she said. "I don't know what to order."

"Wine of the country. I'll order a demi-carafe and we'll split it. How did your morning go?"

Her face lit up. She showed me her sketchbook, page after page of swift drawings of the sculptured pilasters that lined both sides of the nave. It was the first of her work she had shown me. Her face questioned me.

I was astonished. "You draw with such confidence," I said. "I had no idea."

"How could you? You've never seen my work. You never asked to. I was thinking of what you said about your father—that he exploded into those letters from Paris. What if that should happen to me? I have never felt so deeply since I left Edinburgh." She paused. "Or since we met."

"You're no beginner," I said. "Either as artist or—lover."

She laughed. "That's a very nice compliment. This is a relief from life drawings. Such vitality those sculptors put into their creatures! What would Malcolm make of me there in this place that deplores sin so voluptuously—and I with another woman's husband."

"Feeling guilty?"

"Just wondering about myself. How unexpected my life has become after years of doing the expected!" Her voice rose and she added, "I like it!"

I laughed. "And I like you."

"What becomes of us?"

I shook my head. "Let's leave talking till later."

"Sorry, I'll try. How did your morning go?"

"Like silk. May I read to you this evening?"

"Not this afternoon?"

"Afternoons are for walking. There is a road around the base of the hill. The vineyards are beautiful. We'll join the gleaners. After lunch? You must be hungry."

"Painting and poetry feed only part of me."

"What do you make of Walt Whitman?"

"He's new to me. I've been searching out your mother's markings. She was obviously moved. I wonder if your father was."

411

"We'll never know."

"Did he have time for reading?"

"I'm sure he made time for whatever he wanted."

The afternoon passed as we wandered around the base of the hill, pausing to glean the last sugary grapes among the dead leaves. There was little traffic, an occasional bicycle or peasant's push cart laden with cuttings and faggots. The white Charolais cattle browsed on the scant grass.

Toward sundown we returned to our room, bathed, donned our robes and stretched out on the bed. "My mind is overflowing," I confessed. "Let's snack on bread and cheese and have a late dinner."

"Whatever you want."

I laid out his diary and letters and my notes on the table by the bed.

"This is the only diary that has survived," I began. "It's probably the only one he kept. His life reached a new tempo. If he kept one on his second trip abroad—and I doubt that he did—it was not among the papers my mother left. That first trip opened his eyes and pores to a new world of beauty and feeling. What a pity he was cut down in what would have been his prime and never knew an Indian Summer. Letters drained off what might have filled diaries. He was a faithful writer to my mother and us boys. If he wrote to Mary Pennington—and I'm sure he did—she probably destroyed them before her death, or even earlier when, according to my mother, he had cooled toward her. During the war in Washington there are no letters at all to my mother. Was it guilt? More likely no time or strength after the twelve-and eighteen-hour days."

"Perhaps your mother destroyed some of his papers."

"If so, why did she keep these from Paris and London? They are the most intimate letters of all as far as Mary Pennington is concerned. You asked why didn't I question my mother about them? I didn't know then that they existed. I was full of my own life. Alas, when I was ready to turn to his, it was too late. Those who knew him best were dead.

"It's strange," I mused, "how a life is reduced to essence in a few letters and a little diary. Here in less than a month my father learned who he really was and of his power to shape and control people and events. Everything fused and ignited. You'll hear how confident and joyous he was, compelled to tell his faithful wife back home what had happened to him—his triumph at the Congress. He knew how proud she would be, she upon whom for twelve years he had depended for support and adulation. In telling her of Mary Pennington, he never stopped to think of the effect on her, so swept along was he on a flood of achievement and feeling that was bearing him to a new life."

"How cunningly you have built the suspense," Meg said. "And it *is* strange how it could all flow from this handful of paper and ink."

"I wish there was something in Mary Pennington's hand or letters between them telling how they responded to one another. Or something of my mother's about that final meeting with Mary when my mother had the last word."

I took up the diary. "It opens on January 1, 1908, *At Chicago, en route to California.* I told you that his winters were spent in Southern California in the heart of the citrus country, directing research that led to his new career. We all returned to Washington in the spring of that year. On March 28, *Baby sick with fever at night.* My mother said it was uncertain if I'd live. My temperature went to 104. Then *Paris paper.* That was for the Congress in October. On August 27 *Sailed at 11 a.m. on Deutschland. Stormy and rough. Box of Valencias and one-half box of grapefruit.*"

"He was determined not to get scurvy!" Meg observed.

"He landed at Plymouth." I continued, "went on to London, Paris, Rome, Naples, and Palermo. He was at Messina two months before it was destroyed by earthquake. Years later, after my father had died, an American naval officer called at our home and handed my mother my father's card. He had been in command of a U.S. destroyer in the Mediterranean at the time of the earthquake and had been diverted to Messina for relief work. He had found the card in the ruins of the consulate. He had kept it all those years and when his ship was in port near Los Angeles, he decided to present it, not knowing my father had died."

"Small world!" Meg murmured.

"My father's good angel was with him then and in 1906 when he missed the San Francisco earthquake by two weeks. He returned to Paris via Genoa and Marseilles.

"The diary is mostly names and addresses and appointments

with government officials and lemon growers. These letters home give the details. In Sicily he first encountered the Mediterranean world. From Palermo, Messina and Taormina he wrote her nearly every day as he responded to the classical landscape. Listen to this from Taormina! *'It is a beautiful clear morning. From where I am writing I can trace the wavy coastline to Messina and can see across the straits to the mountains of Calabria; and just at one side and high up on the hill in a clump of olives is the house where Robert Hichens lived when he wrote* The Call of the Blood. *I read it on the steamer coming over.'* "

I paused. "Everything he saw and felt and read was whetting his appetite for what lay ahead. Our consul in Messina and his Austrian wife were his guides and interpreters. The Sicilian lemon growers were flattered by this visit from an American official with practical knowledge and experience who could identify with their problems. From my father's first research on the deciduous fruits — apples, peaches and plums — he went on to become an authority on the citrus fruits. Except for a trip in 1909 to the apple country of Washington and Oregon, he never worked again on the deciduous fruits. In Sicily he marvelled at the lemon, orange, fig and olive plantings, and the way the terraced groves ran almost to the summit of Mt. Etna." I paused and then recalled, "Among my mother's things was a little sachet of orange blossoms, no longer fragrant, with a note in his hand 'To my dearest wife, Taormina, September 27, 1908.' Included were those famous lines dating from Goethe's first visit to Italy, *Kennst du das Land wo der Citronen bluhen; im dunkeln Laub der gold Orangen gluhen.*"

"You'll have to translate for me."

"*Dost know the land where the lemon tree blooms and where in deepest shade the golden oranges gleam.* Sicily was a homecoming for him. I wish I had the letters and cards he wrote from his second trip. Upon his return in the spring of 1911 he asked for the divorce and she had her breakdown. It was probably then that she destroyed everything from that trip, believing that he had again been with Mary. I don't think he was."

"Do you know Sicily?" Meg asked.

"Even before I retraced his itinerary. His letters are passionate and yet precise. He was a poet as well as a scientist and administrator. We would have grown very close if he had lived."

"You must make this your book as well."

414

"It was the impact of Italy and France that determined his tastes for the fourteen years that remained to him. His love for beautiful things came from that experience. Nothing of Western American art interested him until he met that other woman in Palm Springs.

"It is curious," I went on to say, "how my early life followed his—that first impact of Italy and France on us both. My first sight came when I was only nineteen as a member of the ship's orchestra on a round-the-world cruise. We had come up the Red Sea, through the Suez Canal and stopped in Alexandria for two days while the passengers saw Cairo and the Pyramids. We then made the narrow passage through the Straits of Messina between Sicily and Italy and I saw Mt. Etna that had enthralled him years before. We came into the bay of Naples on a cold winter morning and saw Vesuvius plumed with smoke. We had more time in Genoa and Marseilles. Even as he did, I responded to the colors, sounds and sights of the Mediterranean world. It was that impact on the youthful me which led to my life abroad.

"In Naples, his diary grew lyrical. Sunset over the bay! And there is this letter which he warned my mother not to show his mother and father. It tells of the prostitutes who swarmed the streets after dark. How exciting for that Quaker boy! Such things sparked the conflagration that occurred when he met Mary Pennington. He was a sensual man, more so than I."

"Not much more," Meg demurred.

I resumed my narrative. "He arrived in Paris on October 3rd and plunged into the affairs of the Congress which was to open at the Sorbonne. There were 2,500 delegates from all over the world. It was the first ever held. My father was chosen by the American delegates to head their group. He presented his paper on the 6th, a summary of his five years of California field work. Then on the 9th these words: '*Dr. Pennington read paper on poultry. Awakened much interest!*' "

"Poultry?" Meg exclaimed. "Who would dream of romance from poultry?" Her voice softened. "Or of us reliving it long after."

"That's all there is about her in the diary," I resumed, "until they reached London after the close of the Congress. Only in letters to my mother do we read of his rising interest in Mary Pennington. Why did he write to his wife rather than in his diary? Was it indeed an unconscious way of initiating a separation? Three years passed before he asked for a divorce. How does your instinct react to that?"

"You know I need to sleep on things."

"As you see, the Paris letters are all on Hotel Chatham stationery, a hotel on the fashionable Right Bank. The first was written on the day of his arrival. It begins: *I reached Paris this morning and found seventeen of the Americans here. There are four ladies in the party, wives of some of the warehousemen. Dr. Pennington, a young woman from the Bureau of Chemistry, is also in the party.*

"He then tells of having to buy a frock coat and silk top hat for the official receptions. Then, *I am glad to hear about the boys and their school and about Lawrence. I wonder often if he has forgotten me. I was two years old then. I should like to see the flowers in the garden. The anemones, chrysanthemums, marigolds, etc. must be fine. Keep track of the colors in the chrysanthemums as I may want to do some transplanting. Tonight most of them are going to Grand Opera, but I will go to bed early. Tomorrow I will go to the Louvre.*"

"Did you have these 'mums put in our room?" Meg demanded. "So he too was under the spell of their fragrance!"

I resumed my account. "His letters show loving concern for his family and homely details, all the while his response to the young chemist—she was his age of thirty-six—grew stronger. As head of the American delegation, he had duties and obligations and responses to prepare. He also had a dispute to resolve between the government and the lay delegates—the commercial people he called the warehousemen. The French wanted to recognize only the official group and give them the place of honor at all meetings. My father knew however that the men from the refrigeration industries who had done the organizing work were deserving of full recognition, and so he was careful to conciliate them. This was the preeminent talent that distinguished his career—an ability to reconcile conflicting interests."

Meg was silent, and I asked her, "Are you following?"

"It's enthralling—and strange, the drama of it. And you were only two years old!"

I read again from his letters. "*I am getting used to a silk hat and long coat or full evening dress. When I come home you will have to take dinner every night in evening dress, and I will wear my silk hat to breakfast, a common sight in the restaurants here.*"

416

Meg laughed. "Rather nice touch, that!"

"Now listen to this. *Dr. Pennington, the food expert from the Department, is a bright woman. She is going shopping with me tomorrow to get you a blue flannel petticoat.*"

Meg exploded. "Don't you love his innocence! He reminds me of Malcolm."

"Shall I continue?"

"Don't you dare stop!"

"It was very early in the morning on October 8 that he wrote the next letter. *The Congress is progressing finely. Tuesday I attended the official luncheon given by the Minister of Agriculture and was seated at his right. He spoke splendid English and I had a delightful time. Yesterday my paper came and if I can judge from the reports in the papers etc, it is the hit of the Congress so far. I took two and a half hours or nearly the whole of the session, including questions and discussion. The charts and the fact that a government man could talk with authority on practical questions seemed to capture them. We have a great system of team work in our delegation. We all support each other's papers. They don't know how to ask questions over here. I prepared ten questions to ask myself and gave them to the boys and they worked them beautifully.*

"My father's success," I told Meg, "came from his knowledge being both theoretical and practical. The California orange growers had welcomed this. He was a research scientist and also a man who identified with growing things. As a boy I sometimes went with him on inspections of groves and packing houses and would trot alongside as he strode down the rows of orange or lemon trees. He would pick a ripe orange, peel it in one continuous ribbon, then give me every other section of the juicy fruit. He made a ceremony of it I've never forgotten, nor the earthy smell of an orange grove or the sweetness when in blossom."

"Not like a hillside of heather!" Meg said softly.

"My keenest boyhood memories are the smell of earth and growing things. There was a nursery across the street from us. The head gardener would ask my father for advice and he would let me go with them down the lath-shaded rows. I loved the humid atmosphere of the greenhouses where the exotics grew. The gardeners were Japanese who lived there with their families. I went over early one Sunday morning to prowl and came on a naked Japanese man and woman having what I thought was a wrestling

417

match. I ran home and told my father that Sugimoto was hurting his wife. He laughed and said not to go over again without him." I grinned and added, "I did though, but never saw them again."

Meg laughed. "Your schooling began early."

"One summer after the war my mother took me with her back east to the scenes of her girlhood—Cornwall-on-Hudson where she was born and to her grandfather's farm near Buffalo."

"Was her father also a farmer?"

"He was a country lawyer and not a successful one. When her mother died, her father married a younger woman. She and her brother and sister were on their own the rest of their lives."

"How did they do?"

"They all did well. Her brother also went to Cornell and became a civil engineer. Her sister married the Lieutenant-Governor of Delaware, and when he died young, she studied art at Columbia and became a water colorist and art teacher. I was very fond of her and sent her many art postcards from European galleries. Both had more drive than my mother." I paused. "Do you want to hear more about my coming of age?"

"Indeed I do. You must have been a very naughty boy."

"That summer the farmer's boys and girls were an earthy lot, doing with each other what they saw the farm animals doing. The oldest boy also did it with the calves."

"I say!" Meg gasped. "Not you, I trust."

I laughed. "I wasn't tall enough. The boys included me among their games—like seeing who could pee the farthest arc, or ejaculate the most times, or who had the longest thing. Amazing the difference between boys otherwise the same size."

"What a difference from my upbringing!"

"Don't convent girls play games?"

"Only in Glasgow!"

"As you see," I said, returning to the letters, "he couldn't keep her out of them. Hear how he let himself go. *Dr. Pennington is the most unique member of the Congress. She is a charming young woman and the only woman delegate. She has done work in meat investigations. She is a 'good fellow' too. A half dozen of us go out to dinner and lunch together and she is always there and pays her share. She is crazy to go to a real Paris restaurant where you see things. They don't open till after midnight. So after the banquet Saturday night several of the married people are going and*

I am going to look after her and her niece. I wish you were with us though you are rather too young and innocent to be out in Paris after midnight."

"How do you suppose your mother took that?" Meg asked. "Would she have been utterly crushed or madly jealous?"

"I believe she accepted it. She was not a fighter nor, she told me, was she ever jealous of him or of anyone."

"I am like that," Meg said, "although Malcolm never gave me any cause for jealousy. What a good writer your father was! He makes it seem only yesterday. To think that they are all long since dead."

I caressed Meg's hair. "But we're not!"

"Not yet!"

"Then came this letter to *My dearest wife, this is the greatest place to kill sleep I have ever seen. I guess we don't average over five hours a night. Something keeps us up to after midnight and as I waken early, the nights are pretty short. It is six a.m. now and I have been awake since four. I am waiting for Mr. Valmorin, a wealthy French fruit grower with large acreage near Paris, who will take me to the market this morning. Dr. Pennington is going too. It is raining and so he may not come.*

"Night before last he invited Miss Pennington and me to dinner. It was the most beautiful dinner I ever saw. The Austrian minister and wife, and the Portuguese minister and the German consul were the other guests. Mrs. Valmorin is a strikingly handsome woman about thirty-five. She is at least five feet ten inches and built like a French Gibson Girl. She is the most beautiful woman we have seen in Paris. Valmorin is about the same age and a great big fellow. The women had stunning dresses. Mrs. Valmorin's was a pearl grey satin with a lacy train. She wore a black gauzy thing over her shoulders."*

"Your father had an eye for women's clothes as well as for them. Tell me again how large a man was he?"

"Fairly short and solid. Not an ounce of fat on him.

"Two days later after telling of a trip to Versailles and Fontainebleau, he wrote again to my mother, *Saturday night was the big banquet at the Grand Hotel. There were six hundred present and it was a brilliant affair. After the banquet there was dancing. Our Americans girls, Miss Pennington and her cousin Miss Irving from Chester and Mrs. Bellman from Philadelphia were the finest dancers among the women."*

"He referred earlier to 'her niece.' Were there two of them with her?"

"There was only one, but whether she was her niece or cousin,

I'm not sure. Probably the former. Her obituary in the *New York Times* said she was survived by a niece. As Dr. Pennington was thirty-six, how old would that have made her niece? She was no child."

"She could have been the child of an older brother," Meg observed.

"Now things begin to heat up. *Tonight is a big reception by the city. Miss Pennington and I are in the receiving line. We get everything that is coming. Friday morning she went shopping and I did the Bon Marché with her. It was great fun. Everybody wanted to know if her husband didn't like this or that. She is about your size and bought one or two things for me to bring you. Don't you wish you knew what?*"

"I call that cruel," Meg protested.

"Those emotions are blinding," I said.

"You speak from experience?"

"Alas, I do." I continued to read from his letter. "*I have space engaged on the thirtieth on the Hamburg America line. I think there will be eight of us to return together. Voorhees from Boston, Kalischer, Nickerson, Stevenson, Miss Pennington, Miss Irving and I.*

"Then on October fourteenth he wrote as follows: *The big reception by the city Monday night was a brilliant affair. There were 6000 people there. At the concert Miss Pennington and I were in the row just behind the President of France and his family. We were shown all possible attention throughout the Congress. Miss Pennington was the only woman in the Congress, and she was the most unique figure and was highly honored. At the formal closing the president named her paper and mine the only two he honored by mentioning. Miss Pennington is a very lovely girl. I have fallen quite in love with her. She is a Ph.D. and a medically trained woman at the head of the Department's food research laboratory in Philadelphia. She is very charming socially, a camper and all around good fellow. She will come and spend the night with us some time in Washington. She and her cousin Miss Irving went to Germany yesterday. Eight of us meet again on the Kaiserin Augusta Victoria on the thirtieth. I have been to the Louvre several times. Miss Pennington took me once and once to the Luxembourg. She knows all the fine things as she spent six months here. I have cut out the Hamburg trip. I will be here till Friday or Saturday, and then go to Glasgow. I will be there three days and then in Liverpool and London until we sail.*"

At that point Meg demanded, "Whatever took him to Glasgow?"

420

"Spoken like a good Edinburgher! It was to attend the weekly fruit auction, and then the one in Liverpool. There's a single letter from Glasgow, telling of 30,000 barrels of apples sold in one auction. He also saw Glasgow's cultural sights including a gallery and a museum."

"Humph!"

"Here is how that letter ends. *I would like to have Baby in my arms now, and also his mother and the two big boys. I would manage all of you.* He was so passionate about everything. I'm sure only his official position kept him from joining the warehousemen after midnight. One letter tells of the naked women they reported holding on their laps. He adds for his wife's sake that if that had happened to him, he would have read to the *filles de joie* from the New Testament."

"A strange man," Meg observed. "And most loveable."

"Here's a passage from the letter from Liverpool. *Did I tell you about going shopping with Miss Pennington and having a girl pass a dainty pair of pink panties over to her to see how her husband would like them? I said she would be a dream in them. I had a card from her from Canterbury today. Miss Irving is called* The Kid *by the crowd. She calls me 'Father' and Miss Pennington says I have taught* The Kid *to say 'God bless Papa every night.' They are a couple of fine girls, regular good fellows. I would like to take a trip through the Lakes. When we come together, we will do it. Glasgow and Liverpool have been as black and smoky as Pittsburgh since I have been here. The sun hasn't been out once.*"

While I stopped again for a drink of water, Meg leafed through the letters, and when I settled again beside her, she remarked, "I find it incomprehensible how he could write so warmly to his wife and in the same letters tell of being swept along by the other woman."

"Don't you know that a man can have both needs at the same time?"

"Malcolm never did."

"So can a woman," I added.

"I never had ambivalent needs—not until he died, and then . . . "

"Are you glad?"

"Guess! Your father loved to shop for gifts for your mother and toys for you boys."

"I told you about the silk handkerchief and the little pictures he brought me from Florence. He brought my mother a Florentine silver necklace of the twin masks of Tragedy and Comedy, and dozens of reproductions of paintings and sculpture in the Florentine galleries and the Louvre. He also took photographs of landscapes and ruins in Italy and Sicily."

"What a sensitive man he was! I believe you're envious."

"God knows he was magnetic. I can still see his luminous brown eyes.

"What a pace he led!" Meg marvelled, still browsing in the letters.

"It went almost to the end of his life. It was the war that crippled him—those eighteen-hour days. That, and according to my mother, the demands made by Mary Pennington as she experienced his waning desire and her own lost youth. I wish I had a picture of her as she was in Paris: the lavish dresses, hats and furs. By the time I met her, she was wearing a tailored suit, a mannish haircut, and had droopy-lidded eyes. *He looks like his mother*. Those words haunt me, and her look of hate when I said how I loved Paris. Why couldn't she have seen that I was like him in being if not in body? He must have sensed that in me as a boy. That was why I was his favorite. This book will be my thanks to him, and also to my mother. Together they made me."

"Oh Laurie!" Meg embraced me. "You are very loving toward them."

"I realize now what he owed her."

"Do you think he ever sought reconciliation with her?"

"Perhaps when he came back from the war and told her that Mary had become too much for him. That was an ironic turn, wasn't it. Matching needs that endure are rare."

"I know!"

"If he had not met that Mrs. Brown, they might have become reconciled. In the beginning they were a very loving couple. When he was on field work, they wrote to each other every day. He apparently never saved her letters as she did his. They certainly loved us boys. One letter when he was in California and she still in Washington looking after us kids, was written on their wedding anniversary. He told her how his love had grown and been sealed by children of their flesh and blood and bone. It's a tender letter that must have thrilled her deeply.

"Her journal is almost devoid of such feelings, and yet there is one entry written in 1920 when he was recuperating at Palm Springs. I have a copy here in my notes. 'Harold came in unexpectedly tonight, down for the Board meeting tomorrow. He sent me a very dear letter the other day and we talked it over this night after we had gone to bed.' Alas, that letter wasn't among the ones she left. She apparently rose later that same night and wrote in her journal. If he were again proposing a separation, why would she have called it 'a very dear letter'? And why was it Mrs. Brown and not my mother who was with him at his death?

"Would that I could do more than listen!"

"There are these last letters from London. When they reached London, the American delegates stayed at the Dysart Hotel, Henrietta Street, Cavendish Square. Their work was done, and he and Mary were free to go to galleries and the theater without the pressures of the Congress they had survived. As the diary tells, the two were together day and evening, usually dining at the Savoy. His letters give details of places and plays and people. The lead soldiers that my mother kept reminding him not to forget were finally bought by Miss Pennington at the Army and Navy store."

"You were fortunate in the love your parents gave you and your brothers."

"I wish life hadn't ended so early for him and for my brothers. Why have I survived them all, including my mother?"

Meg shook her head.

"Now listen to this," I continued. "*I wish you could see the beautiful things* The Kid *Miss Irving has. She must have spent $250 on dainty laces and lingerie. We will have tea at the Tower some afternoon with the Keeper of the Crown Jewels who Miss Pennington knows. She has spent two summers in London and knows every corner. She says you will be trying to get a divorce if she takes me around much more.*"

"Oh but he was wicked!" Meg cried. "You were right when you said he was, consciously or not, seeking to effect a separation."

"His desire erupted in the frankness of these final letters. Here is what he wrote next: *I feel like a cooked owl. The pace here is murderous and if I don't get away soon it's a stretcher that will accompany me. Last night we spent the evening with Sir Shirley and Lady Murphy. He is the city health officer and a charming Irishman. At two a.m. after two hours sleep, one of his inspectors came for Miss Pennington and me and we spent three hours in the Smithfield Market—the great meat market of London. It is the greatest thing of its kind in the world. I ended the night by sleeping with the lady mentioned above—i.e. we both fell asleep in the cab. This is the last letter and it may get there before I do. I can hardly wait to start. If you don't get eaten up, it will not be my fault."*

"He was certainly not lacking in appetite for life!" Meg marveled.

"On that same day, October 27, the diary bears this entry: *Old man in market after being introduced to M.E.P. said to me 'Does the lady bear your name?' 'Yes.' 'Is this your first trip?' 'Yes.' 'Well, you are a fine looking pair.'* "

Meg gasped. "I call that going all out!"

"He wrote a last time on the next day: *I will send one more note. We had a lovely dinner last night with the Simmons at the Royale. After that we went to the theatre and saw Forbes Robertson in a strong moral play. 'The Passing of the Third Floor Back.' We came home three in a hansom. Auntie had to sit on my lap all the way and The Kid sat in the corner and chuckled. I am getting used to holding the girls on one knee or in any old way. They are game. I never met a better pair of travellers. They pay their share of everything, and as auntie, Miss Pennington, is a doctor and a widely travelled girl, she has an independence and confidence that takes her through anything. They are both anxious to meet you and I told them we would have them come and spend a few days with us."*

"That's rubbing her nose in it," Meg protested. "I couldn't have survived a letter like that."

"On the 29th there is this final diary entry, *Theatre in the evening. 'What a Woman Knows' with MEP and HLI.* The rest of the pages are blank through 1908, save for this last entry on Saturday, November 7, *Arrived in New York.* He and Mary had seven days and nights at sea on the *Kaiserin Augusta Victoria.* What does Meg say? Did they or didn't they?"

She drew me fiercely down to her. "Did!" she cried exultantly. And in a softer voice, "Do!"

The next morning we had breakfast again in bed and talked.

"Does the trail end with those letters?" Meg asked.

"Except for what my mother told me that morning in Notre Dame, there's only a few mentions of Mary Pennington in later letters from California to my mother in Washington before our final move west. If Mary wrote to him—and I have no way of knowing if she were a letter writer—nothing of hers was in the papers he left. He *was* a letter writer, as you have heard—and I'm sure he wrote to her whenever they were apart. I doubt that anything survived her death. God, what I'd give to have his letters to her!"

"Do you believe he broke with her as your mother said he did?"

"I don't know. It could have been wish fulfillment."

"What can you make of it with so little to go by?"

"Needed is belief beyond my own," I said.

"You have mine. Remember Delacroix. Wasn't your father strong, honest and wild?"

"As far as society let him be. It was a different age from ours. Now will the world accept him as he was, clothed and naked? Today he is known only as a public man. Remember I told you of the memorial service after his death and how proud it made me when I realized the esteem in which he was held by those in high places." I went to my briefcase, then came back to bed. "Here is that booklet of the addresses given that day. Mr. Hoover spoke first of the work he had delegated to my father. Herbert Hoover was in charge of all food and distribution throughout the country. He was called the Food Czar. He gave my father responsibility for all perishable foods—fruit and vegetables, meat, fish, poultry, dairy products. The object was to ensure their flow and fair distribution to cities and country and the armed forces—an enormous job which required the commandeering of the nation's railroads and trucking industry. Let me read this paragraph from Hoover's opening address:

> One of the qualities that enabled Harold Powell to make so great a success in so difficult a task was his great capacity in conciliation, his great geniality of character, which amid all the opportunities for a thousand frictions enabled him to carry through the whole organization a certain basic sweetness and kindliness that lifted him through the most terrible discouragements. For these services Harold Powell deserves the gratitude of all the American people.

I told you that he was decorated by France, Belgium and Italy. There is also a memorial in the Department of Agriculture in Washington. Sometimes I stand by the bronze tablet for the feeling of pride it gives me."

"Is he really remembered today?" Meg wondered.

425

"Not as a person. All are dead who would remember him. His work lives, although time has modified it. The Sunkist organization still exists as the country's greatest example of agricultural cooperation. In 1913 my father wrote a text for a series in Agriculture edited by his mentor, Liberty Hyde Bailey, which remains the history of the movement."

"Let me go back to your question, will your book lead to his acceptance as a complete man?"

"First there must be readers."

"Did your father see himself as a conciliator?"

"He must have had a pretty good idea of who he was. Mary Pennington would have confirmed it."

"Was he introspective?"

"He was too busy."

"What do your mother's journals say?"

"Nothing at all."

"One thing's sure," Meg said, "that's the whole man he revealed to his wife, your mother. And the two parts are inseparable. I'd love to have drawn him in his prime!"

"Balls and all?" I asked.

"Yes!" Meg said fiercely. "The way Rodin saw Balzac."

"Bravo!"

"Your mother accepted him as he was, didn't she? She never left him nor allowed him legally to leave her and you boys. And she kept those letters and that diary, and left them to you."

"To do what with them?"

"She knew you intended to write his life."

"That was her last wish."

"Then she wanted all of him in it," Meg concluded triumphantly. "It seems to me you must emphasize what is most lasting, that is the man more than the work."

"Except for the letters, what is there of him as he was? Almost nothing in my mother's journals. A few tributes to his kindness and geniality."

"You have told me a number of revealing insights into the man himself. They will be in your book, won't they? Then his lasting memory is yours to ensure."

"Alas that he died when he did, just as I was leaving boyhood.

I haven't told you everything. There's one more thing that's troubling me, whether or not to include it."

"There *are* more letters?"

"Only an incident remembered only by me. There is no other record of it—nothing in my mother's journal."

"You sound mysterious."

"It has been a live coal in my memory. I have wanted to free myself of it, and yet until now—until you—I have never dared put it in words even to myself."

I held out the first finger of my left hand. "This scar will confirm what I am going to tell you."

"Now I *am* curious."

I got up. "Let's dress and go for a walk."

"You are not going to work this morning?"

"Not until this final block is removed. Now the time has come, if you will continue to be patient with me."

Again we trudged up the hill to the square and around the basilica to the ramparts. A cold wind had risen. Two crows planed crazily over the slope, then returned to light in the highest branches. Meg's cheeks were flushed. A rust-colored scarf muffled her neck. Her tam hid all but a few wisps of her hair. We leaned against the low wall and surveyed the landscape.

I turned her to face me and kissed her lightly. "You are a beautiful woman," I said.

"Am I?"

"Each day more so."

"I'm glad you listened to your river goddess. It is a strange book you are writing," she said.

"Must I include everything?"

"You know you must. What still troubles you?"

"Shall I tell you now?"

"Tell me, my dear. I may not be a goddess, but as you know I am a good listener."

We walked to the far end of the esplanade and leaned again on the low wall. At last I began to speak.

"It was at that meeting when she told me of my father's death and of Mary Pennington and Mrs. Brown. Then she fell silent and we sat on in the emptying church while the organist continued to play. I thought she had finished and I rose for us to go."

427

" 'Not yet,' she said. 'There is one more thing I must tell you if you are to know your father as he was—a strong and complex man I could never understand nor satisfy.' There was another long silence and then she asked in almost a whisper if I remembered an afternoon when I was a boy—a Sunday and my father was home from the office—when she had been in bed all day with a migraine headache and my father had been reading to her from the Sunday paper. I had grown hungry between lunch and dinner and was downstairs in the pantry making myself a cream cheese sandwich on a French roll. It was the cook's day off. While splitting the hard roll with a butcher knife, it slipped and sliced into the first finger of my left hand."

I held out my hand again for Meg to see the scar. "That's why I remember it all these years. There in Notre Dame my mother took my hand to see if the scar was still there. When blood began to flow from my finger, I wrapped a dish towel around it and ran upstairs to where my father was still sitting beside her bed. They were alarmed when they saw the bloody towel. I told them what I had done. My father took me into the bathroom and washed the cut, still bleeding profusely, then bound it with a cold wet washcloth. We went back to my mother's bedside and he showed her what he had done. 'He is going to faint!' My mother cried. I did feel woozy and leaned against the bed."

"What happened?" Meg asked when I paused for breath.

"I probably would have fainted, but my mother reached for the glass of water on the bedside table and held it to my lips. Before I could drink, my father shouted 'No!', seized the glass from her and in the same move rushed me back into the bathroom, poured out the glass in the toilet and flushed it, then filled it with fresh water and gave me a drink that cleared my head. 'Thank God!' I remember him saying. We then went downstairs and he found clean rags in the kitchen closet, tore off strips, soaked them with iodine and rebandaged my finger."

I stopped then and Meg asked, "What did you make of all that?"

"Nothing at the time. I was only a kid, about twelve, I guess. The war had ended and he had come home from Washington. They were both upset by my bleeding and looking faint. I never thought of it again for years until that day in Notre Dame when my mother

428

recalled what happened. Then she added in a whisper, 'From that day on, I never took any food or drink from him.' "

"My God!" Meg cried. "You mean? She . . . "

"I don't know. I should have questioned her. I suppose I didn't want to admit any kind of negative thought about my father."

We walked to the other end of the ramparts.

Then Meg asked, "What do you think now?"

"What *should* I think? I still don't know. It could have been that the glass only held dissolved aspirin tablets prepared by my father for her migraine and he didn't want his precious little boy to have that bitter pain killer. There is absolutely no evidence to support her suspicion and fear. It could have been a dying woman's effort to free herself of a morbid suspicion, and to shift it to me, as she did. I wish she had kept it to herself, had never told me. Now I have burdened you with it."

"I am willing to share," Meg said simply.

"I loved them both."

"Not all three?" Meg asked softly.

"Perhaps if I had met Mary Pennington earlier when, warmed by love, she put him in orbit, before her blood had turned to ice. Now what should I do, what must I do with what my mother told me? There is no way of knowing if my father ever had such an evil thought. It does not seem likely, particularly that late. If he had, would he not have acted on it at the earlier time when she refused him a divorce?"

"That seems likely," Meg agreed.

"My over-riding memory is of his warmth, so different from my mother's coolness and Mary's cold hatred of life denied her. How can I associate him with any such wish?"

Meg said earnestly, "You don't need me or any one to tell you what to do. You know you must write of the whole man, using everything you know and remember about him. It's not for you to judge him, or any of them. To separate parts of him would be a second death. Your task is to integrate and give him life anew. He needed those women, all of them. One gave you to him, the other awakened and made him the man the world responded to and loved. The third gave him peace as his end neared. What they did cannot be compared nor measured. Your task is to render justice to them all, him most of all, you, dear man, who came from his loins and her womb."

With tears in my eyes I took Meg's face between my hands and found her cold lips with mine and held them until they warmed.

We returned to the basilica and I sat at the back of the nave while Meg continued to fill her sketchbook with details of the figured and garlanded pilasters.

When a tour bus arrived mid-morning and a guide led his party around the interior, Meg presently stopped and came to sit beside me.

"Are you all right?" she asked. "I know what it must have taken for you to tell me what you did."

"I feel better after that cathartic."

She took my hand. "Your mother must have felt the same way, relieved not to have to carry her secret to the grave."

"Now the book will have to carry it," I said wryly. "I couldn't have told anyone but you. Strange how she had the last word. Was it her way of avenging herself? Yet she was not a vengeful person. There was no bitterness when she told me about his two women."

"By then she had come to terms with them all. It must have begun when she went away and lay on the beach and read Walt Whitman."

"She was fatalistic," I continued to muse. "New Thought taught her that. Her belief in Reincarnation led her to identify my father with the amorous Samuel Pepys. He too was a great administrator. She never stopped admiring my father. That's why she saved those letters and that diary, and why it was so important to her that I write his life."

"And now you will—and as she wanted you to. Think of me, Laurie, as feeling the pride she would be feeling, in him and in you, their son."

"Who but you will understand why I have written it?"

"One reader is an audience, Malcolm used to say when I asked him who read books about canon law. You'll have to leave it to the reader, whoever he or she may be to decide."

"Perhaps print a few copies to give away. To whom? They're all dead."

"To me then," Meg said softly.

I stood up. "Don't these tourists bother you? They do me. We've had it to ourselves. Let's adjourn to the café. A good strong *au lait* will help."

We took a table on the café terrace, and after we had been served, Meg opened her sketchbook. There on the page were the tourists.

"Good Lord!" I exclaimed. "You do practice life drawing!"

"*Il faut toujours travailler,*" she laughed. "Please find out where the bus is going next. I could get on and make a few pence doing portraits! Could help pay our bill."

I went out to where the driver was re-boarding the group, then returned and told Meg, "They're going to the monastery called La Pierre-qui-Vire. It's a balancing megalithic monument. Legend has it that when it falls, Doomsday is at hand."

"Let's push it over! How far is it?"

"A day's walk there and back."

"You said we might see the cathedral in Auxerre on the way back. I read about it in the book about Burgundy. There are stone angels. I ought to take back more than devils."

"I'll check the bus schedule when we get back to the inn. I wish we had a copy of Pater with us."

"How much longer will we stay here?"

"Are you impatient to get back?"

"I shouldn't be gone too long, and I'm running out of sketch-books. If I had brought my materials, I'd paint the hill from where we walked below." She paused, then said firmly, "I intend to draw you."

"Me?"

"Remember? Pan Awake!"

"My legs aren't hairy enough. Besides I lack hooves."

"No excuses," she said sternly. "I want something to shock my teacher."

"You mean draw me *en toto*?"

"Don't be shy."

"I might catch cold."

For another couple of days we spent the daylight hours in walks in the colored countryside deeply at ease with one another. Before bedtime I read and wrote and lounged in our room while Meg, propped on the bed with sketchbook on her knees, drew with silent concentration. I gave up trying to carry on a conversation when I

431

realized she was not listening. She wouldn't show me her work until the last page was filled. Then I marvelled at the subtle sureness of her line.

"Are there that many Me's?" I asked.

"Ones you've hidden from me. I wanted you to know I can draw more than stone devils. Here's the grandfather of them all."

"What will your teacher make of it?"

"He'll be jealous."

"He's sweet on you?"

She smiled. "He was cross when I told him of seeing the Delacroix."

"He doesn't approve?"

"His drawings, yes — *un grand maître, bien sure* — but not his oils. *Ces bêtes sauvage? Mais non!*"

"Did you like what we saw?"

"The self portrait, oh yes, and the one of his old servant."

"Am I being what you said I should be?"

"You were certainly wild in carrying me off this way."

"Do you know this is our last night?"

"Yes, I know."

"Are you all right?"

"I'm trying to be. I think I am. Yes, I am!"

During the night I was awakened by her crying. I drew her to me.

"Don't worry about me," she murmured. "It's deeper than pain. Joy and pain so mingled I don't know which is which. I'm sorry I woke you."

"Your name will be on the title-page with mine. It's our book now."

"In invisible ink."

"You haven't given me your Edinburgh address."

"Must I get up this minute?"

We went back to sleep.

Morning found Meg her usual self. We waited in front of the inn for the early bus from Avallon to Auxerre. There we were to take the afternoon express to Paris, arriving in the early evening. The morning was cloudy and cold and leaves were flying. The *patron* came out to see us off as the bus lurched to a halt and our same driver leaped down to lend a hand with our bags.

"*Alors, ca irait?*" he winked.

432

"*Mais que pensez-vous?*"

He grinned and we all laughed.

"*A la prochaine fois!*" the *patron* called as we boarded.

"*A bientôt!*" I assured him.

Meg gripped my hand as the bus gathered speed down the winding hill.

This time we had seats up front and the driver kept up a racy commentary for our benefit as we stopped time and again to pick up passengers. By the time we had crossed the Yonne, pulled into the depot and I checked our bags at the railway station, we were relieved to be alone as we toiled up the hill to where the cathedral of St. Etienne dominated the town.

"I'm glad to be out of sketchbooks," Meg said, "even though the angels are beautiful. Drawing takes me away from everything else—even from you," she teased.

"I noticed."

"I want to be with you every last minute," she said earnestly. "You're leaving in a day or two, you said."

"Tomorrow night if I can get a flight to Washington. When do you go home?"

"In another two weeks. I'll have work to make up. I'm glad."

"What do you mean?"

"I want to be so busy I won't miss us." She paused, then said even more earnestly, "I mustn't be foolish. Will you please tell me how one disengages? You're the one with the experience."

"You'll soon be with your sons. You're a grandmother, remember."

"I haven't seen them in a year. I told you Scots disperse. Will you write and tell me how the book comes out?"

I nodded my head and we started up the hill again from where we had been resting. I didn't know what to tell her. I wasn't sure what she was feeling. Nor I.

"You go your way, you told me," she continued. "Is this what will happen now that your book is nearly done?"

I took her arm fiercely. "No more talk. We're going to walk clear around the cathedral before we go in. You need spiritual preparation. There are two side portals as well as the front. The angels are on the sides, and also the Wise and Foolish Virgins."

"Pity me, kind sir, foolish not wise and no virgin."

433

The leaves swirled around our feet as we made our way beneath the bare chestnuts.

"How beautiful!" Meg exclaimed when we stopped to gaze at the sculptures around the portals. "It's what Ruskin meant by architecture as frozen music."

When we had made the circuit and regained the entrance, Meg said, "Those lines of your poet—*La joie venait toujours après la peine*—say what I tried to tell you last night. Thank God something transcends both."

"He wrote another poem, about hunting horns, not bridges. Listen:

Les souvenirs sont cors de chasse
donc meurt le bruit parmi le vent.

"Are you telling me that our memories will die on the wind?"

"What I'm telling you is to go on opening doors. You opened one that led to Paris, then we opened one together. You are the artist, I'm not. Your blind intensity when drawing, alone proves it." I turned her to face me. "Do you want me to move on through?"

"Why don't we have lunch? Then maybe I can answer you. This woman misses her porridge."

We laughed and stepped over the threshold.

"Dear Lord!" she cried as we looked down the long nave. "Distance and height, darkness and light."

"Pure Gothic, the more so from our having come from the Romanesque."

"Again *Monsieur L'Impresario!*"

"There's time to eat and make our train," I said as we left the cathedral and walked quickly toward the town. "The Restaurant de la Gare, although plain and un-adorned, is one of the best in France, famous for its lamb. Shall we share a *carré d'agneau?*"

"*Mille fois* yes, monsieur!"

Back in Paris we slept that night in our separate rooms. In the morning while she was at the school to show her week's work, I left for Orly and the overnight flight to Washington. We had gone beyond words.

Palm Springs, California
18 February

Dearest Meg:

The date reminds me that it was on this day in February that my father died. My instinct brought me to this desert oasis to end the book, as it brought me to Paris where it began. Yes, it is done at last and I'm staying on a few weeks to make a clean copy for a publisher who has expressed an interest.

What is it? What you said it should be, a portrait of the whole man in which his work, important though it was, is of less importance and even less interest as time passes. You kept insisting you were only a listener. Why did it take me so long to realize you were also a teller? Now I know why you first appeared to me on the bridge and why it was crucial that you went with me up near the source. You, *you*, Meg Graeme, were the sibyll I kept listening for. You were the river goddess with the answers I sought. How blind I was!

Is it a novel, as you once suggested? No, but neither is it the usual biography. I have used my material to the best of my ability. There are inevitable gaps, for I have invented nothing. The heart lies in his early work in the groves of Southern California which led to Sicily, Paris and Mary, Sunkist, Herbert Hoover and early death. So exalted did finishing it make me, that now I know for sure that the man will live in my book when his work is forgotten, thus it is a "Portrait of My Father," including all of them, and with love. I came here to make a last effort to learn something, anything about Mrs. Brown. No luck. And to enjoy the isolation in the detached guest house of a former colleague in State. A perfect regimen for work, as Vézelay was for us both.

Palm Springs is now a fashionable spa, overrun at this season by the Beautiful People. Would he have enjoyed them? Wartime Washington had its social whirl, he was gregarious and his tastes had grown rich, and yet I like to think he had sickened of it and at the end wanted only the company of an artistic woman. I fantasize that they became desert recluses. No, Republican politics sucked him back into the stream and he died unfulfilled. Why was she with him at that fatal dinner? Who was she?

Where the Desert Inn once stood is now a high rise hotel, although far above it rises Mount San Jacinto whose snow melt waters this oasis. Despite overpopulation it is still a beautiful place, the mountains behind and the desert before, clear to the Colorado River and Arizona beyond.

There was a great meteor shower last night. They say it presages the return of Halley's Comet. Seeing it when it last came around is my earliest memory. My mother woke me and carried me to the window and I saw the tail streaming out behind the bright head.

Before our family Christmas I went to my father's grave near his natal Ghent. The little Quaker burial ground is on the western slope of the Berkshires, the graves of his parents and theirs — several generations of Powells, Chases, Macys, and Townsends. He and his mother and father occupy the same grave over which stands a granite headstone bearing the additional words IN LOVE THEY SERVED MANKIND. Have I?

It was a cold clear day in December. In the southwest beyond the Hudson were the blue Catskills where Rip Van Winkle went to sleep. It was like the day we went down the Seine. I would have made a bonfire but it had rained the night before and the leaves were soggy.

So I spread my overcoat and had a sandwich and a Pepsi. All the family descendants have moved away and the little cemetery is no longer used for burials. My first cousin comes over once a year from the Massachusetts side of the Berkshires and cleans up litter left by picnickers and rights any fallen headstones. I listened for my father's voice, remembering the last time I heard it, and I told him what I've done to link our lives so that they are now one life.

I don't know when the book will appear. More than anything I want you to read it, to read it to you. When? Where? Italy next summer? We could rendezvous on the bridge over the Arno where Dante first met his river goddess.

Tell me how it goes with you, your Christmas reunion, your work. What did your teacher make of Pan awake? Write to me here at General Delivery — what the French call Poste Restante. I'll be here another few weeks. Au revoir!

LAURIE

TUCSON
BAJADA OF THE SANTA CATALINAS
1983–86